girl in LOVE

a kylie ryans novel

CAISEY QUINN

DELUXE EDITION FEATURING DELETED SCENES AND CHAPTERS

Girl in Love

Cover Design & Layout by E.M. Tippetts Book Designs
Interior designed and formatted by E.M. Tippetts Book Designs
www.emtippettsbookdesign.blogspot.com

Editor: Mickey Reed

Proofreader: Rahab Mugwanja

Published in the United States of America

First electronic publication: February 2014 by Caisey Quinn.
www.caiseyquinnwrites.com

For Emily, who read Girl with Guitar and said, 'You have to publish this,' then held my hand every step of the way.

For the two men I've loved. For my dad, thank you for showing me what real love looked like. I miss you every day. And for my husband, who taught me the meaning of forever.

What's the greatest chapter in your book? Are there pages where it hurts to look? What's the one regret you can't work through? You got it, baby. Mine would be you.

Mine Would Be You

– Blake Shelton

prologue

"SERIOUSLY, thank y'all for coming. I know I'm not great company lately."

Kylie looked down at the glass of champagne she held instead of up into the eyes of the guests of her birthday party. The surprise one Mia and Lulu had thrown her. Biting her lip, she gathered the courage to glance up.

It had been nine months, nearly a year, since he'd walked out of her life. But she was still a shell of the person she used to be. She hid it well. Hell, she had two—well technically three—hit songs to show for it. But the people in this room knew better. And she knew they knew.

The two scheming hosts, plus Carmen and her fiancé, Lily, Steven, and the guys in his band all looked at her with similar expressions. Pity. God she hated that look.

"You've been working so hard lately. You deserved a night of fun." Lulu nudged her shoulder. "You did have fun, didn't you?"

"Yeah, I did. It was great." She forced the biggest smile she could. Lulu's eyes narrowed as she silently called *bullshit*.

"Hey, we should head out. Let you get some rest for your big day tomorrow." Mia threw her a knowing look. Kylie thanked her with her eyes. Of all people, she never would've expected Mia to become the person to pull her out of her own personal hell. But she had.

Not that tomorrow was something she necessarily wanted to be reminded of. *The Other Side of Me* had gone platinum and the label was throwing a party. One she had no desire to go to. Not that she had a choice.

"I'll walk you home, Mia," Chris, Steven's band's lead singer, offered. Kylie's eyes darted back and forth between Mia, Chris, and Steven. Steven's face remained blank, but she saw the slight tension in his shoulders. Now there was a weird little love triangle she was kind of curious about. She grinned to herself as she considered nicknaming Mia *Yoko*.

"We should get going too. Our flight leaves early," Carmen said, pulling Kylie into a side arm hug before walking to the door with her man. "You comin', Lu?"

Kylie had told them all that they could stay in her new place. It was big enough, that was for sure. But they'd insisted on getting hotel rooms. She had a feeling it was because she wasn't much fun to be around.

She spent nearly every waking minute either writing or in the studio. She knew her weirdo behavior made people uncomfortable, and she didn't miss the looks they shot each other when she zoned out and missed an entire conversation. But she had no idea how to help it.

"Um, nah. I'll get a cab later. I'm going to stay and help clean up."

"Don't be silly. You did all this work and you've had a long trip. I can handle it." Kylie gave her friend a lingering hug and whispered, "Thank you," in her ear. She hugged everyone else goodbye as they left. Well, everyone except Steven, who was still leaning on the bar in her kitchen. Part of her was glad he'd stayed behind. And part of her was nervous as to why.

She didn't mind cleaning up by herself. In fact, she preferred being alone. No smiles to fake or forced conversations. But sometimes being alone was...lonely.

Once they were gone, she turned back to the tattoo-covered man in her kitchen.

"I'm staying to help clean up. Like it or not, Ryans."

She laughed. "Okay, *Blythe*." They worked in comfortable silence for a few minutes, clearing beer bottles and washing dishes.

"I'll take this out to the dumpster." Steven pulled the big black garbage bag from its can in her pantry.

"Thanks."

She was bent over, putting the remaining bottles of alcohol into her fridge, when he retuned.

He cleared his throat and she jumped, nearly slamming her head into the top of the stainless-steel door. "God, you scared me."

He gave her a wicked grin, provoking a twisting sensation all through her insides. "I like it when you call me God. Like it when you moan, '*Oh God*', even more."

Her eyes went wide and she slapped him lightly on the chest as he came closer. "I thought we weren't ever going to mention that again?"

Last weekend they'd crossed a line.

They'd stayed up late finishing a song they were writing together and she'd had a few drinks too many. She'd felt bold and made a move. Kissed him. Kissing had led to more. Much more. They hadn't actually sealed the deal, but what they'd done was still more than she thought she had probably been ready for. But since then, they'd both adhered to the strict no discussing drunken making out and inappropriate touching policy.

Until now apparently.

He responded with a cocky smirk that was as annoying as it was a turn-on. "Who's mentioning it?"

Her chest heaved between them as he came closer into her personal space. "Y-you are. I think."

"Do you want me to stop?" He leaned in, the force of his bright blue eyes pressing her back against the fridge as he let his hands rest on her hips. "Say the word and I will."

She should say it. Should tell him it had been a mistake then, and would be a mistake now. She didn't love him. Couldn't love him. Couldn't love anyone since she didn't have enough of a heart left to love with.

But that was what made it so tempting. He didn't love her either. It was just comfort.

Trace had walked away from her. Mia had rejected him. They'd found a way to ease the pain. Together.

She'd felt like hell afterwards. Like she'd cheated on Trace. Or betrayed herself somehow.

But with him this close, she couldn't think straight.

She closed her eyes and she still saw it. The source of her pain. Trace and Gretchen Gibson holding hands as they entered a rehab facility in Dallas. Hugging in a hotel doorway in Georgia. Arms wrapped around each other in a parking lot at a bar in Charlotte, where he'd supposedly come to see her. They'd been blurry photos online and in the tabloids, but the images in her mind were crystal clear. Even nine months later.

She licked her lips, knowing Steven could make them go away, even if it was just for a little while. "Same deal as before?"

"If that's what you want."

She sucked in a lungful of air. He smelled so damn good. Sharp and sweet all at once. Cologne and beer. A hint of men's soap and sugary icing from her birthday cake. "I want—"

She was interrupted by a harsh knock on her door. Well that was frustrating. She smiled at the irritated look on Steven's face. "Wonder which one of them forgot something?"

"I'm kicking their ass, whoever it is."

She snorted out a laugh as they both headed for the door. "It might be Lulu, and when she threatens to junk-punch you, she's completely serious."

Steven chuckled as they reached the door. "Thanks for the heads-up."

She laughed again. It was kind of nice being with him. Easy. "Consider yourself warned," she told him with a grin.

But when she opened the door with him close behind her, the smile dropped straight off her face.

Her world began to pitch hard left and then right as she completely lost her center of gravity. A bright bouquet of peachy pink roses, held by the last person on Earth she had expected to see at her door, greeted her.

Emotions she'd held back for so long slammed into her with the driving force of a runaway freight train. "W-what are you doing here?"

His hair was slightly longer. What had once been stubble was a full-grown beard. But it was him. If she'd thought his hazel eyes had been stormy before, they were currently a tsunami of colors swirling and threatening to drown her that very second.

"Just though I'd drop by to wish you a happy birthday, Kylie Lou."

Pain leaked out into his words, and for a moment. she was confused.

"Corbin," Steven said evenly from behind her. *Oh sweet Jesus.* She'd completely forgotten Steven was there, even though he was so close his

4

chest was touching her back.

"Blythe," Trace said just as evenly as he jerked his chin upward just a little. His greeting was slightly deeper and laced with something she couldn't name. Anger, maybe. Whatever it was, he'd managed to make Steven's own name sound like a threat.

"Anyways, I just wanted to stop by and give you these. I'll let you get back to...whatever you were doing." A muscle in his jaw ticked, and even under the beard, she saw it.

It was taking all of her concentration to breathe normally and remain upright. Her hand shook visibly as she took the flowers he held. "Thank you. I didn't realize you were—"

"Out," he finished for her, making it sound like he'd busted out of prison. "Yeah. I am. Have a good night." His gaze lingered on her briefly before he turned on his heel and disappeared down the hall.

And just like before, he took what was left of her heart with him.

chapter
ONE

3 months later

"PLEASE say you'll come tonight, Kylie. It'll be fun. And if anyone needs to have a little fun, it's you."

"Gee, thanks." She would've rolled her eyes but Jean Claude was prying them open to apply another pound of mascara.

"I'm serious. It's been nearly a year. It's *time*." Mia stepped to the side where Jean Claude wasn't. "*Come on*, Oklahoma. Steven and Chris have been asking us to do something with them forever. It's just a club. We'll have a few drinks, and hell, maybe we'll go crazy and do some dancing."

Now she wanted to glare at her friend, but Jean Claude was working on the other eye and one-eyed glaring wouldn't have quite the same effect.

"Incase you haven't noticed, I've been a little busy." She waved a hand around to remind Mia where they were. Backstage at the CMAs. Where she was about to perform. And be recognized as a nominee in the New Artist of the Year category. In the past year, she'd spent more time in the studio than the people who worked there. She had two hit singles to show for it. *Not a Nice Girl* was up for Song of the Year and *Heartbreak*

6

Town was up for Video of the Year.

"Exactly. You've been busy *working* twenty-four damn seven. It's time to loosen up already." Mia shook her head and stepped aside to let the makeup artist coat her in one more layer of shimmery powder.

She should've been happy-dancing around the dressing room like a maniac. It had been an amazing year.

She'd cried the first time she heard herself on the radio. She'd cried again when she sang an original song of hers for the first time and saw people in the audience singing along. Because they'd already known the words. Her words. She'd been bombarded with messages from fans saying that they loved her and loved her songs.

For some artists, this was a hassle to deal with. But for her, her fans were literally her family. Her only supporters. Everything she did, she did for them.

Tears of joy, she told herself each time she broke down. But deep in the core of her being, there was always that voice. The dark, ugly, honest one.

You're crying because he's not here to share this with you. Because all you want is to tell him about it. And for him to kiss you, congratulate you, and be proud of you.

She closed her eyes and focused on picturing nothing and no one. No one's face with boyish dimples that appeared when he grinned. No one's tan forearms under rolled-up shirtsleeves. No one's muscular back. No one's ass in jeans so tight it should be illegal. Just blackness. Nothingness.

In her twenty years, she'd loved two men. Loved them deeply. Her daddy, who'd died right after her eighteenth birthday in a freak accident at the factory where he worked. And another. One whose name she did her damnedest not to even *think*, much less say out loud. Because that was the past. And she was focusing on the future.

Music was her future. Nothing else really mattered.

"I like working," she said, hopping out of the chair.

Her friend smirked. "Yeah, I get that. So do I. But I also like having a life. And living that life."

"I have a life," Kylie argued as they walked towards her stage entrance.

"Oh yeah? So what are you doing after this show?"

"Stopping by the studio to do one more run-through of—"

"No." Mia shook her head. "I mean it. I'm done watching robot-Ryans work herself to death. You're coming out with us tonight if I have to hogtie your ass."

"Like you actually know how to hogtie anything," Kylie said with a short sarcastic laugh. "You don't understand and I don't need you to. This is me. I'm doing what I love. Just because you would rather—"

Mia put a hand up to stop her. "See what I'm doing here? I'm cutting you off before you say something you'll regret. Because here's the thing. I've been as kind and gentle as I can with you. But I've been talking to Lily and to Olivia and—"

"You talked to Lulu?" Kylie was bursting with excitement about the latest news from her best friend. On the next tour she went on, Lulu was coming along as her personal stylist. But she was kind of pissed that the girls were obviously talking about her behind her back. She could feel an ambush coming on.

"Yeah. And the general consensus is we're all worried about you."

Kylie aimed a pointed look at the stage she was about to perform on in front of several thousand people.

"Not about your career. About *you.*"

Is there a difference?

"So stop it. I'm fine." She raised her arms as two stagehands came to clip her mics onto her dress.

"Kylie, I need you to listen to me, okay? You're not fine. And even if you were, you should be so much more than *fine.* You're dreams are coming true and you're *fine.* Wow. I'm underwhelmed."

"I don't know what you're getting at but—"

Mia cut her off once more. "But nothing. Grief is like your favorite pair of old sweats. You get comfortable in them. So comfortable you don't want to take them off even to shower. They're worn in and fit just right and you never want to let them go, even when they're stained and gross and have holes all in them."

Kylie arched a brow. "I think I'm missing the point of this little speech."

"The point is they look awful on you."

"That was a really shitty analogy. Wish me luck."

Bryce Parker and an actress Kylie didn't know but vaguely recognized were hosting the awards show. They were right in the middle of announcing her as the next performer when Mia touched her on the arm and sighed loudly.

"Sorry if that was harsh. I know you're still hurting, and I can be kind of insensitive sometimes. Good luck out there."

Kylie nodded and turned towards the stage. "Thanks," she mumbled. The weirdest part was she wasn't hurting. She wasn't anything. She was numb and had been for the better part of a year. It's why she wasn't nervous about performances like this. She felt nothing.

Well, she felt Bryce Parker trying to cop a feel when the lights went down. She smacked his hand away. Hard.

But other than that, nothing. No butterflies, no jangled nerves. No worries about anything going wrong.

Except…when the lights came up on her this time, in that split second before the band cranked into her song, she looked down. Because she had the oddest sensation that instead of wearing the five-thousand dollar designer dress she had on, she was actually in her sweatpants.

chapter TWO

"WE probably shouldn't sit by each other." Gretchen shuffled down the aisle around Mike, putting a seat between them. "Unless we want to be engaged with a baby on the way tomorrow."

"You're being paranoid." Trace shook his head.

He hadn't even wanted to come to this. The label was holding all the cards now though, and he was grateful they'd understood about his needing time to step back from his career and get his drinking under control. Plus, he wasn't a complete moron. They weren't really as understanding as they were pretending to be. They just didn't want to send a public message that they didn't want their artists to get help if they needed it.

He knew that at the first sign of any wrongdoing on his part they'd drop the ax over his head so fast he wouldn't even feel the pain of being cut loose.

"No, I'm not," she said. Her voice was a hiss of a whisper because the lights were going down as the show began. "You need to read some tabloids, my friend. There's all kinds of stuff going around about us."

"I'll pass. Thanks."

He didn't care what anyone said. That had been part of his therapy in rehab. Overcoming the impulses that surged when he felt out of control or powerless.

Some things he could control. Himself. His drinking. He was working on his temper. What a bunch of dickheads printed about him in some trashy-ass magazine…there was nothing he could do about that.

"She's right, Trace." The oldest member of his band, Danny, leaned over. "If you want to start clean, then you two need to keep your distance. If it gets around you that and Gretch were in the front row for Kylie's first big performance, you'll be a shoe-in for Asshole Country Artist of the Year."

He blinked at the man. *Kylie's big performance?*

He hadn't paid attention to any of the stuff about the awards show. He'd just shown up because the label said he had to. Before he had time to ask any questions, the room went pitch black. Bright pink lights on the stage caught his eye. They lit up, one letter at a time. K-Y-L-I-E-R-Y-A-N-S.

Aw hell.

"I'm an alcoholic," he whispered to Danny. "An emotional drinker. None of y'all thought it might be a good idea to mention this ahead of time?"

Danny's eyes were glued to the stage as he answered. "Pauly and Noel said not to. Said you wouldn't come."

Trace turned to see her coming from the smoke and fog on stage. The lights hit her and for a second he couldn't breathe. "I wouldn't have."

In nearly a year of rehab, he'd learned a few things. One was that there were certain situations he had to avoid if he wanted to remain sober. Triggers, Dr. Reynolds called them. Tabloids—any media coverage at all, actually—were some of them. He'd yet to determine if Kylie Ryans was a trigger or not.

Guess I'm about to find out.

The woman on stage was something else. Her sound had changed. It was harsher, angrier. But mesmerizing. She was a force of nature up on that stage, stalking towards the audience as her lyrics hit him full force.

I know they talk trash behind my back. But baby I got news for you. Those crazy rumors about me? Well hell, they might all be true. I'm not a nice girl.

He tried to focus on his breathing while her guitar player rocked out. She was doing country-rock crossover? Last he'd seen her perform, she was going more a folksy bluegrass route.

His chest ached as his mind conjured the most probable cause for the change. He hadn't seen Steven Blythe anywhere tonight, but surely if he and Kylie were still a couple, he'd be here. He'd been with her on her birthday three months ago. Alone. In her apartment. Trace had to swallow a few times to choke down the bile that rose in his throat from the memory.

Knowing it was entirely possible that a television camera could be aimed at his face at that very moment, he worked to keep his features expressionless as she began to sing.

I'm not the one that your mama would choose. I'm not the kinda girl that you propose to. Turns out I'm just fine with a one-night-stand. Baby I'm not lookin' for a wedding band. I'm not a nice girl.

The picture perfect moment her lyrics brought to life behind his eyes was a solid chink in the armor of his resolve to try and put the past out of his mind and move forward.

You are not a nice girl, he'd told her when he'd thrown her into his pond and she'd faked him out and pretended she couldn't swim.

Some days he wished someone could punch him hard enough to make him forget. If he knew it would work, he'd take the hit. Happily. And at the same time, his ego swelled just a bit. It could have been a coincidence that something he'd said to her when they were together became the title of her hit single, or it could be that she still remembered too.

There wasn't a single second of their time together—from the moment he'd first laid eyes on her in a smoke-filled bar two years ago—that he'd forgotten. And he'd tried.

She was strutting around stage with the confidence of a superstar. Even if Steven Blythe was the one responsible, he was still proud of her. And as much as a part of him still wanted a drink, wanted to soothe the hurt of seeing her again, of knowing she probably belonged to another man—maybe even a better man—he knew he wasn't going to give in. Not tonight at least. Tonight he was going to focus on his music and taking it one day at a time.

So he thought.

Damn that dress she had on. It was black and tight and light reflected off it all over the place. There was a longish skirt-type deal but it was wide open in the front and the sight of those perfect legs was enough to make him regret everything.

Leaving her. Going to rehab without asking her to wait for him. Going into rehab period, because it meant nine-plus long months without those firm, perfectly toned legs wrapped around him.

The tightening in his pants reminded him *how* very long those months had been. She was still singing, but in his head, she was moaning his name.

He closed his eyes. Hard. Trying to erase those images. It wasn't fair to remember that. To think of her that way. He'd walked away from it. From her.

In place of her lip-biting, please-don't-stop, I'm-coming face, another version of Kylie Ryans appeared behind his eyes. His girl. Kylie Lou. Those gorgeous eyes of hers round and wide and full of tears. Her voice was as clear in his head as it was on stage.

Don't do this. You don't mean it. I don't believe you.

And even though she was wearing a black dress and singing her ass off right in front of him, the Kylie he saw was just standing there. Crying and broken in a red dress.

Just as he'd left her.

chapter THREE

"I CHANGED my mind."

Mia smiled as Kylie made her way to her seat between her and Donovan Taite, their friend Lily's dad.

"About going out?"

Kylie nodded.

"Sweet. I'll text the guys to meet us after their show. It'll be fun. You'll see."

She gave Mia a taut smile. "Can't wait."

The truth was, she'd rather do anything else. Write, record, sleep. Take up knitting. Have dental work done. But fate was cruel and downright spiteful.

Tonight had been the biggest performance of her life and the man she'd forced out of her memory had been in the front damned row.

And he wasn't alone.

"A RE you wearing that out tonight?" Mia eyed Kylie's tattered jean skirt and her Hank Williams Junior T-shirt.

"Hell yeah I am. Why?"

Mia frowned. "I mean, I know you haven't been out in a while but the club we're going to is kind of—"

"I don't have anyone to impress."

"Yeah, well, no danger of that." Mia rolled her eyes and linked arms with Kylie as they left her apartment.

The club was crowded and noisy. From the moment they passed through the roped-off VIP entrance, the music grated against her in a way that made her want to cringe. There was a time when she would've loved it. Would've barely been able to keep still as the bass pounded into her.

Not tonight.

Mia dragged her over to where Steven Blythe and his friend and lead singer of his band sat.

Chris Something. Do I even know his last name? Whatever. Kylie couldn't remember for sure. Not that it mattered.

"Heard you sang the hell out of that song we wrote together tonight," Steven said, winking at her.

"Well if you heard that, it must be true."

Kylie looked past him to where a waitress was delivering drinks at the table behind them. When the woman looked over, Kylie waved a hand. "Can I get an Amaretto Sour please? A couple of them?"

She could tell by the waitress's expression she was thinking about carding her. Twenty was close enough to drinking age. Kylie fished her black credit card out of her wallet and held it up. "I'd like to start a tab please."

The woman took it and nodded. Mia and Steven ordered beers and Chris ordered a soda. Plain ol' soda. Lot of fun he was probably going to be.

Two drinks in, Kylie started to realize what was really going on. This wasn't a night out for fun. This was a setup.

"So *Chris* here is really into animal rights. He organized a protest last year at the university and was able to get them to stop testing non-life-saving products on lab animals." Mia beamed at Kylie as if she'd just said that the dude had invented world peace.

"Cool." *Probably not the time to mention that my daddy used to take me hunting.* Kylie downed her drink. Her stomach twinged a little from the sweetness.

This wasn't a mixed drink kind of night. Not after seeing *him*. When the waitress passed by again, she lifted her hand. The woman raised her head in Kylie's direction. "Can I get two fingers of bourbon please? Heaven Hill if you have it."

In honor of the man who shattered my heart into a million pieces.

"Kylie," Mia hissed from across from her. "What the hell are you doing?"

She raised an eyebrow. "Getting trashed. Isn't that the point of going out? Blowing off steam and all that?"

"Ryans, can I talk to you outside?" Steven asked, leaning across the table.

"After I finish my drink." The waitress returned and sat the squat glass of amber- colored liquid in front of her.

Here's to you, Trace. She reached for the glass but it wasn't where she'd expected it to be.

She looked up just in time to see Steven chug it back in one swallow. "What the—"

"There. Now you're finished. Let's go." He didn't pay any attention to her protests as he wrapped a hand around her elbow and pulled her from the bar.

Once they were outside, she jerked out of his grasp. "I don't know what the hell is wrong with you, but if you ever grab me like that—"

"I'm sorry I grabbed you. But I guess we're even. 'Cause I don't know what the hell is wrong with you either. No, I take it back. I bet I do know." He folded his arms and leaned back against the brick building behind him. "I guess you heard he's back in town."

She wanted to roll her eyes. Deny it. Lie and say that she couldn't care less. But she'd been consumed with feeling nothing for nearly a year. She was too tired to keep up the façade.

She'd sat through her signing party at Capital Letter Records like a zombie. She couldn't even remember a single thing that was said at her birthday dinner a few months ago.

Only what had happened after.

He'd shown up at her apartment. With flowers. Mr. I-Don't-Do-Flowers. He'd seen Steven and bolted. Right back to rehab according to the local rumor mill. Seeing him tonight had jolted her back to reality.

She couldn't help but wonder if it was karma repaying her for hurting him. For causing him to fall off the wagon and run back to Dallas. To *her*.

"I saw him," she said quietly. "He was there tonight. In the front row. Him and her both."

Do not cry, dammit.

She looked up at the dark sky. She couldn't see the stars or the moon. She was glad. A clear night sky unaffected by city lights would've reminded her of a farm in Georgia she couldn't bear to think about.

"Shit. Hey, I'm sorry." Steven reached out and wrapped his arms around her. Tears came without her permission.

And I'd been doing so well.

She stepped back, knowing she'd probably see a cell phone quality shot of this moment in a gossip magazine any day now.

"I'm fine. It's fine." She shook her head and wiped her eyes. "I'm being stupid."

"Naw. You're being human." Steven nudged her with his shoulder. "Good thing, too. We were starting to wonder." He winked at her.

She rolled her eyes. "Guess I made a hell of an impression on my date, huh?"

"You caught that, did you?" He shrugged and put his hands up. "Mia's idea, not mine. Swear."

She gave him a small smile. "I figured."

Steven huffed out a breath and she caught the familiar scent of bourbon in the air. She licked her lips and took a step closer—feeling like a junkie who'd just gotten a hit of her favorite brand. She wanted it. Wanted it to hurt and burn and remind her of everything she'd tried so hard to forget.

"Take me home."

Deep blue eyes widened as she came closer. Who knew five-feet two inches of blonde mess could make a six-foot tall tattooed guy look so panicked? Steven's eyes narrowed as he watched her move in for the kill.

"Oh-kay. You mean take you home as in *walk* you home, right?"

"Are you sleeping with Mia?" Kylie asked, tilting her head to the side.

"Jesus, Ryans. Guess subtly's not your thing, huh?"

"Yes or no?"

Steven shook his head. It was the answer she wanted. For tonight, he could help her remember. Maybe he could help her forget, too. One day. Except…something had flashed in his eyes when she'd said Mia's name.

"You're not." She blew out a breath. "But you want to be, don't you?" It was probably for the best.

He didn't answer right away. His eyes raked over her. Not in an I-want-to-tear-the-clothes-from-your-body kind of way like someone else's used to. More in the I-have-no-idea-what-the-hell-you're-doing kind of way.

Well, that made two of them.

She liked Steven. Enjoyed writing music with him. Hanging out with him wasn't turning out to be so bad either.

They'd crossed a few lines once, months ago after a late night writing session and too many drinks. But it hadn't been like…like it was with Trace. Damn. Even *thinking* his name still stung.

"I don't know yet. We're getting to know each other. Seeing how it goes. Neither of us is really looking for anything serious, you know?"

Kylie turned her face away from his. "Of course not. Don't want to end up like me, right?"

"Hey." She flinched and half-stumbled when Steven reached for her. He steadied her and placed his finger under her chin so she'd have to look up. Her gaze met clear blue eyes when what she wanted to see was stormy hazel ones. "There's nothing wrong with you. You hear me? Nothing whatsoever."

"Yes there is," she whispered.

I gave my heart away and he didn't want it. Now I can't find it anywhere.

Steven shook his head and leaned in close. Close enough to kiss her. Her head swam a little. Their surroundings faded, but it still wasn't the heart-hammering rush she'd once experienced. The one she still craved with every fiber of her being.

"That first night we met, when I saw you breaking into the VIP room at The Texas Player's Club, I had every intention of taking you home. For about five seconds. When I saw the way you looked at him, the way he looked at you…" He stopped and shook his head. "Every person in that room felt that connection, Ryans. I knew I didn't stand a chance."

The bourbon on his breath combined with the power of his words was conjuring a memory she couldn't handle. Causing parts of her to tingle, confusing the hell out of her.

Her eyes began to sting. She clutched Steven's hips and shook her head. "He doesn't want me anymore. I don't know that he ever really did."

"He did. He just…I don't know. I wish I knew how to make it better for you, but I don't. But he knew he needed help and he went and got it. Can't fault a man for that."

"So how do I move on? How do I get help for what I need?" She knew it wasn't fair to demand answers from Steven. But he'd known Trace longer than she had. Surely he knew something.

He stared at her long and hard. She didn't miss it when his gaze dropped to her mouth. "Tell me something. If I take you back to my place tonight, if we do things to each other that you've never even said out loud, who will you be thinking of in the morning? Me? Or him?"

Breathing was suddenly a feat more challenging than she was capable of. She swallowed hard and stared up at him. She could change everything. Right now. This was one of those moments where the whole story that was her life could go in a direction she'd never expected.

She could say, "You. I'd be thinking of you." She could wake up tomorrow and Trace Corbin wouldn't be the last person—the *only person*—she'd ever slept with. But then she'd be lying. To Steven and to herself.

She'd felt nothing for nine long months. Until he appeared on her doorstep, bringing everything back and taking it all away in a matter of seconds. Afterwards, she'd blamed herself for his return to rehab—convinced herself that they really weren't good for one another, as Trace had once tried so hard to explain. She'd thought she'd finally moved on for good.

Then he'd shown up tonight and she'd felt a pain more intense than she thought she was capable of without someone having died.

Steven gripped her wrists and gently nudged her out of his personal space. "Time's up, Ryans." Kissing her softly on the cheek, he sighed in her ear. "I know it's hard. But you're gonna be okay. Just give yourself some time."

"Wait." She reached for his hand, slipping hers into it. "Will you just come over and hang out tonight? As a friend?" It was the contact—his soft, warm lips on her face— that made her ache for more. For a connection to someone. Anyone.

Steven glanced around. "Just me and you?"

She nodded. She couldn't handle much more of Mia's critical evaluations of her clothing, her song choices, or her behavior.

Steven looked her straight in the eyes. "You know what people will say. And honestly, I know myself well enough not to trust myself. I can't promise to care if you're over him or not if you come at me like that again."

Kylie grinned. At least he was honest. "I'll behave. Promise. I just… don't want to sit home alone and rehash the past all night. Maybe we could get some writing in. Please?" She bit her lip and waited for him to respond.

She watched his jaw clench as he contemplated her suggestion. "I'll come hang out. For a little while. On two conditions."

Relief flooded her entire body. The thought of sitting in that empty apartment had been weighing on her even more heavily than she'd realized. She knew she'd give in and spend all night on the Internet, trying to find out everything she could about Trace and Gretchen. Torturing herself if she went home alone.

"Name 'em."

"First, we tell Mia. Explain that we're just hanging out as friends. Or we invite her. Whichever."

Kylie frowned. "I know she means well, but I need a break from 'suck it up and get back in the game' boot camp courtesy of Drill Sergeant Montgomery."

Steven nodded. "Okay then. I'll tell her I'm stopping by your place after this. Condition number two. Ryans, so help me, if you so much as glance in my direction with that come-fuck-me look one more time, you better be ready to follow through."

The intensity of his words hit her full force and she took a step back. "Got it. No come-fuck-me-looks."

Steven laughed. It was dark laughter that warmed her in places only one other man had ever been able to affect in that way.

"I didn't say you couldn't give them. I'm just giving you fair warning. I took the nice guy high road once. I probably won't take it again."

"Duly noted."

She felt much lighter when they went back into the club. Writing with Steven was cathartic and she was looking forward to it. But she had a nagging feeling she was going to have to invite Mia whether she liked it or not. Even though she was driving Kylie a little crazy lately, she knew Mia was trying to be helpful in her own way.

Mia had told her a million times that she wasn't looking for a relationship and that nothing was going on between her and Steven, but she knew it wasn't worth risking it. If Mia even had even an inkling of a feeling for him, then hanging out with him alone was a bad move. A dangerous and probably stupid one.

She was just about to tell Steven that all four of them could go back to her place and just hang out when he stopped so abruptly she ran smack into the back of him.

"What the hell, Blythe?" But as soon as the words were out of her mouth, she saw what had stopped him.

Right next to where they'd been sitting, Mia and Chris stood at the edge of the dance floor. They might have been dancing. Or having sex standing up. Kylie wasn't sure. But she saw that they were firmly connected at the waist, chest, and mouth regions.

She reached up and wrapped her hands firmly around Steven's biceps from behind, pulling him back. He was stiff as a corpse. His muscles flexed under her hands.

"Come on. Let's go. Now we both have something to write about."

But when Steven turned around to face her, his normally playful bright blue eyes were dark and blazing. Apparently she wasn't the only one contemplating something dangerous and stupid.

chapter FOUR

"Where are we going?" Kylie asked as she plowed through sweaty bodies in an attempt to keep up with him.

"I'm going to the bar. You can go wherever you like."

She squeezed onto a stool beside him as he ordered half a dozen shots of tequila.

"Really? Six shots? When you've already been drinking? For someone who doesn't know how he feels about Mia, that's a lot of alcohol."

Steven smirked at her. "I'm not upset about Mia. Not really. I'm pissed at Chris. We don't do that shit to each other. Ever. And he was here to get to know *you*. I told him a little about what you'd been through. That you needed to have a night of fun. Just hanging out and having a good time. So either way you look at it—" he paused to jerk his head back in the direction of where they'd seen their friends—"it's a shitty move."

She raised her eyebrows. Steven Blythe was pissed on her behalf. Well, that was kind of sweet.

"Oh, and these three are for you." He slid half of the shots closer to her. "So you can blame the tequila tomorrow if you wake up with regrets."

So much for sweet. She didn't stop to think it over. Just downed the first shot as quickly as she could. She clenched her eyes shut at the pain. Grenades of burning red detonated behind her eyes.

Holy hell. Why do people do this?

"Here. Open up, rookie." Steven held a lemon wedge at the edge of her lips.

She opened her mouth and took it in. It did help a little, actually. Once she could breathe again, she looked at her drinking buddy. There was something in his gaze she recognized. She knew because she avoided noticing it in the mirror.

No matter what he'd said, he was hurting. Seeing Mia and Chris like that had hurt him, for whatever reason.

He gave her a small smile. She knew her eyes were still slightly watery from taking that shot. "You don't have to drink the other two." He reached out to pull them back, but Kylie put her hand on his.

"I want to."

His eyebrows rose as he watched her take the next two shots in quick succession. He grinned when she grabbed the nearest lemon wedge and bit down on it like her life depended on it.

"Well, look who's a fast learner." He winked and finished off his own shots. When he'd set the last empty shot glass down, he turned toward to face her. "That offer to come over still stand?"

She wasn't sure if *she* could still stand. She bit her bottom lip and glanced up at him. Before she could answer his question, he reached out and used his thumb to pull her lip from her teeth.

The residual tingles from the alcohol and him touching her mouth made her brave, so she nodded. He was different. Nearly the exact opposite of what she thought she'd wanted for so long.

Sometimes different was a good thing.

THE walk to her place was relatively short. But they were both pretty heavily buzzed so it was taking longer than usual.

"I should've probably taken the hint in Chicago," Steven said as they reached the door to her building. "She went straight for him when I called her up on stage."

Kylie resisted her normal habit of blocking memories.

Chicago. They'd hung out. Danced. The pictures and the video from that night were what had sent Trace over the edge. Straight into rehab.

And from the looks of it, straight to Gretchen Gibson.

She tried to pull herself from the past and focus on the present. "I think she did that to make you jealous. Who knows? Maybe tonight was to make you jealous, too."

He shook his head and huffed out a breath. "Thanks for trying, Ryans. But I don't think either of them gives a damn if we saw or not. Notice how no one has called or texted to see where the hell we went?"

The man had a point.

She avoided the elevator when they entered her building. A small, enclosed space was not safe right now. They climbed the stairs to her apartment in silence. It wasn't until she turned the key and opened the door to the darkness that the full weight of the situation came down on her.

"Steven, I don't know if—"

Whatever she was going to say was silenced by his mouth as he pressed it against hers before she'd even turned the lights on. He tasted of tequila and lemons. It wasn't a gentle kiss. Wasn't tentative, coming from smiling lips like their other messing around make-out sessions had been. It was rough and desperate. Angry and hot.

She fought back against his tongue with her own, pulling at his bottom lip hard with her teeth. Her chest burned as if she were setting fire to her own heart.

Good. A heart isn't good for anything but aching anyways.

Steven kicked the door shut behind them. She let him press her against the wall.

Change me. Make the pain go away. Kiss his memory right out of my damn head. A rumble of angry chords played when they knocked a guitar over.

"If you want to stop, now's your chance," he mumbled against her lips.

Kylie took the opportunity to let her head fall back and catch her breath. Or try to catch her breath anyway. Steven slid his hands up underneath her shirt, raking his warmth over her sides and up to the edges of her bra.

Do I want to stop? Her head said yes. That this wasn't the man she wanted this with. But her body said no. That she needed this. Needed to let someone in so she could push someone else out. Someone who'd already left long ago. Her heart was apparently staying out of it. Or maybe she'd burned it to ash already.

"Um."

Steven's strong hands began to drop lower. His right hand snaked up under the hem of her skirt.

"I mean it, Ryans. I warned you. And yet, you followed me to the bar. You gave me come-fuck-me eyes while we did shots. True or false?"

He dropped his head and licked her neck. She shivered when his hand rose higher on her thigh.

"True," she whispered.

His teeth raked the sensitive flesh on her throat, and she whimpered involuntarily.

"See, noises like that will get you fucked. Is that what you want? I need to know for sure."

She couldn't think straight. Every answer that rose to her lips seemed like the wrong one. *Yes. No. Maybe. I don't know.*

When a thick finger slid under her panties and through her slick folds, she cried out. Pleasure, pain, and deep, messy hurt swirled inside of her.

"I need...*oh God.*" Steven sucked the skin just above her collarbone as he pressed a finger inside of her.

"Fucking hell, you're wet," he growled into her ear. "Dammit. I have to stop, Ryans. I have to." He withdrew his finger and leaned into her, dropping his head onto her shoulder. She heard him struggling for breath in her ear.

Her knees threatened to give out. "No. No. Don't stop." She gripped onto him for dear life. She couldn't take any more rejection. Her eyes were starting to adjust to the lack of light. The outline of his frame was broad and muscular. His mussed hair sticking up in every direction from where she'd been tearing her hands through it was a major turn-on. "I need...I need..."

Why can't I just ask for what I need?

"You need to come. I can feel that. How tight and tense you are. The tension is rolling off you so hard I nearly pulled you into an alley tonight."

"Yes, God, yes. I really do. Make me come, Steven. *Please.*"

He groaned loudly from above her. Thick arms braced against the wall on either side of her head. He leaned down and let his forehead press against hers.

"We're messing up, Ryans. We're friends. We're damn good at writing music together. The occasional messing around is one thing. This is point of no return shit we're dealing with here. This will complicate things. It will make things weird."

"I don't…Shit. I don't know if I care right now, *Blythe*." She felt like a trembling mass of raw nerves. All riled up with no relief in sight.

"Trace will kill me if he ever finds out."

Something in her snapped at the sound of his name. She shoved hard against his chest in the darkness but he barely flinched.

"Don't. Don't fucking use him as an excuse. He threw me away. He walked away. Hell, he practically *ran*. He's with someone else. If you don't want to do this, then go. But don't you *dare* make this about him. I'm moving on, dammit." Scorching tears began to roll down her face. Tears of anger.

Something else wet touched her cheek. Steven's mouth. He was literally kissing her tears away. Well that was something no one had ever done before. And it was also extremely hot.

"Shh. Okay. Okay, Ryans. I'm sorry." He licked her last remaining tear. "Tell me what you want. I'll do whatever you want. You want to mess around and then pretend it never happened? Okay. I can try. Want to have meaningless sex until the sun comes up? I can do that too. There are so many ways I can get you off, it'd take all night to list them. But I need to make a few things clear first."

She nodded. Her blood was on fire from his words. She was burning up. Heat spread through her so fast she was losing the ability to concentrate on anything else.

Steven gripped her wrists tightly and pinned them above her head. She squirmed, rubbing her thighs together to relieve the pressure.

"There's a difference between wanting to have sex with someone and needing to come. I can make you come. We can go to sleep after and blame it all on the drinking. If I make you come and you still want to have sex with me, well, let's just say I won't turn you down. But if you so much as think of another man while I'm inside of you, I will know. And let's get something straight right the hell now. You want a mess-around buddy to get you off every now and then? I'm cool with that. But I am no one's fucking rebound guy. Got it?"

"Y-yes." She shivered at the intensity of his words. "Now I need to know something."

"Okay. Shoot."

"Why did you want me? Back then? When we first met?"

Steven pulled back for a second but didn't release the death grip he had on her wrists. "Same reason I want you now." She could feel him grinning in the darkness. "You need me."

The old Kylie would've have told him to fuck right off. That she didn't need anyone. But he was right. She'd needed him then and she needed him now.

"Oh," she whispered into the darkness.

"I'm screwing with you, Ryans. I want you because you're beautiful. And strong. And amazing. There's not a guy out there in his right mind that doesn't want you."

"There's one," she said quietly.

"And he's the only one you can think about, isn't he?" Steven let go of her wrists and they fell to her sides.

"I'm sorry." Her lower lip began to tremble.

"Shh. Hey, come on. I didn't come here just to get laid. I was coming over anyways. As a friend, remember?"

Before she could answer, Steven pulled her into his arms and guided her to the couch. He eased her down with him and she let herself relax on his chest. The silence surrounded them until she whispered her secrets into it.

"I just want to move forward, you know? I want to be able to feel things, do things, without connecting them to him. Think that will ever happen?"

He shrugged beneath her. "No idea. But until you really do get completely over him, Ryans, I'll be here for you in any way that I can. But I told you. I'm no one's rebound guy. Not even yours."

She tucked her face against his side so he couldn't see how much she was hurting. The small sobs gave her away.

"Hey, don't do that." Steven tightened his arms around her. "It's been a long day. Let's see how you feel about it tomorrow. If you still want to talk about this in the morning, then I'll be here. Get some rest, Ryans." She felt the gentle pressure of him kissing her on the top of her head. It was a soothing and yet heart-slicing familiar gesture.

She was weak and empty. Exposed and disoriented. Rest actually sounded really good.

chapter FIVE

"THE venue pulled out, Trace. I'm sorry."

"Great." He raked a hand into his hair and stared at the pile of paperwork in front of him.

While the label was putting on a supportive front about his rehab stay, not everyone else was willing to do the same. Sponsors of his A Hand Up program for single parents were dropping like fucking flies.

"They said they'd made a mistake and double-booked. They're refunding the deposit," his manager informed him. "We have to find somewhere else to do this. Soon."

"Right." Trace huffed out a breath. The benefit concert he'd scheduled nearly a year ago was a week away and he had jack shit. Well, no. He had five hundred people who'd RSVP'd, concert tickets and VIP passes to raffle off from people he actually considered friends, and a truck the local dealership had donated for him to give to one of the AHU families. But nowhere to have the damn thing.

"Look, I hate to say this. But at this point, we might just need to accept that it's time to cancel and—"

"No. No, we're not canceling. We'll have the it at the farm before I cancel."

The program had become even more important to him than he'd realized. He cared about these people, knew them by name. Knew they needed more than he could currently give. But by raffling off signed guitars, tickets, and all the other stuff that had been donated, he could raise the kind of money that could make a difference. Money he could use to do a lot for those families.

Pauly Garrett cleared his throat. "Okay. Well, the label suggested asking Kylie to perform, a way of showing you two are on good terms and maybe even—"

"No. Not an option." Trace took a deep breath. "Look, between you and me, seeing her at the CMAs nearly killed me. I'm not going to play their game and use her to generate publicity. I'm just not. I've put her through enough. I'm done."

"She's made quite a name for herself since you've been gone. Her involvement might help us secure a venue." Pauly's voice was even, matter of fact. Trace knew his own was in danger of shaking.

"No. She's doing well and I'm happy for her. But I can't go anywhere fucking near her, Pauly. You know I can't." Jesus Christ. Just thinking about her was painful. A sharp, stabbing ache tore at his chest and his temples throbbed. She was bourbon and intoxication and freedom from everything that had ever held him captive all rolled into one dangerously enticing package.

He clenched the oak table where the ever-expanding pile of his problems sat.

"Okay, I hear you. Loud and clear. I'll make some calls, okay? We'll figure it out."

Trace huffed out a loud breath and eased his hands off the table. "Thank you. I'll make some too."

After they said goodbye, he stared at the papers in front of him. Some were bills. Some were letters from single parents thanking him for the help they'd received from A Hand Up.

Some were old, some were new. The past and the present, overlapping in a chaotic mess. Just like his fucked-up life.

A year ago, just the sight of the responsibility, the pressure, with no clear answers in sight, would've sent him over the edge. Straight to the bottle.

The irony of it all was so bitter it caused him physical pain.

He'd wanted to be better for her. Gone to rehab so he could be the kind of man she deserved. And he'd lost her in the process.

Two days and two dozen phone calls later, he still had nothing. Nowhere to have his benefit concert and auction. He and Gretchen were the only confirmed artists, and everything was going straight to shit.

"We can do it, Trace. It'll be good. I call some friends and get some help getting things done around the property." His sister's soothing voice reassured him—to an extent.

"Claire Ann, honestly, I don't know if I can handle this. A Hand Up was supposed to be a good thing, but it's turning into nothing but a nightmare."

Somehow, his sister had convinced him to go ahead and have the benefit at his house. His farm in Macon—the one sanctuary he had left. Not that it was much of an escape anymore.

All it was now was an eighteen-acre reminder of Kylie Ryans. Of taking her in the kitchen, the bedroom, the shower, the barn. Waking up with her. Feeding her breakfast in bed. Throwing her in the pond, chasing her around with a handful of mud. Loving the ever-loving shit out of her.

"This is bigger than you, Trace. You get that right? These people are counting on you, okay? So let's do what needs to be done. I'll see you day after tomorrow. I'll handle Cora and Pauly and everything. Just do whatever you need to and get home. We miss you."

"Miss you, too. Thanks, Claire Ann. You're one hell of a woman, you know that?"

He smiled at his sister's laughter on the other end of the line. He couldn't remember the last time he'd smiled. But her next words wiped the grin clean from his face.

"Do you want me to tell them to invite her or no?" She didn't have to clarify who she was referring to.

Trace cleared his throat. Twice. "Er, naw. She's probably too busy for this kind of thing. Especially on such short notice."

Truth was, even though her music had changed pretty drastically, he knew who she was well enough to know how much she cared about the cause. She'd probably come to anything for A Hand Up if she were invited.

She'd been raised by a single parent herself. But seeing her was hard enough. Seeing her in the place where'd they been…whatever they'd been, the place where he'd let himself imagine marrying her someday… That would fucking gut him.

"Okay. Got it. See you soon, big brother."

He forced out a chuckle. "I don't know what I did to deserve you. Or Rae. But I'm glad I did it." Claire Ann was silent for so long, he checked his screen to make sure they hadn't been disconnected.

"You cooked for us, Trace. When Mama couldn't. You hid us in the closet. You kept us safe," she said quietly. "You did plenty to deserve us. I just wish for once you'd find a way to get what you deserve."

"Claire…" Fuck. He closed his eyes and clenched the fist that wasn't holding the phone to his ear. "I don't, I mean…I didn't—"

"She'll come around. If she doesn't, then *she* doesn't deserve *you*." With that, his sister ended the call. Leaving him drowning in a sea of painful memories. But there was no bottle of bourbon to grab. No sweet, burning numbness.

Leaning back into his couch, he let the pain come—let it soak into his skin.

His sisters gave him too much credit. He hadn't always kept them safe. And it was the times he'd failed, stayed out with friends, or worked late to earn extra money and came home to his sisters bruised, bloody, crying, and clinging to each other after his father had taken out his anger on them that haunted him.

The bruises had faded. A few of the marks had scarred. They each had a few. But the deepest one for him, the one he knew he'd never be able to get over, was the one he'd left on someone else.

chapter SIX

"They want me to what? No, hell no." Kylie scoffed at her agent and her manager, who sat across from her in the back booth at the Oak Bar.

She put her burger down, having suddenly lost her appetite, and wiped the napkin across her mouth. Her agent was a traitor, she was damn near positive. But her manager usually had her back. She leveled him with a glare and he put his hands up.

"Kylie, you bailed early on your own release party for *The Other Side of Me*, imitated a soulless corpse to the point we wondered if you were auditioning for a spot on The Walking Dead at the party they threw you when it went platinum, and turned down the tour with Bryce Parker. You're turning into some type of diva who won't play by the rules. The label can support you or let your ass hang in the wind. It's your choice. But they're asking you to do this, to make a quick appearance at this benefit, to generate some buzz for both of you."

She narrowed her eyes at Chaz Michaelson. He shrugged, clearly unfazed by her hostility.

"Bull. They want me to show up there and make some kind of scene so the tabloids can drum up some shit about me and him and his crazy-ass girlfriend. Get him back in the public eye before his next album drops. Pass. They can find a hundred other girls willing to fake a relationship with him for attention. I'd bet my daddy's truck on it."

Her agent pulled her glasses off and rubbed her eyes. "Is this about you not wanting to be a pawn in the publicity game or about your feelings for him? Be straight with us, because we're the ones trying to help you here. Remember?"

Yeah, Kylie remembered. She also *remembered* that her agent was his agent, too.

"I don't want to be involved in anyone's game. Not his and not the label's. That's how I started out, and I've put it behind me. My career is about me. Not about him and not about whatever the label wants to spin us as. He and I are nothing and it's going to stay that way."

"He who?" Maude Lowenstein prompted. "If your feelings for him aren't an issue, then how come you haven't said his name? He's not Voltemort, last I checked. Saying his name won't conjure him out of thin air."

Kylie resisted the urge to fold her arms and glare at the surprisingly sharp and callous woman in her late sixties. And to storm the hell out. She took a deep breath and shrugged.

"Trace. His name is Trace. And while I fully support his A Hand Up charity-thing, I have no interest in being involved in his benefit concert. I'll donate a signed guitar or something. But I'm not going to it. I wasn't even technically invited. We done here?"

She began to scoot out of the booth, but her manager reached out and put a hand on her arm.

"You were invited, Kylie. He's having a hard time. The venue pulled out because of his rehab stay and so did some of his family-friendly sponsors. The event's been moved to his property in Macon and his sister called me personally and invited you."

He's having a hard time.

The words wrapped around her heart and squeezed. Kylie swallowed and looked up at the ceiling. She sucked in a lungful of air and glanced from her agent to her manager.

"All I have to do is show up?"

The other two people at her table exchanged glances and Chaz cleared his throat.

"Um, not exactly. The label was hoping you and Trace would sing *The Other Side of Me*. On the tailgate of some truck that's being donated to his charity."

Kylie's eyebrows shot up in surprise. "Why do they want us to sing it at some benefit? I don't see how that would make any difference to them."

"We don't know for sure," Maude answered. "But if I had to make an educated guess, I'd say they're playing with the idea of sending you two on tour together. Again."

chapter SEVEN

T HE town car's windows were tinted so dark she could barely see out of them. Kylie used the long drive to text Lulu so she wouldn't be tempted to watch the scenery. To smile at the sight of magnolia trees dotting the sprawling land bordered by white fences, and grand weeping willows that made her want to do just that—weep.

This drive used to mean something to her that she couldn't even articulate accurately or aloud without a lump forming in her throat.

It used to be the way home.

Now it was the way to a place she'd sworn she'd never return to. A place where she was pretty sure she wasn't wanted. Not by the homeowner anyway. Obviously some other people had other ideas.

"Shit. Are you going to cry, Oklahoma? If you are, at least get drunk first so we can blame the alcohol."

Kylie glanced over at Mia. "Shut it. I'm tired. It's been a long few weeks."

Mia Montgomery grinned and handed Kylie a bottle of expensive imported beer. "Here. I smuggled these. Pretty sure you're going to need a drink or two to get through this."

"I've got to quit telling people you're a conceited bitch. You're actually somewhat thoughtful." Kylie nudged the girl beside her.

Mia raised her own bottle in a toast. "Nah. Then I'd have to stop gossiping about what a self-centered pain in the ass you are. I think the rivals thing works for us."

Kylie took a long pull of her beer. She vaguely recalled the last article she'd seen about her and Mia getting into a screaming match about both of them being up for Breakout New Artist. They'd been joking around in a crowded bar and had to yell to hear one another. But sometimes the alternate reality the media created was better than the truth.

The truth was, Mia was a tough chick that had somehow become a friend. A damn good friend. One who was willing to accompany her to her ex-boyfriend's house and had brought the liquid courage she needed to get through it.

Not that they didn't still give each other constant hell. But that was the dynamic that worked for them. Just like they bossed Lily Taite around and were obnoxiously overprotective of her because she'd become the little sister neither of them had ever had.

Kylie opened her mouth to come clean with her friend about everything that had happened with Steven. To ask Mia about what was going on with her and Chris. If anything was going on. Mia was so private—it was hard to tell. But then she closed it. There was enough happening today without adding to it.

"Do you think she'll be here?" Kylie asked quietly.

Mia was quiet for a minute. "Gibson?"

Kylie nodded.

The other girl shifted on the seat and lowered the phone she'd been texting on. "Yeah, um, I checked the website. She's going to be here. She's performing."

Of course she was. Kylie fought hard to ignore the throb of pain that swelled through her chest. "Awesome. That's awesome."

She made the colossal mistake of glancing out the window. They were about fifteen minutes away from the farm.

"No offense, Oklahoma. I'm not judging your professional decisions here because I'm assuming you know what you're doing. But why in the hell did you agree to this?"

Kylie polished off her beer and reached into the small cooler between them for another.

"Honestly? I have no idea what the hell I'm doing. Not when it comes to…this. Chaz and I talked about it. Our theory is that if there's drama tonight between—" She cut herself off to take a deep breath. "If there's drama between me and him, the label will feed on it and push us to tour together. But if I can suck it up and just get through this with even an ounce of my dignity intact, then they'll hopefully see there's nothing here. Nothing that would be worth sending me on tour with him."

Mia whistled low and took a slow sip of her beer. "That's one hell of a theory. What do you think your odds of keeping your shit together are?"

A sharp left turn made Kylie look out the window once more. This was the road the farm was on. A few more miles and the car would make another left, pulling her closer. Closer to him. To the past. Tears pricked the backs of her eyes.

When she spoke, her words came out as a whisper. "Not good."

chapter EIGHT

"What in the hell is she doing here?" Claire Ann Corbin yanked the earpiece off and watched as a slender blonde stepped out of a sleek black town car. She jammed her finger down on the button on the handheld. "Somebody find Pauly Garrett—now!"

Jesus. This was bad. So very bad. She was certain that she'd controlled everything. Handled every single aspect of this benefit. Micromanaged the details of the event down to how low the dang grass was cut. But this she hadn't expected. Couldn't have planned for. Prepared him for.

From the area where the sound guys were setting up the equipment, Trace's manager began heading her direction. He glanced to his left and saw the girls emerging from the car in the driveway.

His eyes were wide when they met hers. "I thought you weren't inviting her?" he asked as he jogged closer. "Trace said not to, right?"

"I didn't invite her," Claire Ann hissed. "I swear to God I didn't."

At that same moment her little sister Rae barreled out of the house. Squealing. "Oh my gosh! Kylie! You made it!"

"I am going to strangle her with my bare hands," Claire Ann gritted out between clenched teeth. "So help me God, she isn't going to live to finish her freshmen year of college."

She stormed towards her little sister, realizing exactly how Kylie Ryans had gotten invited to the event.

A warm hand wrapped her upper arm. "Claire. Hold up. A big scene won't help anything. Won't help him."

"Oh, I'm not saying a word to Nashville's precious Sweetheart. My sister, however, I am drowning in the pool before anymore witnesses arrive."

"Shh. There's no need for that. It's fine. It'll be fine. Breathe."

She took a deep breath. "She'll ruin this. He's been so stressed already and seeing her…seeing her will be—"

"He's got this. You're underestimating him. He's going to have to get used to seeing her."

Claire Ann glared flaming daggers at her sister as she tackle hugged Kylie Ryans in the driveway. Then she turned her heated gaze to the man who still had a hand on her arm.

"Oh, so he can handle seeing her but he can't handle seeing us? Which is it, Pauly? Either he's strong enough or he's not."

The man she'd been secretly dating for nearly a year removed his hand from her arm and used it to rub his graying goatee roughly. "That's different and you know it."

She huffed out a breath and whirled to face him. "Is it? Or is that just going to be the excuse you use forever?"

"Claire, please. Don't—"

"You know what? Forget it. I can't do this right now. I have to find my brother."

chapter NINE

"MR. Corbin, they need to know if you want the truck by the pool or by the pond."

Trace glanced up over the amp he carried. A twenty-something brunette with a clipboard eyed him appreciatively. "Uh, pool I guess. Pond is a littler farther out than I expect guests will want to venture."

"Yes, sir. Got it. I'll make sure you get what you want." She gave him a wide-eyed look of innocence, but when the slow smile spread across her face, he saw it. That gleam in her eye that said she would do whatever he wanted. And call him sir while she was at it.

He cleared his throat and nodded as he made his way past her. "Thank you, darlin." His bass player smirked at him as he set the amp down a few feet away. "What?"

Mike grinned and shook his head. "Green Eyes over there has been eying your ass all day. Literally. I made her an offer but I think she's more interested in you. Guess she has shitty taste."

He glanced back at the brunette.

Her eyes were green? Trace hadn't noticed. He actually couldn't remember much about her except that she'd asked about where to put the truck.

"Guess so. Hey, do they have the speakers set up yet? I need to get back up to the house and check in with Claire Ann. She's radioed me ten damn times."

He was grateful for his older sister's help with this, but Lord, the woman was a slave driver.

"We're good here, man. Go on up and see what Hitler wants."

Trace thanked him and jogged up towards the small studio on his property. The golf cart he'd covered with custom Mossy Oak panels and ATV tires was waiting for him. He hopped on it and headed to the house. He stopped twice on the way to check on people helping set up for the event. He was overwhelmed with gratitude at how many people were volunteering to do what they could for this benefit. It was an odd mix of people from home and people from Nashville setting up the tents, buffet tables, and sound equipment.

He'd learned a few things in rehab. One of those things was how to tell who actually gave about damn about him.

When he reached the driveway he parked the cart and got out. A few more cars had arrived, and the valets were beginning to park them out in the pasture. A sleek black town car caught his eye. It was the kind his label, Capital Letter Records, usually sent artists in. Except he was the only Capital artist here.

Gretchen was performing tonight, but she was no longer affiliated with the label. And he was pretty sure she'd run late. She was sober but she was still Gretchen.

He squinted into the setting sun. It was getting late and he needed to get his ass inside and get ready for the show. He pulled the handheld from his hip and hit the button.

"Headin' in the house, Claire Bear. I'll find you after I'm decent." A few catcalls from the guys rang out over the channel. "That's my sister, you sick fuckers." He pressed the button again. "Mike, you can come join me in the shower now."

"In your dreams, Corbin," Mike's muffled voice answered. Trace laughed but he sincerely hoped Mike wasn't bending the brunette over in the barn or something.

He himself couldn't even go in the barn because of what he'd done last time he was in it. Who he'd done. She was the same reason he couldn't use the shower in his private bathroom either.

The memory of Kylie Ryans had become a ghost that haunted his house. And his dreams.

Aᶠᵗᵉʳ showering in the main bathroom, Trace wiped the thin film of moisture from the mirror above the sink. Sober eyes stared back at him.

He sighed, tightened the towel wrapped around his waist, and searched for his razor. Enough hiding behind the beard. The people coming to see him perform tonight were donating to his organization, showing their support when he'd done nothing to deserve it. So he'd do his best to give them the best show possible.

After each stroke of the razor, he rinsed the blade under the rushing stream. When he was done he patted his face with aftershave and met his own gaze again in the steamed-up mirror.

"You can do this." Determination set his features into hard lines. He gave himself a nod and stepped out into the hallway.

Where he was greeted by the sound of his little sister's voice.

"You can get ready in my room. It's right here on the right," she informed someone he couldn't see. Shit.

"Hold up, Rae. I'm not—"

Kylie Ryans—the real-live flesh-and-blood version—appeared right in front of him before he could finish his sentence.

Someone whistled.

"Hot damn, Corbin. You doing a strip tease for cash tonight or what?" Mia Montgomery grinned at him from behind Kylie.

He couldn't answer. Couldn't speak. Couldn't think of anything except, *Holy shit*. There she stood. Less than a foot away. Her wide blue eyes met his and robbed him of his breath. The shock of seeing her unexpectedly jolted every cell in his entire body to life. Except the ones involved in brain to mouth speech function apparently.

"Um, Rae said we could change in her room," Kylie said quietly, avoiding his eyes by aiming hers at his sister.

Her soft, sweet drawl was music in his ears. His mouth went dry as he stared at hers.

Rae stepped between him and Kylie in the narrow hallway. "Oh God. Sorry. I didn't know you were—"

"Yeah, I had to shower. Thought people might prefer the cleaned-up version." His words came out about as choked as he felt.

Rae's expression reflected the same sheer panic he felt as she looked from Kylie to him and back again.

"Well this was sufficiently awkward," Mia deadpanned as she pulled Kylie aside. "We're just gonna go get ready now."

"Right. Got it." Trace backed up into the bathroom doorway to let them pass, never once taking his eyes off of her. When she was out of sight, he leaned against the wall and fought to catch his breath.

He still wanted her so damn bad. Still craved her like nothing else he'd ever wanted.

Great. Just what he needed. Another addiction that would likely kill him.

He clenched his fists and stormed down the hallway.

So maybe he'd learned two things in rehab. The first being you found who actually gave a damn. The second was, it was the people you loved, the ones you needed, who had the power to destroy you. Who could rip everything you'd worked for away in a single second. With a look. A smile. A touch.

Her touch would undo him. Undo everything he'd fought to overcome. But damn if he didn't want it more than air. More than music. More than anything.

The image of Steven Blythe standing behind her in her apartment flashed behind his eyes.

An overwhelming flood of painful images unleashed themselves, tearing through him so fiercely he couldn't stop them. Steve kissing her. Touching her. Holding her.

He couldn't even hit anything to get a modicum of relief from the swirling anger and pain building up inside of him for fear of scaring Rae half to death. And it was his home, for fuck's sakes. This was what it meant to be sober. He had to feel every-fucking-thing. Let it wash over him, pound him down, and beat the living hell out of him.

Once he was safely locked in his room, he dressed in jeans and a black shirt. His fingers fastened the buttons on autopilot. As soon as he was fully clothed and had run his hands through his hair, he pulled the handheld device off the dresser.

"Claire Ann Corbin, if you aren't in this house in five seconds, I'm coming out there to find you. I suggest you find me first."

A few "ooohhhs" answered him.

And then Claire Ann. "Be right there."

He loved his sister. Loved both of them. Very much. But Claire Ann was about to catch some serious hell.

chapter
TEN

CLAIRE Ann rushed into her brother's bedroom and shut the door behind her. Her heart broke wide open at the sight of him sitting on his bed with his head in his hands.

"Rae invited her, Trace. She contacted someone at the label and pretended to be me. She'd overheard us stressing about the event on the phone. She thought it would help." His sister reached out and rested a hand on his shoulder. "Trust me, I don't want her here any more than you do. But Pauly called around and apparently the label was pushing for it too. They asked her to attend and maybe perform. Apparently her attendance drew in some of the last-minute sponsors. I'm sorry I didn't make the connection sooner. I thought—"

"Did she bring anyone?" He looked up, and his eyes were full of an emotion she didn't have a name for. A mix of pain and longing and desperation.

Claire Ann knew he was asking because Kylie had a boyfriend. According to the tabloids anyway. A rocker dude with tattoos all over the place that was from their area. She'd been too many years ahead of him in school to know him, but she was pretty sure Trace did. Rae wasn't the only one guilty of sneaking a peek online now and then.

"Just the American Idol girl."

"Right. Okay. Is she going to sing or what?" His eyes hardened and he stood. Claire Ann knew this meant he was patching up his wounded heart and resuming with business as usual.

She cleared her throat and checked her watch. "Yeah, um, as long as it's okay with you she'll go on right after the auction. She'll sing first. Then Gretchen. Then you. After that, we'll wrap up and you'll thank everyone for their contributions. Some people will want autographs and photos and then we'll shut it down. We could head out now and try and get some of those handled so we can wrap up even sooner. Sound okay?"

Her brother nodded and headed towards the door. "Is she—" He cut himself off with a deep breath. "Is she still in the house?"

"No. Rae just escorted them out."

Relief smoothed his features. "Good."

She wanted to hug him. To soothe him like she'd tried to do when he was a little boy. Tuck him in bed and sing him a song until he fell asleep. They'd grown up in hell, but they'd gotten each other through it. He was going through his own personal hell now and there wasn't a single thing she could do about it.

"Stop." He shook his head before she could say anything. "Stop looking at me like that. I'm a grown man. I'll live."

She sighed. "I'm sorry things didn't work out for the two of you, Trace. Everyone deserves to be happy." Claire Ann bit her lip. She sincerely hoped he believed that too. Her biggest fear was that he wouldn't approve of her relationship with the man who made her happy. "Did she make you happy?"

"She made me..." He closed his eyes, and she watched as her brother swallowed hard. "She made me crazy. She made me want a life I could never have. Made me think I could be a man I could never be." He smiled, but she knew him well enough to know it was forced. "I'm good. I swear. Let's go."

She tried not to be obvious about how closely she was watching him as they headed outside. But she could barely see his face. It was dark now and the lights she'd ordered were mostly focused on the buffet in the tent and the shiny black truck a local dealership had donated to be raffled off. They were using it as a stage tonight. She threw up a silent prayer that

46

once Kylie sang she'd get the hell out of there so Trace wouldn't have to see her again.

Cars were beginning to fill the drive like cattle. They had to maneuver in between them to get over to the area where the sponsors were being seated. Her brother smiled and shook hands like a champ, joking and laughing with high-powered professionals even though she was pretty positive he was dying inside.

Glancing around the tent, she saw Pauly doing pretty much the same as Trace. When he looked up, their gazes met. He smiled apologetically. She looked away.

A girl could only deal with so many broken hearts at a time. She'd have to put her own away for later.

chapter ELEVEN

"THIS was a mistake. I have to get out of here."

"Kylie, breathe. That was an unfortunate encounter, but you lived. Chill."

She paced alongside the back of the barn with her friend trailing behind. "I can't be here, Mia. It's like torture. You don't understand." She shook her head and put her hands on her knees. She took a few deep breaths, thankful that she'd been able to send Rae to get her something to drink before she broke down. "Seeing him is hard enough. Seeing him here…*oh God*. Seeing him with *her* here? I won't live through that. I won't."

"You will. I promise you will. Relax, Oklahoma. Sing your one song and we can blow this joint. I can probably get you an actual joint if you want one."

Kylie laughed quietly. "Thanks. I appreciate that."

"Seriously, do you want another drink? There's a flask in my purse in the car."

It was tempting. Kylie sighed and leaned against the barn. Remembering she had on a sheer top that would probably tear right open if she caught it on a piece of the splintered wood, she stood abruptly.

"I'm okay. You're right. Like my daddy used to say, never let 'em see you cry, right? I'm a big girl. I can do this."

Mia grinned. "Atta girl, Oklahoma. So what song are you going to sing?"

Kylie's eyes went wide. "Oh sweet Jesus."

"That a new one?" Mia's eyes darted in every direction as she tried to figure out what Kylie might be seeing that upset her. "What's wrong?"

"I can't sing any of my songs." She shook her head and closed her eyes briefly.

Her friend scrunched her brow in confusion. "Um, oh-kay. Why not?"

Panic radiated from Kylie's gaze as she answered so low Mia could barely hear her. "'Cause they're all about him.'"

"Here you go!" Rae Corbin smiled widely as she handed her a mason jar of sweet tea. They were taking this down-home thing pretty seriously apparently. "I looked for you but I couldn't find you and then Pauly stopped me to ask if I'd seen Trace. Speaking of Trace, sorry about earlier. That probably sucked for you. I swear I didn't set you up to run—"

"Rae. It's cool. No worries. Thanks for the tea." Kylie took a deep breath and sipped her drink. Caterers behind her served barbecue that smelled like heaven. But her appetite was pretty much dead. Like the rest of her. Every cell in her body wanted to look for him. Which was odd because he was the last person she wanted to see.

Mia raised an eyebrow at Trace's exuberant younger sister. "You remind me of someone."

Rae practically bounced to the top of the tent. "I do? Really? Who? Someone famous?"

"I'm trying to put my finger on it..."

"Lily. She reminds you of Lily," Kylie offered. She knew because Lily had reminded her of Rae.

"Yes she does," Mia agreed. "You a fan of Lily Taite?"

"Oh my gosh, I so am!"

"Figures," Mia muttered under her breath. Kylie nudged her in the ribs.

"I'll have to introduce y'all sometime."

Before Rae could respond or do a cartwheel, Trace's older sister appeared at her side. "Rae, I need to speak with you privately. Now."

"See y'all later," Rae called out as she was practically dragged away. Kylie tried to catch Claire Ann's eye so she could offer the woman a friendly smile but the two women were gone in a blink.

"When and if you introduce her to Lily, please warn me so I can flee the tri-state area." Mia grabbed a glass of wine from the waiter's tray next to them and nodded at someone approaching. Kylie glanced in the same direction and saw Trace's manager.

"Hi, Pauly," she greeted him. He looked as nervous as a cat at a fireworks display.

"Hey there, kiddo. How about you and me head over to the stage and get set you set up? You're going to perform first and then you're free to go. I'm sure you have better places to be."

"In other words, you're herding me the hell out of here as soon as possible. I'm sure he's thrilled about me being here." She snorted even though the truth hurt like hell. She wasn't wanted here. She could feel it. Had seen it in Trace's eyes in the house. Her heart grew heavier in her chest, causing a dull ache as Pauly took her elbow. What stung even worse was realizing a part of her—a tiny, stupid, naïve part—had hoped maybe he'd be happy to see her. Or at the very least, not horrified by the sight of her.

"It's not..." The manager next to her let out a loud breath as they reached the truck. "It's a complicated situation, which I think you're aware of. I mean, you can imagine what all he's dealing with."

Yeah, she could imagine all right. Someone at the label must have pushed her being here. Trace's new girlfriend was probably going to be super pissed and might make a scene, and Trace looked like he'd seen a ghost when she ran into him. But there was something more important to her than whether or not anyone wanted her around. She bit her lip and gathered all the courage she had.

"Is he happy, Pauly? I mean, did rehab work and is everything okay with him and Gr—"

As if she'd been conjured by the mere thought of her name, Gretchen Gibson appeared before she could finish. Which was for the best since the lump rising in her throat was choking the shit out of her.

The statuesque, raven-haired woman narrowed her eyes as she gave Kylie a hard once-over.

"What's she doing here?" Gretchen's flashing gray eyes flicked over to Pauly.

"None of your concern, Gretchen. Let's keep in mind this is a *charity* event. And that Trace needs for things to go smoothly." The manager swiftly guided Kylie behind the lights and around to the metal stool that she'd use to climb into the back of the truck they were using as a stage. But not before she heard Gretchen's bitter words.

"Oh, I know *all about* what Trace needs. What he doesn't need is her here causing him to—"

"Enough," Pauly commanded, using a tone Kylie'd never heard from him. "You're up next, Gretch. The only words I want to hear out of your mouth are the ones you sing when you're up on this truck. Otherwise, you're free to go. We clear?"

Damn. Who pissed in his Cheerios? Not that Kylie wasn't grateful for his intervention. But Pauly Garrett seriously needed to get laid.

"Sure, PG. We're clear." Gretchen glared at Kylie once more before stalking off in the other direction.

As much as Kylie hated to admit it, Gretchen looked good. Pretty, even. Not at all rough and ragged like she had the last time Kylie had seen her. Sobriety agreed with her apparently. *More salt in the wound.*

"You good?" Pauly asked her as a young female assistant clipped Kylie's earpiece in and handed her a microphone.

She couldn't help but notice that her knees were shaking as she stepped up on the stool. She swallowed hard and forced her head to nod. "Pauly, the song I chose...It's...It might..."

The manager shook his head and regarded her with warm, kind eyes. "It'll be fine, kiddo. He knows it will be about him. They're all about him, right?"

Tears stung her eyes. Dammit. She'd put all this away. Behind her. And now it was crashing into her hard enough to make breathing nearly impossible. "I didn't even realize until—"

"Ms. Ryans? We're ready." The assistant practically shoved her forward. The crowd wasn't nearly as big as she was used to and yet it was the most intimidating one she'd ever faced. She was thankful for the blaring spotlights practically blinding her. Because she knew he was out there. And she was about to sing out all the pain he'd caused her right in front of him.

She forced a smile and focused on her breathing. This was it. Put up or shut up. "Hi y'all! Thanks for coming out tonight. What an amazing organization y'all are supporting just by being here." Her voice was a little unsteady so she swallowed once more. Once the applause and whistling died down she grinned again. "A Hand Up is truly something special. I was raised by a single parent and I know firsthand the struggles many of them face. So reach deep into your pockets tonight, y'all!"

There was laughter and a few more whistles.

"Okay. Here we go."

The members of Trace's band began to play. The tingle of the symbols rose goosebumps on her skin. She sucked in a deep breath and threw up a silent plea for the strength to get through this.

I used to believe in make believe. Used to wish on stars. Used to fall asleep at night feeling safe there in your arms. I wanted to believe. That a girl like me…could have everything.

Kylie pulled in more air—hoping additional courage would come with it.

Now I know that life doesn't always work out like I want it to. I get to go and live my dream but I had to let go of you.

The tempo sped in time with her racing heartbeat. *Deep down there's still one thing, one simple wish I wish could still come true. I wish there were two of me. So one of me could live my dream and the other one could stay right here with you.*

Yeah I wish there were two of me. So one of me could lay right here on this old porch swing forever. Where we'd always be together. I wish there were two of me. So I could stay in your arms, chase my dreams and follow my heart. Oh I wish there were two of me.

Thanks to the glaring lights she couldn't see him. But she could feel him. Could feel a heavy gaze boring into her as she finished her song.

When she was done, she thanked the audience and hopped down from the tailgate. Carefully weaving her way around lights and cords, she made it to the back of the barn. Where she put her hands on her knees and threw up everything she'd eaten in the last week to the soundtrack of Gretchen Gibson singing about second chances.

AFTER she'd gone inside and rinsed her mouth out, she smiled and shook hands and posed for pictures and signed autographs while

Trace belted out *Rock It On My Tailgate*. The audience hollered and cheered and sang along as she navigated the path to the car that had brought her here. Once she'd found it, she snuck a lukewarm beer from the cooler in the back seat and looked around for Mia. But she was nowhere in sight.

The really sick part was she didn't actually want to leave yet. Common sense said she should get as far from this place as she could and never look back. But she wanted to hurt just a little longer, ache a little more for what she'd lost. For a life she'd never have.

She didn't feel like she'd so much as taken a breath until she made it down to the pond, away from the partygoers. She'd never thought she'd feel this way. Not here. Not in the only place aside from her actual home she'd ever felt safe. Alive. Loved.

She wondered briefly if he'd arranged this on purpose. Having her here. Making her face him and Gretchen since he'd seen her with Steven. But deep down she knew better. He couldn't have known the label would be so insistent about her going. And how self-centered was she? This was about his foundation, raising money for his A Hand Up charity. He didn't give enough of a shit about her to plan such a significant even just to lure her here.

She took a large swallow of her beer. Thank God for Mia.

She almost laughed out loud. There were four words she never imagined she'd ever be thinking. Plus, she was drinking and Trace was sober. Now there was some irony. But seeing him fresh out of the shower like that, shirtless, and wet and…damn. She really did not need to go there.

Insects danced on the surface of the pond, rippling the water here and there, contorting the perfect reflection of the moon. Whippoorwills called in the distance, and she closed her eyes. For a split second the moon became the sun and she could hear the echo of her own squeals as she was tossed into that very same pond.

She could see him coming towards her, looking panicked at first and then smiling when he realized she wasn't drowning. They'd splashed and laughed and she'd dunked him with all she was worth. They'd made love soon after. Her first time. *Jesus.* It seemed like it was yesterday and a lifetime ago all at once.

"Tellin' your troubles to the crickets?"

She jumped at the deep cadence of his voice. For a moment she thought it might have been in her head. But turning, she saw him. Walking slowly down the steep incline towards the pond. She took another long drink from her bottle and steeled herself, slamming the thick walls back over her exposed emotions.

"You're the one who just bailed on your own party. Who says I have troubles?"

Trace took a step towards her, tentatively, as if he realized he wasn't welcome in her space. "Well I know that when I snuck off to drink it was because I had troubles. Everybody has troubles, Kylie Lou," he answered quietly.

She grit her teeth together so hard it hurt. Asking him not to call her that would make her look weak, and demanding he not call her that would just make him do it that much more.

"Whatever you say. I'm gonna head back up and grab Mia. It's gettin' late."

"Past your bedtime?" he teased.

She was careful to keep the smirk off her face. She had his number, knew his game. But she wasn't playing. Not this time. She'd already gone all in once and lost everything.

"Something like that." She gave him the widest berth possible as she passed. "Party was great. I'm sure it was a success. Best of luck with your foundation."

"Hey." He turned and reached for her but she took another step, just far enough to keep out if his reach. "Come on, it's not that late."

"It is," she said, backing up even more. "It's too late." Her words held a double meaning, and his expression said he'd picked up on the one below the surface. She dipped her head. "It was a great benefit. Thanks for inviting me." She swallowed hard, trying to gather the strength to say the rest. "Goodnight, T-Trace."

Saying his name out loud ripped the air from her lungs. She turned away and stumbled. He reached out to steady her but it wasn't necessary. She steadied herself and shook him off.

"I'm fine."

He stepped closer. "Are you?" He pulled his hat off and ran a hand through his hair before turning it backwards. "'Cause it kinda seems like you might not be."

What the hell is that supposed to mean?

"Well I am." She bit her lip. Hard. But the words still came out. "Not that it's any of your concern." Shit. *Shit, shit, shit.* She was losing control of her mouth. Becoming the person he'd deemed *Hothead* not so long ago. This close she could smell his cologne and his warm woodsy scent. Memories she'd worked so hard to keep at bay forced their way back into her mind.

"Doesn't mean I don't still care," was all he said.

She didn't trust herself to speak again so she just turned and walked away without even saying goodbye. Just like he'd done. Just like everyone else always did.

Somehow it didn't feel nearly as good as she'd expected it to.

chapter TWELVE

"Situations like this are called triggers," Dr. Reynolds reminded him. "Sometimes it's a person, a place, or just a stressor that agitates the urge to drink. We talked about these at length, remember? It's okay to have them. I'd be shocked if you didn't."

The benefit had gone surprisingly well. They'd raised nearly twice as much money as Trace had expected, and the outpouring of support had blown his mind. But…Christ Almighty, seeing her there had nearly destroyed every ounce of self-control he'd had.

When she was on stage, singing a song that'd pummeled his heart six ways to Sunday, he'd wanted nothing more than to grab her up, throw her over his shoulder, and drag her to his bedroom caveman-style. He'd spend all night—and every night afterward—trying to take away the pain he'd caused her. And if he got her back in there, she was never coming out. Neither of them was. Ever.

He'd tried to talk to her and she'd all but run from him. Afterward, he'd spent the entire night sitting alone in his bedroom staring at the bed, picturing her in it. He hadn't downed a bottle of bourbon and let the burn coat his insides with sweet fire and distract him from the pain of missing her. Of having lost her.

But now, having gone more than twenty-four hours on no sleep and an entire night of watching the ghost of Kylie Ryans tease and taunt him, he was on the brink.

"It's more than that, Doc. This isn't a trigger I can avoid. I mean, I can try. Hell, I've been trying, but…" He sat in his truck, rubbing the bridge of his nose with the hand not holding the phone. "I can't outrun my own memory."

He'd left the house as soon as it was daylight and driven to his house in Nashville. Which he knew wasn't nearly far enough from her apartment. The only thing that kept him from going there was the memory of what had happened last time.

"Trace, it's not your memory that's the trigger. It's the situation or your feeling like you can't control it. Can't repair what's been broken."

Yeah, okay. The man had a point.

She wasn't a piece of equipment on the farm, wasn't something he could take a hammer and nails to and fix. Unfortunately. Kylie Ryans was a force of nature—wild like prairie winds that blew past so quickly you couldn't tell which direction they'd come from. She'd blown him the hell away from day one.

"Doc, I'm sorry to have called so early. I have to go. I'll check in again tonight." Before the doctor could protest, Trace hung up the phone. Grabbing a pen from the center console, he began jotting down the song that had just begun to play in his head.

A FTER writing a song he knew he'd probably never have the balls to sing in public, Trace sprawled on his couch and stared at the ceiling fan. The cherry oak blades drifted lazily in circles, but he didn't see them. He saw her.

She was different. Guarded. Less…something.

It was as if someone had coached her. Her sassy Oklahoma accent was less pronounced. She carried herself with the grace of someone older and wiser than he'd remembered. She thought before she acted, before she spoke. For just a moment last night, he'd seen her slip. Caught a glimpse of the Hothead who had turned his whole world inside out.

The Kylie Ryans he'd known was open, honest, and wore her heart on her sleeve. The girl—no, woman—he'd seen last night was closed off, holding everything in, and had her heart on maximum-security lockdown.

Because of me.

Understanding hit him hard, as hard—if not harder—than the urge to drink always did.

I love it… I love you, she'd told him when he'd bought her daddy's truck and given it to her. And he'd said nothing. She'd handed him her whole heart and he'd fumbled it. His fists clenched as he lay there. No wonder she'd hidden it away.

There was still another factor he was trying not to think about. But it was pretty hard to ignore with its tattoos and screaming guitars and the annoying smirk Trace wanted to sucker-punch right off its damn face.

Maybe she wasn't hiding her heart from the world. Maybe he just couldn't see it anymore because she'd given it to someone else.

chapter THIRTEEN

THE next morning, the blaring ring of her phone compounded the hangover from hell. She'd stopped using music as her ringtone and just used a traditional one. It was annoying, but at least it didn't dredge up any painful memories.

"Ugh," she groaned as she rolled over and glanced at her phone. Bright blue eyes greeted her. "Morning, Blythe," she greeted her caller.

"It's noon, Ryans. You missed the opportunity to tell me good morning."

"Damn. How will I ever go on?" She yawned and sat up in her bed. Which she didn't remember getting into. She owed Mia one. Or more than one.

"I'll let you make it up to me. Somehow. Want to have lunch? Or breakfast in your case? I'm in the neighborhood."

Well this was new. Steven Blythe had gone from a once upon a time late-night fool around friend to a writing buddy and just plain old friend. Though he wasn't exactly someone she expected to be asking her on a lunch date.

"Oh-kay. Where do you want to meet?"

"How about at your front door?"

Kylie jumped up and sprinted to her bathroom. "Um, okay. So, like, you're here now?"

She almost cried out when she saw her reflection. Her hair was a mess and her makeup was smeared all over her face. She had no idea if the dark rings under her eyes were from crying her mascara off last night or lack of sleep.

A low rumble of laughter came through the line. "Yeah, I'm heading to the elevator now."

"Okay. See you in a minute." Kylie disconnected the call and splashed some water on her face. Shit that was cold. After brushing her teeth and throwing on an old Rum Room t-shirt and jeans, she met her unexpected visitor at the door.

"Morning, babe. You didn't have to get all fixed up for me." Steven gave her his wickedly adorable grin and an appreciative once-over.

Kylie pulled her hair up into a messy bun and rolled her eyes. "You're welcome," she told him as she grabbed her keys and sunglasses off the table by the door. "So where to?"

"Wanna grab something at the Rum Room? Or hit one of the diners down the street?"

She'd already locked her door when she realized she'd forgotten two of the most important items she owned.

"Oh crap." She sighed and turned back around. "I need to grab my wallet and my phone. I don't know where my head is today. Sorry."

She wasn't one to sleep in, and normally her daily life was scheduled down to the minute. She was beginning to realize why.

Steven's warm hands wrapped around hers. "I'm buying. And you can make it through one meal without your phone, right?"

She froze, wondering if she actually could make it through a meal without her phone. She couldn't remember the last time she had. And he was buying? And holding her hand? So this was a date? Her head swam with questions she was still too hungover to answer.

"Okay. But, um, I eat like a dude, so consider yourself warned."

Steven grinned as they left her apartment building. "Maybe take it easy on me then. I'm out of a job."

Kylie stopped and turned to face him. "You're what?"

Placing a hand on her lower back urging her forward, he continued.

"It's not a big deal. Band's just taking a breather."

"The hell it isn't a big deal. You guys are about to be freaking huge. You're like *the* unsigned band to be right now. I thought there was interest from Eletrick and all that?"

He shrugged as he held the door to the diner open for her. "Things got…complicated."

Kylie raised an eyebrow at him but he didn't offer anything further. She watched as Steven nodded to a pretty redheaded waitress. As she took in his tight black T-shirt and the tattoos banding his thick arms, a slow smile spread across the woman's face. Kylie barely managed to keep from laughing out loud.

The woman gestured to an empty booth Kylie would've bet money was in her section and they slid in.

"So, Miss-Eats-Like-A-Dude, what'll it be?"

"Come on, Blythe," Kylie began, using her hand to lower the menu he held. "Talk to me. What's really going on?"

He sighed, setting the menu aside and turning the full force of his bright blue eyes on her.

"Chris isn't feeling the new sound. He says we're letting the media influence make us too 'mainstream.'" Steven used air quotes on the last word. "I don't know. Maybe he's right. But lately he and I have just…" He smacked his two fists together as an illustration. "Just been coming up on opposite sides of every discussion you know? And BJ is tired of it. He gets stressed out really easily. Kid had a rough home life."

"So what are you guys going to do? Just break up? That's asinine."

Steven ran a hand through his already mussed black hair and shifted in his seat, but before he could answer, the redhead appeared to take their order.

"What can I get for you?" she asked, green eyes locked on Kylie's breakfast companion.

Kylie didn't miss the flirty grin Steven shot the waitress before motioning for her to take Kylie's order first.

She thrust her menu at the annoying chick. "Yeah, I'll have the pancakes and bacon with extra syrup please. And an orange juice and a large coffee, black."

The waitress forced a smile that was more like a smirk. "And you?" she said, taking Kylie's menu and turning back to Steven.

"Same, I guess."

When she was finally gone, Kylie turned back to Steven. He was spinning a saltshaker back and forth between his large hands. "You do her or what?"

"What?" His eyebrows shot upward as he looked at her with wide eyes.

"No? So all women get ridiculous around you like that? Because if they do, this is our last breakfast date. It's too early for me to watch some chick ogle you. Her desperation is making me nauseated." Kylie yawned, which nearly made her giggle at the perfect timing of it.

"Aw, Ryans, you're jealous." With a wink, Steven leaned in closer to her. "Actually, that's kind of a turn-on of mine."

"You're a jackass." Kylie sat back and folded her arms. "For one, I don't do jealous. For two, I'm more interested in hearing what the hell's going on with the band than what turns you on. And for three, can we just focus on one thing for a second? I swear I think you have an attention deficit issue."

He chuckled and slid the saltshaker aside. "For one, I was just messing with you about being jealous. For two, the band is on a break... indefinitely. And three, I actually do. My parents made me take medicine for it when I was a kid but it made me feel dead so I stopped."

Kylie huffed out a breath. "Figures. Okay, so tell me the truth. You and Chris butting heads—is it really over the direction of the band or a certain brunette we both know and have likely seen naked?"

"You've seen her naked?"

"We toured together, so the answer should be obvious. It was a small bus. But I'm guessing from the way you nearly fell out of your seat that you haven't. And that's the issue."

Propping his elbows on the table, Steven regarded her warily. "What if I have? You don't care?"

Kylie tossed her hands up, palms facing him. "Whoa. This isn't about me. This is about you and the band and whether or not you're throwing your career away over a girl."

Isn't it?

Kylie's head swam as the overwhelming possibility that this early morning meeting was about much more than breakfast overtook her. "Steven..." She bit her lip as she tried to find the words to say what she wanted to.

"Relax, Ryans. I know. Jealousy isn't you're thing. Got it. But I wonder, if it was a certain—"

"Don't. Whatever you're going to say, don't." She could feel it in the air when people were about to mention Trace. Everything inside of her tensed up.

"All right. My bad. So yeah, in all honesty, whatever's going on with me and Chris, Mia Montgomery isn't helping matters any."

Kylie nodded. Surprisingly, the admission didn't sting. Not even a little. She wondered briefly if something was wrong with her. "Well, have you talked to Chris about it?"

The waitress reappeared with their food, and Steven waited to answer until she'd gone.

"Yeah, and it hasn't gone over well. Our last conversation ended with us deciding not to tour at all until next year. If even then."

"I'm sorry. That sucks. Seriously. You want me to talk to Mia?" Not that she knew what she'd say, but she could at least let her friend know that her relationship with Chris was causing tension.

"Um, no. What would you say, Ryans? Hey, Mia, at some point between Steven giving me countless orgasms, he mentioned that you and Chris dry humping during band rehearsal was distracting and he'd like for you to quit. Yeah, that should go over well."

Kylie felt her face redden at least ten shades. "You did not just say orgasms and dry humping over breakfast."

"I did. And so did you." Steven snatched a piece of bacon off her plate and crammed it in his mouth. She didn't care. It was chewy and gross instead of crispy like she liked.

"Ugh. How did we get so..."

"Fucked up? Easy. We got rejected by the people we cared about and then we used each other for a distraction of a physical nature."

Kylie shook her head. "You know, sometimes I'm not actually looking for a literal answer." In spite of herself, she grinned when he did.

He shrugged. "Then don't ask me questions."

"You're such a guy."

Steven smirked. "Yeah, I am. Glad you noticed. But you, on the other hand, have barely touched your food. Some dude you are."

"I can't eat with the waitress glaring at us and you talking about your career ending like it's no big deal and tossing around the o-word all while trying to figure out how to get Mia to stop dry humping your lead singer." She rubbed her temples and tried to think.

"Hey," Steven said softly, reaching over the table to pull her hands from her head. "This isn't your problem, Ryans. I didn't ask you here to stress you out."

"Why did you ask me here?" She swallowed hard. If this was the part where he said he wanted more, wanted a relationship or something, she was screwed. She wasn't interested in that—not with Steven or anyone. And turning a guy down when his band was breaking up seemed pretty bitchy, even for her.

She watched as he sucked in a breath. "I just wanted to know if you knew of anyone who might need a lead guitarist. If I don't find something soon, it's back to Georgia I go. There's an open spot on my dad's construction crew with my name on it." His pained expression made her heart ache. Though she was breathing easily since it hadn't been a profession of love he'd blurted out.

"Steven, surely—"

"Look, don't do the pity party thing. Just keep an ear out, okay? If anything opens up, let me know."

She nodded, mentally scanning her brain for anything she might have heard about bands needing guitar players. She stood as he tossed some bills on the table. The fact that the waitress hadn't even had a chance to leave a check with her number on it made her want to snicker.

Once they were outside, she was hit with another fleeting wave of panic. Would he walk her home? Should she invite him in? Would anything happen between them if she did? Did she want anything to happen?

"Um…"

"I've got a few leads to follow up on about gigs this weekend. But I'll call you. Or call me if you hear of anything."

"Okay. Thanks for breakfast."

"You're welcome. Later, Ryans." With a quick kiss on the forehead and a one-arm hug, Steven headed off in the other direction.

We got rejected by the people we cared about and then we used each other for a distraction of a physical nature.

He'd pretty much summed it up perfectly. As much as she hated to admit it, he was right. The reason she didn't feel jealous over the waitress or Mia—or anything really—was because her heart wasn't in it. At least this time she knew Steven's heart wasn't in it either.

Last time, she'd been stupid enough to think the other person's actually had been.

chapter
FOURTEEN

"THIS is the offer. It's not something they're willing to negotiate. It's, 'Here's what we have. Take it or walk.'" Maude Lowenstein lifted a bony shoulder in a half shrug. "It's better than nothing as far as I'm concerned."

"She won't go for it. Not in a million years. All she wanted at the benefit was for me to stay the hell away from her." Trace shook his head and fought the urge to wince at the memory.

His agent and his manager sat across from him in the conference room at Capital Letter Records. He'd thought he'd been called in to sign his dissolution papers. But Noel Davies had sprung one last option on him, one last proposition of the fuck-you-flavored variety.

"She's not in a position to be turning down the label's offers either. She already turned down a world tour with Bryce Parker." His agent lowered her glasses. "Care to know why?"

He fought the urge to grin and cleared his throat. "No. And you probably shouldn't be discussing her with me. She's just as much your client as I am."

"Yes, she is. And if two of my clients are about to be touring together, I can discuss it with whomever I so chose." The woman paused as if waiting for him to challenge her. When he didn't, she continued. "So here's why I think she'll be more agreeable than you suspect. In the meeting when they offered her a spot on Parker's tour, she said, and I quote, 'I'm not going on tour with some cheap knock-off Trace Corbin wannabe,' end quote."

"She said that?"

"Yes, she did. So again, she's not really in a position to turn down a tour with the real thing, now is she?"

"I don't think she cares about what kind of position she's in," Pauly chimed in. "She'll probably tell the label to kiss her chart-topping ass if they even suggest she and Trace share a bus for the next few months."

Trace shook his head. Discussing Kylie and positions was doing things to him. Causing him to think things one should not be thinking during business meetings. "Yeah, I have to agree with Pauly. She's not going to go for this. The label can threaten me all they want because I'm on my last leg, but she probably has offers lined up."

Pauly nodded, and even Maude was quiet for a moment.

"What if we let her think it was her idea?"

"What?" both men asked, almost in unison.

"Just think about it. You and she have a history, Trace. Talk to her. Tell her you need a big act for your next tour or the label's cutting you loose. Say whatever you have to."

He thought it over for a split-second. "I won't do that to her. She doesn't owe me anything. She'd be the first to tell you so."

"So make her *want* to tour with you. Take her to dinner. Take her to bed. Whatever." The woman leaned back in her seat as if the matter was settled.

"You're such a romantic, Maude. I'm not going to screw Kylie Ryans into touring with me. And the fact that you're even suggesting it makes me think the only thing I should be telling her is that she needs a new agent."

"Trace—" Pauly began, but Maude cut him off.

"Look, from where you sit, this probably all looks really complicated and messy. But from where I sit, it's pretty damn cut and dry. Here's the thing about this business. The most talented artist isn't always the one who makes it big. You know who is? The one the media pays the most attention to, the one who works the hardest to stay out front, the one who does whatever it takes—regardless of things like fairness and feelings and all that other pretentious preschool bullshit—to make their career what they want it to be. So you want more platinum-selling albums? You convince Kylie Ryans to do this *The Other Side of Me* Tour. Or you can walk away from this and let these twelve-year-olds take over country music and put your ass out to pasture."

She stood to leave and Trace closed his eyes. He'd nearly been plowed down on his way into the meeting by an entourage surrounding some kid whose eyes had been glued to his cellphone.

"That's Collin Hanes," Pauly had informed him. "He's sixteen and his album is number one on iTunes."

The little shit had looked like he was there for Take Your Kid to Work Day.

Trace opened his eyes and let out a loud breath. "I won't play games or trick her into this. But I'll try. I'll do what I can to try and convince her."

"Good," Maude said as she placed a hand on the door. "So will I."

Trace groaned and leaned back in his chair. Damn. This was not good. This was the opposite of good.

Pauly cleared his throat as he stood. "As your manager, I'd say Kylie Ryans might be the best thing for your career at this point. As your friend, one who actually gives a damn about you and your sobriety, I'd say she's probably the worst person you could involve yourself with— personally or professionally."

"Thanks, Pauly. That's real helpful."

His manager squeezed his shoulder lightly as he passed. "I know. But I also happen to know she's recording at Bluebird Studios tonight if you wanted to swing by there. Maybe a heads-up from you would come across better than Maude or the label blindsiding her."

Maybe. Or maybe she'd tell him to go straight to hell where he belonged.

BLUEBIRD Studios was empty save for a few cars in the parking lot. Trace let himself in the entrance for artists and nodded at Molly at the front desk.

"Hey, sunshine. Would you happen to know which studio Kylie Ryans is in this evening?"

"Hm. Well, Mr. Corbin, that depends. Is she expecting you?"

He gave the blonde a wink and a grin. "I don't know if anyone could ever be expecting me, darlin'. I'm kind of hard to handle."

The receptionist eyed him appreciatively. And then her face transformed into a mask of disappointment. "So the rumors are true then? About you and her?"

"Where there's smoke, there's fire, sweetheart. Is she in D? I know she prefers D." He was guessing, but he preferred it. He figured she probably did, too.

"Yeah, she's in D. Go on back. But you snuck in if anyone asks. And you owe me," she called out after him.

He made a mental note to send Molly some flowers or chocolates. She was a sweet girl. Pretty, too. Just not the one he wanted.

Once he'd reached Studio D, he stepped into the listening booth and nodded at Kylie's manager, a guy with glasses he'd seen around a few times. Before he had time to introduce himself properly, her voice filled the room.

I'll set your night on fire. I'm a live wire. I'm a live wire.

Boy, was that the truth.

He watched as she belted out the rest of her song, a fast one about how she was untamable. Watching her while being surrounded by her sultry voice made it hard to swallow. Or think. Or breathe. So he glanced down at his phone and pretended to give a shit about something on it until the music stopped.

"Mr. Corbin?" Kylie's manager came over and shook his hand. "Chaz Michealson. Kylie's manager. What can I do for you?"

"Nice to meet you, Mr. Michaelson. Kylie's said nothing but good things about you." The man cleared his throat and Trace grinned. "Don't feel bad if you can't say the same thing to me. I deserve it, whatever she's said."

"She has a bit of a temper," her manager said, glancing back to where she stood glaring at them on the other side of the glass.

"That she does." Trace raised his hand in a small wave that she didn't return. The force of her stare should've shattered the glass between them. "Listen, I was wondering if I could speak with her privately for a few minutes. No doubt she'll be filling you in on every aspect of the conversation once we're done. Or you can stick around and hear it through the door when she yells at me."

"Think I'll sit this one out, if it's all the same to you." The manager opened the door as Kylie came through.

"Hey, pretty girl," Trace greeted her. His heart began beating in overtime at the sight of her.

Her blue eyes gleamed in the lights of the studio. He didn't know if her face was flushed from singing her heart out or from seeing him. Either way, she was beautiful as always.

"What are you doing here?"

"It's nice to see you, too. I was in the neighborhood." Trace leaned against the side wall as Chaz and the other men in the room let themselves out quietly.

He watched as Kylie chugged half a bottle of water. "Oh yeah? Well, I'm all done for today, so if you need the studio, knock yourself out."

"Actually I need you. I mean I need to talk to you." Jesus. Sometimes he wondered if his life would be easier if he'd just cut out his own tongue years ago.

Kylie raised an eyebrow. "Okay. Talk."

"Here? You don't want to go get some dinner or something?"

She snorted. "No, thanks. Steven took me out for a late breakfast and I'm not hungry."

Shit. That did not feel good to hear. It felt as if she'd socked him as hard as she could right in the chest. He lowered himself onto the couch and looked up at her. The lights surrounded her, making her look like a vision he was having. His hands twitched, aching to reach out and touch her. It was an urge more intense than the need to drink had ever been. And she was even more off-limits.

"Thanks for performing at the benefit. I appreciated that."

Her eyes widened in surprise, but she seemed to shake off her reaction before she spoke. "You're welcome. Is that what you came to the 'neighborhood' to tell me?"

"No. I came because…" *Because I love you. I miss you. I need you and I can't stand having to be on the same planet as you if I can't have you.* The words stuck in his throat. What he actually said was, "Because the label has some ideas for us. They're pushing hard and I wanted you to hear it from me, wanted you to know it wasn't my idea."

Her brows dipped downward and she took another drink before responding. "What wasn't your idea? The tour?"

"So you know then?"

She wiped a drop of water from her perfect mouth and then glared at him. "Yeah, I know. I'm not the same girl I was...before. I'm not all wide-eyed and excited about the opportunity to tour with *Trace Corbin.*"

The way she said his name, with false enthusiasm, made his stomach churn.

"All right. Well, I didn't figure you'd be too thrilled. Gotta say, I'm not sure why the hostility is directed at me though. I just told you it wasn't my idea."

Her glare intensified before she finally looked away. "I knew this was coming when they asked me to do the benefit. It was pretty obvious that you didn't want me there."

Trace opened his mouth to tell her that wasn't exactly how it was, but she rushed on before he could.

"Chaz and I kind of talked it out. In a way, it makes sense. The media thinks there's something going on between us—or that there was—and you can't turn the radio on without hearing that damn song. We'd probably sell out every venue."

"There's a but coming." He could see it on her face, in her stance.

"You bet your ass there is. Just because it might be the right move for both of our careers doesn't mean I want to take a tour down memory lane. I'd rather be bound and gagged and dragged naked through town than share a bus with you. Again."

If it didn't hurt so much to hear, he might've laughed. He barely resisted the urge to tell her that if she said yes, he'd be happy to get her naked and tie her up. But as hard as she was trying to stonewall him, he could see the hint of pain flashing in her beautiful eyes.

"Say no more. Message received. Well, that's that then." He rubbed his sweaty palms on his jeans and stood to leave, but there was one more thing he had to say. "For the record, I didn't come here to talk you into it. I came here to tell you that if you did decide to go through with it, for professional purposes only of course, then I would do my best to make it as easy for you as possible. I know what you think, but I promise, I'm not the same person either. I wouldn't stand you up or bail on shows and leave you to deal with the fallout. And I wouldn't cross all those lines like I did before. You're with someone else now. I can respect that."

He could tell her breathing was becoming labored even though he was staring into her eyes. Her face contorted from what he figured was the effort to keep any of her actual emotions from showing. His hand reached out to stroke her smooth cheek, but he pulled back at the last second. He'd just said he wouldn't cross lines and here he was, wanting to trample all over them.

"Kylie Lou, I—"

"Don't. I heard what you said. I'll consider it. I'll talk to the label and let them know I'm thinking about it."

"I guess that's all I can ask for." He shrugged. "You sounded great in there, by the way." He nodded towards the sound booth. "And at the CMAs, and at the benefit. I know I haven't had time to tell you, but I'm really pro—"

"I have to go," she blurted out. Before he could finish his sentence, she grabbed her belongings from the couch and barreled past him out of the room.

chapter FIFTEEN

BREATHING had become nearly unbearable. Existing was painful.

He'd just appeared at her recording session without warning. She couldn't handle Trace Corbin without some time to prepare herself. And then he'd been all "Hey, pretty girl." And then nearly telling her he was proud of her? It was too much. Way too much.

The tears came unbidden down her face as she leaned against her daddy's truck and tried to steady herself. Damn Trace Corbin to hell for making her feel this way. He hadn't even looked as if talking to her in such close proximity had affected him in the least.

Well, up until she mentioned Steven.

Steven, she realized, was her ace in the hole. Her shield that backed Trace Corbin out of her space.

The idea of having at least a tiny bit of protection from her own feelings and irrepressible reactions allowed her to breathe a little more easily.

Once she'd regained the majority of her equilibrium, she got in her truck and drove to her place. It was huge. Huge and empty. And lonely.

Trudging to her front door of her building, she did what she'd told Trace she would. She thought about it. Pondered the possibility of being on a bus with him, performing together, touring together.

Business-wise it made sense. There was a great deal of buzz around the both of them, their duet was a hit, and you couldn't stand in line at the grocery story without seeing photos of either of them in a tabloid or two. But…

She just couldn't put herself through that again. She couldn't and she wouldn't. Not when seeing him for all of five minutes had nearly wrecked her.

She'd worked her ass off to make it in this business, and she'd only gotten this far by putting her feelings about him, about everything that had happened between the two of them, in a small, dark corner far away where no one could reach it. Not even her and sure as hell not him.

The label would just have to take no for an answer.

KYLIE woke up next to her guitar. She'd fallen asleep on her couch as usual. Despite the fact that the bed she owned was enormous, she rarely slept in it.

She rubbed her eyes and stretched, blinking until her eyes adjusted. In the distance, she heard a ringing sound. It was the standard ring she'd set her phone to. Scrambling to her feet, she dug it out of her purse and answered.

"Morning, sweetheart. I just wanted to remind you about the meeting at the label this afternoon. They're pulling out all the stops today I bet, so don't be late."

"I got it, Chaz. All the reminders you put on my phone helped." She chuckled until she caught her reflection in her bathroom mirror. She definitely needed to get her hair cut sooner rather than later. "Hey, do you think you could call Emelle and see if she can come by and do something with my hair today before the meeting?"

"Nooo, I can't. Because I'm your manager, not your assistant. However, I was talking to my boss last week and she mentioned that on your next tour you need a day-to-day manager, kind of like an assistant. But since sleeping on a bus is not something I ever plan to add to my bucket list, we're currently looking for someone who'd be a good fit. Any requests?"

"Hmm." Kylie stared at her reflection in the mirror as she contemplated the prospect of having an assistant. Boy, life was strange sometimes. "I'm not really picky, I guess. Just as long as they're not too like…perky. Just someone efficient and professional."

"Sounds good. I'll pass that along to the boss lady. See you at three."

Since she didn't have an assistant yet, she hung up with Chaz and dialed her stylist. Who thankfully was available to come over in a few hours and help her look presentable before meeting with Noel Davies and the rest of the peanut gallery.

Kylie knew she wasn't exactly playing well with others as her manager had pointed out, but she also knew that she wasn't going to be forced on some lame tour that would keep her out of the studio. The options the label had presented so far just hadn't felt right.

Her biggest fear was that today's meeting would be the one where they asked her to go on tour with Trace. And her second biggest fear was what she already knew to be true.

As much as it hurt to think about and as terrifying as it was, that was the one option that actually did feel right.

AFTER Emelle had trimmed and highlighted her hair, Kylie felt better. Less world-weary and somewhat refreshed. The past few weeks had been draining, both physically and emotionally, and she'd needed the pick-me-up even more than she'd realized.

As she dressed for the meeting, a startling realization forced itself on her. If they were going to push the tour with Trace on her today, he might be there.

Suddenly every option in her entire wardrobe fell into two categories. Not sexy enough and trying too hard.

Standing in the center of her bedroom in her underwear, she texted Mia.

Meeting today. Pretty sure Trace will be there. Feeling a little nervous. Clothing suggestions?

She waited a few minutes and had almost given up and texted Lulu. But the then phone buzzed in her hand.

Wear good lingerie in case you guys do it in the parking lot afterwards.

Ignoring the excited panic that rose in her stomach, Kylie texted back.

You are not helpful.

Mia responded almost immediately.

Isn't your BFF going to be your new stylist soon? Ask her.

Kylie sighed out loud. This was true. But she'd also made every effort to convince the whole world, with the exception of Mia—who'd seen her freak out firsthand—that her past involvement with Trace Corbin was a non-issue in her life. Admitting that she cared what she looked like around him seemed like a dead giveaway.

She stared at her closet once more. This was dumb. She was twenty years old and he'd seen her naked. She could pick out an outfit for a meeting for God's sakes.

After three changes of clothing, Kylie settled on a short navy blue dress, a cream-colored wrap, and brown knee-length riding boots. It was a little shorter and tighter than what she'd wear to a meeting if he weren't going to be there, but it wasn't an overtly obvious cry for attention. At least she hoped not.

The last thing she wanted to do was send mixed signals.

Not that she could even send clear signals, because she hadn't exactly figured out what the message was for herself.

chapter SIXTEEN

"W̲E̲'R̲E̲ going to get one shot at convincing her that this is a good idea. Y'all know that right? Because once she makes up her mind, there won't be any telling her otherwise. From anyone." Trace made eye contact with Pauly, Maude, and Noel Davies.

"Leave it to me. I can handle her," Noel informed him.

Trace barely fought back a snort. Kylie Ryans was not the type to be "handled" by Noel Davies—or anyone else, for that matter.

Even Maude gave the Record Exec a doubtful smirk. "Again, if we just let her think it's her idea, that it's what's best for her career, then none of us will have to convince her of anything." The woman eyed each of them as if they were complete morons. "If any of you had half a brain, you'd bring her in here and tell her the label doesn't like her new grown-up sound. That the only way to get fans on board is to have her tour with Trace and appear to be in a serious adult relationship with him. Present it as an opportunity instead of an ultimatum. It's not that hard, boys."

"It's not that easy either," a female voice broke in. "It's the damnedest thing, but if I didn't know better, I'd think I actually had a mind of my own and could just make decisions all by my lonesome."

The sound of her voice, even her angry voice, softened something inside of Trace. For as steely as her solid glare at all of them was, he'd detected the note of hurt when she'd spoken. He met her stare and offered her an apologetic shrug. Like she'd said, she wasn't the same girl. She knew how things worked now.

A part of him hated that. That she'd lost that wide-eyed innocence about the music business. That this was no longer a dream come true for her, but a job. A minefield to navigate.

"Kylie, we weren't—" Noel Davies began before she cut him off.

"Yes you were. But that's okay. I suspected I was walking into an ambush. Looks like it's a perfect day for playing Manipulate the Bitchy Artist into Submission apparently." She walked all the way into the room with her manager close behind. Trace nodded at him as they sat across the table.

"So where were we then?" Noel said, eyeing each occupant at the table. "No, you know what? This is so formal and unnecessary. How about we all head over to my office and sit comfortably so we can discuss this like civilized professionals?"

Trace shook his head. He knew what was up. This was Davies whipping out his dick and putting himself at the head of the table. He would show Kylie just how big and bad his office was, intimidate her with his power. He couldn't stand by and watch that.

"I think we're good here, Davies. How about we just get on with it?"

"Are we keeping you from something, Mr. Corbin?" Kylie asked, turning to him with raised brows and a look of feigned interest.

What the hell was her problem? He was trying to move things along without the dog and pony show. For her benefit. So much for chivalry.

"Okay. Since you've all decided to play hard-asses today, how about I just give it to everyone straight?" Davies cleared his throat and when no one interrupted, he continued. "The label has decided that the best way to launch Trace's comeback and Kylie's *Not a Nice Girl* album is to send both of you on an arena tour. You'll both have *The Other Side of Me* on your next albums, so that'll be the headline for the tour. One bus, some promos hinting that the two of you might be romantically involved, joint interviews, and then afterwards, you're both free to do whatever you want."

Noel's words hung heavy in the air and silence descended on the room.

Until everyone began talking at once.

"That's not even—"

"I don't see how that will—"

"Maybe we should just—"

"Well then, I see you all have some things to discuss. Feel free to stay in here as long as necessary until these contracts are signed." With that, Noel Davies stood, slid two stacks of paper to each side of the table, and left. Trace's hatred for the smug bastard intensified.

Once the door closed, he took a deep breath and met the gorgeous blues of a girl he knew would wreck him. In more ways than one.

"What do you think, Kylie Lou? Can we do this?"

He could hear the voice of Gretchen Gibson in his head.

No. You can't handle this. You aren't strong enough and she's not worth your sobriety. You'll only be repeating the same mistakes.

Kylie was out of reaching distance, but it didn't stop him from seeing the memories flicker through her expression. They were the same ones playing behind his eyes. The fights. The laughter. The lovemaking. The goodbye.

And when it ended, pure, unadulterated fear slipped past the bravado and she was as exposed to him as the first time they'd slept together.

A year ago, a look like that would have brought him to his knees. Even now, if they'd been alone, he would've dropped down and begged for forgiveness, pleaded once more for the right to kiss her, to hold her.

But as it was, they weren't alone. And this was business. Kylie cleared her throat and broke their stare. Turning to her manager, she nodded.

The man nodded back and then at Maude. Suddenly Trace had the feeling it wasn't Kylie who was being ambushed at all.

"So here's what we have," Maude began. "Kylie is open to this possibility. Contingent upon some specifications, she's willing to co-headline on this tour."

Trace felt his eyes widen. So she had just been playing reluctant for Davies? Or was Maude playing everyone? He wasn't sure, but he damn sure wasn't up for being played.

He stared at Kylie, but she kept her gaze focused out the window. He wondered what Nashville looked like through her eyes now.

"Let's hear these *specifications*. I might have a few of my own."

That got her attention. He leaned back in his chair as she turned towards him.

"One," Maude began, "she wants it in the contract that there is to be no drinking on your part. And if you're so much as one minute late to a soundcheck or a show, she walks."

He cocked a brow and tried to pretend it didn't sting that she still didn't trust him. Not that he'd done much to deserve her trust. But he could work on that.

"Two," Maude continued, "no fake promos about your relationship or lack thereof, and you are to have separate living spaces of equal size on the bus. And in any hotels you stay in during the tour."

Tilting his head, he continued to listen as their agent discussed the rest of Kylie's conditions. He did his best to put off an air of boredom. As if these things were inconsequential to him. But in reality? Separate living spaces or no, this was not something he was sure he could handle.

He'd been depending on her to shut this whole crazy thing down. Even if she agreed to tour with him, she was a big damn deal these days. Sharing a bus was the biggest fake promo there was.

It said to the world that they were practically living together. Which they would be. Sharing a bus with her, knowing deep down that what he felt for her was bound to burst through the surface any second, might be the death of him. He was going to have to risk hurting her feelings and saying so in a room full of people.

But when she stood and he got a glimpse of her tight little body in that tiny dress, those smooth, tan legs that he'd once had wrapped around his waist while buried so deep inside of her he couldn't remember his own name, all he could think was, *What a way to go.*

chapter
SEVENTEEN

"DON'T you think I know that?" Kylie said into the phone wedged against her ear as she balanced precariously on one foot while trying to put a boot on.

"It's just, it's him, you know? And after everything the two of you have been through…after how bad things ended last year, I'm not sure this is the best idea. For either of you."

"Lu, I'm aware of this. Believe me. But he agreed to all of my conditions, and the truth is, I think this tour is what my fans want. So even though it might be hell getting through it, I owe it to them. Without them, I'd still be waitressing at The Rum Room."

She heard her friend huff out a breath. "Kylie—"

"Remember when I called you from Nashville? The first time?" Her friend didn't answer right away, so she rushed on. "Remember how worried you were? And what did I tell you?"

"That you were going to be okay. You promised."

Kylie grinned even though her friend couldn't see. "Right. And I am going to be okay this time, too."

I hope.

"And this time I'll be with you," Lulu added. "So if you and Country

Ken Doll get yourselves into a mess, I'll be there to junk-punch the both of you."

For the first time in days, Kylie laughed. "Well thank God for that."

"So my flight gets in tomorrow morning. I hate that I can't be there tonight."

Kylie's laughter died in her throat. Tonight was the kickoff party for the tour. At The Rum Room. And she was going alone. "Yeah, um, no big. Promise I'll be fine."

"You do realize what happened last time you said those words to me, right?"

She swallowed hard and secured her other boot onto her foot. "Yeah, Lu. I know. I ended up on tour with some hotshot country music singer in tight jeans."

"And here we go again."

A LOW whistle greeted her when she got out of the white SUV the label had sent to drive her to the party.

"Well I'll be. If it isn't our very own Kylie Ryans." The manager of the bar stood next to the back entrance, shaking her head.

"Hey, Tonya." Kylie did her best to exit the vehicle without flashing Tonya her crotch. It was damn near impossible in the entirely-too-short red dress she was wearing.

"Hey, hot stuff. There's quite a crowd in there. You ready?"

She looked up into Tonya's eyes as she approached. "Can you really ever be ready for something like this?"

The woman bit her lip and gave her a sympathetic look. "Probably not. But on the plus side, you're a big deal now, right? Equal footing and all that."

"If you say so." Kylie was grateful that they were alone. She could feel the blood rushing to her head, and it was becoming increasingly difficult to breathe normally.

"Hey, hon. Seriously. You okay?" Tonya's sympathetic look morphed into one of concern.

Kylie forced herself to nod as they entered the back of the bar. "Yeah, I'm fine."

"Kylie, listen to me. Whatever's going on in that head of yours, shut it out. You are gorgeous, talented, and just as successful as What's-His-Ass in there. Don't forget that. You've worked hard and you deserve this. So go knock 'em dead."

"Thanks," Kylie breathed out. "Tonya, could you maybe grab me a water? With some vodka in it?"

The other woman let out a small laugh. "Yeah, sure. I've been manager for a year now. Probably about time I got fired for serving minors." She reached in a cooler and grabbed a bottle of water, which she handed over without adding anything to it.

The walk down the hallway behind the stage felt like a death march. Her legs grew heavier with each step. Kylie shook her hands, stretched her neck, and sipped her water—trying to do anything for a distraction.

"So how's the kiddo?"

At that, a wide grin broke across Tonya's face. "She's good. She's three handfuls but I can't complain. Starts kindergarten this year."

"That's awesome, Tonya." A smidge of the tightness in her chest loosened. She was happy for her friend. Glad that the woman finally had the life she wanted, the life she and her daughter deserved.

Tonya retrieved her phone from her pocket and pulled up a picture of a little girl with a high ponytail wearing an *I heart Kylie Ryans* T-shirt.

She grinned at the picture. "Wow, she's adorable. And she obviously has excellent taste in clothing and music."

"That she does. Gets it from her mom," Tonya said with a wink. "Hey, one last thing then I'm turning off my momdar and letting you be." She stopped walking and placed a hand on Kylie's shoulder. "You okay, hon? I mean really, *really* okay? Because you seem…different. And not too-big-for-your-fancy-designer-britches different like I expected. Sad different."

"I'm still just a girl with a guitar, Tonya. Not much has changed except that people actually pay to hear me sing now."

Her friend studied her intently. "Okay, if you don't want to talk about it with some lonely old bar manager with no life of her own to speak of, then I understand. But you could talk to me if you needed to vent. Honestly."

"Honestly?" Kylie glanced down the empty hall. "Honestly, no. I'm not okay. Honestly I have no idea what I'm doing and I feel like I've been playing the 'fake it till you make it' game and I can't do that with him. Every time he looks at me, I feel like he can read my mind or something and I just can't—"

Her sentence was interrupted by someone clearing his throat. Loudly. She closed her eyes. *Please let that be Clive. Please, pretty please.*

"They're ready for us," Trace said softly. "House band is warmed up and ready to go."

Kylie knew her eyes had widened at the sight of him. The dark blue button-up he wore tucked into his jeans fit him perfectly. His hair was fixed differently. As in, he did more than rake his hands through it. Or maybe it was just that there wasn't a worn-out trucker hat covering it. Either way, he was the Hollywood version of himself that she wasn't quite used to. Not that any version of Trace Corbin didn't have the uncanny ability to knock her senseless.

"Um, okay. Be right there."

"Equal footing, cuz," Tonya whispered from beside her. "Breathe."

She did as she was told and forced a smile in Trace's direction. He nodded once and walked towards the stage.

"Oh, my poor, sweet cousin from Oklahoma," Tonya said, shaking her head. "You, my dear, are in big trouble."

"I am?" Kylie asked, turning to her friend, wearing her panic all over her face.

"You're in love. And as I've said before, this shit ain't for amateurs."

chapter EIGHTEEN

T RACE greeted the crowd, trying his best to focus on them instead of who stood beside him.

Every time he looks at me I feel like he can read my mind.

He'd overheard her talking to the waitress-turned-manager that he knew she was friends with. What he couldn't figure out was if she had been talking about him or the guitar-wielding asshole behind them.

What the fuck Steven Blythe was doing in The Rum Room's house band was beyond him. Besides screwing up Trace's entire life that was.

"Thank y'all so much for coming out tonight. I can't tell you how much it means to me. And to someone else who is very special to me. Ladies and gentlemen, Miss Kylie Ryans."

The crowd hooped and hollered and whistled as she stepped up into the spotlight. Trace couldn't take his eyes off of her. Jesus Christ she was beautiful.

For a moment, he forgot she wasn't his. Forgot he'd given up the right to touch her, kiss her sweet, smiling mouth. Reflexively, his arm reached out and wrapped around her. The shock was clear on her face and he removed it as smoothly as he could manage.

"Hi y'all," she greeted the audience, taking a step away from him as she did. "Thanks for having us tonight." When the cheers and applause died down, she continued. "Trace and I are so excited about this upcoming tour and we couldn't wait to share the news with our friends at The Rum Room."

She paused, and he knew it was his cue, but the words escaped him. She was wearing a red dress. It wasn't the exact same one she'd had on the last time they'd been here together, but it was similar.

"Trace," she prompted. "Would you like to tell our friends our exciting news?" Her expression indicated that she'd barely been able to not call him a dumbass for gaping at her like an idiot.

"Of course I would." He turned and flashed his panty-dropping grin at the audience. "Our exciting news is that Kylie and I are expecting."

The response was almost deafening.

A hand smacked him hard in the chest. "We're *expecting* y'all to come see us on the road. Because tonight we're kicking off our *The Other Side of Me* tour," she clarified, practically shouting into the mic over the bedlam.

He winked when she glared at him.

"Ah yes. *That* news," he agreed.

At the confirmation that he was just kidding, the audience both cheered and booed them good-naturedly.

Kylie nodded over at Steven, which forced Trace to muster all of his self-control. But even all of his self-control couldn't keep the smile on his face. He prayed he wasn't glaring at least.

The opening chords of the song they'd written together started up, and before he knew it, he and Kylie were well into it.

The world wants fun and shiny and new. But I save the best of me for when I'm alone with you.

Tumultuous past or not, they sang in perfect harmony.

I'll keep all in, hide it under a grin, but you're the only one who sees. Yeah you're the only one who sees, the other side of me.

Once they were done, the crowd begged for an encore. Trace began singing *Waitin' for You to Call* and Kylie chimed in along with the band. But just like everything between them had always gone, it was over too soon for his liking.

He knew he shouldn't look at her, shouldn't let himself fall into those pools of blue he'd nearly drowned in once before. But he'd always had issues with addiction. So he looked. Stared, really.

She didn't say a word. But her voice filled his head. "I was broken. Dead inside," it whispered. "You made me feel alive."

It was a funny thing about addiction. During his stint in rehab he'd learned that addicts couldn't really ever be cured. They just learned ways to abstain. Resist temptation. And even years after abstaining, the smallest taste would put them right back where they started.

He hadn't fully believed it until that very moment. Until he'd gotten a taste of making music with Kylie Ryans and realized that since that day he'd walked out on her in this very same bar, he'd been dead inside. Going through the motions.

But being here, with her, again…had brought him back to life.

chapter NINETEEN

"Whⁿ the hell was the meaning of that?"

"Of what?" Trace looked at her like she'd lost her mind. But she saw it. That spark in his eyes, that mischievous, triumphant gleam.

"You know what. It was supposed to be one song, Trace. One. And that whole 'we're expecting' thing. Do you have any idea what kind of rumors you probably just started?"

He smirked, and she felt her blood pressure rising.

"Relax, Kylie Lou. It was a joke. And about the encore—so what? It's just a song."

Her fists clenched at her sides as she stormed out the back exit of the bar. "You are such an ass. What happened to being professional and not crossing lines?"

"Ky—"

"No, forget it. I don't know what I was expecting. Same old selfish Trace. Just do whatever the hell you want and don't bother considering how it affects anyone else."

It had been nearly a year since she'd gotten this upset over anything. She was practically shaking with rage. He was so damn arrogant. She was almost overcome with the urge to slap him. Hard.

"This really about the song? Or you all worked up about something else?"

She narrowed her eyes at him. "Well, I don't love that you told everyone in there that I was pregnant either." She folded her arms and glanced around in hopes that her ride would be there. She just wanted to escape to the safety of her apartment. But the back lot was empty.

"It was a joke, for God's sakes. You know, something people say sometimes to break the tension?"

"Oh, you're a comedian now? Guess everyone needs a fallback plan." She tried not to watch as he unbuttoned his sleeves and rolled them up his muscular forearms, but it took serious effort to keep her eyes elsewhere.

"When did you get so damn uptight? Am I imagining things or did you used to be more fun?"

She'd been so carefully holding it together with everything she had. But all of his comments in the bar and his whole 'let's just make jokes and have fun' attitude was more than she could handle at the moment.

"Fun? You want to talk about fun? Yeah, Trace, it was real fun falling for someone who didn't actually give a damn about me. And it was even more fun watching him run to someone else, someone he'd sworn meant nothing to him, via every tabloid and gossip website known to man."

"Kylie, you know how the media is. And I never said she meant nothing—"

She took a step closer to him, despite how much being in his space scared the crap out of her. But she knew her limits and if he finished that sentence she would break apart in a pile of messy pieces.

"You know what's really fun though? The most fun I've ever had in my life *fun*? This sick, twisted joke that fate is playing on me where my dream—everything I've worked so hard for, sacrificed for, and damn near lost my mind over—is totally one-hundred percent dependent on some self-absorbed ass who thinks this is all one big joke and that I was put on this Earth solely for his sheer amusement."

She squeezed her eyes shut and tried to focus on her breathing. She would not—*could not*—let him get to her like this. She was a professional. She could do this. No matter what kind of spectacle he tried to turn this tour into, she would keep her head up and get through it. Hopefully maintaining her career and her self-respect.

"Hey," he said softly.

She opened her eyes and saw him reaching out in her direction.

No. Hell no.

She put a hand up to stop him. "I'm fine. I don't know why I'm surprised that you aren't taking this seriously. But I'm over it now."

His mouth dropped openly slightly as if he were going to say something, but the back door opening behind him cut him off.

"Ryans, you okay?"

Kylie smiled at Steven, thankful for the interruption. Now that her nerves had calmed, she was completely humiliated that Trace Corbin had gotten the best of her.

"Yeah, I'm good," she answered, forcing the biggest smile her face could manage. "Great, actually. You guys taking five?"

"Yeah, we are. I was going to see if I could buy you a drink."

Trace huffed out an annoyed-sounding breath from beside her. "She's underage, so all you can buy her is a soda."

She refused to so much as glance at Trace Corbin or acknowledge his snide comment. She was done letting him get to her. If any one man had used up all of her emotions, it was him.

"Don't worry. I know the owner," she told Steven as she breezed past Trace and back into the bar.

An hour later, she stood with Steven outside the bar. The SUV taking her home had arrived and she was slightly tipsy.

"Thank you," she said, holding on to the lapels of his jacket for support. "For being here tonight. For keeping me company. I had a good time."

"I can see that." He chuckled softly and regarded her warily. "You okay, Ryans?"

She sucked in a deep breath of outside air and took a wobbly step backwards. "Why do you keep asking me that?" Shaking her head, she waved off Steven's attempts to help steady her. "You know, it was a year ago. We weren't even really together. It was a stupid fling and I was a stupid kid with stars in my eyes. Feels like a whole different life. I am *so* over it. Over him."

Clearing his throat, Steven took a step into her personal space. "Yeah," he said quietly, "I meant, are you okay getting home? Because you were tossing them back pretty hard in there."

She felt her face flush in embarrassment. "Oh god." Suddenly it was hilarious. She dissolved into a fit of laughter. Burying her face into Steven's shoulder, she had a sobering thought. "Blythe, can I ask you a question? A serious one?"

"Sure. Shoot, crazy girl."

Kylie pulled back just enough so she could look into his eyes. Their faces were so close, their noses almost touching. And yet, he was still a little out of focus. "Am I fun? You can tell me if I'm not. I can take it."

A slow grin curved Steven's lips. "Yeah, Ryans, you're fun. Tons of fun. But I think you've had enough fun for tonight."

"Boo," she heckled at him as he put her into the SUV. "Come by later tonight when you're done?"

He sighed and shook his head after buckling her in. "You really think that's a good idea?"

Kylie bit her lip and held her breath. Rejection—even rejection from a mere hookup buddy—hurt like hell. And on the night when she'd had to face the man who'd broken her heart into more pieces than she could currently count, it hurt worse than she expected hell might.

"I'm all out of good ideas, Blythe. But I think it would be fun. And I want tonight to be about fun."

"I'll call you when I get off work." He kissed her gently on the forehead before tapping the top of the SUV to let the driver know she was in safe.

Kylie frowned at him as she pulled away. She had a feeling she wasn't going to be having much more fun tonight. Because she was going to lie in bed and watch the Earth spin while replaying every second of tonight's interaction with Trace Corbin.

God, he'd been so…infuriating. But ever since Steven interrupted her and Trace earlier, he'd kept his distance. That was something.

Settling back into her seat, she remembered something Trace had said before.

You're with someone else now. I can respect that.

She almost laughed out loud at the thought of a light bulb switching on above her head. Trace thought she and Steven were a couple. Like a *couple* couple. Instead of just a couple of people who messed around on occasion.

And Steven filling in for Andy, the normal Rum Room guitarist, had obviously put Trace off his game.

On an impulse, Kylie dug her phone out of her purse. Her manager picked up on the first ring.

"It's nearly one in the morning, Kylie."

"Chaz, I need you to take care of something for me. Like now."

"I told you, I'm not making your hair appointments. You need to do an online search and look up what a manager actually—"

"Didn't Aiden and his wife just have a baby?"

Her manager paused for a moment before answering. "Yes. They had twins. Why is that important at this hour? You already sent a gift."

"Because, with two new babies at home, he probably doesn't want to go back out on the road, right?" The briefest sensation of panic at what she was about to propose struck her, but she ignored it.

"Well, his wife isn't exactly thrilled. But it's his job. Besides, who could we get to replace him on this short of notice?"

"I have a guy," she replied. "And I know he's up for it."

"Kylie, if it's who I think it is—"

"He's a friend, Chaz. A good friend. He needs a job, and I could use a friend on this tour."

"A tattooed friend with a reputation of leaving your apartment in the middle of the night?"

She snorted. "A talented guitar-playing friend who will have my back so I don't lose my composure while on tour with someone who pushes all my buttons."

"And you're sure about this?"

Was she? It felt like she was. Her liquor-fogged brain couldn't conjure up a pro- con list at that particular moment, but for the most part, she was sure.

"I'm sure."

"I'll let Aiden know he can sit this tour out. But, Kylie?"

"Yeah?"

"I just want to go on record as saying I think this is a bad idea. One of your worst actually."

"Noted." Yawning, she hung up with Chaz.

Less than thirty minutes later, she was in the process of passing out on her couch. The night was kind of a blur, but she was pretty sure it had been a success. Mostly.

The nagging feeling that she was supposed to stay awake for some reason kept her from succumbing immediately to exhaustion. But just as her phone began to ring, she fell into a peaceful sleep.

The last one she would have for a long time.

chapter TWENTY

KYLIE woke up with a start that landed her ass on the floor next to her couch. Her head pounded steadily in rhythm with her ringing phone.

She crawled over to where her purse was dumped out next to the coffee table.

"Hullo," she answered sleepily once she'd located the source of the incessant ringing.

"I'm guessing you forgot about picking me up and I should grab a cab," her best friend snapped.

"Oh shit."

"Nice. I feel the love."

"Lulu, I'm an ass. Forgive me?" Kylie rolled on her back and waited for the floor to stop tilting.

"Yeah, yeah. I'll see you in a few. Wait. There aren't going to be any pantsless men in your apartment are there?"

Her friend's question sent her reeling even harder than the hangover. Had Steven come over last night? She glanced around the apartment. No sign of any pantsless men.

"Nope. Just me."

"Lame. I guess I might forgive you, though hearing you'd spent the night having great sex would've made your forgetfulness slightly more redeemable."

Kylie sighed. It always came back to that. Sex.

The tabloids had it wrong. Her manager had it wrong. Even her best friend in the whole world had it wrong.

The truth—the cold, hard, painful truth—was that Trace Corbin was still the last person she'd had sex with. And that sucked. It sucked even harder when a picture of him and Gretchen Gibson having lunch somewhere made the front page of the Nashville Star. Made her want to run out and grab the first guy who was willing and beg him to make love to her.

But every single time she and Steven had come to crossing that particular threshold, one of them always held back. Or passed out. Their encounters rarely occurred when sober.

"Sorry to disappoint," she told her friend. "See you soon, Lu."

"Move your ass, Country Queen," Lulu said as she banged on the bathroom door the next morning. "We have to leave in an hour and I need to shower."

"Nice rhyme. Maybe you can write my songs from now on," Kylie teased as she exited the bathroom.

The two of them kept up the constant witty banter all morning in an attempt to avoid discussing the situation at hand. The one that was about to become their reality for the next few months.

Stepping out of her apartment building and into the unforgiving glare of the sun, Kylie squinted and slid on her aviators. Beside the black SUV picking her up stood her manager and a slender exotic-looking girl with a chin-length haircut that looked as expensive as her designer suit.

"Kylie, this is Hannah, the day-to-day manager we discussed accompanying you on this tour. Hannah Reagan, Kylie Ryans," Chaz said gesturing to each of them.

Kylie shook Hannah's hand briefly. "Nice to meet you, Hannah. Not sure what you did to get stuck babysitting, but I'll try not to get gum stuck in my hair. Not too often anyways." She smirked but then forced her lips into the most genuine smile she could manage. Wasn't this poor girl's fault her management company thought touring with Trace was more than she could handle on her own.

"I'm Olivia," Lulu said. "Stylist, best friend, life coach, and owner of Kylie's embarrassing middle school pictures should you need them."

Kylie snorted at her friend's 'life coach' comment and watched as Hannah took them both in. Lulu, with her short, bleached-out boy haircut with pink and black streaks, and then her.

She wondered what she looked like to someone who didn't know her. The jeans she wore were ripped, but they'd come that way and she didn't even want to know how much they'd cost. She'd stopped asking long ago. The vintage T-shirt she had on wasn't one from her dad's collection, it was designer too and probably worth more than what the band featured on the front had made in their entire career.

"Hannah's from the New York office and is really excited to be learning the ropes of artist management." Chaz continued discussing Hannah's qualifications until Kylie was tired of nodding and smiling.

"We'll be fine, Chaz. Someone is making sure my truck makes it to each show, correct?"

Kylie prided herself on not being a diva. She didn't make people fill her trailers or green rooms with roses or champagne or bowls full of M&Ms with all the brown ones removed.

She just had one relatively simple request. Wherever she went, her daddy's truck went. It had its own special trailer that blended right in with the ones carrying tour equipment and luggage.

"Yes. Jackson Ashford is in charge of it. He has the spare key and will handle anything you need. I'll text you his contact info."

"Sounds good. Thanks, Chaz. I'll keep in touch." With that, she nodded at the driver who'd opened her door and slid into the vehicle.

"Hey, Kylie," Chaz called out just before the door closed between them.

"Yeah?" She leaned forward so she could still see him.

"Make good choices, okay? This is bigger than you now. You get that, right?"

She rolled her eyes behind her sunglasses. "Yes, sir. No getting caught with hookers or blow. I got this. Peace out, Chaz."

She didn't have to see him to know he was shaking his head in that exasperated way he had.

"So you were kind of a major bitch to Hannah Banana back there,"

Lulu said as she hopped into the SUV from the other side.

Thankfully the new chick was riding in a different car. Kylie wasn't really in the mood to keep up the forced small talk and fake smiles. She pulled a prescription bottle from her purse and dropped two oval-shaped tablets into her hand. She could feel her friend's steady gaze on her as she retrieved a bottle of water from the mini-fridge and took her migraine medicine.

"I wasn't trying to be," she mumbled over the pills she was trying to swallow. "Guess my *life coach* should've taught me better manners."

"You don't pay me enough for that." Lulu nudged her elbow off of the armrest they shared. "Anyways, she seems nice enough. Little out of her element, but nice. Maybe take it easy on her. Remember how out of place you felt when you first came to Nashville?"

Leaning back in her seat, Kylie closed her eyes and took a deep breath. "Yeah, I remember. And you know damn well I spend the majority of my time trying *not to* remember. Thanks for bringing it up."

"You're welcome," Lulu responded, as if Kylie's appreciation had been genuine and not laced with sarcasm.

The drive to the lot where the tour bus and the rest of the convoy waited was quiet. Until they pulled in and Lulu broke the silence. "Hey, speaking of reminders, did you forget to mention something? Maybe something kind of important?"

Kylie stretched her neck and rubbed her temples. Obviously the meds hadn't kicked in yet. "Not that I know of, why?"

"Because that guy waiting by the bus looks a hell of a lot like Steven Blythe. Unless you know another tattooed guy with black hair and a habit of carrying a guitar case around."

Kylie lowered her sunglasses and looked out her window. Dear God. That damn sure was Steven Blythe.

What the hell is he doing here?

The question had no sooner entered her brain than the blurred memory of why he was here came back to her. He was here because she'd drunkenly decided he could fill in for her guitarist on this tour. Because Trace Corbin apparently wasn't enough drama to deal with.

"Um, did I forget to mention he was filling in for Aiden on this one?"

"Um, yeah. Apparently you did." Lulu gaped at her in disbelief. "Do you really think this is a good idea?"

No. "Sure. Why not? He's a friend. He needed a job."

Lulu snorted out an obnoxious laugh. "I bet. Didn't realize you were giving out *jobs.*"

"It's not that big of a deal." She wondered if she said it out loud enough times if it actually wouldn't be. Or if Lulu would believe she believed herself.

"Sure it's not. Who better to bring along on a tour with your famous ex than your current fuck buddy? It's genius really. This should go swimmingly."

"He's not my—" Kylie began but didn't get to finish because Lulu was already out of the SUV and had slammed the door. "Fuck buddy," she said, completing her sentence for her own benefit as she got out of the vehicle. She ignored the puzzled look of her driver as he held her door open. She lugged her carry-on bag onto her shoulder and made her way to where Lulu was waiting.

"I might've been slightly intoxicated when I made this particular executive decision," she whispered to her friend as discreetly as she could.

Lulu checked Steven out blatantly and nodded he approval. "Well…at least he's nice to look at."

chapter TWENTY ONE

*Y*ou *have got to be kidding me.*

The thought repeated itself half a dozen times in Trace's mind as he watched Kylie greet Steven Blythe. By *their* tour bus.

He'd told himself that he was probably just there to say goodbye. It wrenched a knife into his gut, but he'd prefer that option to what was really happening. The motherfucker had his guitar with him. And was currently being introduced to Kylie's band. A band conspicuously missing one member.

He knew it was possible that he was imagining it—wishful thinking and all that—but Kylie's smile appeared tight from where he stood. The creases in her forehead could've been from the sunlight in her eyes, but the giant shades she had on were probably providing sufficient protection her from that.

No, he was almost positive she was uncomfortable. Well, that made two of them. He turned to his manager and jerked his head towards Kylie and Steven.

Pauly Garrett scratched his chin and shrugged. "Aiden Rogers and his wife just had twins. Guess she decided to give him some time off," he said only loud enough for Trace to hear.

Or she just wanted to give her boyfriend some time on.

The thought provoked a painful tightening in his chest.

"Think he actually gives a shit about her or he's using her to get ahead in the business?" He felt his jaw flexing as his manager cleared his throat.

"I think it's none of our business either way."

He nodded once. "Right."

After Pauly had left to board the bus he'd be riding on, Trace spent the next few minutes helping the crew load equipment into the trailers.

Despite the magnetic pull he felt towards where Kylie still stood with her friend from home he'd met a few times before, an attractive dark-haired girl he didn't recognize, and Steve, he did his best not to glance over his shoulder in their direction.

He hadn't even looked up until his bass player came over to lend a hand.

"Who's the blonde?"

"Friend of Kylie's from back home, Mike," he answered without removing his eyes from the equipment he was loading. "Do me a favor and don't bother, okay?"

The other man held his hands up. "Now wait just a damn minute. Since when does your shitty love life have to interfere with everyone else's?"

"Since now."

Mike frowned at him from under a mess of blonde hair. "You know, if it were me in your position, I'd be thinking that this tour could be the perfect opportunity to—"

"Thin ice, Brennen," Trace practically growled at him. "Drop it."

"You don't even know what I was going to say."

Trace slammed the door to the last trailer shut with a bang. "And I don't want to know."

Without another word on the subject of Kylie Ryans, her friend, or what might or might not happen on this tour, Trace turned away and stalked over to his bus. Granted, it was only half his. But it was half *his*. Not half Steven Blythe's. Dammit.

"Hey," Kylie said softly as he approached. "Um, I haven't gotten on yet so I didn't know if you'd already picked which room you—"

"Take whichever room you like," he said shortly as he blew past her little entourage without slowing.

Take the room, take my heart, take my life. He would've written it down and used it for lyrics later but he didn't have the ability to think straight at that particular moment. Seeing Kylie and Steve together was his kryptonite. It hurt. It sucked out his soul and made him feel weak and vulnerable and pissed the hell off about it.

Dropping the one bag he carried in the booth in the middle of the bus, he plopped down into the seat and lowered his head in his hands.

For a few moments, he sat in silence, alone with his thoughts. Thoughts of calling his sponsor because he wanted a drink so bad he could taste it. But that wasn't the want that was overpowering him.

He wished they'd had rehab for Kylie Ryans addiction. He never would've left.

The sweet sound of her laughed chimed through the bus as she boarded and greeted the driver. He hadn't even noticed the man before. He only caught a few words of their conversation, but the ones he did were, "Oklahoma, my daddy, this guitar, and of course I'd love to sign that for your daughter."

Yeah, she was different in a lot of ways. But she was still the same girl who had stepped tentatively onto his bus two years ago.

His mind's eye conjured the image of her greeting him on the bus during his *Back to My Roots* tour. He'd known even then that there was *something* about her. But he'd had no idea how drastically she was going to change his life. And he'd been completely clueless about how much she was going to change him.

He dragged himself back into the present and watched her smile and nod during the exchange with the driver, wishing for the first time ever that he'd never met her. He wished that he was a stranger to her and that this was their first encounter. So that she could get to know him as *this* man. A sober one who valued his career, his relationships, and more than any of that, *her.*

He wished for those things even more when she turned towards him and the smile dropped from her face at the sight of him. She was a professional though, so she plastered it right back on before his very eyes.

"I'll take the suite in back if that's all right with you. It has the attached bathroom I hear."

Trace tried to make eye contact with her, but she wasn't having it. "Okay." He could give a damn about which room she took. There was so much to say, so much they needed to discuss, and yet neither of them could admit it out loud.

"Okay," she parroted back in the same tone. Apparently that was all she had to say because she disappeared into her room without another word.

The second he heard her door close, he made a decision.

He wasn't going to try and get Kylie Ryans back. She clearly had moved on and if she was happy, he had no desire to take that away from her. But he was damn sure going to find out if she truly was happy, and if Blythe was into her for the right reasons. And like it or not, he was going to find out whether or not he could handle being on tour with a woman he still loved.

IT was 2:42 a.m. and Trace had an answer to at least one of his questions. The answer, unfortunately, was no. No he could not handle being on tour with her. Kind of a shitty time to be realizing this, that much he knew for certain.

Knowing she was less than twenty feet away, probably scantily clad in one of her favorite threadbare T-shirts under her covers was killing him.

His blood burned in his veins as he lay in his own bed sans covers. Somehow her scent had infiltrated the entire bus. He wasn't sure if he was actually inhaling that sweet warm vanilla-honey smell he loved so much or if his memory had become so vivid that it included all five senses now.

But it wasn't his memory keeping him awake. It was his inability to tell the future that had him all twisted up inside.

Questions swarmed and stung him in all his weakest spots. *What if she brings Blythe on the bus? What if he sleeps in her room? Or worse—doesn't sleep in there?*

The thought of hearing even the tiniest sound of pleasure coming from her room while another man was in it stoked the fire she'd lit inside of him. The intensity was like nothing Trace had never known.

He'd never been possessive or concerned about the love lives of any women other than his sisters. And that was just because he had their best interests at heart and because, naturally, he didn't want to know anything about their sex lives. Despite the fact that Claire Ann and Rae were thirty and nineteen respectively, in his head, they'd never had sex—nor would they ever.

But Kylie Ryans had. He knew firsthand that she'd had great sex. Earth-shattering, mind-blowing, ruin-your-whole-damned-life-for-anyone-else-ever sex. He knew because she'd had it with him.

WHEN the bus stopped moving, Trace roused himself from the half-ass version of sleep he'd been in. His head throbbed from not getting nearly enough rest. He stood and stared at his reflection in the mirror.

Swollen bloodshot eyes, pounding head, and blurry memories of Kylie walking past him as if he were a stranger on the street. It was like having a hangover minus the fun of the night of drinking that led up to it.

He didn't have an en suite bathroom so he had to step out of his room to take a shower. Which he did. A long and hot one that nearly scalded his skin right off.

But apparently painful memories didn't evaporate as easily as shower steam. Because when he stepped out of the bathroom, he was once again wrapped in a towel from the waist down and standing face to bare wet chest with a fully clothed and fully startled Kylie Ryans.

"H-hey. Um, I just came to tell you that we're all heading to breakfast. At the diner here in Columbus. And then we have soundcheck."

He couldn't help but grin. She was fighting the good fight to keep her eyes off of his chest. But she was losing that fight.

"Got it. I'll be out in a few."

"Okay."

His grin widened when she didn't move. "So, uh, if it's all right with you, I'll get dressed now." He tilted his head towards where she stood.

"Yeah. Of course. Please do."

"You're blocking my bedroom door."

"Oh God. Sorry." She nearly tripped over herself in her attempt to get out of his way. "I'm going to go now. To the diner. For breakfast."

She muttered something under her breath that he didn't catch.

"Hey, Kylie Lou?" he called out as she left.

"Yeah?" She turned and met his gaze with wide eyes.

There was so much he wanted to say to her. Apologies and desperate pleas for another chance came to mind. But the words wouldn't come out of his mouth. So he chickened out.

"Enjoy the view?"

Her eyes narrowed and she glared at him briefly before storming off the bus.

Leaning back against the wall, he let out a breath.

It was going to be a long few months.

chapter
TWENTY
TWO

"Enjoy the view? Enjoy the view! I mean, what the hell?" Kylie leaned her head down and turned her face towards her best friend so no one else in the diner would hear. "We've barely spoken, despite the fact that we've been on the same bus for nearly twelve hours, and all he can say to me is, *Enjoy the view?*"

She tried her best to whisper despite the fact that she really wanted to yell her frustration at the top of her lungs.

"And that's why I believe in equal opportunity junk-punching," Lulu responded just before taking a sip of her coffee.

Kylie gave a subtle shake of her head to let her friend know that was the end of the conversation when Hannah slipped into the booth across from her. She wasn't exactly thrilled about having a day-to-day manager. But she knew Lulu was right—it wasn't Hannah's fault she'd been sent to babysit her. After her run-in with Trace on the bus she was starting to think maybe she did need one after all.

"So next week the reporter from Rolling Stone is meeting us in Connecticut. The photo shoot is at nine and he'll be with you every minute up until the show. So be mindful of what you say, even if you're speaking to someone else or on the phone. Pretty much everything is fair game."

"Good morning, Hannah," Lulu began. "Please, feel free to jump right in with the shoptalk. No need to waste time on niceties."

Hannah's face darkened with what appeared to be embarrassment. "Sorry. There's just so much to cover and I realize Miss Ryans's time is precious."

Lulu smiled warmly at the other girl. "Very true. But I think Miss Ryans can handle it. She's done okay so far, right?"

Kylie barely managed to keep her eyes from rolling back in her head. "I'll try to keep my potty mouth in check. Thanks for the reminder."

Before any of them could say anything else, the bell above the diner door chimed alerting them that new patrons had entered. Kylie glanced up and nearly spit out her black coffee when she saw Trace and Steven coming through the door at the same time.

Her face must have given her away because Lulu turned to look at what had caught her attention.

Kylie watched as Trace gave Steven a hard glare before moving aside to let him pass. Both guys joined the tables where their bands were seated without even glancing in her direction.

"You okay, Miss Ryans?" Hannah asked softly.

"What?" Kylie worked to keep her face blank. "Yeah. I'm fine. Sorry. I was, um, lost in thought."

"Bet I can guess what you were thinking about." Lulu snickered and Kylie kicked her under the table.

"Anyway," Hannah continued, "after the official interview, the reporter will hang around for the concert, and the review and cover will run in next month's issue. You're one of very few young female country artists to be featured, so keep in mind that you're representing—"

"Hey there, pretty lady," a male voice said. "Sorry to interrupt your breakfast."

All three girls looked up at the man standing at the edge of their booth. Kylie greeted him with a warm smile.

"No problem, Danny. I was wondering when you were going to come say hi to me." She slid out of the booth and gave the older man from Trace's band a hug. He gave her a firm squeeze in return and the familiar ache of missing her dad pinged through her chest.

"Well, I don't want to upset any of your gentlemen suitors over there," he said with a wink and a nod towards Steven and Trace. "But I did want to let you know I brought my banjo along in case you felt like singing that song you wrote."

The lightning flashes of discomfort became thunderous vibrations of agony at the memory of the song she had written and sung about her daddy.

"Um, okay. I don't really play that one much anymore. But thanks for letting me know."

"Anytime, sweetheart. You ladies have a good one." With a parting nod, he headed back towards Trace and the others.

Kylie felt the blood draining from her face. Danny was a painful reminder. A living, breathing reminder of just how much she missed her daddy. And the fact that there had only ever been one man able to soothe that painful ache rattled her even harder.

Suddenly she couldn't swallow, and a dull ringing sound began to radiate from inside her head.

"I'm not feeling so great, y'all. I-I'm going to go lie back down on the bus for a while. Here, breakfast is on me." She slid a black credit card towards Lulu and bolted out of the diner as quickly as she could manage without making a spectacle of herself.

A few feet outside of the diner, she heard the chime of the door a second time, but she didn't look back to see who had followed her out. It could've been Lulu or Hannah or Steven. Or…someone else.

Her chest tightened and her stomach clenched at the realization that there was only one person she wanted it to be. He was the absolute last person she should want it to be. And yet…she hoped and prayed it was him.

Tears stung her eyes as she focused on making it to the bus without looking back.

The ground beneath her blurred through the moisture. She blinked in an attempt to dry it up. "Stop it. This is ridiculous," she whispered to herself. "Grow up already."

"You look pretty grown up to me," his voice said from behind her.

Her entire body went rigid at the sound of his voice, but there was a part of her—a small part—that relaxed.

"I just needed some air. It was getting kind of crowded in there," she said without turning to face him.

"Agreed," he said low and practically in her ear.

When did he get so close?

"So, um, I'm fine. No need to escort me. I'm just going to go lie down on the bus for a while."

"Turn around and tell me you're fine and I'll go."

She swallowed and pressed her eyes shut, blinking out any remaining tears. Roughly swiping her hands beneath them to clear the evidence, she turned.

"Trace," she said slowly. She really wished she didn't have such an intense physiological response to the sound of his name on her lips. It was difficult to hear herself speak with her heart hammering in her ears. "I'm fine. I don't want everyone to think I'm making some big dramatic scene and you had to console me. Go enjoy your breakfast."

"Come on, Kylie Lou. Since when do we care what everyone thinks?" His hazel eyes gleamed in the sunlight. He even smelled light sunshine. Like a clear day on a Georgia farm. Tears threatened from the backs of her eyes once more. The urge to reach out and wrap her arms around him nearly overtook her.

Thankfully, his phone rang just as she was about to speak. Good thing, because she had no clue what the hell she had been about to say.

"Answer it," she said softly.

He frowned at the screen, but did as she'd said. "Hey, Gretch. What's going on?"

Kylie's knees went weak at the sound of his girlfriend's name. She wondered if this was how he felt about her and Steven. Then she realized it didn't even matter. They were done. The past was the past and Gretchen was Trace's present. And probably his future, too.

He turned slightly to the side as he spoke, just enough for Kylie to step out of his line of sight and tap on the door to the bus. The driver, Reggie, who went by Tiny—despite the fact that he was anything but—opened the door. She greeted him quickly and darted back to her room.

Shutting the door behind her, she leaned against it and slid to the floor.

Everything was different. And yet the thing upsetting her most, the cold, hard fact that had a cold, hard lump wedged in her throat, was the fact that nothing had really changed.

Her daddy was still dead. She still missed him so much it was damn near debilitating. And she was still in love with the only man besides him she'd ever loved.

And she still couldn't have him.

THE show in Columbus had gone well. Lots of college kids had shown up and the crowd had been amazing. She'd successfully avoided Trace since the incident at the diner. They'd sung *The Other Side of Me* together without so much as making eye contact. So not a total success as far as performances went, but she'd done the best she could.

Driving past the local campus, Kylie wondered briefly what her life might have been like if she'd have gone to college. Not that she ever could've afforded it. But it was fun to think about what it might be like if she got to pick a major or take a class on human sexuality just for the heck of it. Or art history, or film studies. It sounded kind of exciting to her.

The only frat party she'd even been to had resulted in Trace punching Steven and carrying her out over his shoulder just before she vomited all over the place.

Maybe college wasn't for her.

As much as she often wondered what it would be like to have a life apart of touring and music and recording, she knew she wouldn't really have it any other way. This was her dream come true. But it was a funny thing about dreams.

Without someone you loved to share them with, to be proud of you, happy for you, cheering you on, achieving them felt kind of empty.

Mia often criticized her for working too hard, but she stayed busy for a reason. It was easier that way. Easier to keep at it than to sit home by her lonesome and wish for things she'd never have.

Days when things had gone terribly in the studio, or God, that time her ear piece had malfunctioned and shot feedback through her ear and she'd screwed up on the National Anthem at a hockey game, it would've been really nice to have had someone to come home to. Someone to wrap her in his arms and tell her it would be okay. That these things happened and that she'd get past it.

As it was, she ended days like those alone, drinking wine from a box, fighting tears so she could see to scrawl out lyrics to songs she knew she'd never sing.

Which was pretty much what she was doing on the ride to Detroit. She leaned her head against the window when they stopped for fuel.

"Knock, knock," she heard Steven's voice say through the door to her room.

"It's open," she answered, scrubbing away residual tears and pasting a wide smile on her face.

"So I heard a rumor," he began, stepping into her room and lowering himself onto the chair across from her bed.

"Just one?" Kylie put her pen down and let it roll off her notebook.

He grinned at her. "Well, just one that concerns me."

"Ah. Are you pregnant?"

"Not that I know of. But I could've sworn you said your guitar player asked for time off. According to the other guys in the band, he's not the type to do such a thing." Kylie didn't respond right away so Steven continued. "Which leads me to wonder, why exactly did you ask me to come along on this tour, Ryans?"

"Aiden's wife just had twins. You were looking for work. It seemed like the best solution for everyone," she said quietly.

"Uh huh. For everyone? Or for you?"

She took a deep breath and met his gaze. "If you don't want to be here, Blythe, I can call Aiden and tell him he's flying to Detroit to meet us. You're not on contract. Feel free to leave at any time."

Steven gave her a sad smile. She wasn't sure, but his expression reminded her of the one people gave when they found out her dad had died. Or that Trace had dumped her for Gretchen Gibson. The pity grin. She hated it. More than anything.

"I wasn't saying I wanted to bail on you, Ryans. Relax. I just don't like being lied to and I don't want to look like an idiot out here. Or a charity case. If I'm here because you needed a guitar player, then okay. If I'm here because you needed a buffer between you and Corbin, then that's okay too. But if I'm here because you felt sorry for me or something, then I wish I would've turned you down. I just want you to be straight with me. I don't feel like that's too much to ask."

Kylie sighed. "No, it's not. I'm sorry I wasn't completely upfront with you." She glanced down at the lyrics she'd written. It was a song she'd started the day Trace had walked away from her. She didn't know why she felt the need to finish it, but she did.

"You know you don't have to hide stuff from me, right?" Steven asked, angling his face beneath hers so she had to look at him. "If you're not okay, you could tell me."

"Yeah, I know. And I promise I'm fine." She felt like she was constantly reassuring everyone of this lately. "The truth is…" She paused to gather as much courage as she possibly could. She could tell him, she knew he would understand or at least try to. She was just worried it would sound stupid out loud. So she edited it a bit. "The truth is you're here because I needed a friend." His expressions softened and she shrugged. "I mean, Lulu is great and I love her. She's been my best friend forever. But sometimes I just want to hang out with someone who doesn't know everything about me, you know? And someone who gets this business, this lifestyle. Like you."

"I get it, I do. And honestly, your band could use some eye candy for the ladies, if you know what I'm saying."

"If only you weren't so modest." She laughed as Steven leaned forward and kissed her on the forehead. At the exact same moment that his lips met her skin, she heard someone clear his throat.

"Sorry. There was a fresh market stand at the last stop so I, uh, got you these because I noticed there weren't any on the bus. I'll put them in the kitchen."

Kylie watched Trace take the bananas he held out of her room. She opened her mouth to thank him but he was gone before she got the words out. She shot Steven a helpless look and he shook his head.

"You're right. You do need a friend." He sighed as she leaned her head on his shoulder. "I'm just not sure I'm the one you need."

chapter TWENTY THREE

"YOU straight?"

Trace raised his eyes to meet the ones of his bass player. "Yeah, man. I'm good."

"Thinking about drinking?"

He raised his eyebrows and opened his mouth to lie. But he saw the truth in Mike's eyes. "Yeah. Little bit."

"Call your sponsor, Tray. Call him now. Tell him what's going on. Or call Dr. Reynolds and tell him to meet up with us. Don't wait until it's too late."

He grimaced. Damn. He'd promised himself he could do this. He'd been so strong for so long, but seeing another man kiss her, even on the fucking forehead, hurt in a way he didn't know how to heal.

So he'd been sitting backstage at her soundcheck in Detroit letting her thick voice wash over him, tearing into all those old wounds. Which was where Mike had found him looking like a kicked puppy.

Through the break in the curtain he could see her—well the back of her. A shot of bourbon sounded good about then. An entire bottle of it sounded even better. But there wasn't a brand of liquor in the world that would douse the pain having a girl like Kylie Ryans and losing her caused.

So he took a sip from his bottle of water and listened to her voice echoing in an empty stadium.

You might wake up with a smile on your face, but you'll reach out to find an empty space. I don't do waking up in your arms, won't be impressed by your smile or your charm. I'll set your night on fire. I'm a live wire. I'm a live wire.

She shimmied over towards her guitar player and rubbed her body against his as he performed his solo. Trace forced himself to look away.

"You know," Mike began quietly, "I don't think I've ever seen you back down like this. You were always a take-what-you-want kind of guy. I admired that about you."

Trace sighed and leaned back in his chair. "It's more complicated than that."

"Is it? Or are you just too chicken to throw your hat in the ring because you're afraid she won't pick you?"

"You suck at minding your own business, you know that?"

Mike chuckled. "Yeah I know. Hey, you remember that time she hustled us all in poker?"

Trace grinned at the memory. Kylie had played the guys in his band and taken them for all they were worth when they were on tour together. None of them had complained much since she'd done a sexy little victory dance afterwards. "She didn't hustle me, Brennen. I wasn't playing."

"Right," Mike agreed. "And once again, she's holding all the cards and you're sitting out on the sidelines. Why is that you think?"

Before he could answer, his manager appeared.

"Okay, thanks for letting me know," Pauly Garrett said into the phone before disconnecting the call.

"Everything okay?" Trace looked up at the man who was shaking his head.

"Nothing for you to worry about."

"Well that's a sure sign it probably is something for me to worry about."

Pauly's expression tensed. "Naw. You just focus on your show. Let's try and see if you and Kylie can't manage to look more like human beings and less like robots during your duet, shall we?"

Trace shrugged. "Maybe you should discuss that with her." If she wanted to rub herself against her guitarist like a cat in heat and then pretend he didn't exist when they were singing together, that was her issue. Not much he could do about it.

"Maybe I will," Pauly said as she came off the stage and towards them.

Trace didn't miss the way Blythe whispered in her ear or placed his hand on the small of her back. He felt his anger rising to a dangerous level.

So this was jealousy. He wasn't a fan of it. And it was owning his ass at the moment.

A slap on his shoulder snapped him out of his trance. "Doesn't look all that complicated to me," Mike said with a smirk as he stood.

"Kylie, can I have a minute?" Pauly asked, pulling her aside as she passed.

Trace didn't listen to what was said as he made his way to his own soundcheck. But the fact that Pauly had distracted her from Steve kept a smile on his face through rehearsal.

THE crowd screamed his name as he wrapped up his show. It felt good. Damn good. Trace handed off his guitar in preparation for his final song before his duet with Kylie.

He wasn't sure what Pauly had said to her earlier and he hadn't seen her since. Her show had gone well as far as he knew. He'd missed it because he'd been warming up for his own performance and taking pictures with some fans. He hoped whatever his manager had said had gotten through to her and that she would at least look at him when they sang together tonight.

The two girls who had been hired to dance on the "tailgate" the stage had been made into during *Rock It On My Tailgate* were conspicuously absent as he sang the opening lyrics. Alexis and Camilla were twenty-two-year-old twins and professional dancers. Mike had taken to calling them the Tailgate Twins.

He hit the first chorus and the audience went wild. Even wilder than usual. That was unexpected. Everyone in the crowd held up camera phones and people were shouting and pointing behind him. He turned as he sang but the sight behind him nearly stopped his ability to breathe, much less sing.

It wasn't the Tailgate Twins shaking their asses on the tailgate behind him. It was Kylie Ryans.

Seeing her up there with a tiny shirt that left little to the imagination and a jean skirt that barely covered her perfect ass nearly killed him. Right in front of a live audience.

He shook his head and grinned when she pulled a microphone from God knows where and began singing his song along with him.

With the regular dancers, he was supposed to jump up on the tailgate and let them grind all over him. But he had no fucking clue if that would be the plan now.

He knew his voice was probably shaking as he hopped up on the tailgate to stand next to her. He kept his eyes on her to see if she'd give him any clue as to what the hell was going on. And also, because she looked really fucking good up there.

Her sweet voice took over, and he decided to switch places with her. She could sing and he'd do the ass shaking.

She smiled when she realized what he was doing and he smiled back.

It felt like he could breathe, really breathe, for the first time since he'd walked out on her at The Rum Room over a year ago.

After they finished his song, they sat on the tailgate and sang their duet.

Looking into her eyes as they sang the lyrics they'd written together did something to him he couldn't explain. Or understand. He wasn't sure if he wanted to understand.

But one thing was for sure. Mike was right. He'd never been one to back down or walk away from what he wanted. And what he wanted was her.

So when the song ended and the stage light began to dim, he placed his mouth on hers to the sound of thousands of screaming fans.

chapter TWENTY FOUR

"**W**HAT the hell was that?" Kylie whirled on him once they were backstage and their mics had been removed.

"What?" Trace looked genuinely shocked and slightly amused by her outburst.

"Are you kidding me? What do you mean, what? You can't just go around kissing people in front of the whole damned world!"

Her heart pounded so hard she could barely hear herself yelling over the sound of it pumping blood into her ears.

Trace stepped into her personal space. "I'm going to have to disagree with you there, darlin'. I don't know what you're so mad about. You were the one shaking your ass in the middle of my show. What did you think was going to happen?"

A small crowd had gathered around them. Lulu tugged at Kylie's arm, but she jerked free. Pauly stood off to the side with Hannah and the guys in Trace's band. She might have imagined it, but it looked like Danny and Mike were smiling.

"I thought," she said, trying her best to lower her voice, "that maybe, *just maybe*, you'd grown up and were going to be true to your word about not crossing lines. But I can see that I thought wrong."

"Relax, Kylie Lou. It was fun for the crowd. Do you hear that? That's the sound of all those satisfied people feeling like they got their money's worth."

"You're an asshole." She folded her arms and glared at him. She couldn't figure out how in the world he could act like such a selfish jerk and still somehow make her feel like the childish idiot in the scenario. It was like he had a super power. And to make matters worse, her lips—well, her entire body, really—were still tingling from his kiss.

"Call me whatever you want, baby. But you kissed me back out there."

She wanted to slap that stupid handsome smirk right off his stupid handsome face. "Whatever. In the future, make out with the Tailgate Twins and keep your lips off of mine. And man up and talk to me if you want to change the show instead of having your manager plead your case." With that, she stormed back to her room on the bus.

As she left, she heard Trace yelling for Pauly. She felt slightly bad about getting the man yelled at, but she was too shaken up to care much at that particular moment. She paced back and forth, rubbing her temples in an attempt to rub the memory of that kiss out of her head.

"Hey," Lulu said softly as she peeked her head in the room. "You all right?"

Kylie stopped pacing and met her friend's concerned stare. "No. No I'm not all right. What the hell was he thinking? Why did he do that to me?"

The other girl looked like she was fighting off a smile as she shrugged. "I think he was throwing his hat in the ring."

"What?" Kylie was starting to wonder if the whole world was going crazy. She had the distinct feeling she was missing something.

"Never mind." Lulu waved her hand. "Something Mike said. Anyways, Kylie, have you considered that maybe you and Trace need to have a real conversation? About why you agreed to surprise him on stage and why you're so upset about that kiss. I mean, I could probably lay one on you right now and you wouldn't bat an eyelash."

Kylie shot her friend a wary grin at the mental image. "Please don't."

"Watch yourself. I'm an awesome kisser. But that's not the point."

"Do you have a point, Lu?" Kylie sighed and rushed on before her friend could answer. "Because I feel like there's some private joke going around and it's going to be on me. And honestly? I'm doing the best I can here. This isn't easy for me. But professionally, this tour was the right choice."

"Right." Lulu nodded. "Professionally. That's the only reason you agreed to this, right? Because you thought it was the best choice for your career?"

She frowned at her friend. "Why else would I put myself through this? Do I look like a masochist to you?"

Her friend put a hand up. "Hey, I don't need to know what kind of kinky stuff you're into. But I do know that I have my own opinions about why you agreed to this tour specifically. Want to hear them?"

"No," Kylie pouted, plopping down on her bed.

"Well, too bad," Lulu said as she sat down beside her. "So I have a few theories. The best one I have is that you still have feelings for him, and maybe you really do think this is the best professional decision and you don't want to disappoint your fans. But then there's the issue of rocker boy."

Kylie side-eyed Lulu. Her friend rolled her eyes and tossed her hands up.

"Come on. You wouldn't have invited all that tatted-up hotness if you weren't afraid of your feelings for Country Ken. But after what I just saw during that show and after, I'm pretty sure there aren't enough tattooed guitar players in the world to stop this runaway train." Her friend gave her a sympathetic look and then hit her with the naked truth. "You and Corbin have shit to work out, Ky. And the only way you're going to make it through this tour is if the two of you *actually* work it out."

"How?" Kylie whispered, afraid of hearing what else her friend might have to say. Pretty much everything so far had been dead-on.

"I'm not sure. Maybe just tell each other how you feel and get it out there. Who knows? Maybe by the end of this tour you'll ride off into the sunset together and live happily ever after."

Kylie pulled her knees to her chest. "Or maybe we'll destroy each other and everything we've worked so hard for in the process."

And there was one thing she couldn't even bring herself to tell her best friend.

She couldn't tell Trace exactly how she felt.

She'd avoided dealing with it for so long, it was all she knew how to do. She couldn't tell him exactly how she felt, because wasn't sure she exactly knew.

And even more terrifying than not knowing, was the idea that she knew exactly how she felt. But she was pretty sure he didn't feel the same.

chapter TWENTY FIVE

"**Y**OU kissed her? Like on the mouth? Full-on kissed Kylie Ryans?"

Trace held the phone away from his ear. Good news traveled fast apparently. "Yes, Rae. I did. And she was pissed."

His little sister laughed. "That's a good thing, Trace. It means she felt something at least. But, um, next time, maybe do it in private in and not in front of thousands of screaming fans. You know, take her to dinner, walk her to her door. That sort of thing."

"Like I'm a normal guy instead of a self-assured jackass?"

"Precisely. By the way, I'm watching it on YouTube right now. And it is kind of hot. Or it would be if you weren't my brother."

He practically growled at his sister. "Rae, what have I told you about looking me up online? Shouldn't you be studying or something?"

Rae was a freshman at the University of Georgia. She'd enrolled under his mom's maiden name—at his request—so that people wouldn't give her hell about him and his rehab and all that. He didn't make any appearances on campus but he was pretty sure her roommates knew who he was because there was a lot of squealing in the background every time he called.

"Or something," she said, sounding distracted. "Anyways, stop stressing about it. I saw how she looked at you at the benefit. And I've texted her a few times. She hasn't responded, but I'm pretty sure that's because she knows I know you two are going to get married and have me lots of adorable nieces and nephews."

"Rae—"

"I'm just sayin'. But back to, um, studying, I go. Later, big brother. Good luck with my future sister-in-law." With that, she hung up.

Trace was pretty certain she wasn't studying. If her grades were low this semester, he was going to take her car away. He was paying for that and her tuition after all.

He sat on his bed and rubbed his neck. Rae had a point. He and Kylie had a history. He shouldn't have just sprung that kiss on her in public like that. Especially when he'd promised not to cross lines if she came on this tour with him.

He'd made it all of two days.

What he couldn't figure out was why good ol' Steve-O wasn't busting his door down to kick his ass. He almost snorted out loud. The kid could try anyways.

If the situation were reversed and Blythe had kissed his girl—in front of people or otherwise—there would be some serious ass-kicking happening. But he hadn't heard a peep. The only person who'd said anything at all about it had been Kylie. And he was pretty sure she was more shocked than actually pissed.

Lying back on his bed, he smiled at the memory of her sweet mouth moving against his. Soft, and then more firmly. Urgent, like she knew it couldn't last.

His dick jerked to attention in response to the thoughts about her mouth. Damn she'd looked good up on that tailgate. The view he'd had of her from below hadn't been half bad either.

She was lucky he'd stopped at a kiss and hadn't carried her off like a crazed maniac to have his way with her. The things she did to him with just a look would break a lesser man. As much as he ached to do something about the tension between them, he had no idea what course of action to take.

In addition to the tattooed complication, there was one other thing stopping him from demanding the bus pull over at the next jewelry store so he could buy the girl a ring and beg her to change her last name to his.

He'd called his sponsor. The urge to drink had passed. But there was no denying that seeing her and being a part of her universe was a trigger.

It wasn't fair and it wasn't her fault, he knew that too. But he knew that if he tried to explain that being around her was tempting him to drink, she wouldn't see it that way. And she'd probably call the whole damn tour off.

So he'd keep it to himself.

For now.

"Morning," he said through a mouthful of cereal as Kylie walked out of her room. "I made you some coffee. Black with two sugars, right?"

"Morning. And, um, yeah. Thanks."

He extended the black mug as a peace offering. "So we should talk."

"Trace—" She regarded him intently.

He used her momentary pause to appreciate how truly beautiful she was. No makeup. Long blond hair falling softly past her shoulders. Bright, clear blue eyes taking him in as well. Her plain blue T-shirt made her eyes look even brighter.

This was his girl. His Kylie Lou who haunted his house in Georgia. The one who had mud fights and made love in barns and showers. The one no one else got to see but him.

He put his hand up. "Before you say anything, I wanted to apologize. For last night. You were right. Kissing you in front of everyone like that was inappropriate."

She cleared her throat and reality hit him like a sledgehammer. Well, him and one other guy maybe. God, he hoped it had just been one other guy. He didn't have the balls to check online to see who else she'd dated while he had been away.

Her mouth opened slightly, but he rushed on before she could tell him it was okay, or to go to hell, or whatever she intended to say.

"And I broke my promise not to cross any lines and that was a dick move. I hope you can forgive me."

She sipped her coffee. He held his breath.

"Kylie? You forgive me?"

She took a deep breath and pursed her lips. "I don't know yet. I'm still waiting for you to apologize."

Trace scoffed. "I just did."

"No," she said slowly. "You just admitted that you *needed* to apologize. And rehashed some of the things you did wrong. Now you should *actually* apologize. And then I'll decide if I forgive you."

He couldn't believe his ears. What the hell was her problem? He smacked his head, intentionally over exaggerating the gesture. "How did I forget? You're impossible."

"And you're arrogant and hard-headed. Now that we've covered that, feel free to apologize."

"I did!" Jesus, she made him crazy.

"Well if that was your apology, then I don't accept." He watched as she slammed her coffee cup down on the counter. "I swear, I see things so clearly now. Never once have you ever actually said you were sorry and meant it."

"That's not true," he said, lowering his voice.

"When? When have you actually said the words and genuinely been sorry for what you'd done? Name one single time." She folded her arms over the soft cotton T-shirt straining against her chest and glared at him.

The moment his eyes met hers, he knew they were living a shared memory. The day he'd walked away from her, he'd kissed her on the head and told her was sorry. Sorry for hurting her, sorry for putting her through everything he had, and sorry for having to be the one to end it.

He knew she remembered because her narrowed eyes suddenly widened and filled with tears. He slid out of the booth and stood.

"Don't," she whispered, putting her hands up between them. "Forget it. I-I forgive you. Just don't touch me. And no more kissing me. Or flirting with me, or whatever. Respect me like you would any other artist or I'm done with this tour. I mean it, Trace."

He nodded once to let her know he would. Or that he would try his best.

"Kylie—" he called out, but she disappeared into her room before he could stop her.

He dropped back into the booth and placed his head in his hands. Why couldn't he have just said he was sorry?

Oh yeah. Because he wasn't. He wasn't one bit sorry for kissing her, for wanting her, or for wanting the opportunity to love her again more than he wanted anything. But yet again, instead of being honest and putting his heart on the line, he'd been an idiot and pissed her off.

She was right. He was the same old Trace.

He was beginning to wonder if he was capable of doing anything other than hurting her.

chapter

TWENTY

SIX

"SHE wrote a what?!" Kylie tried to distance herself from where she'd been chatting with Hannah, Steven, and Lulu as she spoke to her publicist on the phone. She plugged an ear so she could hear over Trace's soundcheck in the arena in Connecticut they were performing at that night. "And they're going to publish it? Why?"

"Money, Kylie. We've been through this. People don't care if she's full of shit. They care if the book will sell." Her publicist reassured her half a dozen times that she would do her best to take care of the situation she was calling about before they hung up.

Jane Bradford was a tough lady who had approached Kylie immediately after her tour with Mia Montgomery and Lily Taite had ended. Seeing how the media was portraying Kylie as the cause of Trace's rehab stay and then turning her relationship—or whatever it was—with Steven into something that made everyone hate her, Jane had contacted her with a plan. A plan to turn Kylie into Nashville's Sweetheart—even though she wasn't entirely sure that's what she wanted to be. But it worked. And she had Jane to thank for a lot of her success.

Kylie had let Cora—the publicist she'd shared with Trace—go because it was a conflict of interest for Cora to try and spin his rehab stay positively for both of them.

She planned to find an agent as soon as possible so they wouldn't be sharing one of those anymore either. It was bad enough they shared a bus.

And now, some dude named Josh from Rolling Stone magazine was tagging along on her every move. While she freaked the hell out about what her publicist had just said and the fact that she couldn't stop thinking about Trace Corbin's mouth on hers. And her phone had been ringing constantly all day.

"Sorry, I know I'm being rude. It's just a weird day," she told Josh in hopes that he wouldn't write that she was a self-absorbed bitch who spent every waking second on her phone. They still hadn't made it through the interview they'd started that morning. "I know you probably have a ton of questions left. I have thirty minutes until I go on if you want to squeeze the rest of them in."

"No worries." Josh smiled and she wondered if it was genuine or if he was compiling a list of reasons to slam her. This business was tough, and she'd learned the hard way not to trust anyone.

"So how has touring with your current boyfriend and your ex affected your performance?"

Kylie took a deep breath. "Um, that's a difficult question to answer."

"Give it a shot," Josh prompted.

She forced a smile. "Oh-kay. Well, for starters, I don't actually have a boyfriend exactly. Despite what everyone seems to think, technically I'm single."

"That so? Well, that's interesting, considering."

"Considering what?" Kylie asked.

"Oh, you know. The reports that your guitar player leaves your apartment at all hours."

"We write together," Kylie said through gritted teeth. "And we're friends. Like, actually friends. Not pretend friends for the sake of the media."

"Is that a dig at someone specifically?"

Josh was starting to irritate her.

"No," she said evenly. "It's just, sometimes you read that people are in a relationship or just friends or enemies, or whatever, and really it's just media hype for their next album, or a tour or something."

"I see. Care to give an example?" Josh arched an eyebrow under his over-styled-to-look-intentionally-messy brown hair.

Suddenly she felt extremely stupid. As if stringing words together into sentences was a feat more complicated than she was capable of. She'd never liked talking things out very much. She preferred to write songs about her feelings.

"I don't have one." She sighed and watched Trace warming up on stage. "I just meant that I'm not playing anything up or down with Steven Blythe. We're friends. We hang. We have a good time. My regular guitar player's wife just had twins. He needed some time off and Steven's band was taking a breather. It was perfect timing and it's nice to be on tour with a friend."

"Would you call Trace Corbin a friend?"

Geez. This guy. Kylie stared at Trace on stage. A few VIP fans had won tickets to some promotional thing he was doing before the concert. They were all female and squealing and jumping up and down. She was pretty sure one of them started crying when he hugged her and signed her shirt.

"No, I probably wouldn't." She bit the inside of her cheek harder than she meant to and tried to think. It was important not to say anything that could be twisted into something negative later. Or that the label would give her hell for. "But not because I have bad feelings towards him or anything. Just because at one point we were sort of involved and now we're not. It's like dating someone you work with and then breaking up. But you still have to work in the same office. You don't hate each other, but the dynamic of your relationship has changed. So it's not something I can label for you. It's not friendship and we're not a couple. We're just on tour together."

"And why is that?"

Kylie pulled her eyes from Trace. "Why is what?"

"Why are you on tour tog—"

Before he could finish, her phone rang again. She offered him an apologetic smile. "Sorry. One sec."

Glancing down at her phone, she didn't recognize the number. But the way this day was going, it could have been anyone.

"Hello?"

"Kylie? Kylie Ryans?" The voice was female and super high-pitched.

"Um, yes? Who is this?"

She heard squealing in the background. "Oh my gosh! It's really you! Can I ask you a question?"

"I'm sorry, who is this?"

"Are you and Trace Corbin really getting back together? Because you should know, he hooked up with my friend Kelly and she—"

Kylie hit the disconnect button and did her best to smile at Josh. "I'm so sorry but I need a minute. I need to make a phone call."

As she was pulling up Chaz's number, Hannah appeared in her line of vision. She hung up before Chaz answered and waved the girl over.

"What's wrong?" Hannah asked as soon as she was in hearing distance.

"I need a new phone number," Kylie informed her. "Like now."

"On it," Hannah promised, retrieving her own phone from her pocket.

"I'm sorry, you were saying?" She turned back to Josh, who was busy jotting something down in a little notebook. "Damn. Now you're going to write that I'm a huge diva who orders my assistant around, aren't you?" She smiled her sweetest smile and winked at him.

"Nah," Josh scoffed. "Not in those words anyway." He winked back, and she sincerely hoped he was kidding.

Her phone rang again and she glared at Hannah's back. Again, it was a number she didn't recognize.

"Hello?"

"Is this Nashville's Sweetheart?" a deep, male voice asked. "Because if it is, I just wanted to tell you that if I was Trace Corbin I'd come into your room at night and lick—"

"I'm not Nashville's fucking sweetheart, you sicko," she yelled into the phone. She wanted to thrown the damn thing into the nearest river.

"Hannah!"

The girl turned and came running back in her direction. "Kylie, I'm so sorry. It looks like Lily Taite lost her cell phone in a club and someone leaked all of the numbers in it online. I'm doing everything I can to get yours changed right now."

"Great. That's just great." She silently vowed to kick Lily's ass both for being in a club and losing her phone the next time she saw her.

"Kylie," Pauly Garrett called out to her. "Trace is all done. You're up, darlin.'"

Turning to Josh, she apologized a dozen times. "I know today wasn't the greatest, and I appreciate your time. If you want to continue this by phone later, I can have Hannah get you my new number as soon as I have it."

"I think I got everything I needed. Have a great show."

She tried to ignore the lump in her throat as she thanked him again. The entire day had been a disaster, and she was damn near positive she was not about to have a great show. And she was cancelling her subscription to Rolling Stone magazine immediately.

Four hours later, Kylie slid into the back seat of a black SUV with windows tinted so dark she couldn't see out of them.

"Just the nearest place with greasy fast food where no one will see us." She'd wanted to drive her daddy's truck, but in this part of town she would've stuck out like a sore thumb in an '88 Chevy pickup.

"I'm sure it wasn't that bad," Lulu reassure her. "I mean, he has to know you can't help that your number was leaked and you were getting prank calls all day."

"And," Steven chimed in, "the interview was supposed to be about your music. Not your love life. He shouldn't have even been asking those questions."

She sighed and leaned her head against the blackened window. "He's a reporter. He can ask whatever he wants. And he can write whatever he wants. And I was a bitch to Hannah."

"You're a celebrity. You can be bitchy. Totally acceptable," Lulu said, shoulder bumping her.

"Yeah right," Kylie mumbled. It didn't matter how many albums she sold. She would never think of herself as a "celebrity." They were an alien race she had no plans to join.

"For the record, I wouldn't be mad if you went around telling people I was your boyfriend. I've been called worse." Steven slung an arm around her shoulders.

"I was trying to be honest. Fat lot of good that probably did me."

"Let's just say you're portrayed in a negative light in his article? You really think it's the end of the world?" Her best friend got out her cellphone. "Watch this." With a few quick touches, she pulled up a screen with search results for Kylie's name.

Kylie let her eyes roam over her friend's findings. A few YouTube music videos, her official website, social media sites, a few fansites, some mentions on TMZ, and celebrity gossip sites.

"Your point?" she asked, looking at her friend.

"My point is, this is just the part of you that you let people see. It's the public version. The private version of you is yours. And it belongs to you and whomever you decide to share it with. For God sakes girl, you're on a tour named after a song you wrote about the fact that you don't let everyone see that side of you. The real side. So to hell with what one reporter or one magazine prints. You know who you really are, and at the end of the day, that's what matters."

The lyrics she and Trace had written floated through her head. At one point, he'd been the one she shared that side of herself with. And that hadn't turned out so well.

It still hurt. Hurt bad. Deep down in that private part of herself she kept hidden away, there was nothing but pain. There was a reason she kept it hidden.

She'd opened her heart and soul to someone who'd chosen to walk away from everything she'd had to give.

One of many memories she'd shoved out of her head with all her might forced its way back to the surface. *I love you*, she'd told him in the cab of her daddy's truck.

That look on his face, the shock and the panic, was one she'd never forget. And it wasn't what he'd said afterwards that still stung. It was what he hadn't said.

She forced a smile for Lulu and Steven. They were sweet and they cared about her. But for reasons she couldn't explain even to herself, she took that part of herself, the part she didn't share with the world, and tucked it away.

Silently, she promised herself she'd never share it with anyone again.

chapter TWENTY SEVEN

"So this is it," Trace told the girl stepping onto the bus behind him. "Kylie and I each have our own living quarters, which I can't show you. But we do have a kick-ass media room and big screen." He grinned at the lady from the radio station and she blushed. It was kind of nice to know he still had it. Touring with someone who was completely immune to his charms didn't do much for his ego.

The camera guy followed them onto the bus and Trace waited for him to give the thumbs-up signal before he began talking. He flirted and cracked a few jokes during the interview.

Just as they were about to wrap it up, the door to Kylie's room opened. He turned and looked at her. Red-rimmed eyes told him she'd been crying. He did a mental recall of the last few days. He couldn't think of anything he'd done that might have upset her.

If Blythe had screwed around on her, he would kick the little fucker's ass. And then dance a jig probably. But only because he'd be out of the picture.

He moved to block the camera guy's shot of her. "Well, thank y'all so much for coming. See y'all at the show tonight."

The lady with the microphone protested as Trace all but shoved them off the bus. Once the crew was gone and the doors were closed, he headed back towards her. Her pain was apparent on her face, and it weighed him down. The urge to reach out and wrap his arms around her was powerful and overwhelming, but she'd asked him not to touch her and he was trying his damnedest to respect her wishes.

"You okay?" He wanted to slap himself. That was a stupid question since she'd obviously been crying. People who were okay didn't cry.

"I'm fine," she answered, stifling a sniffle but not completely. "Just tired." She pulled her oversized sweater around herself. He was kind of grateful that he couldn't see her body so he wouldn't be tempted to do things to her that he shouldn't.

Yeah right. He was pretty much always tempted around her. She could wear a brown paper sack.

"You've been crying." *Master of the obvious, here.*

She shrugged. "Do you know if there's any ice cream on the bus?"

"Um, hang on. I'll check." Trace turned and beat it into the kitchen. He was grateful to have a task. Crying women made him feel helpless. What the hell were you supposed to do? Ask them about it? Not ask? Get tissues? Shut the hell up? Be there for them or get out of their sight? He never knew.

After checking the freezer thoroughly, he returned to her empty-handed. She was sitting on the couch, curling her legs up to chest. She looked so…lost. The need to make whatever was upsetting her all better was more than he could handle.

Dropping to his knees before her, he looked up into her eyes from below. "Mint chocolate chip?"

Her lower lip trembled and she nodded.

"Okay."

Trace sprang into action and practically sprinted off the bus. He grabbed the first person he saw. It was Hannah, Kylie's manager slash assistant or whatever she was.

"I need ice cream. Now. Where the hell are we?"

"We're outside of Lubbock. Drivers needed a rest. We got fuel about an hour ago and I haven't seen any places since. I'm guessing she saw it?"

"Saw what?" He was scared to even guess.

"The article. It wasn't great." The short dark-haired girl retrieved an iPad from her purse and pulled up the latest issue of Rolling Stone.

Trace let his eyes drink in the vision of perfection on the cover. It was Kylie. She was in a tight plaid button-up but none of the buttons were buttoned. A lacy black bra thrust her full breasts up just below her collarbone. Her eyes were sultry and her fingertips lingered by her full, pouty lips.

The wanton expression on her face made him want to run back onto the bus and do unspeakable things to her. Well, unspeakable in front of Hannah.

The idea of the entire world seeing it made him want to hit something. Hard.

"She looks…amazing," he choked out.

"It's not the picture she's upset about. It's the headline."

He looked at the bold print on the bottom of the cover. **Kylie Ryans: Not Nashville's F@#*ing Sweetheart**, it read.

Aw hell. Trace swiped the screen until he came to the article about her. There was another picture of her scantily clad body sprawled out next to a guitar. She was smiling this time. Again, he was struck dumb and breathless. He forced himself to look away from her and skimmed the article.

Very concerned about how she's portrayed and whether or not the world thinks she's a diva.

Below that was a breakdown of a day in the life of Kylie Ryans, and the writer had taken the time to add that she "barked" at her assistant every other hour and that she "handled" people like equipment. He called her performance with Trace that night in Connecticut "cold and automated." He even hinted that she herself had said that the whole tour was a farce and she and Trace had no chemistry. Which the asshole made sure to mention he agreed with.

Trace let out a low whistle. "Ouch."

"Yeah. I tried to steer her away from the magazine stand at the last few stops but I guess she ventured online. How is she?"

"I need ice cream, Hannah. A large amount. Mint chocolate chip, stat. Can you help me with that?"

She nodded. "I'll see what I can do." She pulled out her phone and he left her to it.

Trace headed back onto the bus. His heart sank when he saw that Kylie hadn't moved an inch since he'd left her.

"Hey, um, Hannah's working on the ice cream situation now. Anything else I can do? Order a pizza? Put on a movie? Kick the Rolling Stone reporter's ass?"

She sighed. "I guess you saw it then."

"Eh, I'm half illiterate according to that guy so I could barely read it."

"He called you illiterate? I must've missed that part. What a dick." She frowned and Trace couldn't help but smile at the cute little thing her forehead did when she was mad.

"Not in your article. A long time ago when I was first starting out. He made a reference to hillbillies and the inability to read. He was surprised that one of my songs contained a reference to a Keats poem. Said I couldn't have written that myself because surely stupid ol' me had never read anything other than girls' phone numbers on bathroom walls in bars."

Kylie's expression melded from annoyed to outraged. "I'm sorry. I never would've even given him an interview if I'd have known he said that about you."

He shrugged. "No big. Trust me, in this business, you learn to let things like that go." Their gazes met as he spoke. "But I guess you know that already. You're on tour with me, after all."

He heard her sharp intake of breath, but before she could say anything, the sound of several people boarding their bus distracted them both.

They turned to see Lulu, Mike, Steven, and Hannah all clomping onto the bus. Mike held a brown paper sack that Trace hoped contained ice cream.

"There wasn't any mint chocolate chip at the Stop-N-Shop we found," Mike began. "But there was chocolate chip cookie dough, double chocolate chunk, and chocolate fudge swirl."

"Which one did you get?" Kylie asked, looking slightly amused.

"All of them," Steven said, pulling out several spoons from a drawer next to Trace. "We figure you can mix them all together. If you want, I'll squirt some toothpaste on it and it will taste just like that disgusting stuff you love so much."

Kylie laughed, really laughed, and the sound both warmed Trace's heart and cut into at once. Steven made her laugh. Steven made her happy. She needed that. She deserved it.

So he did what he knew he should. He moved out of the way so Steven could sit next to her.

"Ohh, let's make milkshakes," Lulu suggested as he made his way off the bus.

"If there's not a blender on this bus, you guys are up a creek. I'm not procuring a blender just because—"

He didn't hear what else Hannah said. He couldn't be a spectator in Kylie Ryans's life.

After what had just happened in there, he was pretty sure he couldn't be a part of her life at all.

T RACE woke up in the floor. The covers were wrapped around him as if he'd been wrestling them into submission. He was covered in sweat. He racked his brain and tried to remember if he'd had anything to drink earlier that night.

He hadn't.

It was another nightmare then. Great. They were back. Another highlight of sobriety.

Yanking himself out of his bed sheets, he stood and smoothed out the fitted sheet that had rolled off his mattress just as he had. He tossed his comforter back onto the bed. Just as he was about to step out into the kitchen for a glass of water, his door opened.

"Trace?" her soft voice whispered.

He froze. Kylie stood in his doorway, illuminated by the light behind her. Her legs were bare under her over-sized T-shirt.

He swallowed hard and worked to locate his power of speech. "Yeah?"

"Um, you okay in here? I heard yelling and then a loud noise."

He closed his eyes and took a deep breath. Fantastic. Just what he wanted. For her to know what a weak-ass baby he was. "I'm good. Must've been dreaming. Rolled out of bed."

There. Hopefully she'd go on back to her room now.

"Another nightmare?" Her voice was soft, tentative and alluring. His dick threatened to go hard on him. But the shame of the situation kept his erection at bay.

He tried to swallow but couldn't. Not easily anyways. "What do you mean, another one?"

"You have them sometimes. I hear…through the walls. You shout and moan and sometimes you cuss. Like you're fighting with someone."

Dammit. He knew exactly what she'd heard. His nightmares were always the same. Always had been. Well, sort of.

All his life he'd dreamt about his dad beating the hell out of his sisters and his being powerless to stop it. But after he'd left Kylie and gotten sober, sometimes the girl being hurt in his dreams was her. The shrink in rehab had himself a field day dissecting that one.

"Yeah, sorry about that. I didn't realize you could hear."

"You want to talk about it?" She took another step into the room.

Trace was torn. He wanted to pull her into his bed and bury himself deep inside of her until he forgot everything else. His past, his present, his name. Everything. But he knew that wasn't what she was offering. And he damn sure did not want to talk about it.

"Naw, I'm good. I'll try to keep it down. You go back to bed and get some rest."

The next words out of her mouth were the last ones he'd expected.

"Earlier tonight, I wasn't upset about the article. I mean, it hurt that he called me a diva or whatever. But I was upset because my publicist had called me back about something that I thought was handled. Darla wrote a tell-all book. *Confessions of a Wicked Stepmother*, she's calling it."

"No shit?" Well this was news. Even though he was surprised by this information, his body was one hundred percent aware that Kylie was coming closer to his bed. In his room. In the dark. In nothing more than a T-shirt. On the bus on which they were mostly alone as far as he knew.

"No shit. A small press picked it up and the demand for it has led to five thousand copies being printed."

"Jesus. I'm so sorry, baby." He almost clamped his hand over his mouth. He had no right to call her that. The darkness was fucking with his head. Confusing him and warping him back to a place in time where she was his.

It must've been confusing her too, because she didn't correct him. Or yell at him. In fact, the only thing she did was come one step closer. Her legs were touching his bed. And for the first time in his life, he had no idea what to do with the woman in his bedroom.

So he stood as still as possible in an attempt not to fuck up whatever spell the dark had them both under.

"I never thanked you. Earlier…for the ice cream."

"Well, I never technically said I was sorry for kissing you on stage in Detroit."

"So we're even then?" she asked quietly.

"Can we ever really be even, Kylie Lou?" He lowered himself onto his bed. "Can you ever really forgive me for all the pain I caused you?"

"I don't know," she whispered. "I should go now."

"You don't have to." *What the fuck?* He hadn't thought the words before saying them. They'd just shot out of his mouth. A pathetic plea he hadn't meant to utter. Damn nightmares. They made him feel vulnerable and fucked up. Even more fucked up than usual.

She was silent for a moment. Not that he could've heard her over the screaming in his head anyway. He held his breath until she spoke.

"If I stay, what do you think will happen?"

He exhaled. It sounded entirely too loud. "I have no idea. I don't want to make promises I can't keep." Screw it. They could go back to pretending they were over everything tomorrow. Tonight all he could be was honest. "I could tell you I'll keep my hands to myself or that I'll respect the fact that you're with someone else. But none of that would be true. The truth is I want you so bad it hurts. I swear to God, if I ever get to hold you again, I will never let go. Ever. I want to be inside of you so damn bad. I fucking *need* to be inside of you."

She was quiet for so long that, if his eyes hadn't adjusted to the dark and he wasn't staring at her silhouette, he would've thought she'd left.

What was it about whispered conversations in darkness that made people honest?

"I want that too sometimes," she answered, barely loud enough for him to hear. The pain in her voice, in her confession, raked over him like razor blades. He was raw and exposed, and he wanted nothing more than to feel her naked body against his.

"You're not staying though, are you?"

"You know I can't." Her words lingered in he space between them.

He let his rigid muscles relax. She was leaving. He was going to have to let her go, whether he liked it or not. "Goodnight, Kylie Lou. Sweet dreams."

"Goodnight, Trace."

He didn't move a muscle until she was gone and had closed the door behind her.

I want that too sometimes.

Her words echoed in his head until the sun came up. One thing was for sure. If even a small part of her still wanted him—despite everything—if she still had any kind of feelings for him, then he had to try. And try he would.

Later that afternoon, he was exhausted as he helped unload equipment in Texas. But her words were still fresh in his mind.

"What's with the goofy grin, man? You drunk?" Mike asked.

"Naw." Trace's eyes found Kylie standing with Hannah and Lulu. She offered him a smile that was worth more to him than any amount of money would ever be. He winked at her. "I'm throwing my hat in the ring."

"Good for you, man." Mike clapped him on the shoulder. "Good for you."

chapter
TWENTY
EIGHT

"Do you know most musicians don't help set up for their own shows?" Kylie watched Trace's muscles strain and flex as he and Mike worked alongside the stage crew to set up for their show in Austin.

"I didn't know that," Lulu said absently as she put the finishing touches on Kylie's makeup.

"Not that it's a big deal or anything, but most of them just stay on their buses until soundcheck and then performance time. I mean, not that there's anything wrong with that. Hell, I do that. But there's something about a man who knows how to work, you know?"

"Yep," her friend agreed as her own eyes made their way over to where Trace's band was setting up. "I know exactly what you mean."

"Who are you ladies talking about?" Hannah asked as she glanced up from her phone for the first time in an hour.

"No one," they both replied quickly.

Hannah's own gaze followed the path the other two had made. "Oh. I see. Nice." She nodded her approval and went back to her phone.

"You got a fella in New York, Hannah Banana?" Lulu asked her.

"What?" Hannah looked up again. "Oh, no. No fella."

"Why not?" Kylie asked, glad to be involved in a conversation about someone else's love life instead of her own for a change.

Hannah sighed and put her phone away. "Well, for one, my job keeps me really busy. At one time I was helping manage three different bands and interning at a record label. I usually prefer work to the crappy blind dates my friends always try to set me up on."

Kylie clapped her hands and then leaned out of reach of Lulu's makeup brush. "Ooh! Tell us the worst one ever!"

Hannah let out a light chuckle and shook her head. "Well, there was this one guy, Shawn. Ugh."

"Did he hit on other girls during your date?" Lulu put the makeup away and focused her full attention on Hannah. "'Cause I had a guy do that once and I left to go to the bathroom and never came back."

Kylie laughed. "You never told me about that!"

Lulu waved her hand. "He was a douche. Not much to tell. Anyways, Han, about this Shawn character."

Hannah stepped closer into their circle. "Well, I should've known it wasn't going to work out when I ordered a beer and he ordered a Cosmopolitan."

Kylie laughed out loud at the thought of Hannah sitting with a dude with a fruity umbrella drink.

"And as if that wasn't bad enough, when the check came, he slid it over to me and kept talking about how he was saving for his own apartment, blah, blah. Because he still lived with his mom. In his childhood bedroom. So by the way, we'd have to hook up at my place."

"Dear Lord," Lulu muttered.

"He was twenty-eight!"

"What are you three gossiping about?" Mike Brennen asked as he approached.

"Boys," Lulu informed him.

"Of course," he said with an eye roll. As Lulu stepped aside to chat with Trace's bass player, Kylie resumed the conversation with Hannah.

"So do you ever meet anyone at work that you think you might like to date? I mean, you're young and pretty. And you seem like a smart chick." She paused to swallow her pride. "I should've listened to your advice about the Rolling Stone interview."

Hannah shrugged. "It's okay. I know sometimes I'm kind of singularly focused with work and I forget to say things like 'hello' and 'good morning.'"

Kylie smiled warmly at her. "I'm like that too, actually. Music is so…I don't know. All consuming, I guess. My job isn't nine to five. It's twenty-four hours a day, seven days a week, and then some. I have a hard time pulling myself out of that mindset."

"Totally understandable. To answer your other question, that's why I haven't met anyone at work that I'd consider dating."

"Because…"

Hannah looked as if she were nervous about what she was going to say next. She met Kylie's eyes with apprehension. "Because I don't date musicians. Hard rule."

"Really? Because we're awful people or something?" She tried to ignore the hurt feelings Hannah's words had caused.

"No, not at all," Hannah reassured her. "I love working in this business because people who make music are passionate and creative and they never cease to surprise me."

"But you wouldn't date one? Ever?"

"Nope," Hannah said matter-of-factly. "Because music always comes first. And I got tired of competing with it. True artists don't have an off switch, like you said."

Kylie glanced over at Trace as he chatted with some roadies. He was simultaneously tapping out a beat with the hand he had propped on the back of the bus behind him. She couldn't help but smile.

"Good point," she told Hannah as she did her best to tear her eyes from him.

Her experiences with both Trace and Steven had revolved around music. But that was what had drawn her to them.

She didn't mind that they didn't have an off switch when it came to music. It was as much a part of them as their hair or eye-color. Same as it was for her.

"HEY you," Steven said as he and Kylie's drummer, Ty, headed towards her after the show. "Do you remember Ben, the guy who used to be the lead singer in my band?"

Kylie had to stop and think for a second. "Yeah, I think so. Him and his girlfriend kicked our asses at that game the night we met."

Steven chuckled. "Yeah, that's him. Well turns out he's starting a band. He's married now so it's just a side thing, mostly small-time stuff, but he's looking for a guitar player. And he knows your drummer and sent along a message for me."

"Nice." Kylie forced a smile. "Does that mean you're ditching me?"

Steven put an arm around her shoulders. "No way. It's just good news is all. It means after this tour ends, I'll have a steady gig."

"Well that is good news. We should go celebrate. Wanna grab dinner somewhere? We've got a while before we head to Atlanta."

Steven glanced over at Ty. "Actually the guys are having a poker tournament and I told them I'd play. That cool?"

"Sure." A night of kicking some ass at cards sounded kind of fun. Kylie hadn't really ever connected with her band the way Trace had with his. She hoped maybe this would be an opportunity to do so. "Tell everyone I'm in too. I love poker."

Ty cleared his throat and shot Steven a look before walking a few feet ahead of them to catch the rest of the crew.

"Um, actually, babe, word on the street is you're a hustler. So I don't think you're invited."

"I see." Kylie bit her lip in an attempt to contain the pout that threatened to expose how much that stung.

"You can come give me some pointers if you want," Steven said, giving her a squeeze. "So the guys don't take all my money."

"Nah. You have fun. I'm gonna spend some time with Lu and Hannah. Do some girly stuff."

"Sounds good, babe. I'm going to go find out everything I can about who bluffs and who—"

"Ty won't make eye contact when he's bluffing. And Lenny Vasquez, the roadie with the naked lady tattoo, he starts twitching in his seat when he has a good hand."

Steven chuckled. "See? That's why they don't let you play." With a quick kiss to the side of her head, Steven followed the rest of the band to the area where the buses were parked.

Kylie walked to her bus alone. She pulled out her phone and texted Lulu.

Where are you?

She waited a few minutes but no response came. So she texted Hannah.

You busy?

Her response was instant.

Just catching up on emails. Do you need something?

Kylie sighed. Yeah. She needed something. She just didn't know exactly what it was.

Just checking in. Want to grab some food or something?

Again, Hannah's response came so quickly Kylie wondered how she'd had time to even read the text much less type out a reply.

I already ate. Is everything okay? Want me to have someone go get you something to eat?

She typed out a quick no thanks text, telling her that she was good and to have a good night.

She'd only take a few steps onto the bus and back towards her room when she heard it. The moaning. The unmistakable sounds of people having sex. It sounded like extremely good sex from what she could hear.

She gasped out loud without meaning to. Her hand flew to her mouth to cover it.

Inexplicable tears filled her eyes instantly.

Trace was having sex with someone. On their bus. And not discreetly either.

"Yes, harder. Oh god don't stop," she heard a muffled female's voice cry out. A hard thumping sound came repeatedly from the back of the bus.

A sob choked its way out of her throat. She gripped the door to stay upright. She couldn't fall apart. Not here.

Her chest ached and it was too much pain to keep on the inside. She let the tears fall freely since there wasn't anyone around to see.

She caught a glimpse of the bananas he'd gotten her and wanted to slap herself. She'd thought he'd still cared for her. All because of some stupid bananas. And because of the words he'd whispered in the darkness.

I swear to God, if I ever get to hold you again, I will never let go. Ever. I want to be inside of you so damn bad. I fucking need to be inside of you.

Obviously he'd found a replacement. And she'd lost an entire night's sleep because she'd felt guilty that he'd seen Steven kissing her on the forehead.

He probably wouldn't give two shits that she'd heard this. Clearly he wasn't too concerned when it came to being faithful to Gretchen either.

She wasn't sure how that aspect of it made her feel.

She wiped her sleeve under her nose and began to run off the bus. She would never forget those sounds.

Pulling her phone out of her pocket, she scrolled through Chaz's messages until she found the contact info for the guy who was responsible for keeping up with her daddy's truck. His name was blurry through her tears but it was the last message Chaz had sent so she knew that had to be it.

She was just about to dial the number when she slipped on the top step of the bus and crashed into something hard.

Whoever it was grunted at the impact and wrapped strong arms around her so she didn't fall on her face. Strong, familiar arms.

She looked up into hazel eyes watching her from under a dark ball cap.

"Trace?" Well now she was just plain confused.

"Hey there, Kylie Lou. What's your hurry?"

The sight of him made her want to kiss his face. But she restrained herself. Instead, she wiped the remaining moisture from her cheeks and pulled herself together. Straightening out of his grip, she shook off her temporary insanity. "Sorry, I was just, um, going to check on my truck."

His face scrunched under his cap. "Uh huh. And you were crying because..." he prompted.

"I wasn't crying," she answered quickly.

Trace climbed the bus steps, forcing her backwards. She didn't hear the moaning and thumping anymore, so she figured whoever was getting it on must have been finished. She was kind of curious to see who it was.

"Yes you were. Is someone on the bus? Steve do something to you?" His tone went from concerned to lethal in a split second.

She waved her hand between them. "No. Not at all. He's playing poker with the guys. I'm fine."

"Fine minus the crying part?"

Before Kylie could deny her breakdown, the bathroom door opened and Lulu stepped out with Trace's bass player close behind her.

Kylie couldn't even begin to contain her shock. Or her laughter.

"What the hell, Mike?" Trace didn't seem to find the situation nearly as amusing as she did.

"Um, hey, man. I was looking for you."

"Oh yeah? In my bathroom with Kylie's friend? How long did it take you to figure out I wasn't in there?"

Kylie watched Lulu's face turn ten shades of red. She couldn't resist embarrassing her friend a little more. "Sounded like they were looking really hard. Like slamming cabinets and everything."

"Cabinets, huh?" Trace glared at Mike, who shrugged apologetically and yet didn't appear to be the slightest bit sorry.

"I was going to see if Kylie wanted to grab some food and then I ran into Mike and…" Lulu's eyes met hers.

Kylie nodded. "Well I'm here now if you're still hungry. Sounded like you worked up quite an appetite."

"Yeah. Starved. Let's go." Lulu ducked past all of them and was off the bus before Kylie could blink.

Kylie grinned and shook her head. She felt fifty pounds lighter. "Well, boys, care to join us for dinner? Might be a tight squeeze in my truck but I'm guessing Lu could sit on Mike's lap."

"Sounds good to me." Mike took a step towards her but Trace's hand on his chest stopped him.

Trace glared at his friend. "Thanks, but I think we're gonna stay here and have a chat. And Mike's going to sanitize my bathroom. Now."

Kylie nodded. "All right. We'll bring something back in a doggie bag. See y'all later." She practically skipped towards the exit. Until his voice stopped her in her tracks. She hadn't even realized he'd been following behind her.

"You were crying," he said low practically in her ear. An uncontainable shiver danced up her spine. "Because you thought that was me in there. You really think I'd screw your best friend? Right next to where you sleep?" His face told her exactly how much that assumption had hurt him.

She glanced over his shoulder to where Mike was sitting on the couch and turning on the Xbox. Clearly he had no plans of cleaning Trace's bathroom. Once she was sure he couldn't hear them, she met Trace's wounded gaze.

She sighed, knowing he wasn't going to drop it. "It caught me off guard, is all. I had no idea who was in there. I didn't even know it was Lu until they came out." A faint smile hinted at his lips. "I know it wasn't in the contract or anything, but I thought we had enough respect for each other not to do that on the bus."

"So you were crying because you thought it was me in there with someone? Why do you care?"

Kylie's eyes narrowed. "Why are doing this?"

"Because I want to know. I want to know what bothers you and what makes you cry. Just like I want to know what makes you happy and what makes you laugh."

She huffed out a breath. "Why do *you* care?"

"Why do you think?"

She rolled her eyes. "Well this is getting us nowhere. It was fun playing twenty questions, but I'm starving and Lu's waiting."

She turned to leave but Trace surprised her by reaching out. Strong hands pulled her to him and she didn't fight it. After Steven ditching her, her own band not wanting to hang out with her, and hearing what she thought had been Trace with another woman, she didn't have the strength to fight it anymore.

Breathing him in, allowing herself to savor in the warm woodsy scent she hoped would linger on her skin, she lost the ability to hold herself upright. She trembled in his arms as he lowered his mouth to her ear.

"For future reference, you don't have to worry, darlin'. If I make anyone moan on this bus, it will be you."

His lips barely grazed her earlobe and she shivered involuntarily.

"What are you doing?" she whispered.

"Just being honest. I'd hate for you to waste any more of those sweet tears of yours for no good reason." He straightened up and winked at her.

For a moment, all she wanted was to kick Mike Brennen the hell off that bus so Trace could make a good on his promise.

"Kylie, you coming?" Lulu's voice startled her out of her trance.

"Not yet," Trace answered just loud enough for her to hear. Her body responded to the heat in his words but she forced herself to ignore him.

"Yeah, on my way."

She practically sprinted off the bus. She'd had to, or she wouldn't have been able to control herself for one more second.

"So...I think I maybe still have feelings, deep feelings, for Trace Corbin," she told her friend as they got into her truck.

"No shit," Lulu answered on a laugh. "Remember how you said it felt like everyone was in on this big joke except you?"

"Yeah," Kylie said slowly as she cranked her truck.

"Well, welcome to the party. You two are like...I don't know. This couple that's toxic and combustible but somehow need each other to function. And everyone can see it, Ky. And everyone can see how hard you've both been trying to fight it. But no one really understands why anymore."

"You know how bad it was," she said softly into the dimly lit cab of the truck. "You saw me...after. I can't go back to that, Lu. I can't be like that again."

Her friend sighed loudly. "I know, hon. I do. And I don't want to see you get hurt again. But unless you two plan to live on different continents, I don't see how you can keep avoiding it."

"He has a Gretchen. And Steven and I—"

"Mess around every now and then," Lulu finished for her. "And you're friends. But believe me, Steven Blythe knows exactly what the two of you are and aren't. And he's cool with it. If you walk up to that boy tomorrow and tell him you don't want to hook up anymore, he'd be just fine with just being friends. I'm pretty sure there are plenty of girls waiting in the wings to soothe his wounded pride...among other things."

It was the truth. She knew that. And she also knew that it should've bothered her, at least a little. But it didn't.

"Okay, but that still doesn't change the fact that I tried with Trace before. I tried hard. I put myself out there and he chose someone else. Period."

The neon lights of a strip of fast food restaurants caught her eye so she pulled into the nearest one.

"See, that's the thing. Mike and I have been talking," her friend began.

"Uh, sounded like y'all were doing a whole lot more than *talking*."

Lulu shook her head. "Let's order our food first. I need a full stomach for this conversation."

After they'd gotten a sack full of tacos and demolished nearly half of them on the way back to the lot the fleet was parked at, Lulu began her in-depth analysis on Kylie's situation.

"So. I have a question for you. My revealing the top-secret intel I've uncovered is dependent upon your answer."

"No pressure then," Kylie said after taking a large swallow of her soda.

"Right. So here's my question. When were you happiest? Like the absolute happiest you've ever been."

Kylie tried to think while focusing on not getting lost as she drove the unfamiliar roads. "Um, happiest as in…in my entire life?"

"Ky, I don't want to sound like an insensitive ass here, but let's be realistic." Lulu paused to give her friend a sympathetic smile. "Happiest as in since your dad died. At what point in your adult life have you been happy, truly happy, since then?"

The answer presented itself in Kylie's mind in vibrant Technicolor. It was a brief period of time in her life, but it was amazing. Full. Everything since felt faded out. Even performing had lost a bit of its spark. Not that she didn't still love it. She did. It just didn't give her that same high it once had. She told herself that it had nothing to do with him. That the newness always wore off. It was totally normal.

"Your silence is more informative than you think," Lulu said softly. "And honestly, I think your music is too."

A small, sad laugh escaped her. "All my songs are about him or my dad. I didn't even realize it until I had to pick one for the benefit." Kylie shook her head. "So what am I supposed to do? Beg him to dump Gretchen and try again with me? I can't, Lu. I just can't. I don't know what it's like to be an alcoholic. I can't understand him like she does. Can't be there for him like that. I tried…He wouldn't let me."

"I know. I know you did." Lulu scooted slightly closer on the bench seat. "But I think now you have some understanding of what it's like to want something that you know you shouldn't. Of having that want feel like a need. And that need being more powerful than reason, than sense."

Yeah, she was a recovering Trace Corbin addict. This much she already knew. One day at a time and all that.

"Are you going to charge me for therapy sessions in addition to the stylist gig?"

Lulu regarded her with a straight face. "I'm like a bartender with a makeup brush, my friend."

Kylie laughed. "I love you, Lu. I do. And I appreciate what you're trying to tell me. I think deep down I know how I feel about him and that, to some extent, I'll probably always be kind of mixed up inside where he's concerned. But the truth is, I've also learned my limits. And putting my heart through that kind of hell again…It's just not something I'm willing to do."

Lulu sighed. "I promised Mike I wouldn't say anything because Trace made him promise to stay out of it." She bit her lip and then took a deep breath. "But Kylie, I think you deserve to know. Trace and Gretchen—"

Before she could finish, Kylie's phone rang loudly in the cab. She glanced down to the center console where it was glowing. She answered and switched on the speakerphone.

"Hi, Hannah. We got tacos if you want some. What's up?"

Her manager's voice sounded strained when she spoke. "Um, hi. I'm good, but thank you."

"Is everything okay?"

In the moment that the woman hesitated to answer, Kylie's chest felt like it was seizing up. She had the strangest sensation that Hannah was about to deliver terrible news. Her traitorous heart prayed it wasn't anything to do with Trace.

"Um, not really. Can you just get here as soon as possible?"

"Hannah, you're freaking me out. What's wrong? Did something happen to someone? Is someone sick or hurt? Should I call 911?"

"No, nothing like that. Just come see me when you get here, okay?"

"Okay, be there in a few." Kylie pressed her foot down on the accelerator as she hung up the phone.

"What do you think the deal is?" Lulu asked while buckling her seatbelt.

"I have no idea. But something's definitely up. Hannah sounded really stressed out."

"Chick's kind of uptight anyways. It's probably nothing."

Kylie nodded in agreement, but the tight bundle of nerves in her stomach didn't feel the same way.

chapter TWENTY NINE

"I'M telling you, it was him. I saw her come out from behind the bus and then he came out right behind her. And he was adjusting his zipper. His zipper, dammit!"

"Trace, we've been over this. What goes on in her love life, or any aspect of her life, really, is none of our concern."

Trace yanked his hat off and raked a hand hard through his hair before replacing it. He paced outside of the bus his band road in. "Pauly, swear to God, I don't care if it's my concern or not. If he's screwing a Tailgate Twin behind her back, I'll fucking end him."

"And what do you think that will solve, huh? You think she'll come running back to you if you defend her honor?"

Trace sighed and leaned against the bus. "No, but at least she'll know."

"That her boyfriend cheats on her? How's that helpful?"

He shook his head. "No, then she'll know that I care about her and won't let anyone or anything hurt her if I can help it."

His manager frowned at him for a long minute. "I need to make a call. Promise me you'll stay out of it for now, okay? It's dark. He could've been taking a leak. Or it might not even have been him. At least wait until you know for sure."

"Oh, I'm going to find out for sure. I'm going to go ask his sorry ass. I've known that kid since before he hit puberty. I'll know if he's lying."

Pauly sighed. "Anything I can say or do to stop you?"

Trace was already turning to head towards Kylie's band's bus. "Nope."

The entire walk over, he tried to calm his nerves. Pauly had a point. Steve could've been taking a leak. But there were bathrooms on the buses. Or maybe it wasn't him. Except Trace was nearly one hundred percent positive it was.

Adrenaline pumped through him fiercely as he marched up to the bus door and rapped on it. His pulsed ramped up so intensely it felt like his entire body was throbbing.

The door opened and Kylie's drummer greeted him. "Hey, man. Come on in. Want us to deal you in?"

He didn't bother with an answer. Because his eyes had already found their target. Steven Blythe was sitting in one of the captain's chairs around the card table. And he was showing his cards to one of the Tailgate Twins. Not that he could've avoided her seeing his cards since she was on his lap and all.

"You," was all he said. He pointed a finger at Steve and then jerked it towards the door. "Outside. Now."

Steven's eyes widened at the sight of Trace's rage. But then he rolled them. "Here we go. Pistols at dawn."

His sarcasm only served to make Trace even angrier. He was starting to wonder if he was in danger of having a heart attack.

"Be right back. Keep my seat warm, will ya?" he said to the Tailgate Twin as he shifted her off his lap.

Trace stormed off the bus and glared at the tattooed jackass as he followed him.

"Let's have it, Corbin. Unburden yourself."

Cocky little shit. "I'm just trying to figure out why a guy who has someone like Kylie would be screwing around with a backup dancer. I mean, do you just not care about her at all, Steve?"

"Says the guy who dropped her for trailer trash like Gibson. You're one to talk, buddy."

"First of all," Trace began, squaring his shoulders and placing himself directly in Steven's line of vision, "I didn't drop her for anyone. And second of all, you don't know a damn thing about Gretchen Gibson. In fact, you have no idea what the hell you're talking about. But I'll tell you what I know. I know what I just saw in there. And I know that no matter how cool you think you are with the band, someone in there is going to tell Kylie what you're doing. And if she sheds a single damn tear over it, I am going to knock your fucking teeth down your throat."

"You're the one who doesn't know what the hell you're talking about. And you know why that is? It's because you weren't here. You left her. Remember?" When Trace didn't respond, Steven continued. "You left the rest of us to pick up the pieces of her that were shattered to hell and back. Which we did. And she's just now getting over it and really moving on with her life. But you come in acting all 'knight in shining armor' and making me the bad guy. If that's what helps you sleep at night, Corbin, you do what you gotta do. I'm going back to my card game."

"The fuck you are." Trace grabbed his shoulder and whirled him back around to face him. "I'm not done here."

"Well, I am." Steven shrugged Trace's hand off his shoulder. "And I'm telling you right now, man, I'm done with this bullshit game the two of you play. I grew up looking up to you, wanting to be like you. But you put your hands on me again or hit me like that shit you pulled before, I'll hit your ass right back. I don't care how she feels or doesn't feel about you."

Steven turned around and left Trace simmering in his own anger. He was just about to march right back up onto that bus and coldcock Steven Blythe just because when he saw Mike running towards his bus.

He threw his hands up in an attempt to ask Mike what the hell was going on but he didn't stop.

Mike jerked his head so Trace followed.

"Why are we jogging to my bus?" he asked when he caught up to Mike.

"Olivia texted me. Said it was an emergency."

It took Trace a second to realize that *Olivia* was Kylie's friend that she called Lu. Once they arrived at the bus he stopped and stared at his friend. "Whoa, seriously? Dude, you have sex with her once and suddenly you're her beck and call boy?"

Mike gave him a strange look. "That was round three, brother. Not that I'm counting. But no, I was running because she said it was an emergency involving Kylie and I didn't know if it was, like, medical or what. Or if they just maybe wanted to have a threesome." He shrugged, and Trace stared him down.

"You know I'd kill you, right?"

"You know I'm kidding. Mostly. But she really did say to find you and get over here. Something about Kylie's mom or something." He looked as confused as Trace felt.

It made zero sense. Kylie's mom had died when she was a little kid. That much he knew.

Aw hell. The fucking stepmom. He'd met her. She was a nightmare. If she was here giving Kylie a hard time, he was going to have police escort her off the premises.

He followed Mike onto the bus and reeled at the difference between the atmosphere on her band's party bus and the somber one on his.

Lulu sat behind Kylie as she watched the television screen. Hannah was finishing connecting the laptop to it. A recorded interview with Kylie's stepmom, a busty blonde woman who wore entirely too much makeup, was playing.

Trace watched the screen as a table full of women who couldn't shut up fawned over Kylie's bitch of a stepmother. They mentioned her *bestselling* novel and her insight on the *real* Kylie Ryans.

He turned away from the screen and watched the parade of emotions marching across her beautiful face.

Anger. Hurt. Sadness. Anger again. Disgust. Disbelief.

"Turn it up, please, Han," Kylie said evenly.

"Kylie," he began, but she just shook her head without looking at him.

"What no one knows," he heard the woman's grating voice from the speakers as Hannah turned the volume higher, "is how truly *ungrateful* she has been for everything I've done for her. I mean, her dad left us with nothing and I worked two jobs to keep a roof over her head."

Kylie didn't cry or scream or cuss. She just sat with her back straight as a board and watched.

Trace felt sick. And pissed off. Fighting off the overwhelming urge to comfort her the only way he knew how was damn near impossible. And now he had no idea how he could tell her what a piece of cheating scum her boyfriend was when she was dealing with this. That was the worst part.

Because now he couldn't tell her.

"Her father was no prize himself," the woman's irritating voice continued. "I mean, I tried to teach her manners but he just let her run wild. It's no wonder that she got her start in the music business by seducing older men. Her relationship with her dad was always very odd to me. She's a perfect case study for a celebrity with daddy issues."

Everyone's eyes went to Kylie. Trace braced himself. If she wanted to hit something, he'd let her hit him. He could take it.

Her eyes widened a fraction, but other than that she was kept her expression blank. She'd always had one hell of a poker face.

When the crazy bitch on the screen began dabbing her eyes and discussing Kylie's late father's supposed impotence, Trace reached forward and turned the damn thing off.

"That's enough," he said to everyone. "Out. All of you. Go get some rest. We're about to be heading to Atlanta anyways."

Kylie remained frozen and mute. Until Hannah turned to leave.

"I want a copy of her book, Hannah. As soon as we get to Atlanta."

"Kylie, are sure you should—"

"Get me a copy of the book, Hannah, or your fired," Kylie said evenly.

The girl nodded once before following Mike and Kylie's friend off the bus.

"That's one way to treat your assistant," Trace said once they were alone. "Though I think you might keep her longer if you try a more civil approach."

"Why would she say those things?" Her voice was thick with pain and barely above whisper. She looked up at him with a helpless expression. "He's dead and gone, Trace. Why do that to his memory?"

Her eyes were full of tears he wished he knew how to stop.

He pulled a chair over so he could sit across from her. "I don't know, darlin'. I don't even try to figure out why people do the things they do."

She turned her eyes upward in what he assumed was an attempt to keep the moisture in them from leaking onto her face. Instinct told him to reach out, wrap his arms around her. But he didn't know if she would want that. Or if she'd want it from him.

He figured he'd lost the right to comfort her the way he wanted to. But he vowed he'd do the best he could—as her friend. As someone she could trust and depend on. He wanted so badly to be that for her. To not let her down this time.

"Hey, look at me," he said, angling himself closer. He placed his hands gently on the tops of her thighs and leaned into her. "What she says, it doesn't change anything, Kylie Lou. Your memories of your daddy are yours. And she can't say anything that changes who he really was or what he was to you. Understand me?"

Her pain spilled over onto him as she lost her battle with her trembling lip and tear-filled eyes.

"I-I just don't understand why they're listening to her. Why are they taking her seriously? She's lying, Trace. None of that stuff was true."

He lifted a hand and wiped the few tears that had fallen. "Because the world is a big place. And there's plenty of room for the all the crazies." He leaned his forehead onto hers. "Sooner or later, they'll see that she's a desperate nutjob trying to get attention. But until then, you don't give her that power. She can't hurt you or him anymore."

His strong girl, the one who'd held her head high all the times he'd hurt her, faced the media and the world head on, bared her pain on stage not so long ago, crumbled in his arms.

"I hate her," she whispered through her sobs into his embrace. "I hate her so fucking much."

"Shh, I know. I know you do." He tried not to breathe in her warm, sweet scent, but fucking hell it was hard. He stroked her hair, rubbed her back in calming circles, and did everything he possibly could to resist the tempting urge to kiss her. To pick her up and carry to his bed where he could soothe her pain all night long. And then some.

"God, you must think I'm so pathetic." She sat up suddenly and scrubbed her hands across her face.

"What the hell are you talking about?" He held her firmly by the shoulders. "You're the strongest woman I know."

She huffed out a breath that sounded like disbelief. "Yeah. That's why you left, right? Because I wasn't strong enough to hold on. Strong enough to handle what you were dealing with."

Trace's head swam from the abrupt turn of topic. "Kylie, I left because I was a mess and I needed help. *I* wasn't strong enough to be what you deserved and I would've just dragged you down. You never would've gotten where you've gotten if I'd have let you get tangled up in my problems."

"You didn't even give me a choice, Trace. You just…left. Just like my dad did." Another sob racked her body and his temples throbbed. "Jesus. She's right. I do have daddy issues, don't I?"

"No, she's not right. Fuck her, Kylie Lou. She's not even worth your tears, and honestly, neither am I."

"Why do you do that?" She stood angrily and moved away from him. "Why do you get to decide what you're worth? You were worth it to me, dammit." She broke down again and moisture blurred his own vision. Her voice was barely audible, but he still heard her whisper it again. "You were worth it to me."

Her words broke his heart. It felt like it was literally cracking apart in his chest.

He reached out but she swatted his hand away. "Kylie—"

"Just get out, Trace. Walk away. It's what you're good at."

"No."

She was glaring when she looked up at him. "Get out. I don't want you here."

He shrugged. "Too bad."

"Perfect." She shook her head. "I want you to stay and you bail, I want you to leave and you won't. I wish I'd have known this was the way you worked. I would've used reverse psychology on you years ago."

"Babe, it'd take you a lifetime to figure out how I work." He winked at her, and the corner of her mouth threated to give her away. She wanted to smile—he could feel it. "But I have you all figured out."

"Oh you do? Let's hear it then." She crossed her arms and leaned against the counter.

"I hurt you," he said softly. "More than I even realized. More than you'll probably ever admit. So now you screw around with punks like Blythe that don't really mean anything to you. Because they can't hurt you like I did."

She glared at him like a bull about to stamp its foot in anger, and he knew he was right. It made him strangely happy to know that whatever Blythe was doing with the Tailgate Twin wasn't going to break her. His girl was tougher than that.

"But, Kylie, I swear to God, I will never hurt you like that again if I can help it." He looked up into her eyes and gave into the pull he felt. The one he was constantly fighting. He was tired of fighting it. She was made for him. Everything in his entire life would be wrong without her.

Standing slowly, he walked towards her, expecting her to stop him at every step. But she didn't.

"Tell me to stop," he whispered when there was no long any space between them. "Tell me this isn't the time or place, or that you don't want me anymore."

She reached out and placed her hands on his chest. He didn't know if she was going to pull him closer or push him away, but he knew her touch would break him and he'd lose the dangerously thin grip he had on his willpower in an instant. He clutched her wrists in his hands and held them between their bodies.

"I can't," she told him in the breathy little voice that reminded him of the way she sounded when they made love. She broke the intense stare down they were having by shaking her head. "I can't do this again."

chapter THIRTY

"You told her? Wow. Didn't waste any time making your move, did you, Corbin?"

Kylie would've stepped back, but she was pressed against the cabinets so there wasn't really anywhere to go.

"Told me what?" she asked, looking from Steven's face to Trace's.

Trace released her wrists and turned toward Steven. Even from the side, Kylie could see the heated anger in his stare.

"Watch yourself, Blythe," he practically growled.

The sound of the driver lumbering up onto the bus distracted all three of them.

"Okay, folks. Atlanta here we come. Wheels up." Kylie watched as Tiny closed the doors and cranked the bus.

In a way, she was glad Steven was going to be riding with them. If ever she'd needed a buffer between her and Trace, it was now. She'd lost control with him before. The moment she let him in, both literally and metaphorically speaking, she knew she'd be right back where she started. In over her head.

Steven came over to where she stood. He ignored Trace completely.

"Olivia told me the deal with your bitch of a stepmom. And I have an idea for a song. You feel like writing?"

She could feel Trace's glare on them but she needed some space. And writing sounded like a great way to work through the mess in her head.

"Yeah, um, head on back to my room and I'll grab us some Red Bulls."

"Cool." Steven winked at her and walked to her room.

"Kylie, I need to tell you—"

"Trace, it's been a really long day. I just want to get lost in some music and forget it all for a while, okay?"

His jaw flexed, and she could feel the tension radiating off his body and onto her. She was wound pretty tight herself. Which was why she needed him to back off before she said or did something she'd regret.

"Fine. But later, when you're pissed at me for something that isn't my fault at all, please remember that I tried to tell you."

She had no idea what in God's name he was talking about. "Oh-kay. Night, Trace."

She was already at her bedroom door when she thought she heard him say, "Goodbye, Kylie Lou."

"Goodbye?" She turned around, bewildered as to why he'd say goodbye instead of goodnight, but he'd already closed the door to his room.

THE smell of stale beer and cigars made Kylie wonder if she'd fallen asleep in a bar. But when she opened her eyes, Steven was sprawled out and snoring next to her.

They'd stayed up until almost sunrise writing music. Some of it worthwhile and some of it garbage. But it had helped her clear her head.

Sort of.

She rolled over and checked the time on her phone. It was nearly ten. She knew soundcheck wasn't until two, but she felt strangely panicked anyways. She rarely slept late when on tour. There was always work to be done.

She took a quick shower and dressed, careful not to disturb the man-boy still sawing logs in her bed.

Walking out in to the main area of the bus, she listened for any sounds of life. But there weren't any.

She made her coffee and grabbed a banana. The show in Atlanta had sold out in record time. She guessed it was because it was near Trace's hometown. She hadn't checked yet to see how tickets for next week's show in Oklahoma City had sold.

As she finished her breakfast, Steven stumbled from her room.

"Morning," she greeted him.

"Umph," he groaned as he went through the cabinets in search of sustenance.

"There's cereal," she informed him as she polished off the last of her banana and tossed the peel in the trash.

"This will do." Steven grabbed an oatmeal cream pie and ate it in two bites. He pulled a soda from the fridge and slid into the booth. "Ryans, can I ask you something?"

"No, you cannot borrow my toothbrush. We're parked. You can go back to your own bus now." She smirked at him.

He didn't laugh. He just downed a few swallows of his soda.

"Joke," she said, nudging him as she sat down beside him. "Well, not the toothbrush part."

"You're hilarious. Anyways, serious question time."

She forced herself to focus on him and ignore the remnants of last night's encounter with Trace that kept threatening to take over her mind.

Steven cleared his throat and pinned her with his stare. "Which of the Tailgate Twins do you think is hotter? Because Alexis is my favorite, I think. But Camilla's ass is like—"

Kylie slung a throw pillow at him, and he leaned to the side to avoid it.

"This is why you should only go on tour with dudes. I do not want to hear these things."

"I thought you didn't do jealous?" He winked at her over the top of his soda can.

"I don't." She rolled her eyes. "But I don't want to hear about other girl's asses either."

"Okay, okay," he said, throwing his hands up in surrender when she grabbed another throw pillow. "But for real, on a scale of one to ten, how mad would you be if I maybe hooked up with one of them?"

Kylie took a second to gage her own reaction. She wondered if it would hurt Steven's feelings if she said zero. "Egh. Depends I guess."

"On?"

"If it's your favorite one you're leaving me and our three illegitimate kids for or just the one with the nice ass."

Steven chuckled and she breathed a sigh of relief. Things with him were so…easy. She totally understood the lure of friends with benefits.

But after last night, she couldn't deny that Lulu was right. All the tatted-up sexy brooding rock stars in the world couldn't hold a candle to the arrogant, tight-jean-wearing smartass she couldn't seem to force her heart to move on from.

"So, uh, did I interrupt something last night? I know I've been kind of a shitty friend lately, but sometimes I think it might be best if everyone else just got out of the way and let you and Trace fight to the death."

"Not really. I mean, kind of. But it was for the best. Sometimes things escalate quickly between me and him, even though neither of us would be ready for the fallout."

"You still have feelings him?" Steven didn't look hurt or worried. He looked mildly amused and intrigued by what was probably a ridiculous concept in his mind. "Even after everything?"

Kylie shrugged. "It never really felt optional, you know?"

"Ah. Well, in that case, I'm going to go see if I can find a Tailgate Twin to ease my wounded pride. And maybe I'll go try on some nut huggers and shake my ass around town a bit. See if that works for me as well as it does for him."

"You're an idiot." Kylie was still laughing when he left. Despite the residual pain she felt from Darla's talk show circuit media circus, she was excited about tonight's show. She hoped Rae and Claire Ann were coming so she could finally talk to them about everything. Especially Rae.

After the Lily Taite Cell-Phone-Gate scandal, Hannah had gotten Kylie a new number. She hadn't had time to let everyone know the new number yet. Kylie had ignored all of Rae's messages, mostly because she never knew what to say. And it hurt, talking to Trace's sister. It reminded her of a future and of a family she'd wanted so badly and would never have.

But Steven's honesty had reminded her of the person she used to be. The girl who spoke her mind no matter what. She had to find a way to stop avoiding people and her feelings. She knew the dangers. Loving people meant risking letting them destroy you. She knew. She'd been destroyed a time or two.

But keeping them out, shutting herself off from everyone and pretending not to care, well, that just wasn't really working so well for her either.

She went back to her room and perused some of the lyrics she and Steven had written the night before. She was halfway through reading the words to a song she knew she'd never sing when she realized what she'd done.

After getting all emotional about Trace having a woman in his room, which turned out not to be his room—or his woman for that matter—she'd let Steven sleep in hers. Granted, nothing had happened. But the door had been shut and there was no way Trace could've known for sure either way.

And he'd been the one to comfort her about the whole Darla thing. Her stomach sank and the nausea hit. There was no denying it.

She owed Trace Corbin an apology.

chapter THIRTY ONE

"CLAIRE Ann, I have to get back to Encore Park like now. Kylie gets a little crazed if I'm late for soundcheck."

The coffee shop where they'd met for breakfast was crowded. His sister propped her elbows on the table and sighed. "Oh, so we're worried about what makes *Kylie* happy now, are we?"

"Come on, Claire Bear. You know I've always been worried about that. Just like I worry about what makes you and Rae happy." He shrugged like it wasn't a big deal. But it was the first time in a long time he'd admitted how he felt about her out loud.

"Trace, do you ever stop to think about what makes *you* happy?"

He didn't answer right away. He stared down into his half-empty cup. He didn't even like the taste of coffee really. Just used it for the much needed caffeine.

"Music makes me happy," he finally answered. "Knowing the people I care about are taken care of makes me happy. Is that so wrong?"

"No, I just worry—"

"We've been over this. Stop worrying about me. I'm fine." He pulled his worn- out trucker hat off of the table, glanced at the faded Yeti logo, and slid it back on his head. "Well you can relax. Tour's going as good as can be expected. No one's died. No one's been arrested. And no one's pregnant—that I know of." He winked at his sister who returned his grin with an annoyed sigh.

"Well, in that case, I kind of need to talk to you about something. Two somethings actually. One is kind of...er, not good. But the other one makes me happy. I'm just worried it's going to make you unhappy."

"Let's hear it. Whatever it is, get it out. I'm personally about to explode from holding things in all the time. So go for it." He had an uneasy feeling about both things she was about to tell him. Her forehead was creased and her eyes looked tired. Too tired for a happy, healthy thirty-year-old woman to look.

His sister ran her finger around the rim of her empty coffee cup in her hands several times before meeting his gaze. She took a deep breath and spoke in a hurried rush.

"I'm worried about Rae. I think she's doing more partying than studying and she won't tell me her grades. I don't think Mom is even checking in with her and it's bothering her more than she lets on. I'm pretty sure the last few times we talked she was three sheets to the wind."

Damn. He'd had a feeling from how quickly she always rushed off the phone with him that she might be getting the full freshmen experience at college. "Okay, I'll talk to her."

Claire Ann bit her lip. "Yeah, that's the thing. I don't think either of us will make much difference because we're just nagging older siblings. And Trace, you trying to tell her to take it easy on the partying is like—"

"The pot calling the kettle black. I get it."

"Like it or not, she looks you up online every now and then. So, um, I was kind of wondering if you could ask Kylie to talk to her. Just maybe get her to say a few things about how much your drinking hurt her and how important it is to stay focused and reach your goals. That kind of thing."

He sighed. "Sure, Claire Ann. I'll interrupt her and her cheating piece of shit boyfriend's next make-out session and ask if she wouldn't mind giving my little sister a pep talk. No problem."

"Her boyfriend cheats on her?" His sister's eyes filled with surprise.

Trace lowered his. He hadn't meant to blurt Kylie's business out like that.

"If Kylie Ryans can't even find a decent man, what hope is there for the rest of us?" she muttered under her breath. As soon as she realized what she'd said, her head snapped up and she reached across the table to touch his arm. "Crap. I didn't mean it like that. You are a decent man. You're more than a decent man. I just meant—"

"It's fine. I know what you meant. I'm not going to start crying in my coffee over here. Even though it does taste like motor oil."

She laughed and then glanced down at the contents of his cup. "Ugh, that's because you don't know how to doctor it up. Cream and sugar, little brother. It works wonders."

"Yeah, yeah. I've always preferred everything straight up with." *Liquor, coffee, the pain of Kylie Ryans moving on.* He managed to force his face into an expression of nonchalance for his sister's benefit. "So what was the other thing? The one that makes you happy?"

Her eyes clouded over briefly and he wondered if she wasn't going to tell him after all. But then the hint of a smile playing on her lips spread into a huge grin.

"I met someone, Trace. Someone I care about. A lot. And he cares about me, too."

Trace arched a brow. In his entire life, his sister had never been one to date much. She'd been so busy with him and Rae while they were growing up that she'd never had much time for boyfriends. A small part of him wondered sometimes if she preferred women. Which he would've been fine with. He truly did want her to be happy. She deserved it more than anyone he knew.

"That so? Well, when do I get to meet him?"

He might have imagined it, but it looked like she'd cringed.

"Um, so I wanted to talk to you about that. He travels a lot for work and he's kind of a little bit older than me. I'm really hoping you won't be weird about it."

"How much older?"

Her eyes narrowed. "Remind me. How old was Kylie when you two met?"

Trace snorted. "Touché, big sister. But I'll have you know, she was a legal adult."

"As am I, little brother. And try to keep in mind, I'm the one in this family who makes levelheaded decisions. And you know I'd never do anything to hurt—"

Whatever else she was about to add was interrupted by Trace's phone vibrating on the table between them.

"It's Pauly," Trace said, glancing at the screen.

"What?" His sister's voice rose a few octaves and her eyes were wide with what looked like panic.

"Calling me," he answered slowly, eyeing her warily as he stood and grabbed his phone. "Probably to tell me to get my ass back to the park for rehearsal. Listen, tell your guy I want to meet him as soon as possible. Bring Rae to the show tonight and I'll see if I can get Kylie to talk to her. It'll all be fine."

With a kiss on the top of her head, he walked out the door.

chapter THIRTY TWO

YOU **did that on purpose.**

Claire Ann typed the text to her boyfriend while glaring at her screen.

His response was slow.

Did what on purpose?

She frowned as she texted back.

Trace just left because you called. We were still talking.

Pauly's response took a full minute. He'd always preferred talking on the phone to texting. She could picture him squinting at the screen. Watching him text always made her giggle. And then she wanted to make him an optometrist appointment. He was far sighted and in denial about it. She tried not to tease him about his age, because then he got all sensitive and pulled them *I'm too old for you* card on her.

He was running late so I called to tell him to get a move on. I'm guessing you didn't tell him yet.

She sighed. The couple at the table next to her made her want to hit something. They were leaning in close to one another and kissing every other minute. The young dark-haired woman smiled at the man like she knew a secret.

Claire Ann was sick of secrets. She'd told Pauly that and she reminded him once more.

It's time he knew. I don't want him to feel like we were hiding from him. We're not doing anything wrong.

Her phone rang, startling her since she was waiting for a text.

"I'm not mad at you," she began.

"Good, because I have a favor to ask." Rae's voice caught Claire Ann off guard. She'd been expecting her boyfriend.

She sighed. "What is it, Rae? If you tell me you're not coming tonight, you can forget the whole me not being mad part. And you can call your brother and tell him yourself."

"No! Of course I'm coming! I just wanted to know if I could bring a few friends. And if we can go backstage. I have exciting news and I'd really like to tell you and Trace together."

Claire Ann's stomach tightened into a hard ball of nerves. "Rae, if your exciting news is that you're pregnant and running off with a biker named Bones that you met at a bar off campus—"

Her sister's loud peal of laughter cut her off. "No, silly! I picked a major!"

"Celebrity couple gossip aficionado is a major at UGA?" Claire Ann joked, but how that freckle-faced kid with knobby knees that were constantly scraped from falling off her bike had become a grown woman with a college major was beyond her. And a little sad for some reason.

"Yep, you guessed it. I'm going to be the first one with that degree in the university's history. Y'all are gonna be so proud."

This time Claire Ann laughed. Rae was always able to cheer her up. "Well it looks like we'll all be sharing news tonight then."

"Really?" Rae practically squealed. "So you and PG are going to tell Trace? Finally?"

"Yeah, I think so," Claire Ann said quietly, as if anyone in the coffee shop would leak the news of her dating her brother's manager.

"'Bout time," Rae quipped. "So, uh, how do you think he'll take it?"

Claire Ann closed her eyes for a moment and tried to picture the multiple scenarios. Trace might hug them and wish them the best. Or he might punch Pauly in the face. She winced. "Not sure. Guess we'll find out soon enough. Don't be late tonight. Especially if you have a bunch of drunken college kids to sneak backstage."

"Love you! See you tonight!"

"Love you, too," Claire Ann said to dead air since her sister had already disconnected the call.

When she looked at her phone, she had another text.

It's better to tell him together tonight anyways. That's how we'll be doing things from now on. Together.

She smiled.

She couldn't remember the last time she felt so light. She'd always been the one to take care of everyone. But when Trace had gone into rehab, and the media hounds had descended upon them, Pauly had stepped in and taken care of things. He'd taken her to dinner or brought Chinese food over when she didn't have the energy to deal with it all. He'd kept her up to date on how Trace was doing. And when she'd lost her grip on everything and broke down in front of him, he'd done the one thing she'd needed more than anything.

He'd listened.

Men had never been creatures she could count on. Not her father, and though she loved him, even her brother was like a big kid sometimes. But Pauly Garrett was a different breed. He was a grown up with a real career, a big warm heart, and a sense of loyalty like she'd never known.

And the things he could do with his hands. No matter how stressed out she was he was always able to both calm her and make her pulse race with a simple touch.

She shivered at the simple idea of being able to hold hands in public, to invite him to family dinners, and maybe one day, start a family of their own.

chapter THIRTY THREE

KYLIE finished her soundcheck and scanned the area backstage for Trace. She didn't see him anywhere.

A few crewmembers were radioing on walkie-talkies and requesting his presence as well. She'd hoped they'd have a few minutes to talk so she could tell him the truth and apologize for the night before. The possibility that Steven being in her room the night before might have sent Trace straight to a bottle had her on edge.

She wanted to get a few things out in the open before either of them hurt the other any more than they already had.

It was time to stop hiding behind her pretend boyfriend.

"He's here," she heard one of the security guys say. She whirled around in the direction the voice had come from.

From across the open area backstage, she saw him getting out of an SUV. He was smiling broader than she could remember seeing lately. There was a determined set to his jaw. Memories of trailing kisses along that same perfect jawline had her slightly off balance.

Her heart began to race and she licked her lips as she walked to the front of the platform. She wondered if her knees were going weak because she'd hadn't eaten much or if it was something else.

Something else grinned when he saw her watching him from up on the stage.

"Hey, pretty girl," he greeted her. She didn't miss the way his eyes lingered on her bare legs when he pulled off his sunglasses.

"Hey yourself." All thoughts of what she'd wanted to talk to him about flew right out of her head the instant he'd spoken. There was a familiar heat in his eyes that reminded her of the first time they'd made love. It was effectively scrambling her brain.

She took a deep breath in hopes of snapping out of whatever weird Trace trance she was in.

"Come on, Corbin. We're wasting daylight here," she heard Mike Brennen say.

Trace looked over his shoulder.

"Trace," she called out as he walked towards where his band was setting up.

He turned with a confident smirk on his handsome face. "What can I do for you, Kylie Lou?"

Nothing I can say in polite company. She had no idea what had her suddenly so off-center. She wiped her sweaty palms on her cutoff shorts. "Um, can we talk? Later, maybe?"

"Sure thing. Meet me on the bus after?" He nodded at the stage, so she assumed he meant after his soundcheck.

"Okay."

His gaze burned into hers and her entire body warmed from the inside out. When it became too hot for her to handle, she looked away.

She knew something was shifting between them. She couldn't explain it if her life had depended on it. But she could feel it.

Kylie hadn't paid much attention to the outside of the buses before. Well, she'd sort of purposely avoided looking at them when she could help it. But as she got back on hers, the larger-than-life picture of her and Trace standing back to back next to the title of the song they'd written together what seemed like a million years ago, had emotions she'd held off for so long swirling inside of her.

She didn't know how bad the storm that was Trace Corbin was going to be this time. All she knew was that it was coming. What terrified her the most was that she knew the precautions she should take, knew there were ways to avoid it. She just couldn't seem to make herself hunker down and hide from it.

Her heart and her head were at war as she waited for Lulu to join her on the bus and help her get ready.

On one hand, she wanted to be honest with Trace, with Steven—with everyone.

On the other, she wanted to keep her already scarred heart locked away where it would stay safe.

But the way he'd looked at her moments ago, he was changing the game. They'd both had walls up. Or she had them up and he'd respected them. She'd thought it was for the best. But she hadn't felt as alive as she did right that second since…since he walked away from her a year ago.

She closed her eyes. Remembering the pain helped keep her sane. It kept her from losing control and throwing herself into his arms. Besides, his arms belonged to someone else now. Or did they?

She wondered if Gretchen was at all concerned about them being on tour together. She'd heard Trace on the phone with her a few times. He always stepped away to take her calls. But it never sounded like they were professing their love or even arguing for that matter. Mostly, the few tidbits she'd overheard sounded like business talk. She could've sworn she'd heard him saying things about building permits.

Feeling overjoyed at the fact that she hadn't yet overheard them making plans to meet up or for Gretchen to catch a show, she wanted to slap herself. It was dangerous and stupid to be this invested in his relationship. If Gretchen did join them at some point, Kylie knew damn well she'd be bunking in a roost on a different bus.

My, how the tables have turned, she thought to herself as she hopped up and sat on the kitchen counter. It wasn't too awfully long ago that she was the girlfriend visiting him on his tour with Gretchen. And yet, in some ways, it felt like a lifetime ago.

She leaned back on the counter as she decided that no matter how painful the outcome might be, she was going to tell Trace there wasn't anything going on with her and Steven. And she was going to ask him point blank, straight-faced with no tears or sobbing nonsense, what exactly was going on with him and Gretchen Gibson.

She wasn't sure how long she spent lost in thought, but when the noise from Trace's soundcheck went quiet, she snapped out of it.

Just before she could work herself into a full-blown panic attack over the fact that he would be back any minute so they could talk, Lulu burst onto the bus.

"I have a surprise!"

Kylie nearly jumped out of her skin. "You startled the piss out of me, Lu!"

"Sorry, but look who I found!"

Before Kylie could even begin to guess, Mia Montgomery and Lily Taite bounded onto the bus behind her.

Lily squealed and hugged her like they hadn't seen each other in a hundred years.

"Hey, Lil. Lose anything lately?"

She pulled back and gave Kylie an apologetic grimace. "Kylie, I am sooo sorry about that. I heard you got tons of prank phone calls."

Mia grinned at her. "Oklahoma probably liked all the attention."

Kylie nodded. "Oh, I did. Lots of heavy breathers and dirty talkers. My favorites."

"Speaking of heavy breathing and dirty talking, have you and Mr. Hotpants got it on yet?"

"Lily!"

Lulu and Mia cracked up laughing while Kylie gaped at them.

"I'm starting to think I might be on the wrong bus," Trace said as he ascended the steps.

"Sweet baby Jesus," Kylie muttered. Mortification swept over her. She was pretty sure he knew they'd been talking about him.

"Well if it isn't Mr. Hotpants himself," Mia said, giving him a quick hug.

If he hadn't known before, he did now.

Kylie couldn't bring herself to look at him directly as the other girls chatted with him. When she did meet his eyes, they were dark and hooded. The warning in his look confused her. Until she realized she was still sitting on the countertop.

They'd had a few bouts of making out and more on a similar countertop. She felt her face heat with the realization, and she was pretty certain he noticed.

"Talk later then?" he finally asked her as he headed back to his room.

"Um, yeah. Sounds good."

When he was out of sight, she returned her attention to her visitors. Who were all three looking at her suspiciously.

"No, they haven't done it yet," Mia said, side-eying her before turning to Lily. "But they're getting there."

"Shut up," Kylie whisper-yelled at her.

Mia smirked at her. But then she suddenly looked aghast for a brief second.

"Ryans, you ready?" Steven poked his head onto the bus.

Kylie checked the time on her phone. It was barely an hour until showtime and she had a few changes to the set list she wanted to run through once more with the band.

"Crap. No. Just a sec. I'll be right there."

Once he was gone, Kylie glanced back at Mia. She seemed to be working awfully hard to keep her even expression in place.

"I didn't know he was touring with you," Mia said quietly.

Kylie's chest tightened. She hadn't mentioned it to Mia for a few reasons. Mainly because she hadn't had time to, and also because she still secretly wondered if Mia knew Steven had feelings for her—whatever kind of feelings he was capable of. She was the main reason his band was taking a breather, after all. But he was her friend, too, and she didn't want to go blabbing his secrets.

She did her best to shrug and appear nonchalant. "He's filling in for my guitar player for a bit."

Lily squealed. "Plot twist!"

"Come on, maneater," Lulu said, tugging Kylie off the counter. "Let's get you ready."

chapter THIRTY FOUR

OF course Mia and Donovan Taite's daughter would appear right when Trace was about to pour his feelings out all over the place.

Because that was the way the universe worked.

The night before, he'd stayed awake mostly to torture himself. He wondered if maybe, just maybe, he could live through hearing Kylie and Steve together, then he could survive anything.

But he also knew that if he really had heard anything more than them discussing alternating time signatures, choruses, and bridges, he was going to barge into her room like a goddamn maniac and kick the shit out of Steve for hooking up with a Tailgate Twin and Kylie. In the same night, no less.

But he hadn't even heard flirtatious laughter. Just them writing music and playing a few chords on her guitar from time to time.

He was pretty sure this was the confirmation he needed. Kylie Ryans and Steven Blythe weren't a thing. Not really, anyway. He knew there was a good chance they'd slept together in the past. But he'd have to find a way to live with that. Hell, he had quite the past himself. And he knew something now, after seeing Claire Ann all lit up about her new fella, that he hadn't realized before.

None of it mattered. The other people, the past, the media, the fights, the ways they'd hurt each other. Those were meaningless details in the grand scheme of life. The fact of the matter was that he loved her. He still loved her and he was pretty damn certain he would always love her.

She was still guarded though, and he'd yet to really see that 'feel first, think second' girl he fell in love with, but he knew she was in there. If he could just get her to come out, then he'd know for sure if she still loved him back. And he had a plan.

Because the Kylie Ryans he knew and loved—the real her—couldn't really contain her true feelings. They tended to shoot straight from her heart right out of her mouth.

That was what he loved most about her.

Or so he thought.

When he was finished getting dressed for the show, he stepped out of his room and nearly ran right into her.

Her tight little body was sheathed in a short silver dress that sparkled when she moved. Her long blond hair was swept to one side, and the smooth strip of her neck that was visible to him practically screamed for his mouth to explore it inch by inch.

She looked up at him from under thick, dark lashes. Smiled at him with pouty red lips. His crotch tightened in response.

Jesus.

Okay, so there were some less virtuous things that he loved about her as well. But that was the point. It was everything. She was everything.

"I was going to tell you that you looked beautiful, but you took my breath away."

Her eyes went wide and he winked at her. Her friend slash stylist made a small "aw" noise.

"Um, thanks," Kylie said softly.

"After you, ladies." He moved aside so they could get through.

His heartbeat sped both at the exquisite view of her perfectly toned backside and the knowledge that his plan was either going to send her running into his arms or running in the other direction.

There was only one way to find out.

TRACE was surrounded backstage by Rae and a few of her friends. When she hugged him, he caught the faintest scent of alcohol and cigarette smoke. He sincerely hoped it was coming from her friends and not from her. Though he knew good and well that was probably wishful thinking.

Looked like he would be pulling the dad card with her after all. Once her friends were busy with Kylie, Mia, and the Taite girl, he took her aside.

"Hey, baby girl, can we talk a minute?"

She looked up at him with pleading eyes. "Can it wait? I haven't gotten to talk to Kylie in forever. And she promised to introduce me to Lily Taite!"

He knew the feeling. He was on tour with her, living on the same bus even, and he felt like he couldn't manage to get a word in. Between Steve, the friend from home, the assistant, and the two newest members of her entourage who had just arrived, he was starting to wonder if he ever would.

He sighed. He'd never really been able to say no to her. "I guess so, Rae. But after the show, I'm coming to the house. Be there, okay?"

"Yes sir," she said with a mock salute before she practically skipped over to Kylie.

He watched as Kylie and Rae hugged and complimented one another's outfits and whatever else women did. Kylie was all smiles as she made introductions until her assistant came over and whispered something in her ear.

He waited until Hannah was walking away to catch up with her. "Everything okay?"

The woman looked slightly affronted by his accosting her. Understandably. "Everything's fine, Mr. Corbin. Can I help you with something?"

"You could tell me why Kylie looks like you just told her you ran over her dog, which I know you didn't because I know she doesn't have one." He flashed his most charming smile. But the woman remained unfazed.

"No dogs have been harmed that I know of. I'll pass your concern on to Miss Ryans."

"Hannah," he called out as she tried to walk around him. "I care about her, okay? Whatever she's said about me, or whatever you think my intentions are, I can assure you, I'm not fishing for information. Just concerned. As a friend."

Thankfully she stopped and sighed. "Actually she hasn't said much of anything about you to me, friendly or otherwise. But you were present when she asked me to make a trip to the bookstore for her. And I do my job. So you can guess what her reading for the evening will be."

Son of a bitch. He'd been so caught up in his own personal revelations about his feelings for her that he'd almost forgotten about her stepmom's bullshit. Before he could calculate whether or not he had time to jog back to the bus and light that damn book on fire before she saw it, he caught a glimpse of Pauly and Claire Ann out of the corner of his eye.

Judging from the way Claire Ann was standing, arms folded and face turned away from whatever Pauly was trying to tell her, they appeared to be arguing. He scratched his head. That was odd.

When he'd gotten out of rehab, Claire Ann had gone on and on about how helpful Pauly had been. He'd asked his manager to keep an eye on his sisters and protect them from any paparazzi assholes who might come sniffing around.

Before he could head over to them to find out what the problem was, Kylie appeared at his side. "Not to alarm you," she began quietly, "but I think Rae might be slightly intoxicated. She reeks of booze and she's told me she loves me about a dozen times."

Once again, he felt like the universe was hell-bent on interfering with his plan to confess his feelings for her. Apparently his little sister didn't have any trouble with it though.

"Yeah. Claire Ann thinks she's been partying a little too hard at college. It wouldn't be a big deal, but given our family history…well, you know." He huffed out a breath and ran a hand through his hair. "Not like I can really say much to her. Some role model I am."

A gentle hand on his arm caused him to stiffen. Fucking hell her touch undid him. He had to clench his own fists to keep from reaching out and grabbing her.

She pulled her hand back, clearly misinterpreting why he'd tensed. "I could try and talk to her."

Before he could tell her how much he would appreciate that, she rushed on.

"I mean, it's none of my business, and I know it's not my place, but—"

"That would be pretty great actually. I'd owe you one."

"No you wouldn't. I care about Rae, too," she said, her gaze drifting over to where the girl was laughing among her friends. One of them was an extremely tan bottle-blonde who was eye-fucking him pretty blatantly.

Seeing Kylie narrow her eyes at the girl almost made him smile. His eyes dropped to her mouth and he remembered kissing her on stage a few weeks ago. And how pissed she'd gotten. His plan was beginning to look like a terrible idea. He decided to give her at least a little warning.

"Hey, Kylie Lou?"

"Hm?" She glanced up at him, seemingly lost in thought.

"I want to change up our finale a little. Sing a different song, a new one of mine—if that's okay with you."

She sucked on her lower lip for a second and his own mouth ached to do the same. "You don't want to sing *The Other Side of Me*? But this is the *The Other Side of Me* tour…" Her expression said that she was concerned for his mental well-being. That made two of them.

"Just come out like normal, okay? I promise not to do anything inappropriate."

She arched a brow and leaned slightly closer to him. "I thought you didn't make promises you couldn't keep?" Her face reddened.

He suspected she hadn't meant to say that out loud. The grin on his face was impossible to contain. She was already slipping. He could almost see his girl underneath all that protective body armor.

"Well, I promise not to kiss you again. Unless you tell me to."

She scoffed. "Trace."

He stepped back when the stagehands came to retrieve her.

"Have a good show, pretty girl," he said softly.

The small smile she tossed him over her shoulder as she was pulled away told him she'd heard.

chapter
THIRTY
FIVE

"How you doin', Atlanta?" Kylie shouted in her mic after her first few songs.

A stagehand brought out her guitar and she grinned at the screams that greeted her as she strapped it on.

"Hey, y'all. These damn stilettos are killing me." She kicked off her heels and began playing *Not A Nice Girl*. Then she launched immediately into *Live Wire*.

The crowd was insane. It was one of the biggest she'd ever played for, and it seemed as if every single person in the audience sang along with her songs.

She forced her mind to stay in the present and give them the best show she could. But as she danced around and sang her ass off, the knowledge that Darla's book was waiting for her on the bus, Rae was very likely developing a drinking problem, and her traitorous heart was inching closer to the surface every time she came within five feet of Trace Corbin assaulted her repeatedly.

And her stomach was in knots about whatever he was planning for the finale.

When she finished her set, Steven followed her offstage. "You could've told me she was coming," he said low in her ear.

She met his eyes with an apology in hers. "I didn't know, Steven. I swear."

They stepped aside as the crew switched her equipment out for Trace's.

"It's not a big deal or anything." He crossed his heavily inked arms and glanced around. "Wonder if she brought lover boy along."

"I have no idea." She leaned even closer to him in case Mia was nearby. "Listen, why don't you just talk to her?"

"Or I could have you pretend to be my girlfriend so I don't have to face her. We could pretend to be madly in love, because that'd be the adult way to handle it." He smirked at her. "How's that sound to you?"

"I'm starting to grasp what an idiot I am, okay?" She shook her head. "Learn from my mistakes. Man up and tell her how you feel."

"It's not like I want to propose to her. Jesus, Ryans."

She smacked him playfully on the shoulder. "I know that, smartass." She spotted Mia standing by Lily and Trace's little sister. "Go," she told him with a shove.

"All right, I'm going. Wish me luck."

She shot him a quick thumbs up. Once he was out of sight, several fans stopped her for autographs and photos. She posed and smiled and signed for several minutes. It was fun and took her mind off all the other craziness for a while. Until a security team member came and informed her that it was time for the finale.

Her stomach pitched forward before she took a single step. Taking several deep breaths, she did her best to steel herself for whatever was coming.

Once she was on stage, an eruption of cheers nearly deafened her.

Her eyes met Trace's. He looked as nervous as she felt.

Oh God.

A sinking feeling hit her so hard her legs began to tremble as he helped her sit up on the tailgate on his stage.

She could practically see Noel Davies rubbing his greedy little hands together. If Trace was going to propose to her as some type of media stunt for the label, she was going to vomit on him in front of all these people. And then she was going to tell him to go fuck himself. Surely he knew how hurtful something like that would be.

"What are you doing?" she mouthed silently at him.

He just winked at her. And then he turned to the crowd.

"So, normally we close the show with a song we wrote together. You might've heard of it," Trace said into his mic.

The cheers and whistles rang out for several minutes.

"But I'm a Georgia boy," he began before he was interrupted by another eruption of screaming and cheering. "So I wanted to sing a new one for y'all if that's okay."

When he turned back to her, his entire face was lit up. He looked so different than he'd been looking lately. Young and carefree. Excited.

For a second, she didn't care if it was just a publicity stunt. She was glad to be a part of something that made him so happy.

Until he started singing.

It wasn't just the fact that he was literally serenading her in front of thousands of people that shook her to her core. It was the words. Each one of them sliced into her like shards of glass reopening old scars.

There's a girl from Oklahoma that I can't get out of my head. Can't seem to get her back in my arms so I put her in a song instead.

She stared at him as the shock of it all seeped in. *What. The. Fuck.*

Something was seriously wrong with him. He was clearly missing a vital chip in his brain that alerted to him to situations that would cause severe pain to others.

She's wild like the prairie wind that blows fast across the plains. She's sweet like the mornin' sun risin' slow after a night of rain. And I did everything I could do to push her away.

Kylie fought the stinging pinch of tears and forced her mouth not to turn down. She couldn't figure out why would do this. She shook her head, silently begging him to please stop this, even though she knew he couldn't. Or wouldn't. But he was too busy singing to notice.

But if ever there was someone ever made for someone, that girl was made for me.

She did her best to block his words out, and when that didn't work, she tried to pretend she was a random fan and he'd pulled her onto the stage. She told her brain that this song wasn't about her. That there was no way a man she'd once loved with all her heart would be capable of such malicious torture and public humiliation.

They say I have a wild streak, a fire burning in me. A fightin' side, too much damn pride. None of them could tame me. Boy they've damn sure tried.

She's water to my fire, a lover to my fighter, and she cuts me down to size. There's not another one like her. Man I gotta find her. 'Cause if ever there was someone ever made for someone, that girl was made for me.

She refused to meet his eyes as he finished his song. The ringing in her ears was finally drowning him out.

But she did look at the audience, and they were enthralled. Trace might've been a heartless bastard, but he was one hell of a performer. She sucked in a deep breath and slammed those cold steel walls over her wounded heart.

"Kiss me," she told him when the song ended.

"What?" Now it was his turn to be shocked.

She nodded towards the crowd full of screaming fans. "Kiss me. That's what they want, right? That's all you care about—giving them a good show. So do it."

He flinched back like she'd slapped him.

She hadn't, but a part of her desperately wanted to. Hurt flashed in his eyes as if he could read her mind.

He didn't kiss her, so she crushed her mouth to his.

Damn him to hell. Her anger and hurt poured out against his mouth. She bit down on his bottom lip hard enough to cause pain. She hoped it hurt.

Once the lights went out she jerked out of his arms. She knew his mic could possibly still be on so she didn't say a word. She just stalked away from him without looking back.

chapter THIRTY SIX

TRACE brought his fingers to his mouth to check for blood. He didn't see any on his hand but he could taste a faint hint of it on his tongue.

He'd put his heart out there in front of thousands of people and she'd stormed off. The tears in her eyes had confused him to hell and back.

He thought maybe they'd been tears of joy. But the harder she'd fought them, the more they'd looked like tears of pain. And her teeth sinking into his lip indicated they might've been tears of anger. Or rage.

Every single person in Encore Park seemed determined to get in his fucking way as he tried to find her backstage.

People congratulated him, some clapped him on the back, a few asked for pictures with him, but he just kept plowing through the crowd.

He caught Claire Ann's elbow and told her he'd see her and Rae at the house in an hour or two. She nodded with a sympathetic expression, so he figured she'd seen Kylie bolt after his grand gesture.

She'd misunderstood. That had to be it. Maybe she thought he was just putting on a show and didn't realize he was putting his heart out there for the whole world to see. He knew she still felt something for him.

He knew because he felt it in her eyes, in her smile. Without even consciously meaning to, he'd begun to study her—paying close attention to each small movement, each laugh. He would earn a damn degree in Kylie Ryans before this tour was over. He didn't miss the little things anymore, like the way she angled her body towards him when he came near and then forced herself to turn away.

He caught a glimpse of her hair and gleaming dress over by the bus, and he was just about to break into a sprint when he saw something that stopped him cold where he stood.

Steven Blythe was leaning up next to a magnolia tree and he had Mia Montgomery in his arms. Their mouths were damn near touching. They weren't kissing, but it clearly wasn't innocent either.

His blood felt like it had caught fire in his veins.

This motherfucker was really starting to piss him off. And if Kylie was going to choose her bullshit charade of a relationship with this dick over him, then he was at least going to confront the cheating bastard. With his fists.

He stalked over to where they stood and whirled Steven around by his shoulder. "Do you even give a damn about her at all, man? I mean, just how many women are you screwing behind her back?"

"Back off, Corbin," Steven warned, turning to face him. "You don't know what the hell you're talking about."

"Well, by my count, there's the Tailgate Twin and now Mia. You planning on nailing her assistant next?"

"What's he talking about, Steven? A Tailgate Twin?" Mia asked from behind him.

"Nothing, Mia. He's just—"

Before Steven could finish, Trace's fist shot out and struck him in the mouth.

Steven took a swing in return, but Trace ducked and wrapped him around the waist—driving his body back against the tree trunk.

Steven shoved him backwards. "Dammit, man. I warned you not to fucking hit me again." He swung hard and connected with Trace's right cheekbone. The two of them surged forward at the same time and wrestled in the dirt until two members of the security team broke it up.

Trace straightened and shrugged off the grip of dark-skinned guy yanking him backwards.

He threw his hands up in the air. "I'm good. I'm done."

Through his one good eye, he saw her.

Kylie stood there among the crowd, looking utterly horrified.

"What the hell is wrong with you?" she screamed at him. His mouth dropped open when she ran to play nurse on Steven's busted lip.

"Me?" he shouted back. "Me? What the hell is wrong with *me*? Your boyfriend here screws everything that moves and you're asking what's wrong with *me*?"

He wiped his face and wasn't surprised that this time, blood damn near covered his hand when it came into view. Trace clenched his fists at his sides as he watched Kylie wrap her arm around Steven's waist while they both glared at him.

"You know, every time I start to think that you might've grown up, that you might actually keep your promise to behave like an adult on this tour, you go and remind me why I never should've trusted you in the first place." She shook her head and turned towards the lot where the busses were parked.

The small crowd that had gathered around them dispersed as quickly as the security team could herd them out of there. Pauly and Claire Ann appeared at his side.

"Let's go home now," his sister said softly.

"No." He began walking towards the bus. "I have to talk to her. She needs to know what's going on. And she can be pissed at me all she wants, but I'm not going to watch that little shit do this to her."

"I don't think she cares what you have to say right this minute." Pauly's face twisted into a grimace. "Listen, give her some time. Tomorrow, after everyone's had some time to sleep on it, you can talk to her about whatever you like."

"I'm not leaving here until I talk to her, Pauly." He turned to his sister with desperation in his pleading gaze.

"Oh no," she said, taking a step back. "Do not drag me into this. You're on your own."

"Please? Just go knock on the bus door and ask her to give me five minutes. It's five minutes, Claire Ann."

She shook her head. "Trace, I told you I needed help with Rae. You promised to talk to her tonight."

"And I will," he promised. "Swear. But I can't leave it like this. Don't make me beg."

"Fine. Five minutes and then we are out of here." His sister led the way to his bus, mumbling about feeling like she was in seventh grade. She knocked roughly on the door. Kylie's friend Lu opened it and stood with her pink-streaked head cocked to the side.

"He wants to talk to her for five minutes," Claire Ann said evenly. "Then we're heading to Macon."

"Hang tight," the girl said, shooting him an annoyed look.

Trace folded his arms. What the hell was wrong with everyone? Blythe had gotten what he'd deserved. Meanwhile, his right eye was ready to throb right out of his skull.

A moment later, Kylie appeared at the door to the bus.

"What in God's name could you possibly have to say to me?" Her blue eyes blazed into his. "Wait, why don't you just wait a few days and sing whatever it is to me in front of my entire hometown?"

She folded her arms, which only functioned to thrust the swells of her breasts visible above her dress even higher. He forced himself to focus on her face.

"I need a few minutes. I'll meet y'all at the car," he told his sister and manager.

Once they'd gone, shaking their heads and giving him disappointed glances as they went, he turned to Kylie and sighed.

"Look, I don't know what I did to—"

"Are you kidding me?" She came down off the steps of the bus and forced him backward. "You don't know what you did? I was all stressed about letting Steven stay in my room last night. Even though all we did was write. I was planning to *apologize* to you. Then you went and humiliated me in front of a huge crowd and attacked my guitar player."

Trace stepped forward into her personal space. "Humiliated you? Kylie, it took every ounce of courage I had to sing that fucking song. Do you have any idea how hard that was for me? But I wrote it for you and I wanted you to know how I felt. I was throwing my hat in the ring, dammit."

She eyed him warily and he swallowed hard. "What about Gretchen?"

"What *about* Gretchen? If you want to ask me something, anything, fucking ask already. But you should know I've got some questions of my own." He waited a beat to give her a chance to say something but she just

186

averted her eyes from his intense stare. "And what the hell is the deal with Blythe? Is he your boyfriend or your guitar player? Because I can't figure it out and I don't think he can either. One minute he's crashing in your room and the next he's got a Tailgate Twin or Mia Montgomery hanging off his dick."

Her eyes filled with tears and Trace felt like a complete ass. Pauly was right. This was none of his business and he shouldn't have made such a public display of her personal issues.

"Dammit, I'm sorry. I'm so sorry. All I do is hurt you." He reached out and she pulled back so fast she backed into the bus.

The girl he'd known couldn't have kept quiet for this long. She would've chewed his ass out ten different ways by now.

It began to dawn on him that maybe she really had changed. Maybe the version of her that he'd fallen in love had disappeared somewhere along the way to her becoming a huge star.

"You," she began, her tone dead even despite the fact that her lower lip trembled. "You have no idea what goes on in my personal life. And I plan to keep it that way. You don't see me giving you hell about Gretchen. And that's because I'm an adult and can behave like an adult."

He wasn't entirely sure why she kept bringing up Gretchen. He thought she of all people knew better than to believe any of that tabloid bullshit. He huffed out a breath. "Adult my ass. It's because you've turned into a fucking zombie who shuts her feelings off like a damned water spout."

"If anyone's an ass, it's you." She looked at him as if she didn't even recognize him. "I don't know how I ever saw you as anything else."

She wanted an ass? Well then, he'd give her one.

"Oh yeah? Well, let's see. When I was buried deep inside you and making you come over and over again, you seemed to like me just fine."

She reached a hand up to slap him and he caught her wrist.

"Easy, Kylie Lou," he said low, with a warning in the depth of his voice. "Play nice."

"Stop calling me that," she practically growled at him through clenched teeth.

He pressed her up against the bus, letting his body rest against hers. "Stop calling you what, Kylie Lou?"

"That. Just...just stop."

"And why would I do that?"

She huffed out a breath and glared at him. "Because I hate it."

At that, his face broke into a knowing grin. "No you don't."

She tightened her jaw and her fists. "Yes. I do."

He released her wrist and braced both his hands on either side of her head. His voice was a quiet and full with the promise of something dark and sinful when he spoke.

"See, here's the thing. Maybe you've forgotten, but I've looked into those beautiful blues when you were coming hard and begging for more. So I know what they look like when you're enjoying something."

She sucked in a shocked breath, but he wasn't done.

"And it's the damnedest thing, but you get that exact same look every time I call you Kylie Lou. So you should know from previous experience that I won't be stopping anytime soon."

He saw sheer panic battling with ravenous need in her eyes when she responded. "I want you to leave. Now."

"Oh, I am," he told her, pausing to let his eyes trail appreciatively down her body. "I'm going home…to my house…to take a long, hot shower. You've spent some time in my shower, haven't you?"

He almost winced at the pain that flashed in her eyes. But he couldn't stop. He needed to push her until she broke. Until she admitted that she remembered, that she still cared. He couldn't let go of the belief that his girl was still in there somewhere.

"And tomorrow morning I just might clean out the barn before I come back to the bus. You remember the barn, right?"

"Go to hell," she said, practically hissing at him. Her entire body seemed to vibrate in his arms. Her sweet, savory scent surrounded him and he was pissed off and turned on all at once.

He'd tried the nice guy route. He really had. But he wasn't that guy, and apparently that flowers and serenading bullshit wasn't going to work on her anyway. He'd crashed and burned repeatedly using that method. It was time to change tactics. He'd always preferred a more direct approach anyhow.

"I'm already there, sweetheart. And I will be there until you stop playing whatever fucking game you're playing and admit that there's still something going on here."

Her chest pressed against his in time with his own pounding heart as she struggled to breathe.

"Oh, there's definitely something going on here. You're being as ass. Why can't you just let me be? What the hell do you want from me? I already gave you everything once and you walked away."

Her words hit him straight in the heart. They were enough to back him up a step. "I know. I know I did. And I'm sorry for that, Kylie Lou. Truly I am. But I don't regret it. It was for the best. It was what was best for you, for both of us, and if I had to, I'd do it again."

Tears began to fall down her face, and he wanted nothing more than to wipe them away. He reached his hand up to do just that, but she smacked it away.

"You don't get to decide anymore what's best for me."

"Please just talk to me. Be angry, hit me. Scream at me. Whatever you need to do. Just don't shut me out. I can't do this with you anymore. This isn't you."

"Has it occurred to you that maybe you don't actually know me anymore, Trace Corbin? Stop acting like your some freaking expert. I was young and stupid and—"

"You're right. I don't know you anymore. Because the Kylie Ryans I knew made her own damn decisions. And since we've been on this tour, I don't know that I've seen you make a single one without your fucking entourage."

She glared at him so hard he was thankful that looks couldn't actually kill.

"Well, watch real close. I'm about to make one right now." With that, she turned her back to him and marched herself right back onto the bus.

Just before she disappeared from his sight, she glared at him once more over her shoulder and hit him with a parting shot.

"Enjoy the view."

chapter THIRTY SEVEN

"THAT went well," Lulu said when Kylie returned.

She didn't even bother with a witty comeback. She was emotionally exhausted from the draining events of the entire damn day.

She dropped onto the couch and looked over at Steven, who was still holding a hand towel full of ice to his mouth.

Trace and Steven had been the ones to whale on each other, but she felt just as battered at they looked.

"Can we have a minute?" she said to Lulu and Mia and Lily.

"Yeah, um, we're actually going to head on to our hotel. We're driving back to Nashville early in the morning," Mia said.

"Thanks for coming. I'm sorry it was such a crazy night."

"I'm pretty sure my dad could get you a reality show," Lily informed her with a grin. "Just sayin'."

"Very funny."

"I'd watch it," Lulu added with a shrug. "I'm going to go see what Mike's up to. And if the backstage brawl has made it on YouTube yet."

"Keep your head up, Oklahoma. This tour will be over before you know it." Mia gave her a gentle smile as they left. Kylie didn't miss the lingering look she cast in Steven's direction either.

Kylie sighed loudly once they were gone. "I think I owe you an apology," she told Steven. "Pretty sure this is all my fault."

"You think?" He tried to smile but winced in pain instead. Kylie nearly winced right along with him.

"For the record, I wasn't trying to make him jealous or make him want to hurt you." She closed her eyes for a moment. "I was trying to protect myself. I thought maybe if he thought we were dating he would respect that enough to keep his distance."

"That really what you want, Ryans? For him to keep his distance?"

She looked up at her friend's already bruising face. "Truthfully, I have no idea what I want. And that's part of the problem." She lifted a shoulder and let it drop. "But I shouldn't have used you like that. I agreed to this tour and I should've handled whatever he threw at me head-on instead of hiding behind you."

Steven came closer and dropped down next to her. "Don't beat yourself up. I came along for the ride knowing what I was getting into." He lowered the ice pack from his face and aimed a pointed stare at it. "Well, maybe not *exactly* what I was getting into. But I've known since day one that you were just killing time with me. And I was cool with it."

"That still doesn't make it okay. And I really am sorry. I don't know how I let it get so...messy."

Steven shrugged. "Love is messy."

Kylie's eyebrows dipped in confusion. "Uh, who said anything about love?"

He chuckled softly beside her. "You did. And so did he. You both practically shout it from the top of your lungs every time you get with in five feet of each other. You just have really fucked-up ways of showing it."

She shook her head and stared at her hands in her lap. "He doesn't love me. Regardless of how I feel or felt about him, he never loved me."

"Did you even listen to the lyrics to his song tonight? The whole damn thing was about how much he loves you. I'm starting to think you both need some fucking therapy. My parents saw a couple's therapist for a while. I could get you the number."

"Gee thanks."

He laughed again and bumped her shoulder with his. "To tell you the truth, I was really just hoping to finally get to have sex with you. You know, strictly for bragging rights."

"You better be joking or I'm going to bust your other lip."

He laughed again. "You never know, Ryans. Maybe if we do it, I'll blow your mind and you really will finally get completely over him."

She tilted her head and tapped her lips with her forefinger, as if she were actually contemplating his offer.

"Just kidding," he said, standing. "Pretty sure it's just a dick in my pants and not a magic wand. But if I could wave it and help you get over him, I promise I would."

"You're such a good friend, Blythe."

"I know, right? A regular humanitarian ready to donate my body to the cause. There should be an award." He gave her a one-arm hug as she walked him off the bus.

She felt the shift when his demeanor changed. "I have to ask you something. Something serious."

Kylie contemplated making a joke about one of the Tailgate Twins, but his expression said he was actually serious this time so she didn't. "Shoot."

"Would it be okay if I got a ride home with Mia and Lily? I think this is my last stop, Ryans. I know a few guys who can be here tomorrow to replace me."

It should have upset her for yet another guy to walk out on her. But it didn't. She understood.

"Yeah. It's probably a good idea. And no worries. I can call Aiden and see if he can meet up with us at the next stop." She couldn't even remember where that was off the top of her head. The whole damn tour was becoming one big fucked-up blur.

Steven breathed a visible sigh of relief. "For the record, whatever you decide to do or not do, I hope you and Corbin get your shit worked out."

She smiled as he kissed her goodbye on the cheek. *Me, too,* she thought to herself. *Me freaking too.*

AFTER a long, hot shower, Kylie wanted nothing more than to crawl in bed and forget the entire disastrous day.

But that wasn't the way her life worked.

Darla's book stared at her from her nightstand. Mocking her. And she had to call her guitar player and let him know he was needed after all. Surprisingly, Aiden wasn't upset. He told her that his mother-in-law had been staying with them to help with the twins and he was mostly in the way at home. She couldn't tell if he was kidding or completely serious.

After calling Hannah and telling her to arrange his flight to the next tour stop, which Hannah informed her was in South Carolina, Kylie sat on her bed and began to read three hundred and fifty-odd pages of lies and bullshit. Twenty pages in, she seriously considered calling the publisher and suggesting they change the title.

By chapter six, she'd lost count of the twisted mistruths. Darla detailed screaming fights where Kylie called her terrible names. They'd happened, but it had been her wicked stepmother calling the names.

The passages reminded Kylie of some of the disgusting words she'd been called by Darla when her dad wasn't around, long before she'd even known what they meant. She thought of how she'd feel if someone had called Lily or Rae those terrible things when they were that age. A sudden swell of heartache for her own pre-teen self washed over her.

But that was nothing compared to the scathing fabrications Darla's story contained about Kylie's daddy.

She'd called him an alcoholic, a liar, a cheater, and impotent—which really didn't gel with the whole cheater thing—but clearly there was no one involved in publishing the monstrosity that actually gave a damn about fact-checking.

Tears streamed down Kylie's face as she read defamation after defamation.

She didn't miss the fact that so many of them were eerily similar to things the media had published about Trace. So much so that she began to wonder if whoever had helped a woman—who, as it so happened, couldn't read and interpret the directions to make macaroni and cheese—write a book, maybe had a vendetta had been purposely trying to draw a parallel.

Trace's name was never mentioned specifically—the non-disclosure agreement Trace had made her sign two years ago must've made sure of that—but Kylie was accused of using her daddy issues as an excuse to sleep her way through Nashville repeatedly throughout the chapters she'd read so far.

When she couldn't take any more, she set the book aside and pulled her knees to her chest. Pulling her daddy's faded blue button-up work shirt around her, she let her fingers follow the thread path of his name sewn into the front pocket.

She didn't have much to remember him by. A few old shirts, his truck, and her memories. Good memories. Memories of fishing and camping trips, ballgames, and learning to play guitar on the front porch after dinner.

The falsehoods Darla spun were just that. False.

He'd drunk a beer every now and then and he'd been tired a lot once he had a high-maintenance hag of a wife to deal with. But he was a good man. The best man Kylie had ever known.

And no one would know. Because she'd put herself in the public eye, and Darla had found a way to exploit that for her own benefit. She wondered if there was any possible way she could've stopped this from being published. Called a lawyer or sued the publisher or something. Anything to keep her daddy's memory from being tainted in this repulsive way.

But it was too late now. It was already out there—this bound book of lies about him and her both.

A hard sob forced its way out of her throat and she threw the book across the room. It hit the wall with a dull thud and landed open on the floor.

"Kylie Lou," a soft voice called. She went completely still, briefly entertaining the ridiculous idea of hiding in a closet so she wouldn't have to face him. She hurried to erase the evidence that she'd been crying. "You okay?" Trace stepped into her room and picked up the book she'd thrown.

She lifted her chin in an attempt to appear perfectly fine. "What are you doing here? I thought everyone was staying at your place tonight."

She didn't add that it stung like a dozen angry hornets that he'd invited everyone except her to his place for a home-cooked meal after the show. Not that she would've gone. But it stung nonetheless.

"They are. I think the better question is, what are *you* doing here?"

She gave him her best that's-a-stupid-ass-question face. "Well, I wasn't invited to the farm last I checked. So where else would I be?"

"I didn't ask why you were here. I asked what you were doing. I meant specifically."

She sighed loudly and closed her eyes for a moment. With a light shake of her head, she opened them and looked at him.

"Trace, between your big productions tonight—you know, the one on stage and the one where you attacked Steven for no good reason—and then our argument outside where you decided to rehash painful memories just for fun, I'm kind of tired."

"You're tired?" He eyed the book in his hands. "So you decided to read a book that you knew would keep you up all night?"

An explanation came to mind, but she bit her tongue. She didn't owe him anything.

"What I read is none of your business."

"Fine. So why are you all alone on this bus reading that piece of garbage? Where's Steve? I saw Mia and Lily leaving earlier and I could've sworn I saw him leaving with them. Care to tell me what the fuck is actually going on with the two of you before I make an even bigger ass of myself?"

"Not that that's any of your business either, but he left. He's done with the tour. Congratulations. Mission accomplished. You can rest easy now."

Pushing off her mattress, she stood and placed a hand out for her book.

He frowned and ignored her gesture. "I wasn't trying to run him off. I just didn't want to see you get—"

"I swear to God, if you try to somehow spin this into you being some big damned hero, I am going to scream." She shook her head and stepped back towards her bed. "And the idea of *you* protecting *me* from getting hurt is laughable."

She expected him to say something back. But he just looked at her intently, as if she were a puzzle to piece together and he was struggling to make it all fit. Her patience ran out before he said anything else.

"Can you just grab whatever you forgot and go on back to Macon? I'm really not in the mood for this right now."

"Okay. I'll do that then." Without warning, Trace leaned down and lifted her off the bed. Before she had time to say a single word in protest, she was upside down over his shoulder and they were bounding off the bus.

"Pants," she squealed. "Trace, I'm not wearing any pants!"

"I know." He gave her a firm smack on her ass, which was right next to his head. "Thank God for that. It was the only reason I could stand listening to all your whiny baby nonsense in there."

"Nonsense? Where the hell do you get off?"

He sat her down in the kitchen. "Well, it used to be inside of you. On a good day, anyways. Otherwise in the shower mostly."

"Something is seriously wrong with you." Her mouth threatened to let a small smile creep out and she wanted to slap herself in the face.

"Lots of things are wrong with me, darlin'. Surely you get that by now." He looked at her as if she were the one acting like a crazed lunatic instead of the other way around. "But I can't fucking sleep in my big empty bed knowing you're here on this damn bus all alone. So get your shit and let's go."

"I'm not going—"

"Spare me the toddler fit, okay? It's late. It's been a long day, like you said. And I have something I want us to do before we head back to the farm."

"Oh no, Trace Corbin. If you think for one second that we're going to—"

"Going to what, Kylie Lou?" His face was the picture of innocence. She knew hers was likely glowing with embarrassment. "I see you have your mind in the gutter."

"I'm going back to bed." She turned to storm back to her room, but he caught her by the arm before she'd made it out of reaching distance.

"Oh no you don't. Look, we can do this the easy way, where you throw on some pants and bring your ass on. Or I can carry you out of here kicking and screaming and tomorrow you'll have to borrow something from Rae to wear." He shrugged. "Come to think of it, doesn't actually make much of a difference to me either way. Welp, up you go then."

He bent down to grab her again and she gave him a solid shove.

"Okay, okay. For God's sakes. I'm coming."

"Sure, we can make time for that too." He reached for her again and she slapped him away.

"Dammit, Trace. Can you stop acting like a fourteen-year-old for five damn minutes?" She could feel her blood pressure rising. "I can't do this if I have to constantly think about everything I say being turned into innuendo."

"Doesn't matter what you say. I'll turn it all into innuendo regardless."

She folded her arms across her chest. "Great. And when will you be stopping that childish habit exactly?"

He made a big show of appearing thoughtful. "When you admit that you still have feelings for me, you still think about me, and that you missed me terribly every second that we were apart."

"There'll be figure skating competitions in hell before that happens."

He nodded as if it made no difference either way. "Well, then I hope you enjoy my little jokes. I got plenty."

She decided to give him a taste of his own medicine. "Actually, I do have a confession to make. It's kind of embarrassing though."

He turned his head slightly. "And what's that, darlin'?"

She took a step towards him. "Do you remember that night on the bus, that one night when you told me to go back to my room and lock the door?"

She watched his Adam's apple rise and fall as he swallowed. "Vaguely. Why?"

Steeling her own nerves so she could go through with her plan for getting him to back off, she reached out and ran a finger down the chest of the tight gray T-shirt he was wearing.

Lowering her voice enough to be seductive, she glanced up at him from under her eyelashes. "Well, sometimes…at night…and even sometimes during the day, I think about you and I…I *touch* myself."

His eyes went wide and then narrowed with suspicion. "You do?"

"Yes. I do." She paused to bite her bottom lip. His eyes dropped to her mouth and she grinned. "I rub my temples. Because you give me a fucking migraine."

His mouth eased into a slow smile while she grinned triumphantly. He shook his head and touched her lightly under her chin. "You're something else, pretty girl. You ready to go or what?"

Locked in his gaze, all sense of having finally beaten him at his own little play on words game vanished. The truth was, she may have finally made it to equal ground where their careers were concerned, but where anything sexual was involved, she knew he would win every time. He'd shown her many, *many* times the way he could rob her off every single ounce of self-control she had with just one touch.

She took a deep breath and stepped out of his space—relenting because she knew he wasn't going to.

"Give me two minutes. I'm gonna go grab some pants."

"Don't bother on my account. I prefer you without them," he called out after her.

She did everything in her power to ignore the way her heart raced. Flirting with him was a terrible idea—one she had no recollection of deciding on and wished she could take back.

She lost control of herself around him, a control she'd worked so hard to keep her white-knuckled death grip on. Her heart was doing its best to try and warn her. It had taken it a year just to regain the ability to function normally.

It definitely wasn't strong enough for anymore of the Trace Corbin heartbreak special.

chapter THIRTY EIGHT

H E had the fire started by the time she got off the bus. Giving her a quick glance over his shoulder, he saw she'd pulled her hair up into a messy bun and put on jeans that begged to be peeled right back off of her.

"Um, what's this?" She gestured to the fire as he pulled out a plastic chair for her to sit in.

"We're having a bonfire. It's a campground after all." Without any further explanation, he tossed the book he was holding into the flames.

"I was reading that!"

"Yeah, I know you were. That was the problem." Trace handed her a stick. "You like s'mores, right?"

Kylie gaped at him as he pulled the items he'd gotten at the gas station from the brown paper sack.

"What are we doing?" she asked softly. The vulnerable plea softened the hardened wall he'd been holding up with all his might.

He sighed loudly as he lowered himself into his own chair.

"I'm trying here, Kylie Lou. I really am. But I don't know what you want or need from me. And if the answer is that what you want and need from me is for me to stay the hell out of your life or pretend like I don't give a damn, well…I don't know if I can."

He turned and let his stare sink into her gaze. For a brief moment, he felt as if he really could read her mind. Hope, fear, and honest to God pain flashed from the depths of her wide expressive eyes. Whatever she was feeling, he was right there with her.

"Why not? I mean, why can't you?" The glimpse at that girl, that same vulnerable heart-on-her-sleeve girl, caught him off guard, and he had to look away to keep from taking her face in his hands and claiming her mouth as his.

"Hell if I know. I just know I can't."

Never in his life had he been this invested in the life of any other woman he'd been with. And of all of them, she was the one who actually had her shit together and truly didn't need him. Didn't even seem to want him. Or she didn't seem to *want to* want him, anyway.

The song had been too much for her to handle. He saw that now and judging from the way she was looking at him—doe-eyed and held captive by something she was obviously terrified of—he was going to have to back it down a notch or she was going to bolt before he could blink.

He cleared his throat and made a pathetic attempt at shrugging. "Maybe we could call a truce. Try being friends. You know. People who spend time together, work together, without any old vendettas or bad memories getting in the way? Clean slate?"

Glancing out of the corner of his eye, he saw that she'd turned to face the fire and was staring intently into the flames. The pages of her stepmother's book were turning to ash as the cover curled and wilted around them.

Sparks and glowing embers floated into the night sky. Trace watched them go, vanishing into thin air, and wished he could figure out a way to do the same thing to the pain he'd caused her.

"They weren't all bad." Her voice was so low he wondered if he'd imagined it. "The memories, I mean."

Her confession nearly gutted him. It took him a minute to recover the playful demeanor he was hell-bent on maintaining. She'd had enough stress for one day.

"Well of course not. I'm awesome in the sack." He turned and gave her his panty-dropping grin. The one she'd always been immune to.

Apparently she still was.

She rolled her eyes and reached for a marshmallow. He watched as she speared it on her stick and thrust it into the flames.

"Last I checked, I wasn't so bad myself."

It was his turn to lose himself staring at her as her full lips blew on her flaming glob of sugar before pulling it gently from the stick. He would've handed her a graham cracker or the chocolate bar he'd bought, but he was unable to move.

Emotions he'd never felt before—well, before her—threatened to strangle him then and there as she worked to build her s'more.

Damn straight she wasn't so bad in bed. She was downright fucking amazing.

His head swam with the memory of parting and filling her, holding her in his arms while she let out those breathy whimpers that sounded better than any song he'd ever played. Or ever even heard for that matter.

His warm memories began to burn with the raging heat of jealousy of knowing he hadn't been the only one to have her that way. But the other guy had thrown in the towel and bailed on her. Just like everyone else.

He still wasn't sure how he felt about that. It made him happy. It made him miserable. Knowing he was yet again responsible for her pain twisted him into an incomprehensible mess of a man.

"Hey," he began, "I know this is more than you want to hear right now, but I..." Panic had him choking on his own words. He took a deep breath.

Kylie regarded him warily once again. "What is it?"

I love you. I can't live without you. I need you to forgive me more than I need to breathe to survive.

He couldn't tell her any of that. Not yet. So he said the one thing he could.

"If there's anything I can do to help with the stepmom situation, you just say the word." He wanted to slap himself for chickening out. "And, uh, for the record, there isn't a limit to what I would do to keep from hurting you again." He swallowed hard and watched the pain dance across her face. "I'm not perfect—you know that better than anyone. And I will screw up. But hand to God, if I can keep from hurting you or keep anyone else from hurting you, I will move mountains and hell itself if I have to."

Her mouth dropped open just enough that he knew he'd surprised her.

"So...I just wanted you to know that." The obstinate fist that constantly gripped his heart in her presence loosened a fraction. Breathing slightly easier, he leaned back and began to roast his own marshmallow.

"I can't go to Macon tonight," she announced into the darkness without looking at him.

Her words were soft but even. Firm.

"Kylie, I know we—"

"No, Trace. You just said you wouldn't hurt me if you could help it. So I can't go." Her chest rose and fell with the weight of whatever she was about to tell him. She lowered her voice to a whisper. "It hurts being there, in that place where we were…you know."

He knew he might have imagined it, but her hands appeared to be shaking. He wanted to grab them and hold them more than anything. Hold her. Reassure her. Love the ever-loving hell out of her.

"Okay, Kylie Lou. We won't go then." He returned his attention to the fire. Without waiting for her response, he confessed his darkest secret. "But the truth is—even if you never set foot on that property again so long as you live—you're always there."

SHE was dead on her feet by the time they finished with their messy marshmallow roast. But he was pretty sure her stepmother's bullshit excuse for a book was a distant memory.

He walked her to her room wondering if he lived a normal life, if this was what a date might be like. After his suggestion of friendship and everything that had happened the past few weeks, he knew better than to expect a goodnight kiss. Didn't keep him from wanting one. Badly.

But when he wiped the sweet, sticky remnants of dessert from her lips, a hint of a smile played on them. He smiled back because even though he wasn't getting a kiss tonight, he'd accomplished his goal. He wanted to make her smile, help her forget, even if it was just for a little while.

His fingers ached to remain on her skin, but they'd turned a corner tonight. Sure, they'd mostly sat in peaceful silence. But there had been no anger, no frustration, and no blatant hatred rolling off of her in his direction. And he was desperately hoping that damned wall she kept between them was coming down slowly but surely. So he removed his finger from her soft lips and took a step back.

"You don't have to stay. Security team is in place. I'm fine, really." At least that's what her mouth said.

But Trace was catching on. Her mouth said, *Go, I'm fine.* Her eyes said, *Stay, I don't want to be alone.*

He was also smart enough to know she would hate that he'd figured that out.

Doing his best to not lay it on too thick, he let a yawn out and stretched his arms over his head. Gripping the top of the doorframe at the entrance of her room, he leaned forward.

"Eh, I'm kinda beat. Too tired to be driving anyways. The crew will make their way back in the morning without me."

"So you're staying then? On the bus?"

There it was, that mix of hope and fear that tended to show in her eyes when she was trying so hard not appear vulnerable.

"That okay with you? I'm just gonna crash in my room. I'll try not to snore too loud or have any disruptive nightmares."

Hope and fear turned to pity. Which he hated.

He scoffed. "It was a joke. It's not a big deal. Unless it really does keep you up. I could sleep on the—"

"Trace," was all she said.

It was enough to shut him up. She walked towards him with a determination that would've made a lesser man retreat. The sight of her hips swaying gently made his entire body stand at attention.

"Thank you," she said, catching him so off guard he couldn't respond right away. "For tonight. For what you said and did. For…coming back."

She was close enough that her sweet honey-vanilla scent enveloped him. Close enough to touch. Close enough to pick up and press against the wall. To tear her clothes off and sink himself inside of her.

He blinked the images away and focused on the present. Or tried to at least.

"I'll always come back." The words had just slipped out without his permission. He didn't even have time to wonder if she recognized them as her own. Her reaction was immediate.

Judging from the tears that sprang to her eyes and the way her entire body jolted, those words were an unwelcome reminder.

"Well, um, goodnight," she said quietly, turning away, dismissing him and busying herself by searching for something in her dresser.

He sighed, certain that he'd screwed up his mission not to hurt her once again. "Goodnight, Kylie Lou."

chapter THIRTY NINE

"**Y**OU'RE seriously telling me nothing happened?" Her best friend gaped at her in disbelief. "Like nothing as in no *bow chicka wow wow*, or nothing as in absolutely nothing? Not even a kiss or one of those damn spine-tingling, shiver-inducing, panty-combusting one-liners he's so good at?"

"Nothing as in nothing, Lu. He tossed Darla's book in the fire. We roasted marshmallows. We ate s'mores. We went to bed. Separately. The end." Kylie kept her voice low as her friend did her makeup. She hoped the girl would take the cue and lower her voice as well before someone heard.

"Well, that's...disappointing."

Kylie snorted. "Sorry. Guess you'll have to try and be satisfied with your own love life since I don't actually have one. Speaking of which—"

"Nope. Not talking about it. Don't even ask."

Kylie leaned back out of her friend's reach. "What the hell do you mean you're not talking about it? I tell you everything!"

Lulu nodded. "Exactly. And I have this theory."

"You and your theories," Kylie grumbled under her breath.

"Yeah. And they're usually right. This one I'm serious about."

"The theory or the guy? 'Cause, Lu, I gotta tell you, Mike Brennen is a—"

Lulu put a blue glittery manicured hand up in front of Kylie's mouth. "Nope. This is what you do. You overthink things, which is something I never thought I'd say about you. But ever since—"

"I got it. You think I'm being too careful." Kylie knew her voice had taken on a harsher tone, but she didn't care. Her heart pounded in her chest and she had to speak louder to hear herself over it. "But when you fall for Mike Brennen, who, by the way, is an alcoholic known for nailing anything that doesn't move out of the way fast enough, and he screws the next thing that comes along behind your back and you have to watch their entire relationship play out in front of the whole world, then you can come talk to me about being too careful." She propelled herself out of the chair.

"Kylie, wait." Her friend called after her. But she didn't.

She fled her best friend's tiny room without looking back.

As soon as she stepped off the bus and into the warm South Carolina sunshine, she was blocked by a solid wall of red and blue plaid.

"Okay, Gretch. Hate that you can't make it tonight. We'll catch up later then," Trace said into his phone before lowering it and disconnecting the call.

Literally running into him when he was on the phone with her least favorite, or maybe her second least favorite—she hadn't taken the time to weigh Gretchen Gibson against Darla yet—person in the whole world, set her nerves on edge. The peaceful truce they'd reached the night before felt like a distant memory.

"Jesus. Do you not own any other shirts?" She squinted up at him. His dark sunglasses hid his eyes, but his mouth quirked up in amusement.

"My bad, Joan Rivers. You have a complaint about my wardrobe?"

Kylie sighed and tried to move around him. "Too many to list. What are you doing over here anyways?"

"I was looking for my bass player. You seen him?"

"No. I haven't. And can you do me a favor when you do?"

Trace folded his arms over his broad chest. She refused to let herself notice the enticing way his forearms rippled and flexed. He'd just been on the phone with his girlfriend for god's sakes.

"What's that?"

"Tell him to leave my friend alone? Seriously. I need her, and if he does something to hurt her and she leaves then—"

"Yeah, I hear what you're saying. I do." Trace adjusted his bright red trucker hat, lifting the bill just enough to scratch his head before lowering it back down. "But I tried telling him to back off before anything even happened between them. You saw how well he listened."

"How well he listened to what?" Lulu inquired from behind her.

Kylie cringed. *Shit.*

"I'm gonna let you gals discuss this amongst yourselves. Either of you see Mike, tell him to get his ass to soundcheck, please." With that, Trace beat it out of there.

Thanks for the support, Corbin.

Slowly, Kylie turned to face her friend. "Lu. I'm sorry. I know I'm being a control freak and paranoid—"

"And ridiculous." Her friend shook her head as she came down off the bus. "Ky, I'm not you, and Mike's not Trace. We're not madly in love or starting some angst-filled, ill-fated, overly drawn-out romance. We're hooking up for lack of anything better to do. It's fun. We're having a good time."

Kylie frowned at her friend. "So you've said. Look, I know it's totally none of my business but—"

"But you plan to stick your perfect little nose in it anyways."

Kylie bit her lip and grinned. "Um, I might've told Trace to tell Mike to back off. Not that he'll listen, obviously."

Lulu made a big show of tossing her hair over her shoulder. Even though it was too short to really toss. "Well of course not. Who could resist this?" She gestured with mock confidence at her body.

Kylie laughed at her friend's lighthearted take on the whole thing, but the tinges of worry remained as the two of them headed over towards the stage where Trace and his band were warming up. Kylie heard the unmistakable thrum of Mike's bass guitar, so apparently he'd been located.

It was still a few hours until showtime so the arena was sparsely populated. They sat in front-row seats. When Mike winked down at Lulu, Kylie looked over at her. The expression her friend wore was hard to read, but she was pretty sure it said more than "hooking up for lack of anything better to do."

"Hey, Lu?" She waited until she'd reluctantly dragged her eyes from the stage before she continued. "Just, um, be careful, okay? I know you're a big girl and can make your own decisions, but I also know how fast hooking up can turn into a whole lot more. And the next thing you know, you're face down in a vat of mint chocolate chip." She attempted a smile. It wasn't easy with the object of her own heartbreak strutting his ass up and down the stage right in front of her face.

"I appreciate the concern. Really, I do." Her friend nudged her shoulder. "And I get where you're coming from. But I promise, it's not anything to stress over. Just two people enjoying each other's company while it lasts."

For a few minutes neither of them said anything. They just watched the private show as Trace and his band worked to get the sound equipment and their earpieces working correctly.

"So…we never got to finish our talk the other day."

Kylie had to work to pull herself out of the song Trace was singing. It was a warm day and she was beginning to feel kind of strange. Like she was in a fog and was having delayed reactions to pretty much everything.

"Huh?"

"When we got tacos. Hannah called about the Darla thing and we kind of got off track."

She turned and gave her friend her full attention. "That's right. Remind me what exactly we were talking about?"

Lulu's eyes darted towards the stage and then back to her.

"Oh."

"Yeah. So anyways, I was talking to Mike about everything that happened last year and I wanted to tell you what he said."

Every organ in her body had a reaction to Lulu's words. Her heart began the out-of-rhythm-beat-skipping thing it did whenever someone wanted to discuss the part of her life she tried so hard not to.

Kylie pulled as much air into her lungs as she could manage. Letting it out slowly, she forced an easy grin for her friend's piece of mind. "It's fine, Lu. I know he went into rehab with Gretchen. I know they're together or whatever. I've dealt with it."

She knew it was a half-truth, and it sucked telling it to the one person she'd always been able to tell everything to. But she was trying her best to make it the truth. Her hope was that, if she said it enough times, eventually it would be. One day in the very distant future probably, but the only thing she could really do was try.

Lulu's face contorted in either pain or concern. Kylie couldn't tell for sure.

"See, that's the thing. Mike's version is a little, uh, *different* from the mass media version."

Kylie's eyes had drifted back towards the stage. She could feel Trace watching her as he sang. Her inner fangirl threatened to come out and sing along. She stuffed a gag in that chick's mouth and returned her attention to Lulu.

"I'm sorry. I'm kind of out of it today. You were saying?"

"Kylie, I need you to focus, okay? And not on his ass in those damn jeans."

She scoffed. "I have no idea what you're talking about."

Her friend grinned. "No. No you don't have any idea what I'm talking about. Because you're paying more attention to him than me. Wonder why that is, Miss I'm-So-Over-It?"

Heat filled her cheeks and she glanced down at her hands in shame. She was tired, and not just because she hadn't slept a freaking wink last night. She was tired of holding up the heavy-as-hell billboard sign full of lies about how over him she was. So she dropped the damn thing and let it smash into a million pieces.

"I'm not over it, Lu. I'm a freaking mess. Last night he wiped some marshmallow goo off my face and I swear…I nearly melted into a puddle on the floor. From his hand. On my face. I *hate* that he still has this effect on me. What is *wrong* with me?"

Surprisingly, Lulu laughed.

Kylie narrowed her eyes at her. "Thanks. That's really helpful. Some bestie you are."

Once she'd sobered, Lulu pinned Kylie with a serious glare. "Okay, first of all, never call me that. In fact, if you even say that stupid-ass word around me, I might accidentally judo chop you in the throat. Purely as a reflex." She shrugged as if to say *consider yourself warned*, and continued her speech. "Second of all, nothing is wrong with you. You have unresolved feelings for someone you still care a lot about. Honestly, you want to know what the weirdest and most awkward part of this entire past year has been for everyone around you?"

Kylie opened her mouth to say something but Lulu rushed on.

"You pretending *not to* care about him."

"I guess acting is out as a career choice then?"

Her friend nodded. "Most definitely. Thank God you can sing."

Kylie sighed. She ignored the urge to look back up at the stage. Even though she knew there was no way Trace could hear her conversation, she felt as if she'd shouted her confession from the rooftops.

"So you were going to give me the expert opinion of Mike Brennen?"

Lulu shook her head. "No, I was going to tell you what he told me sort of by accident."

"Jesus. If you start telling me y'all talk about Trace in the throes of passion, I'm going to—"

"No. God, no. Nothing like that. I was going to tell you that Gretchen called Mike the other day. They share an addiction specialist dude or something." Lulu waved her hand as if the details were inconsequential. "Anyways, when they hung up, I made a snide comment about why she didn't just called her boyfriend to get whatever info she needed to know about the AA dude."

Kylie couldn't help it. She winced when Lulu referred to Trace that way. Her friend offered her a sympathetic smile and continued.

"And um, here's the weird part. Mike was totally lost. His exact response was 'I didn't even know Gretchen had a boyfriend.'"

Before Kylie had time to register the full impact of what her friend was saying—or the oddly disturbing fact that her face had gone strangely numb and prickly—Lulu put her hands up.

"Ky, I'm not saying you should take him back or run back to him with open arms or whatever. I'm just telling you what Mike said. According to him, Trace and Gretchen weren't together—um *aren't* together. They went to rehab together as friends…like a moral support buddy system thing or something."

"Oh." Her mouth was so dry she couldn't get any more words to come out of it. She licked her lips and snuck a glance to where he stood on stage talking with his drummer.

Her brain said that this was good news. Maybe he hadn't chosen someone else over her after all. But her heart said that she should keep that steel wall around it firmly in place and run like hell.

Because if this were true, if he really had just gone in to get help and so he could be better and then he'd come out only to see her with Steven—

which she was pretty certain had sent him right back into rehab—then she wasn't just a wounded ex-girlfriend who'd been dumped for someone else.

She was a complete idiot who'd basically cheated on the only man she'd ever loved.

But to her, it didn't necessarily matter what the *official* status of Trace and Gretchen's relationship was. They definitely had an intense—and likely very complex—one.

The words he'd said when she called him on walking away from what they had still plagued her.

It was for the best. It was what was best for you, for both of us, and if I had to, I'd do it again.

Those words rang out in her head like a tornado siren screaming a warning to run and hide. Especially that last part.

Because the truth was, dating or not, he'd told Gretchen about his drinking when he couldn't tell her. He'd gone into rehab and away from Kylie most likely at Gretchen's prompting. And she knew Gretchen didn't like her, would probably never like her, and Trace clearly valued her friendship and her opinion.

It was a huge fucking mess. One she couldn't sort through or process with him singing on stage a few feet away and the humidity making her sweaty and confused.

Everything she thought she knew, the clearly defined details of the situation and the images of him and Gretchen in her head, began to blur and fade. Because if Mike was telling the truth, her whole world had just become a strange and unfamiliar place. An alternate universe where everything was suddenly the exact opposite of the way it had once been. She was jaded and closed off and Trace was admitting his feelings and sober.

Hand to God, if I can keep from hurting you or keep anyone else from hurting you, I will move mountains and hell itself if I have to.

"Lu?"

Her friend appeared relieved that Kylie hadn't gone completely mute or into shock. "Yeah?"

Kylie tried to stand and the Earth jolted beneath her feet at the same time. She tried to get her eyes to focus, but it wasn't happening.

"I don't feel so good."

chapter FORTY

"SHE was fine one minute—we were just talking normally—and then she stood up and said she didn't feel so good and *wham*. Down she went."

Trace listened as Kylie's friend Olivia told the paramedics and Hannah what had happened.

"I'm fine," Kylie mumbled as she reached for Hannah. Her face was half hidden behind the oxygen mask they'd strapped on her. "Seriously, Han. Tell them I'm fine."

Her assistant nodded. "I will. I promise. They're just checking to make sure you'll be able to perform tonight."

"Like hell she will," he said, finally speaking up. "She just passed out. We have an extra day. We can postpone the show till tomorrow."

Her friend mumbled something to Mike that he couldn't hear.

"It's kind of late for that," Hannah informed him with a shrug. "She's probably suffering from mild exhaustion and dehydration. Some Gatorade and some rest and she'll be good as new."

"I'm sorry, did I miss the part about you being a doctor?" Trace felt his anger rising to an unstable level. He'd been through this with management professionals. All the ones he'd had early in his career had cared about was pushing him as hard as they could so they got paid. He'd be damned if he'd sit by and watch that happen to Kylie.

"I didn't mean to imply that—"

"Hey, you know what? We're gonna give these guys some space so they can check her out." Mike clamped down hard on Trace's shoulder and tugged him away from where the small group had gathered around the back of the ambulance.

"What the hell, man?" He glared at his bass player.

"You her manager, agent, doctor, or next of kin? No. No you're not. You needed to back up and let the people do their jobs, Tray. Period."

He took a few deep breaths. "Yeah, okay. But when they're done, I'm talking to her. And if she's not up for this tonight, we're postponing. *Period.*"

Mike shrugged. "Fine by me. You might want to call Cora and whoever Kylie's working with before this gets out. Some of the VIP fans were recording that little scene on their phones. And uh, before you go postponing anything, someone might want to check in with Davies and let him know the situation. You know he'll use this to activate that *No fucking up allowed* clause in your contract."

Trace nodded as Mike's advice sank in. A slight tinge of guilt hung around the edge of his concern. He knew he shouldn't have snapped at Hannah. Girl seemed nice enough. And not like a money-hungry leech like some of the ones he'd worked with. Part of it was his own selfish fear that he was to blame because he'd kept her up late last night.

Just as he pulled out his phone to call his PR lady, he saw Pauly Garrett headed his way.

"I called Kylie's management company. Chaz Michaelson said he'd take care of talking to her publicist and the label."

Trace thanked him and watched her talking with the medics. He couldn't ignore the fact that she looked awfully frail. Seeing her like that, weak and tired, brought his every protective instinct to the surface.

"She okay?" Pauly asked, jerking his head in her direction.

"They think it's just dehydration and maybe exhaustion," Mike answered before he could.

"No. Her *manager* thinks that. The medics are still checking her out." Pauly raised his eyebrows.

Mike's hands came up in a defensive gesture. "Yeah, and Trace thinks the entire world should shut down so we can lock the two of them on the bus and he can play doctor with her." Mike smirked at him. "To be honest, she does look kind of pale. I don't think she's up for the kind of *treatment* you probably have in mind."

Trace's fist twitched in anticipation of connecting with his bass player's jaw.

Pauly must've noticed because stepped between the two of them. "Tell you what. Why don't you run to the bus and grab her some waters and crackers or something," he told Trace. "And you," he began telling Mike, but Trace didn't hear the rest.

He was busy mentally berating himself for being such a complete idiot. All he'd seen her eat the day before was two s'mores. Claire Ann had offered to cook for everyone and he'd just figured she knew she'd been invited and hadn't wanted to go. Which was mostly true.

Well, I wasn't invited to the farm last I checked...It hurts being there, in that place...

Her words—her soft, heartbreaking words—filled his head as he searched the cabinets on the bus for some damned crackers. He found peanut butter granola bars and grabbed a few Gatorades and some bottles of water as well.

He really hoped her fainting spell wasn't a result of the fact that she wasn't eating or sleeping. Because if she wasn't taking care of herself— and if her not taking care of herself had anything to do with him or being on tour with someone who'd hurt her like he had—then he'd call the whole damn thing off.

He nearly dropped everything he was carrying when he stepped off the bus just in time to see the ambulance pulling away.

Pauly waved an arm in his direction. He jogged over to where he could see her being led by Hannah and Lulu and Mike back towards the bus.

"What'd they say?" His manager looked grim and his stomach turned. "What's going on?"

"Relax. She's fine. Slight dehydration they said. We're going to stay in a hotel tonight. Show's been moved to tomorrow."

Trace watched as Pauly tapped a few things out on his phone.

"I should—"

"Trace, maybe you should ride with me," his manager said, bracing him back with a hand on his chest. "I think this has been a lot for her to deal with. The fight, the guitar player leaving...And her manager mentioned that her mom wrote a tell-all that's recently been published. You know firsthand how messy those situations can be. You going in there all worked up like this isn't going to be good for anyone right now."

He frowned. "I care about her, Pauly."

The man nodded. "I know. I know you do. I just don't want this to start being a trend. I'd like nothing more for the two of you to finish this tour amicably and for everything to go smoothly. But times like this, I really think it's best if you just keep your distance. The last thing you need is for it to hit the press that you're the cause of her stress or something."

An icy cold wave of dread hit him hard. That was his biggest fear. That this was his fault. He handed Pauly the snacks and drinks he'd been holding.

"Here. Take those to her. I'm going for a walk."

chapter FORTY ONE

"Well that's the last time I tell you anything," Lulu said.

Kylie sat up and sipped more water. "Very funny. I should've eaten breakfast. I just didn't feel hungry this morning."

Mike rode with them to the hotel. He was quietly watching SportsCenter on the flat screen while Lulu sat by Kylie's makeshift bed on the couch.

"Any idea where Trace went?" she asked him.

He looked over at her and shrugged. "Dunno. I guess he got a ride on one of the other buses. He was feeling a little out of it himself I think."

"So y'all just ate s'mores last night, huh?" Lulu arched a brow.

Kylie thwacked her will a pillow. "Shut up. This is embarrassing enough. I can't believe they postponed the show. Tabloids will probably all say I'm pregnant tomorrow."

"Or anorexic," Lulu offered helpfully.

"Or a drama queen making a desperate play for attention," Mike said, waggling his eyebrows at her.

"Nice. Both of you. Thanks a lot."

"Who cares what they say?" Lulu rolled her eyes. "I'm about to Tweet that you were really tired from the orgy you had with your band and needed a day to recover."

Kylie snorted. "No one would believe it. My band hates me."

"No they don't," Lulu reassured her.

"Yeah. Actually they do," Mike informed them both. "Sorry to be the bearer of bad news, but they think she's a slave driver who needs to get a life."

Kylie tried not to let either one of them see how much that hurt to hear. Not that it was surprising, but it stung.

"Okay, Bass Boy, you're like two seconds from being tossed off this bus."

"It's fine. He's just being honest," Kylie told Lulu. "And they have every right to feel that way. I never take breaks, they have to beg for holidays off, and I'm a perfectionist. They pretty much all hate my guts."

Lulu turned her back to Mike and gave her friend her full attention. "You've worked hard for this. It's your ass on the line. Your face on the album. You can be however you want to be. They don't like it, they can find another band to be in."

Kylie shrugged. "My New Year's resolution was to try and take it easier on them. It's not their fault I don't have a life."

"Mia mentioned that you were pretty much living in the studio before this tour. Ky, can I ask why that was? I mean, you have a great apartment, you live in the city of your dreams, your album rocketed off the damn charts, and this is everything you wished for, right? So what's with the constant nose-to-the-grindstone routine?"

A lump formed in her throat. Kylie waited until she could swallow to answer.

"It's all I have, Lu. Music is literally my life."

The pity in her friend's expression made her feel even worse.

"You know, I don't get why everyone acts like it's such a bad thing. In this business, if you take a break, someone younger and prettier replaces you while you're not looking. So I don't like to sit around on my ass and wait for that to happen. So what?" She threw her hands up. "And besides, this is temporary. It's not like I'll be the next big thing forever. The newness will wear off and I'll be old news. So it only makes sense to do as much as I can while I'm in the spotlight, right?"

"What about when you're not in it anymore, Ky?" Lulu's voice was much softer than usual. "When this all ends or slows down at least—because, like you said, it will one day—I'm worried about what your life will be like then. What *you'll* be like."

Kylie wished she could just disappear and avoid this conversation. She knew what kind of life she was going to have. She'd always known.

Holidays alone eating frozen meals on her couch. Pretending it was fine. That she was glad to have some time to herself.

Her daddy's death had left her with nothing but a dream, a dream that she'd chased and caught and would probably have to let go of at some point. She had her dream career, had success she knew many only hoped for and never got. But she wasn't stupid. She knew a career in music wouldn't last forever, wouldn't love her, and wouldn't keep her warm at night. But she'd been naïve enough to hope for everything once, to think maybe she could have her dream and someone to share it with. She'd be damned if she'd make that mistake again.

"What would you suggest I do? I've tried dating and having a life outside of it. You saw how well that worked out for me."

Lulu opened her mouth to answer, but it was Mike clearing his throat that she heard.

"Mind if I take this one?" he asked her friend.

"If you say something hurtful and asinine, I promise you will be hoofing it to the hotel on your own two legs."

"Noted," Mike answered with a grin. He scooted a little closer to where they sat and looked Kylie right in the eyes. "You know what I always liked about you?"

"Probably nothing that's appropriate to say out loud," Kylie muttered.

He laughed good-naturedly. "Well, yeah. But also, you were tough. And anything anyone gave you, you gave right back. You didn't play any bullshit games. Well, minus hustling us all in Hold 'Em in Mobile. But aside from that, you were a straight shooter."

"Are you trying to say I'm some big phony now, Brennen? Because—"

"Eh, eh, eh," he said, cutting her off before she could blow a gasket. "Hear me out."

She huffed out a breath and waited for him to continue.

"What I'm saying is, somewhere along the way, for whatever reason, you changed. And that's probably not a bad thing since this business tends to eat pretty little girls like you for breakfast. But from what your band bitches about and how tight Corbin's been wound lately, I think you probably went a little too far in the *I don't fucking need anyone* direction. And when you work with a band who has your back in the studio and on the road, that's a dangerous move."

Kylie chewed over the things he'd said for a few minutes.

"So you're telling me I should just go with the flow and say to hell with rehearsing, recording, and the rest of it?" She threw her hands up and let them fall back into her lap. "You know as well as I do, this business will toss me out on my ass if I do that."

Mike didn't answer right away. When he did, his question caught her off guard. "Your guitar player, the one that just had twins, what are their names?"

"Uh, his kids' names?"

"Yeah."

Kylie scanned her memory for any mention of their names. "I don't know. He never said."

"Really? 'Cause I've met him all of once and I know their names, time of birth, and weight."

"I've been busy," Kylie said in her own defense.

"Okay, what's his wife's name then?"

Once again, she felt like she should know the answer but couldn't pull it to her lips. "Starts with an M I think."

Mike raised a brow. "Really? They spell Rachel with an M where you're from?"

"Jesus Christ, Mike. She doesn't have to memorize all of their life stories," Lulu broke in. "Give her a friggin' break."

"That's not what I'm saying." He gave a slight shake of his head and shrugged. "All I'm saying is, I can get not letting *everyone* in. The way shit went down with you and Tray, I can see how you'd want to be careful. And it's not easy trusting people in this business, period. But when it comes to your band, you might want to at least make an effort. Let them know you're human and you actually give a shit about them."

She pulled her knees up to her chest. It felt like the man had just torn her skin off and shown everyone her battered heart.

She'd changed. She knew she had. But she also felt like she'd had to. Otherwise she'd just keep trusting the wrong people, giving them everything she had to give, and winding up empty and alone. At least this way she was alone by choice.

"I need to know something. Tell me the truth, Brennen. Please?" She hated the pathetic pleading tone in her voice, but she had to know.

He smirked at her, and she glared hard at him before he made some inappropriate comment.

"Trace and…Trace and Gretchen. Are they a thing or not? Was it all media hype or was there truth to any of it?"

Trace's bass player and friend tilted his head and stared at her intently. Then he ran a hand through his messy blond hair and shrugged. "You and the kid who recently parted ways with the tour. Were you a thing or not? Was it all media hype or was—"

"I got it," she said, putting a hand up. "I shouldn't have asked."

Lulu handed her another bottle of water from the fridge. "Ignore him. What the hell does he know, right?"

"No, he's right," Kylie said softly, taking the drink from her friend. "I shut people out. It seemed easier that way, after everything. Until…" She trailed off, unsure as to how to explain.

"Until you had to face him again. He's not exactly the type of guy you can shut out."

Kylie swallowed, the knot in her throat threatening to choke her for what seemed like the millionth time recently. "Yeah," she managed to get out.

"Well, I don't know that Bass Boy is exactly the best person to be giving life advice, but I do think there's at least one person you should talk to about how you feel about Trace. Get everything out in the open and go from there."

Her brows dipped in confusion. The sham of a relationship she'd faked with Steven was over. Her cover was blown and she was pretty sure everyone knew that.

"Kylie," her friend prompted, giving her a gentle nudge with her shoulder. "I think it's time you talked to *him*."

The bus stopped and she realized they were at the hotel. That wasn't the only thing she realized. Her friend was right. Painfully so.

"Can we stop in the hotel bar before we head to the room? I need a drink."

Mike's eyebrows shot up. "You just passed out from dehydration and you want to—"

"Yes," Lulu interrupted, glaring at Mike as she did. "Yes we can have a drink. It's been a crazy few weeks. You've earned yourself a drink. But just one, Ky. You did just pass out on me after all."

Kylie still felt sick and slightly dazed as they got off the bus and walked towards the hotel.

If she was going to tell Trace Corbin how she felt about him, how she *really* felt, she was going to need a hell of a lot more than one drink.

chapter
FORTY
TWO

Because his manager was a decent guy and also a decent-sized pain in the ass, he'd kept on and on at him until Trace got on the bus and rode to the hotel with the band.

Danny asked if Kylie was okay, and Trace mumbled that he wasn't allowed to check on her apparently.

He felt like he had a babysitter from the second they arrived at the hotel in Greensboro. Danny and Pauly flanked him closely as they passed the hotel bar.

"What the hell is the deal with you two?"

"Nothing," they both answered a little too readily.

Pauly glanced at his phone. "Hey, I'm starved. How about we let the crew unload everything and we go grab some dinner?"

Trace's eyes narrowed. Pauly and that damn phone. He was beginning to wonder if his manager was selling classified government secrets on the thing. "Something going on I should know about?"

He'd had it with whatever overprotective dad shit they were trying to pull. If something was going on with Kylie, if she was worse off than they were telling him, then he was going to find out and do something about it. The more they evaded discussing her, the more hell-bent he became on finding her right that second and making sure she was really all right.

Danny spoke up before Pauly could answer. "How about we all go out to dinner? Round up the band and—"

"Stop. Stop with the distraction techniques." He wasn't entirely sure what was going on, but they were definitely trying to keep him from something. "Tell me what's going on."

He swung his imploring gaze from his manager to his fiddle player and back again. Neither of them met his eyes.

"I get it." His chest tightened, and he was surprised to realize that his feelings were hurt. "There's a bar here. And probably a mini-bar in my room. So naturally everyone's worried I'm going to get wasted and take this whole tour down with me."

He shook his head. When neither of them answered, he pulled the room key he'd been given out of his back pocket and stalked towards the elevator alone.

"Thanks for the vote of confidence, fellas," he tossed over his shoulder. "Really. Means a lot to me."

"Trace. Son, wait," Danny called out, but it was Pauly who reached him first.

Pauly Garrett was a patient man. He was also a smart man who'd been blessed with the gift of foresight. And he'd been Trace's manager for as long as he had because he'd learned to spot potential explosions before the necessary components gathered in one place. Trace usually appreciated that about him. But this time, he just wanted the guy to give him the benefit of the doubt. For once.

"I am worried about you." His manager sighed. "But it's not about the bar, Trace." He nodded to Danny to go on with the rest of the band. "Not exactly."

"Okay," Trace said slowly. He pressed the button for the elevator. "So what is it?

He heard his manager pull in a breath. Jesus. Was someone dying?

"Trace, you know I try not to interfere with the things I don't have to interfere with. But sometimes, I've stayed out of your personal life only to wish later that I'd said something. Something that maybe could've prevented—"

The elevator dinged as it reached them. Trace looked up at the red light to see which door was about to open.

"Get to the point, Pauly."

"It's about Kylie. And I don't want this to come out wrong but—"

"Is she okay? Dammit. I knew I should've—"

"She's fine. I swear," his manager assured him.

"Then what is it? What's going on with her? I'd appreciate it if you stopped jerking me around." The elevator door glided open, and thankfully the plush red velvet cavern of it was empty.

Trace stepped on and his manager followed. He had to hold his room key in front of a black panel to get to the private floor he was on.

"She's looking for you. But Trace's she's been—"

Before he uttered another word of explanation, she was there.

Flanked by her friend and Mike in the same fashion he'd been guarded by Danny and his manager moments ago.

Trace barely registered the curse Pauly mumbled under his breath.

His arm shot out to hold the doors open.

When his gaze collided with hers, her blue eyes burned so bright he couldn't fucking breathe. It was her. His girl. The one who'd given him all of herself, heart and soul, that very first time. Readily and without hesitation.

The walls she'd had up all this time were gone and she was locked in his stare.

She wore a dark blue dress that slid tantalizingly off one of her smooth bare shoulders and her favorite boots, but the way she looked at him, she might as well as have been stark naked.

His world suddenly became a very fragile place made entirely of glass. The wrong move, the wrong word, would send it all crashing down.

"Get off the elevator, Pauly," he said evenly without taking his eyes from hers.

"Trace, I don't think you—"

"Get. Off. The. Elevator." His chest pumped in response to the considerable effort he was making to operate his lungs. "Now."

His manager shook his head and stepped off the elevator.

He didn't look up into the worried faces of the other three. Because all he could see was her. And she was in desperate need of something. He hoped like hell it was something he could give her.

If it was what he suspected it was, then he was going to make sure she got what she needed again and again.

With a slight lift of his chin, he invited her to come to him.

He was either dead, dreaming, or witnessing a miracle, because she came to him. And she kept coming until her body was nearly against his.

Once she was inside, he moved his arm and allowed the elevator doors to close, cocooning them in privacy.

"Heard you were looking for me."

"I was," she said softly. "Looks like I found you."

Holy hell, that look. He couldn't even begin to comprehend what that look did to him. Every ounce of confidence he'd lost, the mistakes and the failures, the disappointment he'd been to so many—it all just ceased to matter.

His whole damn world hung in the delicate balance of that look.

Because he knew now that she still saw him. She still looked at him and saw that man she'd convinced him he could be, the one she trusted, had faith in, and believed was worthy of her.

"So you did. What can I do for you, sweetheart?"

Desire-drenched need flashed in those eyes of hers. "I think you know, Trace. I think you've always known."

He forced his throat to swallow. His hands twitched. As did his dick.

Apparently Kylie Ryans had decided to test him and see if he meant all those dirty things he'd said to her on the bus. It looked like she was about to call his bluff. He'd told himself a million times that if he ever got another shot, he would be careful with her. He would take it slow. Do things in the right order.

But each floor they rose, each breath of hers that he breathed in, his self-control dissipated. Inch by inch, layer by layer, until it was a thin vapor he could no longer grasp onto.

"How are you feeling? Earlier you gave everyone quite a—"

"I'm fine, Trace," she assured him. "More than fine."

She took at step closer even though there wasn't really any more space to move into. He gave up on restraining himself and pulled her to him. What the hell, he figured. All of his cards were already showing anyways.

"I might not be able to take it slow, Kylie Lou. It won't be gentle or sweet like you deserve. I might…hurt you."

God he didn't want to hurt her if he could fucking help it. He wanted to please her, give her a pleasure so deep and undeniable she'd never even think of anyone besides him being inside of her.

"Maybe I don't want it to be gentle or sweet," she breathed against his skin. "I can take it. I think…I think I want it to hurt."

Fuck me. He was a goner.

Her fingers slid up his chest as her lips brushed the stubble on his chin. He bent down and wrapped his hands under her ass as tightly as he could. Lifting her onto his waist, he slammed her against the wall of the elevator hard enough to rattle the whole damn thing.

He groaned as she pressed herself against the rock-hard ridge in his pants. He heard her sweet surprised gasp as she took in a breath.

"Feel that, baby?" he hissed through his teeth.

The whimper that escaped her lips in response said hell yeah she felt it. She gripped the hair at the nape of his neck hard enough to make his eyes water as she nipped and licked his earlobe. Her thighs flexed around him and he groaned in anticipation of her tight heat. He couldn't wait to get inside of her. To give her every single inch of himself.

His hands raked up her hips and back. Her thick, blond curtain of hair surrounded him. He was drowning in her and drinking her in, breathing her in, every way he could.

He was about to hit the emergency stop button and fuck her in that very elevator when the chime sounded and the door opened. Taking a second to catch his breath, he set her down gently and pulled her by the hand towards his room.

"Come on, baby," he said, squeezing her hand as they made their way down the hallway together.

"Trace," she said softly, lust dripping from the ache in her tone.

"Yeah, Kylie Lou?" he rasped when they reached his door.

"I need you. I need you so bad." Her voice broke, as if she might be about to cry. She'd been strong for so long. He knew good and well how much it had hurt her to confess her need.

He planned to soothe that pain and that need. Soon. He turned and pressed his forehead to hers and closed his eyes. "I know. I know you do, pretty girl. You have me."

HE didn't kiss her on the mouth until they were safely locked in his room. But the door had barely closed behind her when she gripped his arms so hard he wondered if there'd be bruises. He fucking hoped so.

His mouth descended onto hers and his knees went weak. His tongue dipped inside to taste her. She tasted like bourbon. *Son of a bitch.*

He figured she'd been drinking. And of course it *had* to be bourbon.

His arms strained to distance her body from his, but she was firmly fucking attached and she was stronger than she looked.

"Kylie. Uh, babe," he tried to say between kisses.

She ignored his pleas, sweeping her sweet little tongue into his mouth, across his teeth, and over his lips.

He couldn't force himself to quit tasting her. There wasn't enough willpower in the whole wide world. He let his tongue massage every inch of her lush, velvet, whiskey-soaked mouth. He sank down onto the mattress, and she straddled him.

Before he could stop her, she stood and pulled her dress over her head. Her skin was the perfect shade of golden in the glow of the lamp that was on in the room. He sat up so he could get the full view of her beautiful body.

And motherfucking son of every cussword he could think of. She was standing there in a white lace bra and a matching scrap of fabric that wasn't substantial enough to be called underwear. And boots. She still had those damn boots on.

In all of his fantasies about her—and he'd had plenty—none of them were this fucking hot.

He knew it would take one finger, one sharp tug at the flimsy string and her panties would be history. His throbbing dick begged him to do it, to remove that tiny barrier and let her wet heat slide over him.

But then she opened her eyes, and he could see the lack of focus in them. She was drunk. Maybe not wasted, but not sober enough to think straight, to make the kind of life-altering decision she was about to.

Clumsily, she began unbuttoning his shirt. She leaned down and brushed her lips against his. Her right leg came up and he grabbed her inner thigh to stop her forward progress.

If he felt that part of her, that warm, pulsating part he knew would be ready for him, against his dick again, he'd be done for.

"Dammit, Kylie. Stop." His deep tenor echoed off the bedroom walls.

A sharp stabbing pang hit his lower stomach the moment she obeyed.

She flinched back and her eyes went wide as if he'd slapped her.

They had a problem. A big one.

He wanted to drink, wanted to pour caramel-colored bourbon down her entire body and lick it off every part of her.

He had his answer. She wasn't a trigger, wasn't a temptation. She was *the* temptation. The old him, the one who got drunk and said to hell with consequence, had room service bring up the bourbon and spent all night fucking her. Long and hard and only stopping when he could no longer remain conscious.

But somewhere along the line, she'd changed him. And that look, the trusting weight of it, was what had sealed his fate.

"You've been drinking, baby. I can taste it on you. We can't do this. Not like this."

Her lower lip trembled, and the cold fear in her expression nearly froze him in place. Her gaze retreated away from him so quickly he could practically hear her reconstructing the walls she'd let down temporarily.

"You're serious," she said softly, tentatively, as if to make sure.

For a split second, he considered smiling and pulling her back onto him. He could play it off like a joke. Act like he'd been testing her to make sure she wanted to go through with it.

"I am."

"Oh, God." She began to wilt right before his very eyes. Her chest caved, like someone had deflated her.

I was broken, dead inside. You made me feel alive.

And now he was doing the exact opposite.

He watched helplessly as she began scrambling to scoop her dress up off the floor.

"Whoa. Hey. Slow down." He stood and wrapped his arms around her. Her entire body shook violently. Her slender arms came up against his expansive chest and attempted a weak shove.

"Let me go," she begged.

"Wait. Just wait a damn second."

Trace made quick work of pulling off his shirt and wrapping it around her. Her eyes met his as he buttoned the few middle buttons for her. The wounded expression in them nearly broke him. But he knew one of them had to be strong. Tonight it would have to be him.

"Kylie Lou, I want you more than you can even imagine. But we need to talk and we need to slow the hell down. Because the absolute last thing

I want is for you to wake up tomorrow and wish this hadn't happened."

She let out a small huff of air. "Well I can pretty much guarantee I'm going to wake up tomorrow wishing *this* hadn't happened."

He rested his chin on the top of her head. "I'm sorry. I'm sorry that I walked away, sorry that I hurt you, and sorry that this is going to be something you regret. But I'd take you regretting throwing yourself at me over you regretting me being inside you any day."

She shivered. He tightened his grip around her. He could feel her heart racing like a frightened animal's.

"Tell me you don't regret it. I need to hear it."

She was quiet for a few long seconds.

He gave her a small squeeze. "I need to know, Kylie Lou. Before anything else happens between us. I need to know if you regret anything. Being with me, giving me your virginity, touring with me, any of it."

He thought his head might fucking explode while he waited for her response. Finally her chest pressed against him. He felt the sob before he heard it.

"Oh, baby, no. Please don't cry."

"No," she said with a surprisingly even voice. "No, I don't regret any of it." Her body went slack against his under the weight of her confession.

"You had a big day. Ambulances and canceled shows and all that. Let's get you to bed."

Trace scooped her up in his arms and carried her to the head of the bed. After tucking her in, he sat in the chair and watched her.

"You're not coming?" she asked quietly, her voice thick with exhaustion. Or intoxication—he wasn't sure.

Apparently not. "I'm good right here. You need to get your rest. Doctor's orders." He propped his elbow on the arm of the chair and rested his head on his fist. "If I get in that bed, you won't get a bit of sleep and we'll just have to cancel tomorrow's show too." He winked at her and leaned forward to kiss her on the forehead before resuming his position.

Her eyes blinked slowly when she turned on her side to face him. "I was looking for you because...because I wanted tell you something. I needed to tell you something."

He was tempted to make a joke. To pretend what had just happened wasn't as monumental as it actually was. But the sexy-as-hell sleepy-eyed look she was giving him and the raw vulnerability she was exuding were compounding the hell his dick was giving him for not giving her what she'd wanted. What they both wanted. And all the blood was still residing south of his brain so he couldn't even think of a good joke anyway.

"What is it, pretty girl?"

"I tried so hard to stop but…but I couldn't." She wrapped her arms around the pillow beneath her and yawned.

He brushed the strands of hair that had fallen over her eyes out of her face.

"Couldn't stop what, Kylie Lou?"

"Loving you," she breathed, effectively sucking all the air from his lungs with the strength of an industrial vacuum. A tiny smile lifted one corner of her mouth as her eyes fell closed. "I still love you, Trace. And it's exhausting pretending that I don't. I thought you should know."

Before he had time to say it back—to tell her that he'd never be worthy of her love, but that he'd gladly take it and try to be—she was asleep.

TRACE woke up with one hell of a crick in his neck. He winced when he tried to turn his head only to find the sun glaring in his face.

He couldn't remember why he'd slept in a chair instead of his bed. He blinked several times and the room came into focus.

It was a hotel room. An empty hotel room.

The previous night's events came rushing to him back all at once.

Where the hell is she?

He let himself hope that maybe she was in the bathroom and now that she was sober and rested maybe they could talk. He could tell her that he loved her, was in love with her. He wanted to do that mushy shit he'd sworn he never would. Tell her every detail of the moment he fell in love with her and why. Discuss the next step in their relationship. And then he could give her what she'd come to him for last night. If she still wanted it. God, he hoped she still wanted it.

He was still smiling at the memory of her in his arms, of their hot-as-hell moment in the hotel elevator.

Until he saw the note she'd left on his pillow. It was written on the hotel stationary.

Thanks for not taking advantage last night. Sorry for throwing myself at you. Won't happen again.

-K

"Dammit," he shouted into the empty room. His open palm smacked the wall above the headboard, sending a screaming pain up his arm in response.

He lowered himself onto the bed. Which was a huge fucking mistake. Because it smelled like Kylie Ryans and bourbon.

He didn't even care anymore. He would drink when he fucking wanted to drink. Because it didn't even matter.

He'd taken the high road, tried to do what was best for her, and he'd still screwed up somehow.

And the cruel joke that was his life, he'd gotten his girl back for what felt like mere seconds. Only to lose her. Again.

Because he wasn't just a fuck-up. He was a *champion first-class* fuck-up. A regular fuck-up would have lost her. But no, not him. He hadn't just lost her.

He'd lost her twice.

chapter FORTY THREE

"My head is killing me. Please, please, if you care about me at all, stop shouting."

Kylie pressed her fingers as hard as she could against her temples. After rubbing them for a solid minute, she pressed the palms of her hands against her eyes.

"I think you're overreacting," Lulu practically whispered, which Kylie appreciated. "He did the right thing. When I said tell him how you feel, I meant when you weren't drunk. I also meant tell him with, you know, words. As opposed to with your vagina."

"Nice," Kylie muttered. Bile rose in her throat at the memory. She was grateful she was in the bathroom of her hotel room incase her stomach decided it wasn't going to hang on to the bagel she'd choked down. "Now you tell me."

Last night seemed like a blurry fever dream-turned-nightmare in her head. But no, the way she'd woken up, half-naked and sprawled out in his bed, confirmed what she'd pretty much known. It was real. And real humiliating.

She'd taken half a dozen shots of bourbon, despite Lulu's and Mike's protests, and thrown herself at Trace. Only to have him turn her on and then turn her slap down. Her head pounded so hard it felt like it was vibrating. It was as if her heart had relocated itself to her skull and was super fucking angry that she'd exposed it last night.

"Where the hell is Hannah? I need something for this headache. Soundcheck is in an hour."

Her friend sighed and sat her makeup brush down on the bathroom sink.

"Look, I know you're upset, and I'm sorry things went the way they did. But I don't think he did what he did because he doesn't want you or care about you. I think it's because he *does*."

"Thank you, Dr. Love." Kylie lifted her head and squinted at the torturous florescent lights in the bathroom as Lulu applied her makeup. "But it was a mistake—one I won't be making again. Trace Corbin made his choice a long time ago, and there are obviously some side effects of dehydration that no one bothered to tell me about. Like clinical insanity."

Lulu rubbed something under her eyes and then grunted her disapproval as she surveyed her work. "The dark circles under your eyes are lighter, but as far as making them go away, you might have to take a nap after soundcheck."

"Sounds like a fantastic idea. Actually, I think I might need to go lie down right now."

"Go," Lulu said, dismissing her with an eye roll. "I've done all I can do for now."

She didn't need to be told twice. Kylie was drifting in and out of consciousness on her bed when Hannah arrived with her pain pills and a bottle of water.

"How about I tell them you're going to sit soundcheck out due to side effects of yesterday's episode?" her assistant asked.

Lulu snorted from across the room.

"Yeah, that sounds good."

She would take a nap and pray that she woke up in a different life. Or maybe a different universe.

Preferably one where she hadn't made a complete ass out of herself.

KYLIE woke up feeling much better than she had the first time. "You know, now that I'm not hungover and I've had time to think about it, Trace did what was best for both of us."

"Agreed," Lulu mumbled as she gave Kylie's hair one last spray with something that smelled like rubbing alcohol and fruit. "As I was saying, it's probably better to talk about—"

"Because really, how much of a nightmare would it have been to wake up knowing we'd done it?" She shuddered.

Being turned down was one thing. Having let him inside of her again, giving him that part of her, just for him to walk away once this tour was over…Now *that* would've been something worth regretting.

"Right," her friend said slowly. "I'm sure you're super thrilled the two of you didn't get it on last night. You don't have to pretend with me, Ky."

"I'm not," Kylie said, nodding her approval at Lulu's handiwork in the mirror. "Last night was a minor drunken episode that only served to remind me of what I already knew."

"Which is?" Lulu prompted.

Trace Corbin was bad for her. Bad for her heart, her body, and her career. She lost all sense of reason when it came to him. That wasn't something she could afford to do in this business.

"It's over." She wasn't going to shrug and pretend it wasn't a big deal, because it was. He was the first man—besides her daddy—that she'd ever loved. "Trace and I aren't going to have some big Hollywood love scene reconciliation. We had our time together and it's time to move on. For good."

And she was going to let him know how she felt. But since she sucked at talking these kinds of things out, she was going to take a page from his book and sing the song she'd never thought she would. She'd literally titled it *The Song I'll Never Sing*.

But she was going to sing it tonight.

Her friend eyed her with blatant disbelief plain on her face.

Trace Corbin was like a huge plate of comfort food. It felt good while inhaling it, but afterwards, she was miserable and consumed painful regret.

She felt ready to let him know once and for all that whatever they'd had, whether it was real love or just some highly intense lust-fueled attraction, was over.

He didn't have to keep giving her that apologetic look he was always aiming in her direction. Or step out of the room when Gretchen called. Or worry about her throwing her stupid drunk self at him.

She was going to sing her piece and move the hell on. Finally.

THE crowd in Greensboro had an energy that brought Kylie back to life. She apologized to them for yesterday and made a joke about the sexy singer she was touring with getting her so hot and bothered that she passed out.

She was proud of herself. Her heart was safe once again.

Her pride was a little wounded though. It cuddled her bruised ego in a darkened corner while she smiled and shook her ass all over the stage.

After what was normally her final song before her duet with Trace, Kylie addressed the audience.

"Any of y'all ever have that person, that one person who deep down you knew you shouldn't love? Knew would only break your heart?"

The majority of the audience cheered in response.

"And no matter what you do or where you go, after that person breaks your heart, it seems like everything everywhere you turn is a reminder of them?"

She was greeted with understanding once more. Out of the corner of her eye, she saw Trace watching her from the side of the stage.

"This one's for you," she said softly into her microphone.

The band played the slow opened chords and Kylie began to sing.

There's a road I never take. It's right past the interstate. It'd be easier to get where I'm goin' if I went that way.

She swallowed hard, startled by the thick knot of emotion threatening to interrupt her.

But I just drive on past. Go ahead and waste the gas. 'Cause I know right where that road will lead. Straight back to the memory of you and me.

For reasons she didn't want to admit to herself, she couldn't even glance to the side of the stage he was on as she continued.

No I don't turn the radio on, 'cause damn if they don't keep playin' our song. There's a shirt in my closet, way back in the back. But I don't even think about that.

No I don't go down that road, don't even turn the radio on, and I don't walk around wearin' your old shirt. 'Cause I know right where all of that will lead. Straight back to the memory of you and me.

Her eyes began to pinch and sting and she prayed the audience couldn't tell that every single lyric was struggling to make its way out over the lump in her throat.

This was therapeutic in a way. It was their final goodbye. She knew it as sure as she knew her own name.

I tell myself one day I'll be strong enough to handle these things, but right now it's the song I'll never sing. You don't have to worry about hearing these words from me. 'Cause you'll always be the song I'll never sing.

The audience erupted into applause when she was finished. He came out onto the stage and her arm brushed his. Trace's entire body twitched as if she'd electrocuted him.

But she felt pure relief.

She wouldn't have to work so hard to guard her heart anymore. She'd left it out on the stage.

This time she didn't have to avoid him as they sang *The Other Side of Me* together to close the show. He didn't even glance in her direction.

When they finished and he left her on stage alone, as if he couldn't get away from her fast enough, her feelings weren't hurt. Because there was only one emotion she could feel, the safest one she knew.

Blissful numbness.

chapter
FORTY
FOUR

CLAIRE Ann had nearly worn a path in the hardwood floor.

Things are complicated. He's dealing with a lot right now. I'll call as soon as I can.

After reading his text for what seemed like the umpteenth time, she turned her phone off. Enough was enough. His last message was from three days ago.

She'd cleaned every inch of the house, the barn, and even Trace's mini-studio.

She didn't know what was upsetting her most. The fact that she and Pauly were still keeping their relationship—if you could even really call it that anymore—a secret, or the fact that something was definitely up with Trace.

Pauly was worried but had kept all mention of his concern vague.

Trace hadn't responded to a single one of her texts or phone calls in over a week. She knew he was in trouble but she had no idea what to do about it.

To make matters worse, she'd missed Rae's last few phone calls due to board meetings with the A Hand Up foundation board members.

This was the part about her life that made her crazy. She was beginning to feel like she spent every minute of it worrying about everyone else, taking care of everyone else, and frozen in some type of time suspension paradox while the rest of the world lived their lives.

The majority of her time was spent attending Trace's meetings, dealing with Rae's mini-melodramas, and wondering if the man she loved would ever be willing to put her first. Or even second.

As it was, Trace was his top priority, his job was second, and she was hoping to beat out traveling the countryside for third place. So far she was running a distant fourth with very little hope of a change, at least not in the foreseeable future.

She'd left several voicemails for him to call her. She texted that she missed him. That she wanted to tell Trace now so that she could meet up with them in Oklahoma at this weekend's show and not have to make up an excuse for being there.

And his response had basically been, **Please hold. I'll get back to you when I can.**

So much for romance.

Trace was getting to live his dream. Rae had her whole future spread out in front of her, not to mention the free ride and no responsibilities thanks to their brother. And Claire Ann had…well, she had the distinct privilege of holding down the fort while everyone else was out living it up.

For one night, she wanted live. To do something crazy.

Except…she'd been out of the loop of the local women her age for so long that she didn't have the first idea what anyone did on a Wednesday night.

Guess I'll go to church. So much for crazy.

Once she was dressed and ready, she studied her appearance in the mirror.

She wasn't a dog, she knew that. She ate healthy foods, organic mostly, and jogged every morning. Keeping up with he property alone kept her in shape. She had thick healthy hair, straight teeth, and nice enough skin.

Ugh. I sound like a horse for sale.

She frowned at her reflection. She hadn't ever wanted much. A family of her own maybe—and not even a particularly big one. A chance to raise a child in a better environment than she'd been raised in. A small house full of love and laughter.

It didn't seem like too much to ask.

But at this rate, if Pauly didn't man up or she didn't meet her soul mate at church, she was in for a nice long life as a spinster.

She really hoped it wasn't time to start taking in stray cats. Trace was allergic to them anyway.

There I go again. It's always about what's best for everyone freaking else.

She was knee-deep in self-pity by the time she grabbed her purse off the kitchen counter. Despite her promise to herself to stop checking the danged thing, she tossed her cell phone into it.

Her hand was on the knob to the front door when a ringing sound made her jump. Her mind couldn't put the pieces together quickly enough. Her cell phone was off—it couldn't have rung.

It was the house phone.

No one called the house phone. Ever. She didn't think anyone besides herself, Trace, and Rae even knew the number. Surely it was a telemarketer. Or a wrong number.

Feeling strangely panicked and not sure as to why, she made her way to the side of the counter where Trace had mounted the receiver when he'd first bought the house.

"H-hello?"

"Mrs. McClain?" a gruff male voice greeted her.

McClain? That was her mom's maiden name. It had never been hers.

"Um, it's Corbin and Miss. Can I help you?"

The man cleared his throat loudly in her ear. She flinched at the abrasive noise.

"Miss Corbin, this is Sheriff Ronald Hewitt. I'm sorry to have to tell you this, but there's been an accident."

chapter FORTY FIVE

THE bus was so dark she couldn't see a damn thing when she slipped onto it. It was late and she didn't want to wake anyone so she didn't turn on any lights and practically tiptoed.

"So that's it then? Planning to avoid me for the rest of the tour?"

Kylie nearly had a seizure at the unexpected sound. She felt the wall and pressed the button for the lights nearest to her. Trace sat completely still at the small table in the kitchenette.

She'd figured he'd be in bed asleep by now. Or at least, she'd hoped he would be.

A brief flashback of letting him have it, telling him off like there was no tomorrow while he sat a similar table, crossed her mind. But that was a long time ago. He wasn't drunk and hateful this time.

Yet, anyway. He appeared calm, but anger rolled off him so hard it backed her up a step.

For the past two days, she'd spent most of her time with her band. Looking at Aiden's baby pictures and getting to know about all of their girlfriends and wives and baby mamas. They were a good group of guys and she was glad she'd taken Mike's advice.

He'd been right. She didn't have to close herself off to everyone.

Just one someone. Someone who'd apparently decided to wait up for her.

"What are you doing sitting here in the dark?"

"Thinkin'," he answered quietly.

"About?" she prompted, despite being uncertain she actually wanted an answer. She swallowed hard and took a few steps towards him. When she was close enough to see, she could make out dark circles under his eyes.

"Things," was all he offered her.

"You been drinking?" She whispered her question, as if somehow that might make it less offensive or upsetting.

He let out a bitter laugh. "No. Have you?"

It was a fair enough question since technically she'd been slightly intoxicated a few awful nights ago.

"No."

"Good. Got a minute?"

Kylie took a step towards her room. "It's late, Trace. We have to be—"

"I'll keep it short then."

"Um, okay. What's up?"

He snorted out a harsh laugh. "Nothing you care much about."

A spine-tingling chill made her shiver. Alarms rang out inside of her. Every cell in her body stood at attention.

This was the way he behaved when he was drunk. But usually when he was angry, he got drunk. This was sober-angry Trace. She couldn't decide which version was more worrisome.

"I-I don't know what you mean by that."

"Don't you?" Trace slid out of the booth and stood in front of her, effectively blocking the path to her bedroom. "Well, let's see, Kylie Lou. From what I can tell, the only thing you care about being up is my dick, right?"

She took a step back. "What the hell is that supposed to mean?"

He glared at her. She worked hard to keep her expression impassive, refused to let him see how much she wanted to break down under the searing heat of his stare.

"I didn't fuck you when you were three sheets to the wind, so you sing

240

that damned song and then blow me off—and not in the fun way, like I'd prefer."

Her blood began to heat, either from her own anger or his fiery gaze. She didn't know and she didn't much care. Her heart threatened to pound straight out of her chest. Which pissed her off even more because she'd thought she'd finally gotten rid of the damn thing.

"I made a mistake the other night. Like you said, I'd been drinking. Oh, but wait, I guess you're the only one who's allowed to get drunk and make mistakes."

"No, but that's the part I can't figure out. Which part was the mistake, darlin'? The trying to impale yourself on my dick part? Or the leaving the next morning part? Because I can assure you, if you'd stuck around, once you were sober I had every intention of giving you what you wanted. Repeatedly."

He knees threatened to give beneath her. "T-Trace," she began, shaking her head back and forth.

"I'm done being pushed away." He came towards her, backing her up as far as she could go. "Tell me, baby. Tell me the truth." She leaned back against the counter, and he braced his arms on either side of her. "There's nobody on this bus but me and you. I made sure of it. No assistants, no band members, not even a driver. Forget the fucking music, Kylie Lou. Forget the label. Forget the tour. Look at me and tell me we're done. Tell me you don't want to be with me, you don't love me, and that you're over it."

She licked her lips and tried her best not to breathe him in. Not to let his manly soap and warm woodsy scent disorient her.

"I'm trying to be. Y-you hurt me, Trace. You hurt me so bad." Blood rushed in her ears so loud she barely heard her own confession.

Wild, tortured eyes met hers. "You think I don't know that? Every damn day of my life has been fucking purgatory since I walked away from you. And I don't just mean the other night. I mean this whole damn year. Don't you see that?"

Instinctively, she reached up and placed her hands on either side of his face. His stubble tickled her palms. It was as if she were seeing him for the first time, or maybe she was just allowing herself to remember what she'd known all along.

She nodded as she dropped her hands and let them rest on his broad, solid chest.

"I see."

And she did. She saw the selfless man who took care of the women he loved, the passionate one who loved with all he had—even when it meant walking away. And she saw the beast in him, the one that led him to drink. He wasn't two separate men as she'd always told herself. There wasn't one who'd loved her and one who'd walked away. They were two parts of a whole. Both parts making him the man that he was.

The man she loved.

She let her eyes memorize every inch of his face. She savored the moment, every single second of it, fearing they'd both reason their way out of this intense stare down before it went much further. Trace's hands came up to her wrists and slid down her arms. She barely stifled the shiver it caused.

"You're still my beautiful girl. Still too damn beautiful for my own good," he said, his voice a soft, tormented whisper. "I knew I could take care of this." He slid a hand down and cupped her intimately between her legs.

Her hands clutched his black T-shirt, gripping him tighter for support as need pooled liquid and scalding where he'd touched her.

"I had to make sure I was worthy of this." Trace's right hand left the throbbing apex of her thighs and came to rest on her heart. "I know you still love me, Kylie Lou. I don't know that I'll ever deserve your love, baby. But I want to. I'll spend the rest of my damned life trying to be the kind of man who does."

She placed her hands over his. Her heart quivered in fear at his words. When he lowered his head and kissed her softly between her breasts her entire body began to tremble under his touch.

His chest expanded as he pulled in ragged breaths. She let her hands roam from his hands to his arms. Smoothing them down his chest, she gripped the hem of his shirt.

"I'm scared," she whispered into the small space between them.

"Me too, baby," he breathed. "But I need you to trust me. We can't do this without trust. I just want you, Kylie Lou Ryans. You're the only one for me. There's no one else. The things the media says about me are—"

"Shh." She brushed a finger over his mouth before lifting his shirt over his head. She'd heard all she needed to.

Once his chest was bare, her eyes drank in the muscular planes. Her hands made a path over the chiseled lines of his abdomen up to the hard ridges of his shoulders.

"When you first left," she began softly, "it was like I had nothing to hold onto. Nothing that mattered anymore."

An apology flashed in his eyes. He opened his mouth to speak, but she placed her small hand over it once again. His eyes never left hers while she spoke.

"And then I grabbed on to music, to the only thing I knew and understood. Even though every note, every chord, every single lyric I played or sang cut deeper into the pain of losing you." She felt his hands massage their way up her back as she worked deftly to remove his belt. "I couldn't save you from yourself. No matter what I did."

His hooded hazel gaze undressed her at the same time his hands did. She felt every barrier she'd put up between them drop away with her clothes. Her sweatshirt hit the floor, but she'd been exposed to him long before it did.

"And then I tried...I tried so hard to find something that didn't remind me of you. Someone who could fill that hollow ache you left inside of me." She felt the wounds she was inflicting on him as his body tensed beneath her hands in response. "And then he walked away. Like everyone else. And I didn't even care."

The sound of his zipper coming down as she lowered it slowly filled the silence.

"And these past few days, spending time with my band and letting them see me—

the real me, the feel-first-think-second me—made me realize I was never empty. I'd kept something no one could take away from me. Not even you."

"What's that?"

A slow smile spread across her face as she shifted his pants down his hips.

"This." Grabbing his strong, warm hand, she placed it in the same spot where he'd touched on her chest. His fingers pressed into her flesh. "Loving you is as much a part of me as my music is. It's not a choice and it's not something I can live a full life without. I love you. I never stopped, Trace. Not for a single second. Even when I tried my hardest. Even when

I wasn't sure if you loved me back."

For the first time since their emotionally charged exchange had begun, he closed his eyes.

"You know," he said softly.

Kylie leaned back against the counter behind her.

"I do." She nodded. "You brought me back to life. You made sure the only one who could record our song was us. You kissed me on stage because I sang a song that hurt to sing. You bought my daddy's truck. You went to rehab and got sober. You ditched everyone, your band, your family, to come have a pity party bonfire with me, you—"

The rest of her words were cut off by his mouth clamping down on hers. She opened for him, moaning softly when his tongue plunged inside.

She felt him stepping out of his jeans as he lifted her off the ground and headed towards his bedroom. Her bare back brushed roughly against several surfaces and doorways in the dark as they made their way to the back of the bus, but she didn't care. As long as his mouth didn't leave hers, she was happy. For what felt like the first time in forever.

When he laid her down on his mattress, she stared up into his handsome face, placing both hands on either side once more and admiring the beautiful angles of it.

"Even though I know, I still want to hear it."

He grinned, that slow, intense smile he gave only to her. Bracing himself above her, he stared straight down into her eyes.

"I love you. God, I love you so damn much, Kylie Lou." His lips danced against hers and she whimpered at the force of the emotional damn breaking inside of her.

"I love you, too, Trace," she whispered against his mouth. "I thought you broke my heart. But you didn't. You *are* my heart," she said with a tremor in her voice.

He kissed her so hard their teeth gnashed against one another's. Panting, she began to shimmy out of the denim that still sheathed her legs.

Trace grabbed her jeans with one hand and divested her of them in one swift movement. He was above her again before she could take a breath.

"I missed you so fucking much, baby," he told between placing frantic open-mouth kisses down her jawline and neck. "Every day. Every damn day I missed you. It hurt like hell being away from you. It wrecked me... having to see you and not being able to have you."

The intensity of his words combined with the damp heat of his mouth stripped away the remaining protective layers she'd kept around herself.

"Show me, Trace. Show me how much you love me. How much you missed me. How much it hurt. I need to feel it. I need to feel you."

"Yes, ma'am." Strong fingers slid her black thong down her thighs.

She let herself let go as he licked and kissed his way back up her legs. When his teeth grazed over flesh, her body jerked in surprise.

A low dark laugh reverberated against her skin.

"Behave yourself, Mr. Corbin," she warned.

He growled—actually growled—at her.

She giggled, a soft, genuine sound she hadn't heard from herself in over a year.

His hands were everywhere at once. Palming her breasts, clutching her hips, spreading her thighs. It was as if he were literally devouring her. She couldn't get enough of him, couldn't get open enough or get him close enough.

He massaged and kissed his way all over her, taking his sweet time on his exploration of her body. She wondered if he'd forgotten how it felt, if he was trying to remember and memorize it with his hands and mouth.

His tongue slid south and moved gently over the center of her, causing her body to bow off the bed. As he licked her gently to her first orgasm, she felt all the tension she'd carried for so long extracting itself from her muscles and floating into the air.

"Now that I've said it, I can't stop." His hands massaged their way up her thighs as he made his way back to her. "I love you. I love the feel of you, the taste of you, the scent of you. I love you so much I lose control sometimes—lose the little bit of sense God gave me. If all I was allowed to do was sit and watch you exist for the rest of my life, I would die fucking happy."

She smiled as his mouth came down on her left breast. "I love you, too. I love the way you touch me, the way you taste me."

He grunted his appreciation of her words and sucked her nipple into his scorching hot mouth before moving to the other side. "I hate myself for not telling you sooner. For walking away without letting you know that I loved you."

"I think I always knew deep down that you loved me, Trace. That's not why I'm scared." Her whispered confession stilled him.

His head snapped up from her chest to her face and his eyes met hers. "Then what are you scared of, Kylie Lou?"

She pulled in a ragged breath of air. "That you won't let *me* love *you*. That you'll walk away again. Like before…" A sob escaped and she laughed at herself as she wiped her tear-filled eyes. "Sorry. I know this isn't the time—"

He cut her off by kissing her on the mouth. She tasted the faint hint of herself on his lips. "It's always the time, baby. You can tell me how you feel, or what you're afraid of, or worried about, or what you need, anytime you want."

"Okay," she whispered against his mouth. Her fingernails raked over his chest, pressing him backward. "Let me love you, Trace. I need you to let me do that. You deserve to be loved. You are more than deserving of my love. It's always been yours."

She grabbed his shoulders and pressed her palms against him until he got the message. Once he'd rolled onto his back and she was straddling him, she slid her wetness along the underside of his steel erection.

He groaned from the contact. His warm hands grazed her breasts and her body responded immediately, arching into his hands for more.

"Tell me what you need, baby."

"I need you inside," she whispered. "I need to feel you inside of me."

Trace sat up with his back against the headboard and pulled her against his chest. His hands pressed a path down the flesh of her back until they gripped her ass and lifted.

She cried out when he sat her down on the full length of him. Despite her body's protest at the blunt force of the intrusion, she began to slide up and down readily. His desperate hold on her was breathtakingly tight as he pulled her legs around him.

Her body surrounded him as if it knew the same thing she did, the same thing she always had.

She was made for him. And he was made for her.

"I can't go slow or be gentle," she warned him. "I might hurt you."

"I can take it," he said against the valley between her breasts.

It was mere seconds before the pressure began to build inside of her.

The force of it was so intense she wondered if it would break her in two. Wondered, but wasn't concerned enough to stop.

Her erect nipples chafed against the smattering of hair on his chest as his hands guided her body, setting the pace of their lovemaking even from beneath her. The light stubble on his face rubbed against the side of her neck as she moved up and down above him.

Words came out of her mouth and were breathed into his ear. Some of them sounded like his name. Some were declarations of love, and some were just sounds of unadulterated pleasure.

She lost count of how many times she came until it seemed to be one endless stream of intensity, wave after wave of ecstasy crashing over her.

When her body went limp and she was certain she couldn't take any more, Trace gently eased her onto her back and began his worshipful treatment all over again.

"*Oh God.* I-I can't. Trace, I can't feel my legs." She jerked in an attempt to move them, but it was pointless. She was boneless.

His fingertips drifted lazily up her inner thighs, one of them venturing dangerously close to her opening, causing her to twitch in response.

He chuckled, that deep timbre warming her from the inside out. "There, baby. See? Your legs just moved."

She was too weak to even open her eyes. His warm, wet mouth placed sweet kisses across her stomach.

"Say it," he murmured against her navel.

She moaned her inability to speak.

"Or don't say it. And I'll just keep turning everything you say into something dirty. I think you like it anyways."

"Say what?" she pleaded weakly.

He trailed a finger through her damp swollen folds, applying pressure where she still tingled.

"Oh my God, *Trace.*"

"Mmm, I do like that. But it's not what I'm looking for. Say, 'You still have feelings for me, you still think about me...'" he began.

Kylie smiled into the darkness. "*You* missed me terribly every second we were apart."

"Oh, you've done it now." With a dark chuckle, he climbed on top of her, sliding the head of his erection up the sensitive path between her legs.

"I said it," she cried out with urgency as her nerves tingled back to life at the contact between him and her overstimulated core. "Now just let me lie here and die happy."

"It's me and you, darlin'." He took her wrists in his hands and pinned them above her head. "I'm pretty sure you already know we're nowhere near done here."

"Trace," she cried out, his name a plea for mercy as his mouth made its way back down her body.

It was all coming back in exquisite detail. Not that she'd forgotten, she'd just forced herself not to think about it. But some things never changed. He took control in bed, took control and never let up, taking her to the precipice of what she thought she could handle and flinging her right over the edge.

Releasing her wrists, he skimped his fingertips down her arms, neck, and breasts with deliberate, unhurried, and feather light delicious torture.

He placed a gentle kiss on the cleft of her mound. "I should've said it before. Should've told you. I try not to have regrets, but I do have one."

His powerful tongue dipped inside of her and parted her swollen folds.

A moan that bordered on being a scream escaped her lips. Her lungs began pumping air in sheer panic as her pussy throbbed hard against his mouth.

"Trace, *please*."

"Please what, baby?" His voice vibrated against her, sending her careering out of control. Her body was no longer hers, but his to do with as he pleased. And apparently what he pleased was pleasing her until she went completely lost her mind.

She couldn't answer so she just shook her head violently against the pillows.

"As I was saying," he continued from between her thighs. "I regret that I didn't tell you, didn't make it *abundantly* fucking clear…" Another intense lick to her clit and her body began simultaneously straining towards him while struggling to get a safe distance from the relentless pursuit of his mouth.

"That you…"

His fingers dented the flesh on the firm swells of her hips as he held her down and paused to run his tongue up the length of her once more before sucking her clit into his mouth briefly.

"Are..."

She whimpered. It was nearly impossible to concentrate on what he was saying with the mindless frenzy he had her in.

"*Mine.*"

"Yes, yes, yours," she breathed. "Only yours."

Before she could reassure him anymore, he was up on his haunches, sliding himself over her sensitive flesh. She came apart so ferociously her body convulsed even under his weight.

The sensation made her needy even as she came from the contact to her clit. Her insides clenched on emptiness. She wanted more, needed more. Needed all he could give.

He seemed to realize this. Teasing her, he placed the head of himself just barely at her entrance.

"Say you're mine, baby," he commanded, applying the slightest bit of pressure.

"I'm yours, Trace." She reached up and dragged his face to hers, kissing him hard and deep. "And you're mine."

He entered her as they kissed, their sounds of pleasure slipping from each of their mouths into the other's.

When he finally gave into his release, squeezing her hard and groaning until the veins in his throat and arms bulged above her, she found hers once more. Their bodies, damp and drained, collapsed together in a heap of heavy breathing and sheer fulfillment.

She rolled onto her side, draping one arm and one leg over him.

"Never leave me. Promise you'll never leave me again," she whispered against his chest. "I wouldn't survive it."

He wrapped his arms around her and squeezed. "Me either, baby. Me either."

She was too weak to point out that he didn't promise.

DESPITE how completely depleted her body was, Kylie didn't fall asleep afterwards. Not really. She was hovering, having an out of body experience in the strange, murky haze of twilight between consciousness and unconsciousness when Trace broke the contented silence.

"I meant what I said."

She tried her best to lift her head off his chest and look him in the eyes to let him know she was listening. But after the earth-shattering sex that had sapped her off all ability to use her muscles, it wasn't easy.

"Which thing?"

"That I'm sorry I hurt you. That walking away from you like that was the hardest decision I ever made. And I'll spend every second you'll let me trying to make that up to you."

She took a deep breath. "Trace, if you ever go back into rehab, then I'm visiting you whether you like it or not, dammit. You don't get to cut and run. No more making those kinds of decisions without me."

She felt the low rumble of his chuckle against her bare skin.

She made the tremendous effort to rise up and glare at him. She pinched his bare side. Hard. "I'm serious."

"Ouch. I know, Hothead. I know you are." He kissed the top of her head and gave her a reassuring squeeze as she returned to her restful position. "Trust me. Losing you was the worst fucking thing I've ever lived through—and for me, that's saying something. I won't intentionally do that to myself ever again."

She didn't know if it was his postcoital honesty, her own recently exposed emotions, or the reminder of the nickname he'd given her, but tears began to slip from her eyes.

"Hey, hey," he began softly. "None of that." Trace wiped her tears with his thumb and leaned down to press his lips to hers. "I'm so sorry I hurt you, pretty girl. Believe me, I hurt myself pretty good too."

"Yeah, well…" she paused to sniffle in an attempt to suck it up before she became an ugly-crying mess. "Don't do it again."

"I swear, baby. I will try my absolute damnedest not to."

She snuggled back down into his arms. Minutes or hours might have passed, she wasn't sure. All she knew was that she was safe and happy with the man she loved, and it was like…like going home after being away for far too long.

"Babe?" He traced a slow circle on her back with a calloused finger.

"Hmm?"

"There is something I should tell you. Something about Gretchen."

Kylie froze. Her body went from a warm, boneless heap to a tight, rigid bundle of nerves. She wanted her warm and fuzzies back.

"Trace, whatever it is, let's just not right now. Okay?"

This was their place, their private reunion, and no one else was invited. Damn sure not Gretchen Gibson.

"Okay," he said quietly. "I guess I won't ask about Rocker Boy either. Not that I even really want to know."

Kylie took a deep breath. She'd hoped after tonight there wouldn't be anyone else between them. But it looked like that might've been too much to hope for.

"He and I never did what you probably think we did." She drew a heart with her pointer finger on Trace's chest.

She felt him raise his head to look down at her. "Seriously? Never?"

"Nope. Not even once."

"Huh." She smiled as he relaxed beneath her. "Well now I feel kind of bad for slugging him."

"Oh, I mean, we *did stuff.* Just not that."

"And magically my remorse is gone."

She couldn't help but laugh. *Boys.*

A violent knock at the bus door startled them both.

"What the hell?" Trace sat up, and so did she. "I told everyone I didn't want to be disturbed."

"Trace! Trace, it's Pauly. I need you to open up if you're in there," she heard Pauly Garrett yell from outside the bus between the pounding knocks. "It's important."

"Shit," Trace mumbled as they pulled themselves from the warm bed. "What now?"

They dressed as quickly as they could. Kylie couldn't find her underwear so she slid her jeans on over her bare skin. She located her bra but couldn't find her shirt anywhere. Trace handed her his. She buttoned it hurriedly as they headed to the door.

"I hope everyone's okay. What do you think is going on?"

"No idea," Trace answered. "But there are cops out there." He pulled back from the window and reached for the door. "You got warrants out, baby?"

She laughed. "Oh yeah. Tons." But the smile fell from her face when she saw the grave expression on Pauly's.

Kylie watched from behind Trace as Pauly introduced the two uniformed police officers.

"What's going on?" he asked, pulling his white T-shirt on over his head.

His manager looked ten years older than usual. And Kylie suspected it wasn't just because he'd been woken up in the middle of the night.

Something was wrong. Something bad. She'd been in this exact situation before when they came to tell her and Darla that her dad had been killed. She didn't know if the next words were actually said out loud or an echo from her memory.

"There's been an accident."

chapter FORTY SIX

T<small>RACE</small> barely resisted the urge to throttle someone until he got some answers.

"What kind of accident? Who? Where?" He looked from Pauly to the uniformed officers next to him. He was vaguely aware of Kylie's arms wrapping around his waist.

He didn't have to ask if it was bad. That much he could tell from the grief etched in his manager's features.

"Trace," Pauly said evenly. "It's Rae."

The blood drained from his face to his toes instantly. A wounded sound came from beside him. Kylie's body sagged forward. He was barely able to hold himself up, much less her. But he did the best he could.

"What happened to her? Goddammit, Pauly, tell me what the hell is going right this fucking minute."

"She was in a car accident. I really think it's better if you just—"

He opened his mouth to yell, but a solid hand on his chest stopped him.

"What condition is she in and where is she?" Kylie interrupted. "And how soon can we get there?"

A million thoughts ran through his head. None of which he could articulate. He was thankful that she could ask the right questions.

"She was with some friends. They were in a head-on collision in downtown Atlanta. She's at Emory and she's critical."

"I have to go," he said, charging forward, not knowing how he could get there but feeling like he could sprint the whole damn way if he had to.

"There's a flight in the morning. I've booked you on the eight a.m. The officers are going to give you an escort to the airport and a car will meet—"

"How long would it take to drive?" Kylie asked.

"Around six to seven hours," Pauly answered. "But she's in surgery and they'll be keeping her sedated so she won't know you're there until tom—"

"I have my daddy's truck. We could get on the road right now," she offered.

Trace turned and looked into her wide, tear-filled eyes. "Get the truck, but you're staying. We can't both leave."

"He's right, Kylie," Pauly added. "We can release a statement saying Trace had a family emergency, but you can't both ditch the tour."

He felt her fingers dig into his arms. "You are my family." The conviction in her voice staggered him.

He pulled her to him. "I know, Kylie Lou. And you're mine. But Rae needs me now and I have to go. I don't know when I'll be back."

"You go I go, Trace. I care about her too." His chest ached at the way her voice broke.

"Mr. Corbin?" one of the officers broke in. "We can escort you as far as the state line. 78 East is going to be your best bet."

Kylie took advantage of the distraction and pulled away from him, moving past all of them. He heard her urgent voice telling someone on the phone to bring her truck around immediately.

"Sounds good, officers. Thank you." He looked over at his manager. "Pauly, I'm going. And odds are, she's going too. Tell the band I'm sorry and I'll be in touch as soon as I can."

His manager nodded and stepped away from the officers. He signaled with a discreet nod for Trace to do the same so he did.

"Look, this might be it for you with the label. Unless you're willing for the details of Rae's accident to be made public. I don't know how else to cover for you this time."

"Details?"

"She was driving. It looks like there was alcohol involved. The girl that was with her is in bad shape. Might not make it through the night."

He ran a hand through his hair and resisted the urge to pull it the hell out in frustration.

"Jesus."

Pauly looked him in the eyes. "I'm not trying to keep you from going. I know you have to go. I just want you to know what it might mean. For both of you," he said, tilting his head toward where Kylie stood waiting.

"I'll call you as soon as I know something," Trace said quietly. The man with Kylie's truck had pulled up. She tossed the keys to him and he caught them.

He watched Pauly walk around the hood and say something to her. She smiled weakly as she nodded. For a split second, he was torn. He wanted her to come, he did. She was right. She was as much a part of his family as Rae or Claire Ann was. But once again, being a part of his life was going to fuck up hers.

His eyes met her panicked ones over the hood of the truck.

"Kylie, I promise, I'll be okay. You can stay and I swear I'll keep you posted on every single thing that hap—"

"Get your tight-jean-wearing ass in this truck right this damn instant, Trace Corbin. Every second you waste arguing with me is a second we aren't there."

Her voice was thick with emotion. Judging from the blazing determination in her glare and her stance, he knew it was time to do as she said or else. He might could dominate her in the bedroom, but that was about it.

This was his girl. She was still his Kylie Lou.

Trace shot a helpless look at Pauly who gave him a what-can-you-do look and shrugged.

"Okay. Here we go."

Four hours in, Trace was extremely grateful she'd come along. He refused to let her drive because he could see the bone-deep exhaustion weighing on her. But she'd been the one checking in with Claire Ann every half hour, and each time they stopped for gas, she grabbed him a large black coffee and every snack food she could carry.

He didn't have an appetite, but the coffee was a lifesaver.

The sun came up as they crossed into Georgia. He pulled his sunglasses on and winced at the skull-shattering headache the glare caused.

Kylie's voice was soft in the cab. "What you're imagining is probably ten times worse than it actually is."

He tried to take a breath. Ever since the words *It's Rae* had dropped like concrete bricks from Pauly's mouth, Trace had felt like they'd landed on his chest.

"You're probably right. It's just..." He couldn't talk about it. Talking about it made it real. Made it terrifying and made him want a drink. He gripped the steering wheel until his knuckles went numb. "If anything happens to her, I swear—"

"She's a tough girl, Trace. She's going to be fine." She placed her hand firmly on his knee.

She sounded like she really believed that. So for the rest of the drive, he focused on making himself believe it too.

chapter FORTY SEVEN

"Hannah, I don't know what to tell you other than I'm sorry. I have to be with Trace right now and I'm not at liberty to explain. All I can tell you is he had a family emergency and I need to be here."

The exasperation her manager felt was palpable even through the phone.

Kylie had talked to Hannah and Lulu both several times since arriving in Georgia. She'd told Lu the actual truth, but Hannah she had to be vague with. The one thing Trace had made adamantly clear was that under no circumstances of any kind were the details of Rae's accident to make it to anyone who might leak it to the label or the media.

"Chaz is not happy, Miss Ryans. The label is going to be even more upset. This just isn't done. Unless you yourself are dying or someone close to you is dead, there isn't a family emergency big enough to justify disappearing in the middle of the night."

Kylie's brain seemed to have switched places with her heart, as there was steady throbbing coming from inside her head.

"I know, Han. Believe me, I know. Just...do what you can. Call Jane

Bradford and tell her I'll be in touch."

"The show in Oklahoma City this weekend is sold out. What am I supposed to say is your reason for canceling it?"

Kylie closed her eyes, thankful that Hannah couldn't see her She was pretty sure this wasn't going to all be over in a mere four days.

"All I can give anyone right now is two words. Family emergency. It's all I have, Han. I'm sorry."

The girl sighed. "Okay, Miss Ryans. I'll do what I can."

"Hannah?"

"Yes, Miss Ryans?"

"Please call me Kylie from now on."

She promised she'd be in touch as soon as she could. But when she heard Trace's voice thundering from down the hall, her conversation with her manager was forgotten. As were the other sixty-three missed calls on her phone.

"Well what *do you know*, exactly? Because we've been here for an hour and I haven't been able to get a single straight fucking answer from—"

"Trace," she said, effectively distracting him from the poor nurse he was yelling at. Kylie placed herself between the two of them. "Hi there," she said, turning to the nurse behind the desk. "Kylie Ryans," she said, extending her hand in greeting.

"I know who you are," the nurse practically sneered as she ignored Kylie's outstretched hand. "But this is a hospital, not the Grammys. So I can't bump you to the front of the line on the red carpet."

Kylie forced herself not to punch the smug woman in the face. "I apologize for our impatience. And please know, we don't expect any special treatment. But we're trying to locate the private family waiting area closest to where his sister is being cared for. I would appreciate it so very much if you could please help us find it so we can get out of your hair."

The woman looked to be about Claire Ann's age but was about fifty pounds heavier and apparently not a fan of country music. Or of the human race as a whole.

All Claire Ann's last text had said was, **Sixth Floor**, which wasn't all that helpful since the sixth floor was enormous.

The woman narrowed her eyes at both of them and clicked a few times on her keyboard.

"I don't have a Rae Corbin anywhere in my patient list. As I told you before, go down to the Patient Information desk on the first floor and—"

"McClain," Trace said suddenly. "I forgot she's been using our mother's maiden name. Her actual last name is McClain."

The woman snorted as if she couldn't be bothered to check again. Kylie felt Trace's body tense beside her.

"Yes, well, be that as it may—"

"Look, lady. We get it, okay?" Kylie did her best to speak plainly through her gritted teeth. "Being a nurse is probably not the easiest job on the damn planet. Long hours, disgusting bodily fluids all over the place, and highly emotional people snapping at you every other second. And we appreciate the job that you do, believe me. But let me make this crystal fucking clear for you. I guarantee that by tomorrow morning, I can have the CEO of this hospital, who's granddaughter happens to be a huge fan of mine, fire your ass. Effective immediately. So do us all a favor and type in Rae Michelle McClain into your computer before I have to call my good friend George and explain how horribly I'm being treated by a staff member at his hospital. Think you can handle that?"

"Here it is. R. McClain. She's in ICU recovery room four. Waiting room's straight down that hall on your left."

Kylie did her best to smile sweetly. "Thank you so much for your help."

She linked her arm in Trace's and tugged him towards the hallway the woman had indicated.

"You really know the CEO?" he whispered from beside her.

"I saw his name on the website when I was getting the address for the GPS," she whispered back.

He let out a small sound. She wasn't sure if it was approval or amusement or both. She gave his arm a squeeze and looked up. His five-o'clock shadow matched the dark circles under his eyes.

When they found the door that said ICU Waiting Room, he pulled it open and she saw Claire Ann sitting in a chair, looking out a window.

The isolation of the scene, the expression of hopelessness on Trace's sister's face struck her hard in the chest.

It was as if she were looking at herself nearly three years ago when she'd found out that her daddy was never coming home again.

"Hey," Trace said, getting his sister's attention. Claire Ann stood and began to cry as soon as she laid eyes on him.

Kylie let go of him so he could go to her. She wrapped her arms around herself as Claire Ann fell apart in his arms.

She lowered herself into a nearby chair and pulled her knees to her chest. Intruding on their private moment of familial grief was uncomfortable, but it was the visceral reminder of her own that felt as if it were going to crush her.

"GENERALLY the goal is twenty-four hours after the sedation has been removed. We'll expect her to wake up confused, disoriented. She may or may not remember the accident. It will be good for her to be surrounded by family when she comes to."

Kylie blinked herself awake and saw the man belonging to the heavily accented voice. The doctor was an attractive Middle Eastern man who didn't look much older than her. She sat up in the same chair she'd slept in as he explained his take on Rae's medical condition.

"And when can we expect that to happen? How long has it been since they removed the sedation?" Trace's eyes were shot through with busted red blood vessels, causing her to wonder if he'd ever slept at all.

"I can check with the nurse to be sure, but I believe you have another sixteen hours or so."

"Thank you," Claire Ann said softly.

The doctor shook Trace's hand and gave Claire Ann a nod as he left. He paid no attention to Kylie, but she understood. She wasn't *technically* family. A fact that had become increasingly clear the past twelve hours.

Claire Ann hadn't spoken five words to her, and Trace had been occupied with doctors and comforting his sister. They'd been able to see Rae, but it was immediate family only for the time being, so Kylie was just about as useful as the piece of furniture she was slowly becoming conjoined with.

"Can I get anyone anything?" Kylie asked. It hadn't been that long since her last coffee run, but she needed to stretch her legs.

"I'm good, baby, but thank you." Trace kissed her softly on the cheek. "Grab yourself something, though, before I have to check you in here as a patient."

Kylie smiled at his concern and stood.

"Claire Ann?"

"No, I'm good. Our mom should be here soon and she's bringing actual coffee instead of that watered-down gunk from the machines." Her entire answer came without so much as a glance in Kylie's direction.

"Okay. Well, I'm gonna go grab myself a cup of watered-down gunk." Kylie turned toward the door.

Trace was preoccupied by something on his phone—probably a text from Pauly. Kylie had no idea how he'd feel about seeing his mom. All she knew was what she'd heard from Rae. They were estranged because his mom didn't approve of his career choice.

"Kylie?" Claire Ann stood to follow her. "Got a sec?"

Kylie glanced over her shoulder as the exited the waiting room. "Well my fan club in the cafeteria is expecting me to sign autographs, but yeah, I can squeeze you in."

Trace's sister gave her a tense smile. Probably not the best time for humor, but the woman made her uncomfortable.

"Look," she began as they stepped into the bright white sterile-looking hallway. "I just wanted to say that I appreciated you coming with Trace. I mean, I'm not super excited that 'Trylie' is an item again, just because I know what it did to him before. But I was glad he didn't have to make the trip alone."

Kylie cringed internally at the nickname the media had given them last year. "Yeah, um, of course. And, Claire Ann? Pauly sort of gave me a message for you, but I got the feeling it wasn't supposed to be passed along in front of your brother."

"Please tell me you haven't said anything to Trace."

"I haven't," Kylie informed her. "But—"

"Just tell me the message."

Kylie took a deep breath. She really didn't want to have any secrets from Trace. But she got the feeling that getting back in his older sister's good graces was going to take serious work and blabbing what was probably her biggest secret wouldn't be a move in the right direction.

"He said, 'Tell Claire Ann I'm doing damage control for Trace and that I'll be there as soon as I can.'"

Claire Ann let out a loud breath. "Oh. Okay."

Kylie didn't miss the disappointment that flashed in the other woman's eyes.

"Um, he also said to tell you that he loves you and to call him when you get a chance."

At that, Claire Ann's mouth hinted at a smile and her eyes brightened. "So Pauly Garrett, huh? You know, I have always thought he was handsome…for an old guy."

"He's forty-three. That's not old," Claire Ann snapped.

Kylie grinned. "I know. I just wanted to see if he meant what I thought he meant when he said to tell you that he loved you."

Realizing she'd told her own secret, Claire Ann stiffened. "Look, it's really none of anyone's business who I—"

"Whoa, relax." Kylie met her panicked stare with what she hoped was a reassuring one. "My lips are sealed. I do think you should tell Trace though before he finds out some other way. But it's none of my business, so I'll just be in the corner practicing my Taylor Swift shocked face for when he does find out."

Trace's sister smiled at her for the first time in as long as she could remember. "Thanks. And, um, I'm sorry I've been so cold to you. It's just…" She trailed off and glanced at Trace through the small window in the waiting room door.

"I understand," Kylie said softly. "And with everything that's going on, being nice to me is not something you should even be worried about."

"Yes it is," Claire Ann argued. "He loves you. Therefore I love you. And Rae actually is your number one fan. If they told her you were here, she'd probably snap right out from under the sedation and start demanding to know every detail of how you and Trace reconciled."

Both women smiled. And then began to tear up.

"Claire Ann, is she going to be okay? I mean, I heard what the doctor said, but aside from being unconscious, is there any other—"

"They don't know for sure." Trace's sister wiped at her eyes. "One of her legs is broken in several places, and with head injuries, only time will tell. So…we'll see."

"She'll be okay." Kylie watched Trace trying to get comfortable on the sofa in the waiting room through the small window in the door. She had no idea how long it had been since he'd slept or eaten. Or if all this stress made him want to drink. "She has to be."

AGONIZED moans pulled Kylie from an already restless state somewhere between levels of unconsciousness.

Rae had been moved into a private suite that was as big as Kylie's living room in her apartment. So the furniture was slightly more comfortable than the ICU waiting room and she was thankful that she was allowed to be in the room now.

But nurses came in and out every other hour, machines beeped constantly, and when the air kicked on it sounded like an eighteen-wheeler was driving through the vent.

She opened her eyes and looked around.

Rae was still unconscious, a fact that had everyone one edge. It was well past time for her to come to. Trace's mom, a fifty-something woman who looked like a world-weary Claire Ann and spoke very little to anyone, was slumped in the chair closest to Rae's bed. Claire Ann's head rested on Pauly's shoulder. They still hadn't told Trace they were dating, but Kylie knew from chatting with Claire Ann that they were planning to once Rae was in stable condition.

The source of the moaning stirred and jerked next to her. Kylie rubbed her eyes. Trace's handsome face was contorted in a mask of pain and fear.

"Ooh," he moaned again. "Stop. Stop it," he yelled out suddenly.

"Trace." Kylie wrapped her arms around him and kissed the side of his jaw. "Shh, it's okay. It's okay. I'm here."

"Get your damn hands off her," he slurred out.

"Trace, hey." She shook his shoulder a little less gently. "Trace, look at me." He twitched, but whatever he was seeing in his sleep kept its grip on him. She slid her hand onto his inner thigh and squeezed. "Wake up, baby."

"Hmm?" His eyes opened slowly and she kissed him again.

"You were having a bad dream."

He rubbed his eyes and blinked a few times. "Oh. Shit. What time is it?" His voice was thick with sleep. He sat up straight and looked at her like she was the most beautiful thing he'd ever seen. Which would've been comical in any other situation because she hadn't showered in three days.

"It's almost seven. In the morning."

He put his arms around her and hauled her to his chest. "I'm sorry, baby. Did I wake you?"

"It's okay. I wasn't really asleep."

Trace glanced around the room. "Well you were the only one." His eyes lingered on Pauly and his sister. "Poor Pauly. Claire Ann's probably drooling all over him."

"Um, he probably doesn't mind." Kylie placed an open mouth kiss on his neck to distract him. She let her hand slide higher up on his thigh.

Trace leaned down and kissed her. She knew they both had god-awful breath as neither of them had had access to a toothbrush recently. But the way he held her tightly, as if he needed nothing more than her in that moment, needed that kiss, that contact, solidified what she already believed.

This was love.

It was not caring if your mouth tasted like month-old coffee. Or worse. It was silence when needed and sleeping on uncomfortable hospital furniture for days without complaint. It was someone to pull you from your nightmares with a kiss.

It was walking away from your dream without a single regret.

It was this.

"You want to talk about it? Whatever it was that had you shouting in your sleep?" She snuggled her head into the nook between his shoulder and chin.

"Not really," he answered, his tone gruff and warning.

"Might help," she said softly.

"Might send you running for the hills."

Her head popped up and she met his tormented stare. His hazel eyes clouded over, causing her heart to hurt for him.

"Trace, if you don't know by now that you are stuck with me no matter what, then you must've missed something."

He chuckled, but it was a low, dark laugh. As if she'd made a cruel joke.

"Hey." She paused to kiss him once more. "I'm serious."

He inhaled sharply and his eyes lost focus, as if he'd gone somewhere else. "My dad was a drunk," he began softly. "Which I think Rae has told you before."

Kylie nodded, afraid to speak for fear she'd say the wrong thing.

"There's more to it. More to me."

She snuggled closer to him. "There isn't anything you can tell me that will change the way I feel about you, Trace."

He cleared his throat. "Yeah, well. It changes the way I feel about me so I try not to think about it. But ever since I stopped drinking, it's been coming back to me. Hence the nightmares."

"I'm sorry, baby."

"Don't be. Not your fault, Kylie Lou. The only person who's to blame is six feet under, may his black soul not rest in peace."

Kylie cringed. They'd had very different brands of dads, that was for certain.

"You think I'm a mean drunk." Trace snorted. "My dad was a monster when he drank. When I was drinking, I lashed out verbally, which, believe me, I know can be just as bad as physical abuse. Which is why I always wonder how you can stand me, much less love me."

A shudder passed through him, and she scooted into his lap. "It's not you when you're like that. I knew that from the beginning. That version of you…It's not the man you really are. Just a part you have to battle with sometimes."

"The man I really am," he said quietly, more to himself than her. He huffed out a small breath. "My dad used to get drunk and hit. He'd use his fists, his belt, whatever he could get his hands on. He beat the hell out of them. Always my mom and usually Claire Ann too."

He clutched her tightly as he continued his story.

"I was ten when Rae was born. Old enough to try to protect her, to know that I was supposed to, but not big enough to really do it."

"Trace—"

"For the first few years, he mostly ignored her. It was a relief, you know?"

She nodded and felt him swallow hard.

"He only hit me when I got in his way of getting to them. Said I needed to learn to be a man."

Kylie wrapped herself around him the best she could in the awkward position they were in on the couch. She felt like they were both in danger of falling off the Earth down into a deep, dark hole neither of them would know how to get out of. But she knew she would go down with him before she'd let him fall alone.

"This one night, when I was fifteen and had started a crappy garage band with my friends, I'd stayed out late." He paused and Kylie looked up at his face. His jaw and throat were working over time to keep the moisture in his eyes from being more. "I knew…I *knew* I should've got my ass home. It was a weekend, he always drank on the weekends."

Her heart ached for him as he laid himself bare. "Baby, you can't blame—"

"I fucking knew. But I was stupid and selfish and so sick of that goddamned house. So I played a few more songs, stood around with my buddies, and shot the shit for no good reason. I walked home the long way."

He stopped talking. She figured it was to compose himself. She could feel the anguish rolling off of him and over both of them as he continued.

"When I got there, his truck was sideways in the driveway. I could hear Claire Ann screaming from inside. We lived on several acres so there weren't any neighbors to call for help."

Kylie took several deep breaths to stave off the quiver that was gaining momentum inside of her. She knew he needed to get this out without her bawling all over him.

"I swear, it was like I had the strength of a hundred men. I flew inside and grabbed him. I slammed him into a wall, and somehow, I literally threw him out of the house. I was puny, and he was a big guy, but I was blind with rage. I threatened to kill him if he stepped foot back in that house. And I meant it."

Kylie kept her arms securely fastened around him. She didn't even know if she was doing it to comfort him or herself anymore. She hoped if their bodies were close enough somehow she could siphon off some of his pain by sharing the weight of this heavy burden he'd carried all alone for so long.

"Claire Ann's face was already bruising and swollen. He'd busted her nose and there were open welts covering her legs. She'd tried to protect our mom while he'd beat her into unconsciousness." His chest rose abruptly as he expelled an audible breath. "Typical Claire Ann. Broken and bloody and trying to take care of everyone else. She kept screaming at me to find Rae." He let go of her and leaned forward. Kylie continued to lean over onto him as he dropped his head into his hands. "She was only five and so damn small for her age. I couldn't find her anywhere. My mom was still unconscious on the floor and Claire Ann was losing it and Rae was just…missing."

A small sob escaped her as the picture took shape in her head, but she choked down the rest of it so he could go on.

Trace's voice was gravelly. She could tell he was doing his best to keep it low as not to disturb anyone else in the room.

"I called the police. They were familiar with our family. They didn't hurry." His voice took on an angrier tone. "And I just started tearing the damn house down trying to find her. I looked everywhere. The girls' room, my room, the bathroom. Every single cabinet, even ones she couldn't have possibly gotten into. And then I saw it. The smeared trail of blood. She was in the space between the stove and the fridge. It was barely big enough for her to fit."

"I'm sorry, Trace. God, I'm so sorry."

"It took me forever to get her to come out. He'd hit her with the buckle end of his belt. Sliced the back of her ear clean open. It took a dozen stitches to close."

She covered her mouth and shook her head to keep the whimpers inside. "Trace, none of that was your fault."

He turned to her with an irate expression. The ferocity in his voice almost sent her reeling backward.

"Are you fucking kidding? Of course it was my fault. I was hanging out with my friends like I didn't have a goddamned care in the world. I might as well have hit her myself."

"You listen to me." Kylie took his face in both of her hands. "You were a kid, Trace. A kid that didn't get a childhood. Because he stole it. From all of you. You know what Rae told me at your birthday party that first time I came to the farm? She told me about your dad but said that nothing had ever happened to her because *you* protected her. *You* kept her safe."

"I didn't. I didn't, Kylie. I messed up. I let her down. It's what I do. I let people down." He let his tears fall and she forced her way back into his lap.

"No, Trace. No, you didn't. You don't." She kissed every inch of his face, tasting both of their salty tears as she did.

"She doesn't remember," a female voice said quietly.

Kylie startled, pulling herself from his arms as a reflex, feeling like they'd been caught doing something illicit in public.

"She doesn't remember that night," Claire Ann continued. "I've asked her about it before. She only remembers you pulling her out of the space by the stove. She thinks you were playing hide and seek and that scar is from where she cut herself climbing behind there."

Kylie gaped at Claire Ann's stoic face, wondering how long she'd been awake.

"Thank God for that. But I can't forget. I remember it like it was yesterday."

She leaned against his chest. His heart pounded rhythmically in her ear.

"Sometimes, I dream it's you. It's you hiding, and I'm him. But I'm watching it happen and I can't stop myself."

It took her a second to realize he was speaking to her. "Trace, I have never, ever been afraid of you in that way. You are not him. You will be never be anything like him."

"She's right, Trace." Claire Ann's soft voice was heavy. "The only reason I have any faith in men is because of you. Because I saw that there is at least one man who can be trusted, who would protect the people he loved from the Johnny Ray Corbins of the world."

He shook his head at both of them. "I grabbed you. I grabbed you in Jackson." The remorse in his eyes sent her on a quick trip back in time. "I had no right to put my hands on you like that. I was angry and I lost control. Just like him."

Kylie shook her head. "Pretty sure it was just all that built-up sexual tension you were harboring for me."

The corners of his mouth twitched and finally lifted. "That may be, but still."

"But nothing, Trace. You're not him. But if you're worried, you know there are people you can—"

"I know." He nodded. "I have a few numbers I got in rehab. People I can talk to, places I can go to get help for the anger."

"Good. Well, speaking of talking," Kylie began, aiming a pointed glance at Claire Ann. "I'm going to go grab some muffins and juice if y'all want to maybe clear the air about, oh, I don't know, any secrets either of you may or may not be keeping."

To her great surprise, Claire Ann grinned. "You can stay, Kylie. I might need another witness in case Trace maims Pauly."

"Why would I do anything to Pauly?" Trace looked at her and Kylie nodded towards Claire Ann. This wasn't her secret to tell.

"Kylie and I've been talking, Trace. And after what I saw this morning when you both thought everyone else was asleep, I owe you both an apology."

"Huh?"

Kylie just shook her head. The last thing she wanted from anyone was an apology.

"I have been so closed-minded about so many things. And frankly, I don't give people enough credit sometimes." Claire Ann cast a long, loving glance at the man sleeping beside her. "I didn't expect you two to work things out because I figured you'd both get in your own way. And Trace, I didn't tell you who I was seeing because I didn't know if you could handle it."

Trace tilted his head as he looked at her. "Claire Ann, I told you I want to meet him."

His sister bit her lip. Kylie felt her insides tighten.

"That's the thing, Trace. You have met him."

"I have? Well, who is it?"

The tension was so thick that Kylie didn't know whether to laugh or cry. The lack of sleep and the heavy emotional climate had her bordering on hysteria.

Claire Ann swung her eyes over to Pauly once more.

"No," Trace said, his voice and his sky-high eyebrows clearly reflecting his disbelief. "Pauly? You've been dating my manager? Seriously? For how long?"

"Since you went to rehab. He checked in on us several times and we just started talking." Claire Ann shrugged. "He's a good man, Trace. You know that. Better than most. Kind of like my brother."

The room was completely silent minus the beeping of Rae's heart monitor.

As if he could feel the attention on him, Pauly stretched and opened his eyes. "Mornin', everyone. Any news on Rae?"

"You're fired," Trace said evenly.

"Trace." Kylie dug an elbow into his ribs.

"You told him while I was asleep?" Pauly gaped at Claire Ann. "Were you thinking it was best to do it in a hospital or what?"

"Okay, you're not fired," Trace said, getting the man's attention. "But really? My sister?"

"We didn't mean for it to happen." Pauly shrugged. "But it did. And after everything..." He paused to wave a hand around, reminding everyone where they were. "Seeing how much you and Kylie are willing to risk for one another, I'm done hiding it. Done being worried about how it will affect everyone else. So, yeah, Trace. Me and your sister." He offered Trace a quick sorry-not-sorry shrug. "Fire me all you want. I've been dating your sister for the past year and the only regret I have is not shouting to the world what a lucky man I was on day one. I love her."

Kylie grinned at the tears welling in Claire Ann's eyes.

"Well, I hate to interrupt this lovely moment, but can someone please get me some water?"

chapter FORTY EIGHT

Aᴸᴸ four sets of eyes swung in the direction of the raspy voice.
"Rae!" Claire Ann and Kylie shrieked at once.

Everyone sprung into action. Kylie poured water from a blue pitcher into a Styrofoam cup as Trace and Claire Ann leapt towards Rae's bed.

Trace held the hand of Rae's without the IV as Claire Ann woke their mother. "Jesus Christ, Rae. You scared me to fucking death." He lowered his head onto the side of her hospital bed.

"Sorry, potty mouth." She squeezed his hand the best she could, which wasn't very hard. "What happened?"

"You were in an accident, sweetheart," his mom broke in.

Trace did his best not to give her a dirty look. Just because he no longer had anything to do with her didn't mean she wasn't still Rae's mom. He knew that. He just wished it weren't true. Kylie touched his shoulder gently as she handed Rae her cup of water.

"We can talk about that later," Claire Ann interrupted. "How are you feeling?"

"I'm going to grab a nurse and let them know she's awake," Kylie said quietly as she edged out of the room.

Trace knew this was probably an awkward thing for her to be a part of, and his family dynamic was a pretty unusual one.

"Thanks, baby." He nodded at her as Pauly stepped out behind her.

"*Baby?* So Trylie is back together?" Rae's eyes were a few shades lighter and her normally tan skin was slightly yellow under the fluorescents, but she was still gleaming. Still his Rae.

"Never call us that again."

"At least not to their faces," Claire Ann added with a grin.

"Rae, how much do you remember about the accident?" His mom put a hand up before anyone could cut her off again. "I don't want to upset you, but the police have been waiting for you to wake up so that they could get your statement."

Rae's eyes went wide as she looked up into their faces. Trace hated that his mom wouldn't drop it, but he had a feeling she was right about the police.

"I went dancing. With my friend Jo. We were…" Rae's eyes were unfocused for a moment. "Downtown. We went to that new place, that new bar on the strip. And then we got some food."

Dread weighed heavily on Trace as she spoke. She'd been drinking and driving. And he couldn't say much to her about it. He and his friends had done that and worse at her age.

Kylie and his sisters painted him as some big protector and savior, but once again, he was plagued by the knowledge that this was his fault. At least in a way it was.

"The last thing I remember is wandering around downtown looking for my car. We couldn't remember where we'd parked."

"Okay, that's good for now," Claire Ann said. "And when you talk to the police, no matter what they say, only tell them what you can remember. Don't let them put words in your mouth."

"I talked to Clancy Ludlow," Pauly said as he re-entered the room. "He's Trace's lawyer and a damn good one. He'll represent Rae if any criminal charges are pressed."

Trace nodded his appreciation to his manager. He still hadn't quite wrapped his head around the idea of the man dating his sister, but there was no denying that he trusted him.

"Criminal charges?" Rae squeaked out. "What's he talking about? Oh my god. Is Jo okay?"

Claire Ann took a deep breath and plastered a mask of calm on her face. "She's got some pretty serious injuries, Rae. Some head injuries and some swelling around her spine. She's got a rough road ahead, and her family knows your Trace Corbin's sister, so they've already got a lawyer and they aren't exactly talking to us."

Tears gathered in Rae's eyes and Trace wiped them as they leaked onto her face. "We'll take care of it, baby girl. It will all be okay."

She sniffled loudly. "I never got to tell y'all I finally picked a major. Want to hear something ironic?" She nodded to her casted leg but didn't wait for anyone to respond before continuing. "It's physical therapy."

More tears fell from her eyes. "Can I see Jo? I just want to tell her that I'm sorry. We should've taken a cab. I'm so sorry." Rae broke down into loud sobs that reverberated in Trace's chest as he held her to him.

"She'll be all right, Rae. I'll pay for her medical care and anything else. It will all be handled. Don't you worry."

"Your brother shouldn't make promises he can't keep." His mother ignored his enraged glare. "Even if the family doesn't press charges, the state still can. And since your blood alcohol level was over the legal limit for someone under the age of twenty-one, the cops are going to ask you what you had to drink. So be honest with them the best you can."

Just as Trace was about to demand that his mom get the fuck out of that room before he helped her out, Pauly spoke up.

"Actually, since she has a lawyer now, the police can't actually take her statement until Mr. Ludlow gets here."

Before Trace's mom could argue any further, a nurse entered the room and shooed them all out so she could get Rae's vitals. A doctor came in as they were leaving.

Trace really wanted to stick around and hear what they had to say, but Claire Ann assure him they'd get briefed after the exam was completed.

He stepped out into the hall where Kylie was fighting to keep her head up on a bench in the hallway. Next to her sat several muffins and juice boxes.

"They hire you to work here yet, Kylie Lou?"

She smiled weakly up at him. "Something like that. Hey, I snagged some stuff for Rae and anyone else who wants it. Everything okay?"

Trace lowered himself down onto the bench next to her. "It will be."

She let her head drop onto his shoulder. "Good. I knew it would be."

For a moment they just sat there together, enjoying the comfort, both of them breathing easier since Rae was out of the woods.

But then Trace's phone buzzed.

"You been blowing up, too?" Kylie nodded towards the pocket his phone was lighting up.

"Yeah. You?"

She pulled hers out and sat it on the bench beside her. The battery was nearly dead. "Mmhm. I'm probably banned from the state of Oklahoma for life."

Guilt crashed into him. They'd been halfway to the show in her home state when all hell had broken loose.

"Baby, go to the house and rest. Then contact your PR lady and tell her I had a family emergency and we canceled the show out of respect for my family situation. See what she what she can do about rescheduling. They can get someone to replace me on the last leg of the tour."

She shook her head. "It can wait. It can all wait. I don't want to leave you."

"Kylie, I promise, everything will be fine. And honestly, the longer you're gone, the more suspicion it will raise and the more people will start sniffing around. The last thing I want is for Rae to get caught in a media shitstorm because she's my sister." He didn't add the part about the alcohol. Because he was still partially in denial and because he knew if it got out, even from a member of the hospital staff, then Rae would get dragged through the mud and she could forget her fresh start in college.

He watched as she folded into herself. Her body began to quiver against him as she fought off tears.

"But—"

"Listen to me. I want you here more than anything. But right now, you need to do everything you can to get back on the road so no one comes to see what's such a big deal we both left the tour. It's for the best for all of us."

She nodded. "Okay. If that's what you want. But will you please give Rae my new number and tell her to text me if she needs anything?"

"If you're sure about that. You know she'll probably be texting you with a nail polish-related emergency five seconds after I give it to her."

Kylie smiled at him and he felt like he could breathe for the first time in three days. "I'm okay with that. Tell her I'm on standby."

He looked into the eyes he loved and pressed his forehead to hers. "I have no idea how we got here, and I would do anything to make this better for Rae, but I can't tell you how much it means to me to have you back in my life, to have you here. To have you…"

Those gorgeous blues widened, and she brushed his lips with hers right there in the hospital hallway.

"Remember what you said about the farm? About how I was always there, even when I wasn't?"

"Mmhm," he mumbled against her mouth.

"Well, I think it's the same way for having me in your life. And having you in mine. You're a part of me. What we have will always be a part of our lives."

"Amen for that," he said, just before he claimed her mouth as his. And tonight, he had every intention of claiming the rest of her.

chapter FORTY NINE

"IF we keep this up, we'll have to find a supply closet soon."

She was kidding, but Trace pulled back from their kiss. "Good point. And not altogether a bad idea."

As thoroughly exhausted as she was, her pulse began to race. An overwhelming and all encompassing truth began forcing its way to the forefront of her mind.

What they had—it was so much bigger than each of them as individuals. Together they could try and survive it, stand together and welcome the pleasure and the pain of the ups and downs that would fill their lives for as long as they were together.

This thing between them—this love—was a force of nature beyond anyone's control. An uncontainable living thing comparable only to the ocean as far as Kylie was concerned. Together they stood a chance. Separately it would crush them both. Fighting it alone had almost destroyed her. It was an exhilarating and terrifying realization.

"Hey, you look worried," Trace said, brushing a hair from her face. "Rae's going to be fine. She's got to give her statement to the police and

I'm going to try to not get arrested. But you should go on to the house. Shower, get some rest. I'm coming home tonight, too. I can smell myself."

Kylie laughed. She wanted to tell him about her revelation, but she had a feeling he already knew. That she was the one who was late to the party.

"Well I love the way you smell. Showered or not, I still wouldn't kick you out of bed." She nipped at his bottom lip.

"Good to know, because I am going to wake you up when I get home tonight. Another reason you should get some rest while you can."

A delicious shiver danced up her spine, and she almost felt guilty. They were in the hospital, Rae was injured and might be in serious trouble, and the label was probably drawing up the paperwork to drop them both like bad habits at that very moment. But somehow, because they had each other, it seemed like it would all turn out okay.

She didn't now if being in love had sent her endorphin and serotonin levels on something like a drug-induced high, or if it was sleep depravation that had her feeling light and strangely optimistic. But as she kissed him goodbye and promised him for the millionth time that she was okay driving to the farm alone, her entire world shifted.

She was practically bouncing out of the hospital as she left. She knew the grin on her face probably made a few of the hospital staff members wonder if she needed a psych eval, but she didn't care. Nothing could take away what she and Trace had.

That much she knew for certain.

"It won't last, you know," a low, raspy voice said a moment after she'd passed through the automatic doors.

Maybe I do need a psych evaluation.

Kylie turned in the direction of the voice, hoping like hell it hadn't come from inside her head.

Trace's mom sat on a bench where the shuttle picked up riders. She took a long drag of her cigarette while Kylie stared at her in confusion.

"Excuse me?"

The woman sighed and gave her a look that bordered on apologetic. "He's just like his father. Sure, it seems like a dream come true right now." She shrugged and exhaled smoke between them. "But wait until his next album doesn't do well or his fancy label lets him go."

Kylie throat constricted, either from the smell of the smoke or the severity of the woman's words.

"Mrs. Corbin, I can assure you that no matter—"

"It's McClain. My last name isn't Corbin. And if you have any sense in that pretty head of yours, yours won't ever be either."

She flinched back like she'd been slapped. What kind of mother spoke that way about her son? Especially a son like Trace. Her heart pumped harder. She felt that version of herself, the hotheaded one rising quickly to the surface. She wondered if that was what it felt like to be the Incredible Hulk.

"I can only hope that one day I'm lucky enough for my last name to be Corbin," Kylie said evenly. She took a step towards the woman so the patients and visitors meandering past wouldn't hear.

Trace's mom eyed her as if she were a lab specimen to be examined and then coughed loudly. "You know, I was like you once. Young. Naïve. And then I married an alcoholic who turned my life into a living hell."

The reminder of the picture Trace had painted of his childhood took shape in her mind and brought tears to her eyes for the second time.

"*Your* life? What about the lives of those kids who had to live in fear? Who grew up still blaming themselves for things that never should've happened?"

"It's easy to judge me from where you stand. But I did the best I could."

Kylie glared at the other woman. "Well, pardon me, but from what I hear, your best fucking sucked."

She didn't appear the least bit fazed by Kylie's bluntness. She just shook her head and stamped out her cigarette on the concrete.

"I tried to stop him from taking this road, from following in his father's footsteps. But he didn't listen. And I see you and him and it's like looking back in time." Her eyes left Kylie's and focused somewhere in the distance. "This little fairytale you're living only ends one way. In the bottom of a bottle. Corbin men can't handle disappointment without it."

Kylie fists clenched at her sides.

"You know, that's funny, considering all Trace has ever had in his life, thanks to you, is disappointment." She pulled in as much as air as she could in preparation of letting this woman have it. The love she felt for Trace surged in her chest, and she was overcome by an intense urge to hit something. The emotions rushing through her were almost too much too contain.

"I bet he was *disappointed* that his mother subjected him and his sisters to someone who was violent and vile and abusive. And I bet he was really *disappointed* when that same mother couldn't support his dream and his decision to move to Nashville. Especially since he'd given up the whole first part of his life to protect everyone else. And you know, I happen to know firsthand from personal experience that he was pretty damn *disappointed* when the same woman who couldn't support his dream didn't waste a minute cashing in on his success by airing his personal nightmare in her very own tell-all book. So pardon me if I don't give a single solitary damn about your opinion of how well Trace handles disappointment."

Trace's mom's eyes were wide as Kylie bore down on her. She opened her mouth to speak, but Kylie didn't much care what she had to say. So she continued on with her speech.

"And if you think my loving Trace is a mistake, feel free to keep it to yourself or save if for your next book. Feel free to mention my daddy issues. Because, yes, I do love Trace even more because he reminds me of the absolute best man I've ever known." She pulled in a breath. "Trace is a lot like my father was, in that he's loving and kind and selfless and strong. He's the kind of man who would give up everything he had for the people he loved. And a man who gets help when he needs it. And he is *nothing* like *his* father." She shook her head, unable to process how Trace's mom could even think there was any comparison. "Trace would walk through fire before he hurt me or Claire Ann or Rae. Hell, probably even you. So for future reference, if your opinion of Trace is *anything* other than that you are damn fortunate to even exist on the same planet as him, I suggest you refrain from sharing it in my presence. And you can quote me on that."

"Okay, Hothead. I think she gets it."

Kylie whirled around to see Trace fighting back a grin.

He held up her cell phone. "You forgot this."

Her face began to burn as she realized he'd probably caught the majority of her outburst. But for the first time in a long time, she felt like herself again.

A sheepish smile snuck across her face and she bit her lip. "Um, your mom and I were just—"

"About to duke it out in the hospital parking lot?"

Kylie shrugged and took another step towards him. "Something like that."

Neither of them even looked up as his mom passed them and disappeared through the hospital doors.

"You really believe all that stuff you said?"

"Of course I do. It was all the truth." She kissed him softly on the lips. "I'm sorry I lost my temper. She just said some really ugly things and I couldn't—"

"It's okay, darlin'. I'm well versed in her lack of faith in me. I read the book." He wrapped his arms around her and she pulled him even closer.

"Well, I have enough faith in you for everyone. To hell with her."

His lips crashed down on hers and she felt her knees go weak. It took all of her self-control to let him go when the shuttle arrived to take her to her truck.

"Come home soon, okay?"

"Yes, ma'am."

AFTER a long, hot shower—one in which she found herself assaulted by the sensual memories of Trace making love to her in the very same shower—Kylie felt slightly more human. She'd gotten to talk to Rae on the phone, and hearing that she still sounded like herself, albeit a very tired and slightly medicated version of herself, made her feel somewhat better.

She snuggled down in Trace's bed in hopes that he would be home soon. The past few days and then the run-in with his mom had left her feeling bereft and alone in the great big farmhouse. She needed him. Needed him badly.

It felt selfish, considering she knew that his family needed him just as much, if not more. But every time she glanced at her phone and saw the many messages and demands of the outside world, a clawing ache began to gnaw at her insides.

She'd spent the majority of the evening on the phone with Jane and Hannah and Chaz. Like it or not, she had one more day until she had to be in Oklahoma to resume the tour. It was either that or lose the label's support on her next album and all the credibility she'd worked so hard to get.

The thought of leaving Trace, of finishing the tour without him, made her sick to her stomach. She knew exactly who the label had chosen to replace him and she'd be damned if she would sing the song she and Trace wrote together with him.

Kylie's head swam with memories of the past and dreams of a future she rarely let herself imagine. She needed him to touch her, kiss her, to soothe that clawing ache inside. To return them to the private bliss they'd been wrapped in before police had come knocking on the bus door.

The memories of her time with Trace in Macon had begun to fade, making her fantasies less vivid. But being in his bed brought them back in full force.

She was still reaching for him, surrounded by memories of their past, when she drifted off to sleep.

"It's kind of hard to explain. Things got crazy and I haven't exactly had time to tell her yet."

Trace's voice roused Kylie from unconsciousness. She rubbed her eyes and sat up. It was barely daylight, and she wasn't sure if she'd slept for a few hours or a few days. But she was in his bedroom. In his shirt. Which was her absolute favorite place to be.

Right up until a woman's voice made its way to her ears.

"Well I'm thinking you're out of time, Tray."

It wasn't Rae or Claire Ann, which she didn't expect it to be since Rae still had at least one more day to stay in the hospital according to Trace.

Kylie grabbed her jeans and yanked them on.

I don't bring women here. He'd told her that the first time she had come to the farm. And she'd believed him. But maybe things had changed, because even though Kylie couldn't tell whose voice it was, whoever Trace was arguing with quietly in the next room was decidedly female.

She ran her fingers through her hair and stepped out of the bedroom.

"Hey, I thought you'd be back sooner..." Her voice failed her as soon she saw the two people embracing in the kitchen. "Oh. God. Wow. Okay, well, I was just—"

"Kylie," Trace began while hastily removing himself from Gretchen Gibson's arms. "Good. I'm glad you're up because we need to talk about—"

"Yeah. Um, actually I've been talking to Hannah and the label and I really need to go because I have like no time to get to Oklahoma. So I'm glad you're here and I didn't have to leave a note."

The words tumbled over each other as her mind raced, trying to process the real-life version of the nightmare she'd been living for the past year. She prayed on everything holy that the feeling of her blood rushing from her head wouldn't cause to pass out. Because this was humiliating enough as it was.

This wasn't a grainy cellphone photo in a cheap tabloid magazine or a pixelated image on a website. This was the real deal. Live and in person.

Adding insult to injury, Kylie looked and felt like week-old run-over garbage while Gretchen Gibson looked amazing. She was practically gleaming as she stood there looking from Kylie to Trace and back again.

Surprise, annoyance, and something akin to amusement sparkled in the woman's eyes.

There is something I should tell you. Something about Gretchen.

"Kylie, wait. Slow down," Trace began, coming towards her as she snatched her keys and cell phone from the kitchen counter. But she couldn't hear him. She could only hear the memory of him trying to tell her something she didn't want to hear.

"I'm gonna run by the hospital and say goodbye to Rae." She swallowed hard and did her best to keep her grip on what was left of her dignity. "Great seeing you again, Gretchen."

She let Trace's back door slam behind her. Running to her truck, she ignored the way the wind ripped through her thin shirt. Just like she was ignoring the way it carried his voice calling her name.

H ER tears were nearly blinding her by the time she hit the main road. The voice in her head screamed obscenities and for her to turn around and face whatever was going on with Trace and Gretchen. Force it all out in the open.

But she just…couldn't.

She'd walked away from her career, her dream, her managers, her label, her band, her best friend—all of it. Thrown caution to the wind to be with him. To be here for him because she thought he needed her.

And for what? So he could offer to let her be girlfriend number two?

There has to be an explanation for why she's here.

Yeah. There did. But she couldn't figure out what it could possibly be. The way they were hugging…Granted, it wasn't like he'd had his tongue down Gretchen's throat, but there was *something* there. Something deep and complex. Something she didn't know about or understand.

How could I have been so damn stupid?

Her hand smacked the steering wheel hard enough to make the truck swerve off the road. She hit the brakes and felt the skid of tires on gravel.

Crying out in frustration, she jumped out of the truck to make sure she hadn't flattened a tire or hit anything.

Kicking a back tire that thankfully wasn't damaged, she broke down in sobs on a deserted Georgia road.

The sound of a truck approaching and squealing to a stop right behind her startled her. She wiped her tears, expecting to wave whomever it was off and let them know that she was fine.

Trace jumped out of the old blue truck and stalked towards her.

"What the fuck, Kylie? What happened to not running out on each other?"

"I'm fine," she pleaded. "Leave me alone." Turning away from that swirling storm of a mess of a man and heading for the safety of her truck, she reached for the door.

"No I damn sure will not leave you alone. Did that once, remember?" He yanked her wrists back and pulled her to his chest.

She slapped at him as hard as she could in an attempt to break free but he didn't even flinch.

"Fucking hit me. You know I can take it." He pressed her up against the truck. "But don't run out me like that. That, I cannot fucking take."

"W-what is she doing here, Trace? Why is she here? What happened to *I don't bring women here?* There a concert happening later that I don't know about?"

She hated the way she crumbled in his arms, the way he—and only he—had the ability to reduce her to this. This wasn't her. This wasn't the Kylie Ryans she wanted to be. She wanted to be a serious musician, the kind of girl who could handle anything that came her way. Not a simpering mess of someone's sort of girlfriend.

Something Pauly Garrett had said to her a long time ago whipped through her head.

If you want to be Kylie Ryans, country music artist who gets taken seriously, it would be unwise to align yourself with an already established artist in any way other than professionally. Trust me, I've seen it happen. Now, if you want to be Kylie Ryans, Trace Corbin's little sideshow fling, then by all means…

He released one of her wrists to run a hand through his hair. "Baby, it's complicated. And it's not entirely my story to tell. But it's not what you're thinking. I swear to hell and back it's not."

She used her free hands to wipe her tears. "How am I supposed to know that? To believe that?"

She took a deep breath and used every ounce of strength to pull those old familiar walls back down over her heart.

"Kylie Lou, please don't—"

"You know, I've been thinking. Your family needs you and I need to get back to the tour, so we should probably take a step back anyways." She forced herself to swallow and look away from the torment filling his eyes. "Everything's been so crazy lately, we haven't really had time to think about what's best for everyone."

"Kylie, I have no fucking clue what you're talking about. I don't really give a damn what's best for everyone. *You're* what's best for me. And I'm trying my hardest to be what's best for you. But if you're having second thoughts—"

"*Second* thoughts is hardly the right term." She tried to smile at him but her mouth wasn't cooperating and it resulted in more a smirk. "More like we've been rushing into things without bothering to have any *first* thoughts about them."

"Don't do this. Don't bail on me, now, sweetheart. I hear the words coming out of your mouth, but you forget I know what's really going on in that head of yours." Trace pulled her close once more and she held her breath so as not to breathe him in.

Her own words echoed around them.

Don't do this. You don't mean it. I don't believe you. She'd once begged him not to leave her. And he'd had to go too. She finally got it. Sometimes it was better to walk away. Painful as it might be, sometimes that was the only option.

"Well unless you're going to explain what the hell she's doing here, I guess we're out of luck. I gotta go, Trace. One of us has to be the grown up and finish this tour."

He stepped back as if she'd shoved him. She flinched as well, knowing that was a cheap shot.

"I didn't mean that." She wanted to hit something. "It's just her…and you. And—"

"She's a friend, Kylie. A good friend. One that I trust and have been through a lot with. That's it. For the most part. But it's not like you think. Not like what you and I—

Kylie put a hand up between them. "Then tell me, this friend you trust, what does she think of us being together? And what are you going to do the next time you slip up and drink? Who are you going to turn to for advice? Let me guess, the good friend you trust and have been through a lot with. Who also happens to despise me."

She couldn't know for sure, but she'd be willing to bet Gretchen was a firm supporter of his decision to walk away from her last year. And she'd been damned if she was getting a repeat of that performance.

"You already planning my next rehab stay, Kylie Lou? Nice. That's hard to hear from the girl who just gave a big speech about her faith in me."

His words broke something inside of her. She was upset and didn't want to keep saying hurtful things. The last thing she wanted was to hurt him when everything was already so screwed up. She needed space. Needed room to think clearly without him disorienting her.

"I just…need some space, okay? Can you give me that? Please?"

His shoulders dropped as he stared at her with an unreadable expression. He nodded slowly.

"Yeah. I can give you that. If that's really what you want."

She leaned up and kissed him softly on the cheek, stilling for a moment so she could feel the rough stubble against her lips.

Slowly, and without another word, she got in her truck and pulled away. But because she'd never really be able to move on from the natural disaster that was Trace Corbin without looking back, she glanced in her rearview.

He stood there with both hands on his head, growing smaller. Looking lost and alone.

Just like she felt.

chapter FIFTY

Oklahoma was a lot prettier when you'd been gone awhile.

It blurred into sight as she crossed the state line. She had three hours to get to Oklahoma City and rehearse for tonight's show. But she had a stop to make first. Two, actually.

Pride is Proud of Kylie Ryans, the sign announced when she entered her hometown.

She'd heard about it, but this was the first time she'd seen it for herself. On one side was her formal senior yearbook photo. On the other was a shot of her smiling for the very first promo shots she'd ever taken when she'd signed up for Trace's *Back to My Roots* tour.

It was like seeing two different girls up there. And then a quick glance in the mirror revealed a third. One she didn't even know herself.

A brief lyric flitted through her head. Something about where you go when you don't recognize the face in the mirror.

Home, apparently.

She rolled to a stop in front of her old house. A late-model mini-van with a handicap tag was parked in the driveway. For a few minutes, she let herself remember.

Sitting on the front porch with her daddy, playing music, catching fireflies, and talking about everything under the sun. But once he was gone, that small faded white house with blue shutters had stopped being home.

She could practically see herself running out the door with nothing other than her guitar case the day Darla had thrown her out. Cringing at the painful words that had accompanied her eviction, she'd walked to work. Where she'd promptly gotten fired and hopped a bus to Nashville.

It felt like a lifetime ago. Or someone else's life.

She placed her hand over her mouth to keep the tears from coming. She'd left that place and she'd found another home.

One with a man who might be more than even she could handle.

For reasons she couldn't justify even to herself, she got out of the truck and approached the front door. Hopefully a stranger showing up out of the blue and saying, "Hey, I grew up here, can I come inside for five minutes," wouldn't creep out whoever lived here. Or at the very least, maybe they wouldn't call the cops.

Just as she made her way up the front walk, stepping over the cracks the same way she had as a kid, the front door opened.

An attractive middle-aged Hispanic lady looked at her and gasped.

"Hi. Um, so sorry to bother you," Kylie began.

"It's you," the lady said, seemingly not surprised, as if she'd expected this random confrontation for some reason. "He said you might come by some day."

"He?"

"We're just heading out. Isabelle has piano lessons at the church," the woman explained as she pulled a young girl in a wheelchair out onto the porch. "But if you'd like to come back later, we'll be home in an hour or so."

Kylie smiled at both of them, trying to cover her confusion. "Um, gosh, no. I have to be somewhere. I just... I grew up here and I was in town so..."

"Pride is proud of Kylie Ryans," the lady said with a wink. "Yes, we know. I'm Marlena Gutiérrez. And this is my daughter, Isabelle."

So someone recognized her then. Well, that made one of them.

"Is that really her?"

Kylie glanced down at the girl, who looked to be around nine or ten.

"It is," her mother confirmed.

"She's really pretty."

Kylie smiled at the girl. "Isabelle was it? I bet you sleep in my old bedroom."

"I do! The kids at school didn't believe me until he put the sign up."

Kylie glanced at her mom for clarification. Marlena pointed to the small wooden plaque by the front door.

Childhood Home of Country Music Singer Kylie Ryans - Official Property of the A Hand Up Foundation, it read.

Below was some small print about restrictions on changes being made to the house, but the water welling in her eyes made it too blurry for her to make out.

"He's a good man, that Mr. Corbin," Marlena said softly. "You didn't know?"

Do not cry in front of these people.

"Yes. He is." Well, that answered the question of who had bought her house. She'd always wondered. And yes, she knew he was a good man, but she was pretty sure that wasn't what the lady had meant. "And no, I didn't know. But I'm glad this old house has so much love in it." Kylie nodded at each of them. "It was wonderful to meet both of you. I hope y'all have as many good memories here as I do." She turned to leave before her tears fell.

"Miss Ryans? Before you go, could you sign something for my daughter?"

She swallowed the lump in her throat once more. "Of course."

Marlena dug an envelope and a pen from her purse. After Kylie had signed it, she thought about Trace, what he would do in this situation.

"Listen, do y'all have plans tonight? I have a show downtown and I can send a car...or a van. Whatever y'all need. Would you like to come as my special guests?"

It was ten minutes before they stopped thanking her. Kylie was pretty sure she'd made Isabelle late for her piano lesson. But it felt good to be able to do something nice for someone else. She could see now why Trace's foundation was so important to him.

It reminded her that she was human.

But Marlena's last words wounded her right down to her soul. After they'd told her they'd come to her show and that she was welcome in their home anytime, the lady added one last sentiment.

"He spoke very highly of you when he visited. Went on and on about how amazing you are and how much you changed his life, inspired him to be a better man. A love like that…" She paused to look at her daughter, and Kylie's heart ached. "It's special. And it's rare. I hope my own daughter is lucky enough to find such a love some day."

"Looks like she already has," she said, nodding at the woman before closing her door so she could have her breakdown in private. Once she was safely in the cab of her truck, she gave up her stubborn battle and let her tears fall.

THE cemetery was empty when Kylie arrived. She made her way to where her mother and father lay from memory.

"Hi, Daddy. Sorry I haven't been home in a while. Life has been… interesting."

It was the first time she'd seen the headstone Trace had purchased for him in person. Running her hand over the cool marble slab and through each of the letters of her last name, she shivered. It was beautiful.

Even her hometown was a reminder. There was no escaping Trace Corbin because her feelings for him, the impact he'd had on her life, was as much a part of her as her DNA.

She crouched down and admired the guitar etched into her daddy's headstone before she sat between his stone and her mom's.

"Bet y'all are surprised to see me." She sighed, wondering if it was possible to pour her heart and soul out until she had nothing left. It was beginning to feel like it was. "I wonder if you'd even recognize me. Sometimes I see a stranger in the mirror."

She watched a few small birds take flight in the distance. Then twirled a blade of grass around her finger as she collected her thoughts and tried to do the same with her emotions.

"I wish you were here tonight. I'd get you front-row tickets so you could finally see me living my dream. Well, our dream, Daddy."

The sound of her own voice startled her. It was hollow.

Nothing at all like the way a girl's voice should sound when talking about living her dream.

"I miss y'all so much. Floating around in the world with no family to speak of… feels like I hatched from an egg sometimes." She shook her head at her own ridiculousness. "But then I remember how I learned to play guitar. And how Daddy always said I had your eyes, Mama."

She wiped her tears from her face and leaned her cheek against he cool marble.

"They call me Nashville's Sweetheart." She let a small laughed escape her lips quietly. "Pretty crazy since being sweet was never really my thing, huh?" Tremors began to rack her body from the inside out. "I just…I just hope you're proud of me."

Using both hands to brush her hair back from her face, she stood. "I met someone. He's…well, he's kind of a mess. We both are. But together it seems like…maybe we're not so messed up. I wish y'all could meet him."

She looked down at the two stones side by side, knowing this was probably not a place she'd return to. At least not any time soon.

"I miss y'all—more than I can hardly stand most days. But I'm glad you're together now." She kissed her fingertips and touched each of their carved names before walking back to her truck.

She'd just pulled onto Main Street when she saw it. The ghost of a girl carrying a faded pink suitcase, a black guitar case strapped to her back.

She thought of warning that girl, telling her to be careful. Explaining that she might have to choose between following her heart and chasing her dreams and that sometimes she might not even get a choice either way.

But she didn't. Because that girl was going to have to learn for herself. And as Kylie drove towards the outskirts, she realized a warning wouldn't have made a bit of difference. That girl wouldn't have changed anything anyways.

"Goodbye, Pride," Kylie whispered into the wind as she drove out of town.

chapter FIFTY ONE

"I SAID I'd pay for it and I will. Claire Ann, I'm not letting this go to court if I can help it." He shook his head. "The media gets so much as a whiff of this and they will destroy her. She's my sister, she was drinking, and someone was hurt. They won't see a sweet kid who messed up. They'll make her a monster."

Trace sat in the polished mahogany-filled office that belonged to his lawyer arguing with his sister for the third day in a row. But Rae's case was finally being closed it seemed. Her friend's family had settled on an amount and it was being handled out of court.

"It's just, the girl is fine. The doctor's said she'll make a full recovery and they're taking advantage because of who you are. It's not fair, Trace."

He looked at his sister and his manager, who was also her boyfriend, as they sat there holding hands. Rusty blades of regret stabbed him deep in the chest.

"Well, fair isn't exactly the running theme in my life, in case you haven't noticed. I'll deal with it."

After he'd signed a non-disclosure agreement and a check with an astronomical figure written on it, he left the lawyer's office. Pauly and Claire Ann had asked him to come to dinner with them, but he could only handle being around people in love for so long. He really wanted to see his baby sister and check in on her physical therapy session, but she lived with his mom and that was a lady he avoided at all costs.

After Kylie had decimated her verbally, in that special Kylie Ryans way she had, the woman had actually offered him a half-ass apology. But he was past caring about that these days.

He'd worked out the things he'd needed to work out with Gretchen, so he had that going for him. But he had a meeting with Capital Letter Records in a week. He was pretty damn sure it was going to be the final 'so long, fuck you very much' from Noel Davies.

And then he'd have nothing left. Not. One. Damn. Thing.

Ripping the tie from his throat, he aimed in truck in the one direction he knew he shouldn't.

"**W**HAT can I getcha, handsome?"

He snorted. The waitress's vision must've been bad. Or she was willing to lie for a good tip. He hadn't shaved in a week. He had a trucker hat pulled low over his bloodshot eyes. He couldn't even remember the last night he'd had a decent night's sleep.

"Just club soda for now, sweetheart." He knew he'd practically snarled at her. But he wasn't in the mood for nice. He'd come into the bar after an hour of sitting outside in his truck and trying to come up with reasons not to.

When he finally worked up the nerve, he'd stepped into his own private hell. The scent of beer and bourbon and cigars had slapped him so hard in the face he'd nearly turned around and walked right back out. But an unrelenting desire propelled him forward. Need. Emptiness. A pain he could only rid himself of one of two ways.

Either Kylie Ryans in his arms, or a bottle in his hands.

Turning to his left, he saw the mirror behind the rows of liquor bottles. He caught a glimpse of his reflection and nearly threw his glass at it.

It was a strange thing to see the devil inside himself. To recognize the tormented creature that thirsted for destruction he was sure he'd chased away for good.

But that was the really screwed up part about being an alcoholic. It was a beast that lay dormant, not one that ever went away.

Everything he'd been through in his entire life twisted together in his mind, as if thrown into a blender that was set on puree.

There was no escape from it. From her.

The smell of her, the feel of her. The sweet honey-vanilla taste to her skin that matched her intoxicating scent. She was blinding shards of light in the darkness of his mind. The memory of being inside of her was cruel and vivid, even more so than any of his nightmares. Having her was like taking a hit of something that took him higher than he'd ever been. Losing her was what he imagined going cold turkey on heroin might be like.

She'd run. Grabbed her heart out of his hands and taken off just as he had when everything had gotten a little too real.

She needed space. And she'd wanted answers he didn't know how to give.

He didn't even blame her.

And he didn't know how to get her back. Gretchen had some theories, but she was the last person on the planet he planned to ask for help with Kylie Ryans.

He winced at hearing her name. And even though he hadn't even had a drop of alcohol yet, he heard her voice. Her strong, melodic voice. The one he assumed would be haunting his dreams for years to come.

"And we have the exclusive, folks. Kylie Ryans, Nashville's Sweetheart, has called off her *The Other Side of Me* tour after a final show in Oklahoma City."

"Turn that up," he hollered to the bartender, an older gentlemen who he was pretty sure owned the place.

"Keep your pants on, buddy," the old man answered as he reached for the remote.

Trace lost his breath when her beautiful face filled the screen.

"It just wasn't right. And the label is upset, and the sponsors will want to be reimbursed, and I know there will be disappointed fans. That's the hardest part, knowing I let people I care about down. But this is the right thing to do."

A perky brunette reporter shoved a microphone in her face. "Kylie, can you comment on Trace's absence from the tour? Surely canceling multiple sold-out shows warrants a bit more explanation than a family emergency. Is there any truth to the rumor that Trace is back in a rehab facility?"

Judging from the look on her face, that rumor was a new one to her. Trace wasn't surprised. He knew that would always be the one that came up from now on. He didn't have any problem being a walking punch line. But he hated himself even more for putting her through this.

"I won't comment on that," Kylie said evenly. "The fact of the matter is things in our personal lives often affect our public ones. And even though we put ourselves out there with our music, it doesn't mean that we don't deserve to be able to deal with difficult situations privately, just as anyone else has the right to. If I were a teacher or a nurse, I'd be given leave from my job to deal with a family situation if needed. This is no different. Trace needed time to be with his loved ones and he deserves that. He gives a great deal to the community and has earned the right to take a break if that's what's best for him."

Kylie slid sunglasses over her eyes and Trace caught sight of her friend Lu and her assistant Hannah stepping up on either side of her. The three of them walked to a black SUV with two security team members close behind, but the reporter clearly wasn't done grilling her.

"Yes, well, can you tell us why you aren't fulfilling your commitment to your fans by finishing this tour with Bryce Parker as planned?"

Kylie stopped and turned. Trace saw Hannah's hand come to signify that the interview was over but Kylie answered the question.

"Finishing this tour—the tour named for a song I wrote with Trace, the tour that was ours from the very beginning—with anyone other than Trace would be a joke. It would be a sad simulation of something that can't be forced or faked or copied. And I won't do that to my fans. I won't sell them a cheap imitation of a man I know to be one of the most incredible performers and musicians of our time. Not for all the money or the labels or the sponsors in the world."

Flashbulbs went off in every direction as she climbed in the vehicle and slammed the door.

When the waitress returned to ask him if he was ready for something stronger, all she found was a twenty-dollar bill and an empty chair.

chapter
FIFTY TWO

"Caught your interview on television," a familiar voice said. "Impressive. I gotta say, I didn't know you had those kind of guts."

Kylie turned as she stepped out of her apartment building and tried desperately not to glare at the woman behind her. "Clearly it's my life's goal to impress you. Guess I can die happy now."

"Don't be so dramatic." Gretchen Gibson rolled her eyes. "It was a compliment."

"Well in that case, gee, thanks." She kept walking towards the car that was waiting. She had a meeting with her band at the studio to talk about the plans for their future. Not that she really had any solid ones. But they'd been so understanding about her reasons for not wanting to finish the tour that she felt like she owed it to them to keep them in the loop.

At the last show they'd all bonded over Bryce Parker's annoying habit of talking about himself in third person and trying to bring back leather vests as if he were a hardcore biker in a motorcycle club instead of an obnoxious pretty boy with a god complex. Mostly, he was just a creep.

"Give me ten minutes," Gretchen called out. "It's about Trace. And me. There are things you need to know before you just write him off for good."

Yeah right. There were things she'd needed to know all right. And yet she always learned them just a little too late. She'd been there, done that, and had the country music break-up album to prove it.

She sighed and stopped walking. "Seriously, whatever it is, the time to tell me about it has probably passed."

Gretchen took another step to catch up before Kylie got into the car. "Look, I know he thinks that impulsive thing you do where you make big dramatic exits without stopping to hear anyone out is real cute. Me, not so much. Personally I find you immature and annoying."

Kylie's raised her brows. "Uh huh. And this is supposed to make me want to hear you out?"

The other woman threw her hands up. "I'm not going to blow smoke up your ass if that's what it takes to be heard. But I am going to tell you the whole story, the part that's mine to tell and that Trace was too much of a gentlemen to repeat without my permission."

Kylie thought it over. She missed him so much that it was a struggle to force herself through mundane daily activities. And it had only been a few days. But even Rae hadn't seen him much lately and was worried. As much as she knew it would hurt to hear Gretchen's depiction of her relationship with Trace, she figured it was better than the gaping black holes she kept falling into while wondering what was going on.

"There's a diner down the block."

Gretchen motioned for Kylie to lead the way so she did.

Once they arrived, Kylie saw the same waitress who had hit on Steven a few months ago. This was so not her day.

"Black coffee, please," she told the woman without bothering to look up.

Gretchen ordered the same and removed the jacket she was wearing. "So, as much of an honor as it is to be having coffee with Nashville's Sweetheart, I'm going to cut to the chase."

"Guess you don't read Rolling Stone magazine," Kylie muttered under her breath.

"Kylie, I can only begin to imagine what you think of me. And thankfully, I don't much care what most people think. But there is one person who I do care a lot about and he deserves someone who can cut him some slack."

She watched as Gretchen dumped about a pound of sugar in her coffee. Kylie stirred a slightly smaller amount into hers.

"I did cut him some slack, for the record. And then you showed up."

The woman sipped her coffee and nodded. "Yes, and if you hadn't run off like your panties were on fire, you might have heard what I had to say and we could've avoided all this."

Kylie ignored her drink and focused her attention on Gretchen. "For the past year, I spent day after day being bombarded by pictures and questions about you and Trace. And when I finally let myself believe that it was just a rebound thing or media hype or friendship or moral support or what the hell ever, I wake up to you. At his house. Where he swears he doesn't bring women."

Gretchen opened her mouth to respond, but Kylie wasn't done.

"And that's the thing. I feel like it's always going to be something. I throw my heart at him, because like you said, I'm immature and impulsive apparently. And he keeps tossing it back at me like a game of hot potato. So excuse me if I didn't stick around for the gory details."

Gretchen nodded again, the hint of smile playing on her lips. "Well guess what, kid? Love is one big mess of gory details. So deal with it."

Kylie eyed her warily. "Meaning?"

"We all have shit in us that we'd rather other people not be privy to. Except that one person who sees that and loves us anyways." Gretchen looked sad for a moment, a fact Kylie tried not to dwell too much on. "And for you, Trace is that person. He doesn't care how much of a pain in the ass you are. In fact, I think he likes it. For whatever reason. The part that concerns me is that you might not be that person for him. Can you handle everything that comes with him? Because I think you know by now it isn't all sunshine and rainbows."

"If he loves me so much, how come every time you called he took it in the other room? Or looked like a deer in headlights when I saw you together in Macon? If y'all are just friends, why all the secrecy, *Gretch*?"

Judging from the way her eyebrows lifted, Gretchen didn't miss Kylie's disdain for the nickname Trace called her by.

"Well, let's see. The media has made us into some alcoholic duo just because we happened to do a stint in rehab together. He knows you and

I aren't exactly friends. And he and I are about be business partner. He was trying to figure out the best way to tell you about it when I heard from a mutual friend that his sister was in an accident and decided to bring myself over to Georgia and check in. Plus I had paperwork for him to sign."

Kylie's head swam at the convoluted information Gretchen was piling on her. "But I saw the pictures. Same as the rest of the world. The two of you didn't just happen to go into rehab at the same time, you walked through that door hand in hand."

"And if we were teenagers, instead of grown adults, that might've been a big deal." Gretchen's pointed expression let Kylie know how big of a deal it wasn't. "But for your information, if you saw a picture of Trace and I holding hands, it was because at the last minute, I panicked. The fear of everyone knowing I was trying to get help, of knowing I might fail, had me retreating. Trace literally pulled me through."

"I still feel like I'm missing something. So were you and him together or not? And what in the world kind of business are you buying? Please don't say a bar or a record label."

Gretchen snorted. "No. Neither of those." The woman took a deep breath and scooted her drink aside so she could prop her elbows on the table. "In order to explain about Trace, I have to tell you some things about me that are really none of your business. So once I do, you feel free to let them slip right out of your memory. Got it?"

Kylie nodded.

She watched as the other woman took a deep breath. "Okay, so I have a son."

Kylie hands gripped the table. Her entire world began to tilt dangerously to one side. "Oh," she whispered.

"Not with Trace. Christ almighty, why does everyone assume that?" Gretchen shook her head. "Anyways. Once upon a time, I was very young and naïve. I met a traveling musician who promised to help me get out of my backwater hometown in South Carolina. He turned out to be a dirtbag and left me pregnant and broke."

Kylie's mouth was dry, and she wished she'd ordered water or straight vodka instead of coffee. "Um, I'm sorry to hear that?"

"Sure, that's an acceptable response." Gretchen continued. "Anyways, I wasn't ready to be a mother. I couldn't even make decent decisions for myself. So my mom agreed to raise my son so I could pursue the one thing I loved."

"Music," Kylie offered softly, thinking they had that in common.

"No," Gretchen said evenly. "Partying. Clubs, musicians, DJs, whatever. I was never like you and Trace. Music was never my be-all and end-all. I was a complete fucking mess with no real ambition."

Or maybe not.

"Classy."

"Yeah, well. I was eighteen and stupid. And then I stumbled into a band one of my loser boyfriends was in with Trace. Even in my stupidity, I knew a decent guy when I saw one. So I tried to ditch my boyfriend and hook up with him, and you can imagine how well that ended."

Kylie tried not to make her internal cringing obvious. She must not have succeeded because Gretchen actually appeared sympathetic for a moment.

"Relax. It was one time, and we were both too drunk to remember. But it was enough to get me kicked out of the band. So I went home."

Where you should've stayed, Kylie thought but didn't say out loud.

"And my mom and Danny—that's my son—had this bond. I felt like this giant third wheel that was just in the way. So I came back to Nashville and threw everything I had into music. I gambled on it, hoping my tiny bit of talent and originality would be enough."

Her mouth turned down in a way that actually made Kylie feel sorry for her.

"I just wanted to be someone my son could be proud of, you know?"

The tears gathering in Gretchen's eyes struck a chord in Kylie's compassion center.

"As someone with two dead parents who would give it all up in a heartbeat to have them back, I can honestly say, I bet your son doesn't care if you're a musician or famous or whatever. My mom was a secretary and my daddy worked in a factory. I don't remember my mom, but I thought my daddy was the most amazing person in the whole wide world. All your son probably cares about is that you're there, that you're his mom."

Gretchen nodded and a few tears leaked from her eyes. She wiped them as quickly as they'd fallen. "Anyways, I didn't ask you here to throw me a pity party. My mistakes are mine and I own them."

"So why did you ask me here?" Kylie sucked in a breath and held it.

"Because I want you to know what's going on with Trace. I think he needs you. And while the old me couldn't really give a shit, the new me, the me who really does want to see him happy, doesn't want to get in the way of that."

"So..."

"So I'm going to tell you something I shouldn't. Something Trace said during a group session in rehab that stuck with me."

Kylie didn't interrupt to mention that Gretchen had said that he'd kept her secrets but now she was revealing his. Because whatever she was about to tell her seemed important. And dammit, she wanted to know.

"We had this exercise we were supposed to do—describe our happy place—the one place where we were never tempted to drink." Gretchen offered Kylie a small smile. "We were supposed to describe it in vivid detail for the group so that if any one of was tempted we could help each other by reminding them of that place, that place where they felt true happiness and didn't want to drink."

"Okay." Kylie's brows dipped as she tried to figure out how this was relevant.

"For most of us, it was a place from our childhood. Not for Trace."

A fist clenched Kylie's heart. No, his childhood didn't contain many happy memories that she knew of.

"For him, the time he was happiest, the one time in his life he never felt temptation to drink…It was being in Macon…with you." Gretchen paused. "I'll give you a minute to let that sink in."

And sink in it did. Kylie just sat there, speechless for one of the first times in her life.

"He described this day, this long afternoon, of just horsing around with you on the farm. He said he fell in love with you that day. We all kind of figured more happened than he'd described. But from the way he looked, lit up and happy in a way I'd never seen him, the falling in love was the most important part."

A tiny sound of surprise escaped Kylie's lips.

"I'm guessing this is a lot to for you to hear all at once. But there's more. You okay?"

Kylie nodded and struggled to suck up the outpouring emotions threatening to escape. "I'm trying to be. Go ahead."

"The facility in Dallas…It was struggling. It's this sprawling, well-hidden place that could seriously be like *the* rehab place for people in need of privacy, like celebrities and such, if it had the funding needed."

"So he bought it," Kylie finished for her. Of course he had. He was always trying to save everything and everyone. Except himself.

"Sort of. He and I agreed to go in half, like silent investors. There's a Board of Directors already in place, so we would literally be just money and maybe do a few figurehead-type things. Kind of like with his A Hand Up Foundation."

"I see." So Trace and Gretchen were going to be business partners. That was major, but not as major as she thought.

"I know what you think—how it looks. But for the record, he didn't leave you for me, and he and I haven't ever been an item like the media makes it seem."

"Why do I feel like there's a *but* coming."

Gretchen was quiet, just long enough for Kylie to feel a panic attack coming on. "There was this one night, your birthday, actually. We had a fight because he said he had to see you and I told him he wasn't ready for that. That he hadn't been sober long enough to go dealing with your unstable ass. But it was your birthday, so he was determined to do something nice, like show up with flowers or take you to dinner so the two of you could talk."

"Oh God," Kylie's heart sank like a heavy stone into her empty stomach.

"Yeah. Turns out you'd moved on. When he came back to my place—"

"No. No I don't tell me." Kylie closed her eyes and shook her head. "I don't need to know."

She didn't. It didn't matter. If he'd turned to Gretchen for comfort that night, well, so be it. She'd have to find a way to deal with it.

"We didn't sleep together, if that's what you're thinking. But I offered. He turned me down, Kylie." Gretchen shrugged. "And not for some noble reason like he didn't want to hurt our friendship. He turned me down because he said he'd tried. He'd almost taken some waitress home after leaving your place, but all he could see was you. All he wanted was you."

"So he went back to rehab?" Kylie had never gotten a chance to ask Trace why he hadn't shown up at the party the label had thrown for their single. The rumor mill had answered the question for her and she'd assumed they were right.

"No. He went to Dallas and got everything in order so we could do the deal with the facility. The Second Chance Ranch we're calling it."

"Catchy," Kylie said absently, still attempting to put the pieces together.

"Yeah, we think so. He's funding this huge redesign to make it as similar to his farm in Macon. Because that's the one place he doesn't want to drink."

"Because of me," Kylie said softly.

The other woman nodded once. "Look, I told you I wasn't going to blow smoke up your skirt and I didn't. I won't sit here and tell you life with him will be easy or even the best thing for either of you. Because who the hell am I to give anyone life advice?" Gretchen put her jacket back on. "But I'll be damned if I'm going to be anyone's excuse. So if you don't want to be with him, then don't. But don't try to pin it on me, because given the choice between me and you, Trace would step over my cold, dead body without blinking."

Kylie frowned. "I don't always make the best decisions in the spur of the moment. Especially when thrown into situations I'm not prepared for, I'll admit that. But I'm not as completely vacant as you seem to think. I could tell pretty early into the tour that the two of you weren't together *together*. That's not why I left Macon when you showed up."

Gretchen raised her eyebrows. "Okay, I'll bite. Why did you?"

Kylie felt her forehead wrinkling as she tried to explain. "Because… because seeing the two of you made me realize that you have something with him that I never will. You understand about his drinking and you're the one who he turns to in a crisis or when he needs help."

"So? You gonna take up drinking so you can room together in rehab?"

Kylie's eyes narrowed. "No. But I'm not going to stick around and wait for him to ask you what you think about he and I being together just so you can tell him to toss me out with the garbage either." She sucked her bottom lip in so it wouldn't give her pain away. "He told me himself that he respects you and values your opinion. And you've made your opinion of me pretty damn clear."

Gretchen surprised her by laughing. "Seriously? That's why you left? Why you're making him give you space or what the hell ever?"

Does he tell her everything?

Kylie shrugged. "For the most part. Yeah."

"Well in that case, I have good news."

Kylie eyed her skeptically, wondering what good news she could possibly have. "Oh yeah? What's that?"

"The truth is, even if I tell him to stay as far from you as humanly possible for the sake of his sobriety, he's not going to listen."

"How do you know?"

Gretchen's eyes left hers and for a split-second she looked slightly ashamed of herself.

"Because that's what I've been doing pretty much every time I've talked to him. I've been a pretty shitty friend to him actually. Telling him that he was a screw-up that couldn't handle being with you because you're young and childish and more than he can handle."

Kylie felt her eyes widen at the grand confession from Gretchen Gibson. She cleared her throat. "Okay. So what changed your mind?"

Gretchen met her imploring stare. "Seeing your interview, and the fact that you basically told the label to fucking deal with it because they can't switch Trace out with a dipshit like Parker and expect you to play along. Hearing you say those things about Trace—that you clearly believe to be true—I realized that I might have been wrong about you."

"I love him," Kylie said evenly. "Of course I believe those things to be true."

"Well, good." Gretchen finished off her coffee and moved her cup to the side. "Look, I'm not here for entirely unselfish reasons. This business deal is the one good thing I have in my life—the one thing I'm hoping will allow me to provide for my son myself. But if you can't handle Trace being involved with me like that, I'm sure he'll say to hell with it if you say the word."

"I wouldn't do that," Kylie assured her.

"I know you and I aren't going to be shopping buddies any time soon, and I won't lie and pretend I think you're necessarily what's best for Trace. But I'll keep my opinion to myself and I'll respect that the two of you are together. I really do care about the rehab facility. That place may have stopped Trace from destroying his life, but it's what kept me from *ending* mine."

Kylie struggled to swallow. She'd never really thought about how bad off Gretchen might've been. She'd been busy hating her.

As the both stood to leave, Gretchen pulled out her wallet and Kylie shook her head and slid several bills onto the table.

"Hey, Gretchen?"

"Yeah?"

"For what it's worth, I hope the investment deal works out for you. For you and Trace both. But even if it doesn't, I bet your son won't think any less of you."

The bell overhead chimed as they exited the diner. The woman smiled at her with gratitude in her eyes.

"Good luck to you, Kylie. I guess if you decide to work things out with Trace then I'll be seeing you around."

"Thanks."

Kylie watched the woman—who'd been the bane of her existence for the past year—walk off in the other direction. She knew she couldn't hear her, but the words came out anyways.

"See you around, Gretchen."

chapter
FIFTY
THREE

"Does one really need to wear a tie for a meeting in which one is getting dropped from one's record label?"

Claire Ann adjusted the knot at his throat. "You don't know that they're dropping you."

"I haven't finished either of my last two tours. I'm pretty much a lost cause. They'd be stupid not to drop me."

His sister met his eyes with her determined stare. "You could tell them, you know. You could get Mr. Ludlow to make them all sign something saying no one would leak anything to the press. Trace, if you just explained what happened—"

"No." He shook himself loose of her grasp. "I've seen what happens when the sharks smell blood in the water. I won't risk that where Rae is concerned and I don't trust anyone there anyway."

His sister sighed. "Well then, you're better off without them. I'll tell Pauly and Maude to start putting feelers out with other labels."

Trace gave her a one-arm hug. "Thank you. But I think it's time I handled these things myself. You have your own life, Claire Bear. I appreciate how much you do for me, but it's time to be a big boy now."

She nudged him. "You know I never minded."

"I know. And that's why I love you."

"Speaking of love," his sister began. "Have you talked to her?"

Trace scrubbed a hand roughly over his face. "I want to. I'm just trying to figure out what I should say."

"Rae thinks you should lead with, 'Will you marry me and have my babies?'"

Trace laughed. "What do you think I should lead with?"

His sister straightened his tie once more and placed her hands on his broad shoulders as her steady gaze met his.

"Your heart."

TRACE walked into the offices of Capital Letter Records for what he knew was probably the last time.

Somewhere in the dark recesses of his mind, he held a very faded, slightly blurred memory of the first time he'd walked through those doors. He'd thought his dreams were finally coming true.

It had been a hell of a lot more complicated than his twenty-year-old self had been ready for.

But his twenty-eight-year-old self had both feet in the real world. This was a day for saying goodbye.

"So Davies is here already and so are several members of the legal team," Pauly informed him as they waited for his agent in the reception area. "They're bringing in the big guns, so I just want you to be ready for anything."

"I am," Trace informed him. "It's okay, Pauly. I've made my decision. I know they're most likely going to drop the ax or give me some ridiculous ultimatum so I end up looking like the bad guy. They can bring it on. I'm ready for anything."

The elevator opened and Kylie Ryans stepped out of it with their agent. Hannah was there too, but all Trace really saw was her.

She wore a short black business-style dress with a zipper in the front that screamed *unzip me* and Trace lost his center of gravity. The fuck-me heels she had on weren't helping matters any either.

"Ready for anything except that, I'm guessing," Pauly muttered from beside him.

"What's she doing here?"

Maude approached them first. "I'm starting to think the label's experiencing budget cuts. Looks like they're going for a two-for-one special with the two of you. Your meeting is scheduled for the same time."

Kylie's face displayed her surprise clearly. Apparently Maude hadn't told her this ahead of time. Sometimes he thought the old woman was going senile and sometimes he suspected she was just screwing with them for her own amusement.

"Well, I guess we'll find out soon enough." He did his best to sound nonchalant, but the truth was, his heart was pounding, his tie was choking this shit out of him, and his dick was twitching in Kylie's direction with a vengeance. Damn that dress.

He felt sweat drip down his back as she approached him.

"Hey, um, can we talk?"

He wasn't sure. He stepped away from the group and she followed.

"We can try, darlin'. Though last I heard I was supposed to be giving you space."

She frowned, and he clenched his fists so his fingers wouldn't reach out and smooth those lines in her forehead. He was pretty sure touching her face didn't constitute space giving.

"Not about us," she whispered. "That we can discuss…later. But right now, here, I'm worried."

Now it was his turn to frown. "Kylie, your debut album sold more copies than most of the other artists at this label combined. You have nothing to worry about."

She rolled her eyes like he was some kind of moron. "I'm worried about you. I think they're going to try and dissolve your contract, Trace. You've got to tell them about Rae's accident. Or I will."

There was literally not another female on the planet that drove him as crazy as this one. Naturally, he had to go and fall in love with her too.

"Like hell you will. Listen to me," he said, lowering his voice to a cross between a whisper and a warning. "I told you about this. I vowed to protect Rae when we were kids and I failed back then. But this time I won't let her down. She will get to recover in peace and without the vultures surrounding her and turning her into something she's not."

She huffed out a breath. He half-expected her to stomp her foot.

"Now you listen to me. I know Rae wouldn't want you to do this. You've worked so hard, Trace, and you don't deserve this. Just tell them the truth." She shook her head and pinned him with those wide blue eyes of hers. "I used to think you were a selfish jackass, and now I know you're just a jackass. All the stuff I thought was selfish was just you punishing yourself for everyone else's mistakes." She stepped even closer to him, making his head swim from her intoxicating scent. "So…how about you fucking quit that now?"

He forced himself to focus the best he could and ignore the urge to grab her to him like a damn animal. "I'll work on it. But this isn't up to you. And if you care about Rae at all—or hell, if you care about me at all—you won't say a word about either of us in there."

"Trace," she pleaded, her eyes growing wider as she looked up at him. "Sometimes you have to choose yourself. Sometimes you need to do what's best for you."

He stared at her for a moment. Part of him understood where she was coming from and part of him knew she'd never had any siblings. Never had anyone she'd felt responsible for.

"And sometimes you have to choose love, Kylie Lou. Even when it isn't the smart choice, or even the best one for all involved parties."

Before she could argue with him any more, a receptionist called for them.

"Here we go, kiddos," Maude said as the doors to the conference room opened.

chapter FIFTY FOUR

KYLIE watched Trace take his seat next to Pauly across from her. He steepled his fingers below his chin and her stomach twisted.

Sometimes you have to choose love.

She agreed. And she loved him enough to see what he was doing today was a mistake.

"Well look what we have here. So the two of you *can* actually show up for scheduled appointments?" Noel Davie paused to glare at each of them. "Good to know. I was beginning to wonder."

"Neither of them have ever missed an appointment with the label," Maude objected.

"Right. It's just performances they can't seem to make it to," Davies clarified.

Kylie glared right back at him. This man made her want to stick her tongue out at him. Right before giving him a solid knee to the crotch. Lulu would've threatened to junk-punch him for sure.

"Do they have detention after school, Mr. Davies? Or is there an actual point to this meeting?"

Sometimes Kylie wasn't sure about Maude Lowenstein. And sometimes she kind of loved her.

"Oh there's a point. Several, actually." He smiled at the members of the table, though to her it felt more like a baring of teeth. "First, there's the matter of revenue lost by the canceled shows and refunded tickets."

The room remained silent.

"For which each artist will be billed individually. They will split the cost of vendor fees, refunded tickets, sponsor—"

"Just put it on my tab, Davies," Trace broke in. "None of it had anything to do with her."

"Oh, but it did," the man countered. "And, Miss Ryans, in the future, if you decide to publically refer to any Capital Letter recording artist as a cheap imitation of another, please know you are opening yourself up to a lawsuit from not only that artist but from the label as well."

She lowered her eyes briefly. She'd known better, but Bryce Parker was repulsive swine. He'd met her at the show in Oklahoma, joining the tour as Trace's replacement, and he'd made more than one inappropriate comment to her on the bus and a few in front of her band, which had almost let to a brawl. Ending the tour then and there hadn't been a tough decision to make.

She squared her shoulders. "Well, Mr. Davies, in the future, if any of your other artists invite me to ride their face or their dick home instead of the tour bus, please know they are opening themselves up for me to bury my knee in their balls. And I'm sure my attorney would love to discuss a possible sexual harassment lawsuit against the label for forcing such a disgusting scumbag on me without my prior consent."

Maude snickered from beside her but Trace was livid.

"He said what to you?" All other members of the room disappeared as Trace's blazing glare burned into her.

She waved a hand and shook her head. "It's handled."

"My ass it's handled. Unless you actually did bury your knee in his balls."

Kylie shot a pleading look at Pauly. He said something low in Trace's ear that seemed to calm him for the moment.

Davies actually looked mildly flustered. As did some of the suits sitting beside him. "Well, if that is true about Mr. Parker's behavior, then we can schedule a meeting to discuss that in the future."

"I won't be discussing anything with or about Bryce Parker in the future. You can add that little stipulation to my contract."

She met the man's beady eyes, challenging him to argue. Which, thankfully, he didn't. He looked down at the papers on his desk and shuffled them a little.

"Moving on. In addition to the financial concerns, there is the issue of legality and bankability. The two of you certainly aren't in high demand where venues are concerned at the moment."

Davies continued to drop legal mumbo jumbo on them for the next several minutes.

Apparently Maude had better places to be, because she was the one to finally call him on his bullshit.

"So what's the endgame here? Do we schedule another tour or ground them or what? Frankly, Noel, I feel like you brought them here to berate them for something that none of us really knows much about. Obviously some type of personal emergency arose that they both felt they had to deal with and prevented the last leg of the tour from being completed successfully. What's done is done."

She leaned back in her chair as she waited. Kylie, on the other hand, was on the edge of her seat. Not so much for herself as for Trace.

Noel Davies smirked at the woman. "Sorry. My apologies if the words I was using were too big for your clients."

"You're a condescending prick, Davies." Trace shook his head. "And clearly one who is enjoying this far more than he should. Kylie and I have both made this label a great deal of money. But all the money in the world won't change the fact that you're a smug little shit who wouldn't have this label if it weren't for artists like us. And yet, you refuse to treat us like actual people."

"You done? Because as far as I'm concerned, you are. The final decision from the Board was release your greatest hits album or dissolve your contract due to multiple breeches. Which one sounds better to you?"

Kylie winced. A greatest hits album was the first nail in the coffin. Or for some, ones much older than Trace, a necessary step towards retirement. Trace's career was nowhere near that point.

"You'll release my greatest hits over my dead body," Trace said evenly, his tone laced with a valid threat.

"Well then, you can sign your dissolution papers on the seventh floor in Legal. I'm sure you can find the door. Feel free to let yourself out."

Kylie nearly fell out of her chair. That was it? No chance to explain? No other options? Just like that?

"No, wait." She couldn't help it. Serious artist or not, she was still that girl who had to say her piece. She stood up to try and stop him from leaving. "Trace, tell him. Tell him about—"

"Kylie, I swear to god, if you say another word—"

"You can't just leave. You can't let them do this."

She watched him look from her to Davies and back again. "Looks like they already did. Enjoy the rest of your meeting."

"You're welcome to follow him, Miss Ryans," Noel Davies informed her. "You seem to have a habit of doing that. Just know that if you walk out of this meeting, you're as finished with this label as he is."

"Stay put, Kylie," Trace commanded on his way to the exit. Before he left with Pauly close behind him, he placed a hand on the door and turned. "Hey, Davies?"

"Yes, Mr. Corbin?" He sighed as if Trace had been nothing more than a giant waste of his time instead of one of the label's bestselling artists.

Trace smirked at him and Kylie dropped into her seat, feeling helpless as the drama unfolded.

"The next time I hear of anyone even affiliated with this label making any kind of lewd or unwarranted sexual comments towards her, you can rest assured, I will find the door. The front door to your house. Hope none of those words were too big for you. Have a good day."

With that, he left and the door closed behind him. For a moment, she was rooted where she sat.

What in the hell just happened here?

She pressed her hands to her temples. This was so wrong for so many reasons.

Noel Davies must not have felt the same way. "Now that that's all taken care of, where were we?"

chapter FIFTY FIVE

"Well, that went about as awful as expected." Pauly patted Trace firmly on the back. "You okay?"

Trace cleared his throat and loosened his tie. "Yeah. I am actually."

"Maude and I were talking and we think there are several other labels that would be—"

The sound of the conference room door opening behind them cut him off. Trace half-expected it to be one of Davies's security minions coming to escort him out. He sighed and turned to check.

"Hey," she called out to him. Kylie stood there, looking at him as if she hadn't just walked out on a meeting that could end her career. Or at least seriously tarnish it.

"Hey yourself. Get your ass back in there before Davies—"

"You bought my house," she said quietly.

Trace tilted his head to the side. "Yeah. I did. It's yours if you want it. I just figured you weren't using it so—"

"Marlena and Isabelle are lovely. I'm glad they live in it."

girl in love

"Well, I'm happy to hear that. Look, Kylie, we can talk about all of this later. You need to get back in there. Now."

His mouth gaped open as she closed the door behind her.

She took a step towards him. "No."

"I'll give you two a minute," Pauly said from beside him. Trace couldn't look away from her long enough to thank him.

Her eyes were flashing into his and every moment they'd ever spent together was playing behind his. God, he loved her so fucking much. And still wanted her so damn bad. But not bad enough to cost her everything she'd worked for.

"Have you lost your mind?"

She bit her lip and his gaze dropped to her perfect mouth. "Maybe. Have you seen it? Pretty sure I left it with you."

He grinned, recognizing the line he'd used on her before. She remembered. "Kylie, you can't just—"

"Yes, I can." Her face spread into a wide grin. "See, I have this habit of feeling first and thinking second. It's kind of my thing."

"Kylie—"

He had no idea what his argument was going to be, but it didn't matter because she ran full speed and jumped into his arms before he could make it.

Her mouth met his, and he felt every single emotion she was pouring into that kiss. Happiness, pain, forgiveness.

"What are you doing, crazy girl?" he asked once she'd pulled back to catch her breath.

"Choosing love," she said, resting her forehead against his. "You okay with that?"

Trace watched her in wonder. He wished someone would pinch him. Or punch him. Something to let him know this was real. That she'd really chosen him, chosen what they had over everything else.

"See, this guy I know, this really stubborn guy, reminded me that sometimes you have to choose love." She kissed him once more as he maneuvered them out of the pathway where people were trying to get to the elevators. "I lost myself for a while," she choked out. "But then I went home and I found myself."

"Home as in Oklahoma?" He wondered if his heart could actually beat out of his chest. Felt like it was a definite possibility at the moment.

314

"Yeah. But when I got there, it was the damnedest thing. It wasn't my home anymore. My home is here."

"In Nashville?" Trace asked, setting her down carefully so he didn't give any other motherfuckers a glimpse at what was under her short skirt.

She shook her head, confusing him momentarily. "With you. You're my home."

"You came back to me."

Her beautiful blue eyes filled with tears even though she was smiling. "I told you. I'll always come back."

"Let's get the hell out of here. They can fax our paperwork to Maude's office." Trace kissed her sweet, eager mouth once more. A deep, lingering kiss that made him need her so badly it hurt. "My place or yours, Kylie Lou?"

She squeezed him so tight it was difficult to walk.

He held on for dear life, knowing that this time, no matter what they faced, neither of them would let go.

"Take me home, Trace."

chapter FIFTY SIX

"**C**AN I open my eyes yet?"

"No, not yet."

His warm breath tickled her ear and Kylie shivered. "Trace, are we in a bar?"

The vibration of his dark laughter rattled her a little. "Relax, it's not even open right now. No one's going to be drinking."

They took several more steps before he removed his hand from her eyes. It took a few seconds for her to adjust to the darkness in The Rum Room. The stage was the only thing with any real light on it. The lights around the island bar in the middle of the room were too dim to be of much help.

She turned in his arms. "What's going on? How did we get in here?"

Trace shrugged. "Eh, I know the owner." He winked and led her over to the middle of the dance floor. "I believe I owe you a dance."

Kylie heard the shuffle of instruments being moved on stage, but she couldn't look away from the man wrapping her in his arms.

A song began to play, one that she had both loved and hated at one time or another.

"Dance with me?" Trace held his hand out and waited for her to accept.

Kylie's eyes filled with tears. She nodded and stepped forward as a singer she recognized as a regular at The Rum Room's open mic night began singing about a woman who loved him unconditionally like Jesus did. He was the same one who'd been singing the night Trace had walked away from her two years ago.

Her own heart faltered in her chest as she listened to his strong, steady one.

"Trace," she whispered, looking up at him as they swayed. "Please tell me you didn't bring me here to tell me you're going back into rehab and I'm not allowed to wait for you."

The last year of her life had been amazing. They'd lived together on his farm in Georgia, had written an album full of songs, while offers poured in from record labels and television networks.

Things were going so well…it was almost too good to be true.

Her entire body tensed as she waited for him to answer.

He swallowed hard and stared down at her.

"No, baby. I brought you here because I needed a do-over. I wanted to do this right."

Her gaze lifted warily as he kissed her on the forehead.

"I brought you here because you changed my life forever in this room. And then I hurt you here, and I want to fix that. That look you get, that panic-stricken fear that fills your eyes sometimes… It kills me."

"Trace, I just… I love you so much, and the thought of—"

"Breathe, pretty girl." He winked and smiled at her, that slow, intense grin she knew he only gave to her.

She nodded and forced the best smile she could. "Sorry. Didn't mean to freak out."

"It's okay." He spun her in a circle and dipped her Hollywood movie-style until she giggled. "There. That's better."

She shook her head. "So, um, you gonna tell me what we're doing here?"

The song ended and silence surrounded them. Her skin prickled as she focused on breathing normally. Trace's eyes were so bright in the glare from the lights of the stage that he appeared possessed by something ethereal.

"We're here because you believed in me when I didn't believe in myself." His voice was thick with emotion. "You loved me when…God." He paused to run a hand through his dark hair. "When I couldn't stand the sight of myself."

"Trace," Kylie said gently. She reached for him, but he backed up and her heart seized in her chest.

"I need to say this. All of it. I need you to hear me."

She swallowed the lump in her throat and nodded. "Okay."

"Seeing you up on that stage that first night, hearing my song, your way…" He took a deep breath. "You brought my world into focus. The mess, the pain. You made me see the things I'd try to blur out, to drink away."

She wiped the tears that had begun to fall as he continued.

"You said you were broken, Kylie. That I made you feel alive… But you really did bring me back to life that night. Seeing you on stage, lit up and so in love with music, with the gift of it changed me."

He let out a small laugh. "And you scared me to death. Because with that beautiful, amazing girl damn near glowing on stage next to me, my every weakness came to light."

"You were never weak," she whispered.

"Yeah I was." He reached out and wiped a tear that had fallen to her lips. "But you loving me, believing in me, having the kind of faith in me that no one had ever had… It gave me the strength to get help. You thought I was better than I was, so I wanted to be that for you."

"I will always love you, Trace. No matter what. Whatever you brought me here to tell me, it's okay. We'll be okay." She pressed her lips to his and drank in his warmth.

"I hope so," he said when their kiss ended. He smiled but she knew it was strained.

Sometimes she could read him so well, could recognize when he was nervous, bluffing at poker, or excited. But in that moment, she had no idea what was going on with him. And it was a terrifying feeling.

"There isn't anything I wouldn't give to make you see how much I love you…to take that fear away. That look you get, the one you have right now, the one that tells me you're still afraid I'm going to cut and run—"

"It's just… In my life, when things seem too good to be true, they usually are." She sniffled in an attempt to keep from full-out crying.

He nodded. She wasn't sure if it was the lights or if his own eyes were beginning to fill with tears.

"Not anymore, baby." He took her hands in both of hers. "I can't promise to be perfect, and I can't promise to never need help for my drinking again. But I can promise that I will never walk away from you. From us. Ever."

He sucked in an audible breath.

"Trace. Please. Just tell me. Whatever is going on, please tell me before I combust."

"Okay, so…you know that song I wrote for you?"

He brought me here to talk about a song?

"Yeah," she said slowly, side-eying him as he walked towards the stage.

"Well I changed a verse a little and I'm thinking it works better in acoustic. But before I record it, I wanted to make sure the new verse was okay with you." He stepped over to the now empty stage and picked up the guitar leaning against the stood. "Promise you'll tell me the truth?"

"Promise," she answered, leaning against the bar and shaking her head. He never stopped surprising her. And she was still a Trace Corbin fangirl. "Let's hear it."

"All right. Here goes." Trace strummed a few chords and cleared his throat.

There's a girl from Oklahoma that I can't get out of my head. Can't seem to get her back in my arms so I put her in a song instead. She's wild like the prairie wind that blows fast across the plains. She's sweet like the morning sun risin' slow after a night of rain. And I did everything I could do to push her away. But if ever there was someone ever made for someone, that girl was made for me.

Her face broke into a broad smile. The first time she'd heard that song, she'd wanted to murder him. But now she could hear it for what it was. His way of telling her just how much he loved her.

She hopped up on a barstool as he continued.

They say I have a wild streak, a fire burning in me. A fightin' side, too much damn pride. No one else could ever tame me, boy they've damn sure tried. She's water to my fire, a lover to my fighter, and she cuts me down to size. There's not another one like her. Man I gotta find her. Cause if ever there was someone ever made for someone, that girl was made for me.

She tapped her foot along to the beat as he repeated the chorus. So far she couldn't tell which verse he'd changed. But when he looked up and his fiery gaze met hers, she knew it must be coming. Suddenly he stopped playing the guitar and sang his lyrics a cappella.

There's not a thing I wouldn't give to hold her. To say the things I should have told her. So if you see my Oklahoma girl, I hope you'll let her know. There's a Georgia boy wants to marry her and he'll never let her go.

Her face went instantly numb as all the blood drained to her toes. She clutched the barstool and tried to stand, but the floor gave way beneath her feet as she lost the ability to swallow. Or think a complete coherent thought.

He stepped off stage and kneeled before her. "So what do you think? Will you marry me, Kylie Lou?"

The entire scene blurred through her tears. She couldn't even see the ring he held clearly. Just something shiny—and possibly guitar-shaped—reflecting light in a dark box.

She covered her mouth to keep from crying out in shock. It muffled her whispered "Yes." She nodded as hard as she could. So that he would know what she'd known for so long.

He was made for her. And she was made for him.

"Yes?" he practically shouted in the quiet as he stood up.

"Yes," she confirming, throwing her arms around his neck and breathing him in. "God, yes."

The bar remained quiet except for their professions of love and mutual happiness as he slipped the ring on her trembling finger.

"Oh my gosh," she began, grinning at him as he watched her with his love-filled gaze. "How am I going to write all those songs about heartbreak now that I'm so damn happy?"

Trace grinned, showing her his dimples and the mischievous gleam in his eyes. "Oh, don't worry, darlin'. I'm sure I'll still piss you off plenty." He winked before kissing her again.

"You know," Kylie began in a whisper between kisses. "I seem to remember you telling me once that you weren't the kind of guy to take me on dates, write me love songs, serenade me in public, and send me flowers. I think you might've been wrong about that, Mr. Corbin."

Trace laughed and shook his head. "Actually, I was going to do this in front of a live audience, but I remembered how much you didn't love that last time. I'm learning." He pulled her into his arms and she laughed along with him.

"I think I might've been wrong, too," Kylie said as they swayed to music only they could hear.

"Oh yeah? What about, babe?"

She looked up and smiled into his eyes. "I told you once that you weren't all that damned special." She placed a chaste kiss on his mouth and let her forehead rest on his. "You are very special. So damned special."

Trace wiped the tears that fell from her eyes. "Well, Kylie Ryans. If I didn't know better, I'd think you were starting to like me."

She grinned at her future husband. "More like love you."

He made a big show of exhaling. "Thank God, because Rae and Claire Ann are already planning the wedding."

They couldn't seem to let go of each other from that moment forward. Kylie's arms were still wrapped around his waist as they locked up and left the bar.

"You know, to some people, this probably looks like the end. Like we finally got our happily ever after."

Trace's bright hazel eyes sparkled down into hers as they stepped out into the city lights. "And what does it look like to you, Kylie Lou?"

She kissed him once more as he held the truck door open for her.

"The beginning."

Epilogue
A Note from Kylie Ryans

IF anyone ever would've told me that I'd love another man more than I loved my daddy or Trace Corbin, I would've told them they were crazy. While laughing in their face.

And yet, as I wait in line to de-board the plane from London back home, anticipation builds in my chest and I know in that moment that the I love the guy waiting for me more than I have ever loved anyone in my entire life. My entire life changed the day I met him. In ways I never could've imagined.

I can barely concentrate on lugging my giant carry-on bag through customs. All I can see in my mind are his bright blue-green eyes and his headful of messy dark curls. I can already picture how wide his smile will be when he sees me.

I'm beginning to think it's true what they say about absence making the heart grow fonder.

I tour a lot less now, since I'm no longer a solo act but part of a group. After a few years of doing our own thing, Mia Montgomery, Lily Taite, and I decided to start a band We just finished our second world tour and Backwoods Belles is currently one of the hottest bands in the country.

But we're about to take a much-needed break. Which I think the love of my life will be thrilled to hear. No matter how little I tour, being apart is still hard on both of us.

But my touring schedule is about to take a significant break. I've got big news. And I know the man in my life is going to be ecstatic about it. At least, I hope he is.

The people in front of me are trudging along slowly and I want to plow them down. I check my phone for the tenth time since turning it off airplane mode. His handsome face is the background on my screen, and seeing it just makes me even more anxious.

The lady in customs at the small private airport looks miserable until she checks my passport. She smiles and asks politely for my autograph for her niece, which of course I give her.

It will never stop blowing my mind that people want my name on a piece of paper. Life is an amazing and strange experience sometimes.

I'm practically jogging to baggage claim where I know he's waiting for me. A few people give me strange looks but I couldn't care less.

Through the crowd I see him and I know that he sees me in that same instant. His bright smile greets me, and I drop my carry-on bag and run.

So does he.

"Mommy!" He squeals as I lift him off the ground and spin him in a circle. "I missed you this much." He throws his arms out as wide as they'll go.

"Well I missed you even more than that," I tell him, choking back tears. It feels like he's grown so much in the six weeks I've been gone. Once I've covered his entire face with kisses, I glance over at my husband. "I missed you too, babe."

He places a chaste but firm kiss on my lips before moving his mouth back to my ear. "Missed you too, Kylie Lou. I'll show you how much… later."

I have to stifle a shiver and set our son down gently.

Trace takes my bag from where I left it and gives me a warning glance when he realizes how much stuff I've crammed in it. "Uh, babe, you probably shouldn't be carrying such heavy stuff since—"

I cut him off with a look because we haven't told Bo he's going to be a big brother yet.

Robert Michael Corbin—Bo, as we call him—reaches out his tiny toddler arm. "I can carry it, Daddy."

"I know you can, big man. But how about you let me carry it so you can hold Mommy's hand on the way to the truck? Make sure she gets in safe?"

Once we've made it to the truck and both my boys have made sure I'm strapped in, Trace buckles Bo in his carseat. They spend the entire ride to our farm in Macon filling me in on every minute I missed while I was away.

Most of it I already know since we video chat every morning and every night before bed, but I could listen to both of their sweet voices forever. God, I missed them.

"Babe, you sure you're up for company?" Trace asks me once we're home.

"It's Thanksgiving," I tell him, confused as to why he thinks I wouldn't want company.

"I know." He kisses me on the head once more before carrying my bags inside. "But you've got to be tired with the traveling and, uh, Bo's present that you've been carrying around all this time."

A smile spreads across my face when we walk into our home. *Our home.* There aren't words to describe what an amazing feeling it is to finally come home where I'm loved and safe and whole. I can't wait to see my son's reaction when he learns he's going to be a big brother.

But it will have to wait, because there are a dozen people coming over for dinner.

"You're sure you defrosted the turkeys and made plenty of stuffing?"

Trace smirks at me. "I think we've established who the cook is in this family."

He's being a smartass, but the word *family* hits me and I tear up again. He misunderstands.

"Aww baby, I was kidding. You cook just fine. Who needs anything other than Pop-Tarts and spaghetti anyways?"

I shove him when he comes in for another kiss. "You're an idiot."

"Yep, and I'm your idiot. Congratulations." He kisses me despite my protests, biting my bottom lip hard enough to remind me how much I've missed him.

"Mmm. So how much time do we have before everyone gets here?" Before he can answer, my phone vibrates with a text.

Be there in a few. Did you tell him yet?

Mia. And I'm pretty sure she isn't asking about whether or not we've told Bo about the baby.

"Not much time. Less than an hour probably," Trace answers.

Bo climbs in my lap and looks at my phone curiously while Trace checks the contents of the oven. It smells amazing. And I'm starving all of the sudden.

It's fine. We're married with baby number two on the way, M. Just get here already.

After I press send, Bo confiscates my phone and begins scrolling through my pictures. I tell him about the ones I took in London. There are a few of my last visit to Lulu in Los Angeles and seeing her blue-haired selfie makes me miss her. I'd hoped she'd always be my stylist so we could hang out on the road, but during a visit with her dad she got hired by some big deal movie company.

"So who all is coming?" I call out to my husband.

"Well, Claire Ann and Pauly, obviously," Trace begins. His sister and her husband live right down the road so it's a given they'll be here. "Rae and that kid with the crappy taste in music she's dating. My mom, I guess."

I don't miss the extra weight in his voice but I hope Bo doesn't catch it. Trace still hasn't completely forgiven his mom for the mistakes she's made over the years, but he's working on it. She's Bo's grandma and he loves her, so I deal with her the best I can.

"Lily and her dad are coming," I inform him.

"I know," he hollers back from the kitchen. "Don told me they were. His son is coming in from overseas, so he'll be here too."

"Is he in the military?" I can't remember Lily mentioning that. But she talks a mile a minute so I might've missed it.

"No, he's a pro soccer player," Trace answers. Now that I did know, just not the overseas part. I forget sometimes that Lily's dad is technically Trace's boss.

After we walked away from Capital Letter Records, Donovan Taite offered Trace his own label. Eventually Trace accepted, provided he could sign a certain trio that included Donovan's daughter, Mia Montgomery, and his wife. It makes Lily's day that she's been signed by a separate label that isn't *technically* her dad's.

Trace is happy with the arrangement since he still has time for his A Hand Up foundation, the rehab facility he's part owner of, and his favorite job, being a stay-at- home-dad.

We still tour together from time to time, but Trace won't go on the road unless Bo and I go with him. He's been sober for almost nearly five years now and I couldn't be more proud of him. But even if he slips and has to go back to rehab, we'd get through it. As a family.

Bo has gone way back in my photo album on my phone. There are still pictures of our wedding on it. We had it here at the farm. Trace wore a tie but I let him wear jeans and boots. I wore my mom's wedding dress with my own boots. The same ones I'd taken on Trace's *Back to My Roots* tour.

It rained on our wedding day, and the guests all took shelter in the tents. But we stayed out in the storm and said our vows. A little rain couldn't stop us. I barely even noticed. We'd been through much worse.

Glancing at the pictures though, I want to laugh. We look half drowned. And that was before Trace threw me in the pond.

"Gretchen and her son and some guy she's dating and his kid are coming," Trace informs me. "She said you invited them at the AHU benefit."

"I did." I bite my lip, wondering if the next guest on the list is going to make him go all cave man on me. "Mia's coming, too. I told her she could bring someone if she wanted. So she is."

Trace steps into the living room with a dishtowel in his hands. "Oh yeah? Who is she bringing?"

I roll my eyes. He can say whatever he wants. The man looks at celebrity gossip stuff online. He knows good and well who Mia is dating. They've been together for a while now. It's not exactly a new thing.

"You know who. Be nice."

Trace eyes the gun cabinet in the corner. "Nice is my middle name. Ask him if he wants to go hunting in the morning."

"You're not right." I shift Bo, whose eyes haven't left my phone this entire time, onto the couch cushion beside me and stand on my tiptoes. I give my husband a lingering kiss. "You know there's only ever been one guy for me."

"Damn straight," he says against my mouth before swatting me on the behind with the dishtowel.

The next hour is a steady stream of guests arriving, and the long day begins to weigh on me. It must be showing because once everyone has arrived, Trace pulls me aside.

"Baby, if you're tired, go lie down. Turkey still has a little while and the kids want to go down to the barn and see the horses."

I wrap my arms around him, resting my head on his chest, and let out a small sigh. It's good to be home. "I'm okay. I'll come down in a minute. I just need to freshen up first."

Looking up into the hazel gaze I love so much, I smile at his darkening expression. He worries about me. It feels nice to have someone who cares so much. Too much sometimes.

"I promise I'm fine." I press my lips to his, and he surprises me by sliding his warm, wet tongue in my mouth. He tastes so good, and I can't get enough.

My arms wrap instinctively around his neck and my fingers rake into his hair.

By the time he ends our kiss, I'm lightheaded.

We have guests, I remind myself.

"Well just be sure you save enough energy for later," he says low in my ear. "I still have to show you how much I missed you."

I nod, hoping my legs are still steady enough to hold me. His lips brush against mine once more and then he winks before jogging outside to catch Bo and the others on their way to the barn.

After I've splashed some water on my face, I follow them out.

From behind and at a distance, they look like one big group.

I can see my son on my husband's shoulders. Next to them, Pauly has one arm around Claire Ann, and in the other he holds Leah, the little girl they recently adopted from Guatemala. Rae and her boyfriend, whose name I can't remember because all Trace ever refers to him as is the kid with crappy taste in music, stand beside them. Trace's mom is slightly at a distance but Bo and Leah are both angling towards her.

Lily and her dad and brother are chatting with Mia and Steven. Looks like Lily's brother the soccer star isn't immune to Mia's charms. I can practically see Steven tightening his grip on her from here. Bet he'll be over that "no need to put a ring on it" thing before the night is over. Gretchen is on the other side of them with her handsome doctor man and each of their kids.

From where I stand, I can see it. Them. The connections. Some are closer than others, but we're all connected. All a part of something I didn't fully understand until now. Something I never thought I'd have.

Walking towards them, I know I'm smiling like a crazed maniac, but I can't help it. In a way, I'm in love with each and every one of them because they're a part of our lives. The roles they've played in helping us get where we are make me love them even more. I place a hand on my stomach and stop to just look at them for a moment longer.

My family.

Panic threatens to send my heart into my throat. Could be the hormones from the pregnancy maybe. But I can't wrap my mind around it. How did I get so lucky? What could I possibly have done to deserve this?

I get to live my dream and I have a family to share it with. To laugh with and fight with and eat meals with. To love and miss, dream and cry with, and drive half crazy.

There was a time when I thought I'd have to choose. One or the other. Dreams or family. And an even darker time when I felt like I had nothing and didn't dare let myself imagine I'd ever have a life like this.

But now I have everything I ever wished for. There's so much to be thankful for that I can hardly breathe.

Someone else has to be responsible. Someone had to be watching over me for me to be this blessed. For me to have everything I ever wanted, everything I needed, and then some, even after all of the mistakes I made.

A light misting rain begins to fall and suddenly I know. My moment of panic subsides and all I am is grateful.

Before I reach my family, I lift my face to the sky and whisper my words of gratitude.

"Thanks, Daddy."

coming soon from
CAISEY QUINN

The Second Chance Series

Love is complicated. Sometimes all you need is a second chance.

Last Second Chance

When Stella Jo Chandler gets an offer to work at the Second Chance Ranch celebrity rehab facility right after graduating from Texas A&M, she's tempted to turn it down. She wants to help real people with real problems, not spoiled celebrities going on vacation for publicity. But growing up on her family's ranch left her with a love of horses that draws her to the opportunity. How bad can babysitting a bunch of strung out celebrities be?

What she didn't count on was being roped into a tangled mess with infamous rocker and three-time rehab drop out Van Ransom on her first day. And she damn sure didn't expect to feel the overwhelming attraction that pulls her to the man who has more issues than she can count on both hands. Like the hotel rooms and tour buses he's famous for trashing, the havoc he could wreak on Stella's heart would be irreparable.

Van isn't at Second Chance for publicity or because he's suffering from "exhaustion". He's on the brink of destruction, and he needs the kind of help Stella isn't sure she can give. But without her, he'll lose everything. Because he's on his last second chance.

thank YOU

Ending this series was probably one of the hardest things I've ever done. I literally couldn't let go of Kylie and Trace until the very last possible second. Being a part of their world has been such an amazing experience. Without the help of so many wonderful and dedicated and supremely talented people, I never could've even begun to think about putting these books out into the universe.

But before I get into my ginormous list of awesome people that I am fortunate enough to know and work with, I have to thank my family. They are the bridge that not only supports me and my dreams, but carries me from the dark recesses of insanity that one must venture into in order to write a book back to reality and then back again many times over. Thank you for allowing me to travel back and forth. For letting me chase my dreams and follow my heart and still have people to share my failures and successes with.

I giggle a lot when I see comments about Trace, because if you hand my husband a guitar, he's basically him. I cheer on the readers who yell at him and shake my head at the ones who succumb to his charms, much like I did nearly ten years ago. I'm a lucky girl to have found someone who can drive me so completely crazy that life is never boring while loving me so unconditionally that I have the courage to simply be myself.

Okay, so moving right along. This is a long list y'all. Brace yourselves.

As you can see in the dedication, Emily Tippetts was the first person to read Girl with Guitar. Thankfully she didn't say, *Stick to your day job, lady*. Instead she said, *You have to publish this*. Then she proceeded to hold my hand, talk me down from ledges, and give me the courage to publish my books. So, if you enjoyed this series, thank Emily (like I do pretty much every day.)

If you did not find dozens of typos in this book, it's due to the diligent work of my editor Mickey Reed and my proofreader Rahab Mugwanja. They are fantastic ladies that I am so lucky to get to work with. If you did find dozens of typos, it's entirely my fault and due to changes I made after their eyes perfected this beast of a book.

So many other authors welcomed me into the indie author community with open arms and advice and just by being their wonderfully sweet selves. Big hugs to the aforementioned Emily Tippetts, Abbi Glines, Anna Cruise, Elizabeth Lee, Rachel Harris, Lexi Ryan, Marilyn Brant, Rhonda Helms, Lauren Blakely, Rachel Brookes, Jen McLaughlin, Heidi McLaughlin, Chelsea Cameron, and the many, many others who I am blessed to call colleagues and friends.

In addition to authors, I could not have survived this process without the love and support and friendship of some AH-MAZING bloggers, reviewers, and readers. I am grateful to each and every one of you who have helped promote my books by beta reading, participating in cover reveals, tours, giveaways, release day blitzes, posting reviews, and all the zillions of other things I've asked of you. Gutter Girls Book Reviews, My Secret Romance Book Review blog, Group Therapy Book Club, SMI Book Club, The Autumn Review, Romance Book Addict, Book Addict Mumma, Smitten's Book Blog, The Indie Bookshelf, Hardcover Therapy, Read This Hear That, Ginger Reads, Reality Bites! Let's Get Lost!, Holly's Hot Reads, GloBug and Hootie, Lovin Los Libros, The Blushing Reader, The Geekery Book Review, Seeking Book Boyfriends, Stuck in Books... I could literally go on forever probably. To those of you who took a chance on some chick in Alabama and read *Girl with Guitar* and then contacted me to say you enjoyed it, I could kiss your faces. If I see you at a signing event, it's likely that I will. You are the reason that Kylie and Trace's story continued. So THANK YOU!

My street team, who share a name with Kylie's band, is made up of 50 of the coolest chicks I know. I couldn't even pay them enough for all of the wonderful things they do to support me. And they do it for free! To each and every one of my Backwoods Belles, y'all are my heart. Thank you for always being there and for your endless love and devotion. There aren't words to express my gratitude. I love you to the moon and back.

I am fortunate enough to be an InkSlinger client and to get to work with my publicist Jessica Estep who understands that my crazy ideas will come at around two a.m. and will respond to emails night and day.

Thank you Erin Kelly for the amazing book trailers that you put together from all of my ramblings.

As most of y'all know, this series recently got a makeover thanks to the lovely and talented Lauren Perry of L. Perry Designs and cover models Teale Murdock (who I swear is actually Kylie Ryans) and Ghent Scott who is not only a smoking hot Trace but a firefighter in real life. Getting to meet and work with all three of them literally made my life complete. Watching my characters come to life is an experience I will never forget and will cherish for as long as I live.

I am so thankful for the county music community and all of the patient people who answered my questions. You are all rock stars to me and I am forever grateful.

Thank you to each of you who came to the Read Like A Country Girl event in Nashville. I hope I get to see each of you again at events this year!

Thank you ladies who orchestrated and participated in the Kylie Ryans Read Along event on Facebook. You made the weeks leading up to the release of this book much more fun and much less stressful than it normally would've been.

Big smothery hugs to every single person who sent me a "When will Girl in Love be available?" message online. You were my motivation and inspiration to keep going and get this book out into the world.

And lastly, thank you, yes, *you* reading this right now, for making it through my blubbering on and on about the people I love. I am thankful for you, thankful that you take the time to read my words and allow my characters into your life.

If you follow me on Spotify, you can find the soundtrack lists for each of the Kylie Ryans novels. They will also be on my website. I am currently working with my real life inspiration for Steven on getting some of the original songs that appear in the Kylie Ryans novels recorded and hope to make those available to you soon.

Music is such a huge part of this series, and a huge part of who I am, but I don't know how to thank music, so instead, I will thank those people who support musicians of all kinds. Parents, teachers, venue owners, producers, managers, interns.

We all have a song, a story, a book, inside of us. Play it loud. Never let your songs stop playing.

To anyone I forgot to mention, you are the ones I love the most, and probably take for granted. Please forgive me!

about the
AUTHOR

Caisey Quinn lives in Birmingham, Alabama with her husband, daughter, and other assorted animals. She is the bestselling author of the Kylie Ryans series as well as several New and Young Adult Romance novels featuring country girls finding love in unexpected places. You can find her online at www.caiseyquinnwrites.com.

This paperback interior was designed and formatted by

Artisan interiors for discerning authors and publishers.

15235471R00189

Printed in Great Britain
by Amazon.co.uk, Ltd.,
Marston Gate.